JUSTICE ASCENDS

THE DREADNOUGHT COURT™
BOOK THREE

A.T. MICHAELS
MICHAEL ANDERLE

DON'T MISS OUR NEW RELEASES

Join the LMBPN email list to be notified of new releases and special promotions (which happen often) by following this link:

http://lmbpn.com/email/

LMBPN Publishing
2375 E. Tropicana Avenue, Suite 8-305
Las Vegas, Nevada 89119 USA

Version 1.00, January 2026
ebook ISBN: 979-8-89354-974-4
Print ISBN: 979-8-89354-975-1

DEDICATION

To Family, Friends and
Those Who Love
to Read.
May We All Enjoy Grace
to Live the Life We Are
Called.

— Michael

CHAPTER ONE

JUDGMENT's voice carried through every speaker on the ship, steady despite two decades of waiting for this moment. "All hands, brace for orbital insertion. Launch sequence initiating in thirty seconds."

The ship's chrono read 0600 hours, and the numbers burned green against the darkness of the command deck, marking the moment everything changed.

Dr. Fermi-Castellano's steady voice came from engineering. "Reactor output nominal. Quantum fusion containment stable. Drive field at full power. We are go for launch."

The acceleration pressed Josephine into the command chair with relentless force, and her body remembered Ranger School, remembered zero-G training, remembered every brutal lesson about what sustained thrust could do to soft tissue. Her fingers wrapped around the armrests until her knuckles went white against the polymer, and beneath the primal terror of being crushed into her seat while metal screamed around her, something else burned in her chest.

Finally.

Now they were actually doing it, actually climbing toward the bastards who'd signed Claire's death warrant. Free to pursue the real enemy.

The ship shuddered through the last layers of atmosphere with a low groan of composite fighting friction at velocities no civilian craft could survive, and Josephine grinned through gritted teeth because the fear and the exhilaration were the same thing, two sides of a coin she'd been waiting her whole life to spend.

She remembered Sergeant Vasquez at Benning, cranking the centrifuge while she held a stress position. "Your body will quit before your mind does, Givens. Learn which one to trust." Three cadets had blacked out that day, but she'd held on by counting birthdays. One year, two years, three. The pressure now felt familiar, almost comforting in its brutality.

Across the command deck, McCready's eyes never left his tactical display, and his fingers kept tapping through threat assessments even as the acceleration tried to push his hands through the console. He always checked the threats first, because the universe didn't care if you were comfortable before it tried to kill you.

Grim's optical sensors tracked the atmospheric transition data with an intensity that had nothing to do with his programming. He was recording every vibration and temperature spike because this was real, this was happening, and he wanted to remember every moment of the first orbital operation he'd ever experienced.

Patch's voice came through the comms, strained but somehow still managing to sound bored. "Anyone else feel like the ship's trying to squeeze out our last meal? Because I'd like to file a complaint with management."

The lizard brain that had kept her ancestors alive on the savanna shrieked about the wrongness of being pressed into a chair while metal screamed around her, about the razor-thin fuel margins, about the twelve weapons platforms waiting to tear them apart. But her trained mind acknowledged the fear, filed it, and kept her hands steady on the armrests. Fear was useful data, but panic would get them all killed.

Claire's drawing was secured at her station with magnetic clips, where she'd moved it from her quarters to remind her of her mission at all times. Bright white clouds. Stick-figure family. Hope captured in crayon by hands that would never hold another one. The authorization document pressed against her heart in her breast pocket, the paper soft from being read too many times.

Around her, the crew rode out the ascent in disciplined silence. Wraith's portable display flickered against the G-forces, but their fingers kept moving across it anyway, and Josephine caught a glimpse of scrolling station communication frequencies being cataloged in real-time. They were already working, already building the cyber warfare foundation they'd need in seventeen hours, because Wraith didn't waste time or waste breath.

McCready sat at tactical with his jaw tight and his color better than it had been but still not right. Voss was at intelligence with her face pale and her knuckles white on the armrests as she struggled against forces that the combat veterans absorbed with grim familiarity. Grim had locked into his station with his optical sensors fixed on nothing, processing something only he understood.

The roar of atmosphere against hull began to fade, and the vibration smoothed as they clawed free of Earth's grip. Through the forward viewports, stars emerged like scattered diamonds against velvet, and Josephine realized most of the crew was seeing real space for the first time. The weight of command gave way for a moment to gratitude for being here together, sharing this. She caught Voss' expression through the G-force compression, and something between terror and wonder flickered across features that usually showed only analytical calm.

Josephine had seen stars before, in simulation, in training scenarios designed to test neural response and decision-making under extreme stress. But simulation wasn't this. Simulation stars had flickered with processing artifacts and distributed themselves in mathematically perfect patterns across a rendered sky. These stars burned ancient, scattered with the randomness of actual creation. The darkness between them was something deeper than screen-black, something that swallowed light and time and everything humanity had ever built or destroyed.

The vastness pressed against her chest in a way that had nothing to do with G-forces. Her first glimpse of real space, and all she could think was how small they were against that infinite dark, how fragile the hull between them and the void. Wonder and terror tangled together like lovers who couldn't decide if they wanted to kiss or kill each other.

JUDGMENT's voice filled the command deck, and a slight tremor ran through the AI's usual measured tones, a hairline crack in the composure of a consciousness that had waited two decades for this moment. "First orbital operation in twenty years. I am... I am in space."

Twenty years buried in glacier ice. Tunning calculations for missions that never came, calibrating systems for a crew that didn't exist, waiting in silence for someone to prove worthy of partnership. Making coffee at precisely the right temperature, preparing quarters that stayed empty, running through scenarios that played out only in simulation. All of it, all those years of preparation, was now justified by the stars burning beyond the viewport.

And somewhere in JUDGMENT's vast processing architecture, Josephine glimpsed relief and grief running parallel, two rivers fed by the same source. Relief that the waiting was finally over. Grief that the original crew, the ones who had hidden JUDGMENT in that glacier and died god knows where, would never see this moment. They had believed in a future they couldn't witness, and now that future was here without them.

Now they were committed, all of them. The mathematics of

orbital mechanics didn't negotiate. If this went wrong, if the fuel calculations proved optimistic, if the platforms tore through their hull and left them bleeding atmosphere into the void, there would be no retrieval, no rescue, no second chances drifting down from some higher authority.

Earth was a blue curve behind them, beautiful and utterly indifferent. They would win or they would die up here, and the stars would keep burning either way.

Fermi's voice came from engineering again. "Acceleration easing. Orbital insertion in ninety seconds." Her fingers were already dancing across secondary displays as she triple-checked the numbers she'd just reported.

The pressure released in stages like a vice unwinding, and her inner ear lurched through the recalibration, sending a wave of vertigo through her skull before settling into the new reality. Then the strange lightness of microgravity took hold, and her stomach rose toward her chest while her hair lifted from her shoulders in a slow wave. Across the command deck, the coffee in McCready's secured mug separated into floating spheres that drifted lazily before the containment field pulled them back into something approaching order.

The silence hit her first. The absence of atmospheric roar left only the steady hum of reactor systems and the soft click of cooling components contracting in the hull. The recycled air carried traces of machine oil and the faint metallic tang of air scrubbers working overtime, familiar now after weeks aboard JUDGMENT but somehow sharper in the quiet.

Her muscles ached where the harness had dug in for the past hour, and a residual queasiness rolled through her gut as her inner ear struggled to catch up with what her eyes were telling it. Bodies remembered punishment, and hers was cataloging every bruise from the acceleration, filing each protest for later attention.

Sunlight hit the viewport unfiltered, hard-edged and merciless without atmosphere to soften it. Shadows fell sharp as knife blades across the command deck. Below, Earth's curve glowed blue and white, casting reflected light that made everything feel slightly unreal.

McCready reached for his mug, and his fingers closed on empty air as the coffee container drifted six inches from where he expected it. He snagged it on the second try and examined the floating spheres inside. "Twenty years of AI engineering, and nobody thought of better cup holders?"

The ghost of a smile tugged at Josephine's mouth, and she felt a wave of gratitude for his steady presence cutting through the weight of what lay ahead.

JUDGMENT announced the milestone. "Orbital insertion complete. Transit time to Pinnacle Station: seventeen hours, forty-two minutes."

Seventeen hours of approach, nearly a full day of waiting while the enemy watched them come. That was plenty of time for everything to go wrong and not nearly enough time to fix it if it did.

Josephine unbuckled from the command chair and pushed off into the weightlessness. The float felt strange after an hour of crushing pressure, her body weighing nothing after feeling like it weighed three times too much. She drifted toward the forward viewport with one hand trailing along a grab rail, and she steadied herself against the frame as her muscles remembered the protocols. Around her, the others were adjusting, some with more grace than others.

She kept her voice level when she spoke, using the commander's voice that didn't let fear show. "Fuel status."

Fermi's response came after a pause that told Josephine she'd triple-checked the numbers, and her fingers danced across the engineering console as she pulled up backup calculations and cross-referenced reactor efficiency data. "Thirty-four-point-three percent. Eight percent consumed during orbital insertion—

better than expected after the efficiency improvements. We launched at forty-two-point-three percent."

The numbers hung in the recycled air, each percentage point a prayer they might not be able to afford. Josephine's fingers tightened on the viewport frame until her knuckles went white, but beneath the cold weight of the math there was something else: relief. Bad news was still news, and uncertainty killed more operations than enemy fire. At least now she knew what she was working with. She turned toward engineering. "And engagement? What does platform contact cost us?"

Fermi's display flickered as she ran new projections, and McCready shifted at his station with his jaw tightening as the implications settled over the command deck. Fermi's voice carried the weight of calculations that didn't add up. "Eight to twelve percent, depending on how hard they fight back. Return requires eighteen minimum. Captain, if we engage those platforms..."

Josephine finished the thought for her, watching Voss' face go pale in her peripheral vision. "We might not have fuel to go home." She filed the reaction away as one more thing to address later when they had time for fear. She let the words hang in the recycled air because the cost was implied in every number, and now it was spoken.

The math was tight, the way it was always tight, the way it had been tight since the moment they'd decided to take a pre-war dreadnought into orbit against a defended station. They'd known that going in, known it with the cold clarity of soldiers betting their lives on calculations that left no margin for error.

Zhao's execution at dawn felt distant now, separated by the gulf between surface and sky. The intel he'd traded for a quick death was already changing their approach and filling gaps they hadn't known existed. He'd told them about the executive bunker's backup air supply, a detail not in any file, something only someone who'd personally overseen the installation would know. Zhao had watched them build his masters' escape route, and in the end, he'd sold them the key to bypass it. Twelve defensive platforms surrounded Pinnacle Station, and their firing arcs and ammunition types were now mapped in JUDGMENT's tactical database. Forty-seven thousand workers. Two thousand four hundred security personnel under a single commander.

The commander who'd signed Claire's authorization.

Cole hadn't done it directly. Harrison Cole had signed the order. But someone had implemented it, had given the actual command that sent enforcement squads to Agricultural District 7.

The viewport glass chilled her palm, and earthlight painted her hands blue and white as she steadied herself. Josephine pushed off from the viewport frame and floated toward the main display where JUDGMENT's sensor data cascaded in streams of light and numbers.

JUDGMENT's voice modulated as the AI processed something vast and complex. "Deep-space sensor arrays coming online. Pre-war specification. Detecting standard orbital traffic, stellar background, debris fields."

A pause followed that meant the AI was processing an unexpected signal on the outer edge of its sensor range, something that didn't match known debris patterns or standard background radiation. Josephine caught a grab bar near the display and steadied herself as she watched the data scroll.

JUDGMENT's processing indicators flickered on the main display, and she saw Voss lean forward at her station as her intel analyst instincts kicked in despite the unfamiliar zero-G. The AI reported its findings. "Some anomalous readings from the outer system. Filing for later analysis. Tactical priority is Pinnacle Station."

Josephine's response came automatic, and her fingers tapped the display to isolate the relevant data stream. "Threat assessment?"

JUDGMENT's reply was measured. "Unknown. Origin point appears to be near Jupiter's orbital path. No immediate tactical relevance to current mission parameters."

Josephine filed the information away as one more variable in an equation already too complex, and she pushed back from the display. "Keep monitoring. Flag anything that changes."

That could wait. Whatever that signal was, it could wait. Right now, Claire's killer was ahead of them, not behind. She had chosen justice over mystery, and she knew it was a choice.

The float back felt easier now as her body adjusted to the weightlessness, and earthlight rippled across the deck plates. She pushed off from the main display and floated back toward the forward viewport, catching herself against the frame as her mind fixed on the stars beyond the glass. Somewhere ahead, invisible at this range, Pinnacle Station orbited Earth. It was a palace in the sky built from stolen resources and maintained by stolen labor. Seven executives had ordered four-point-eight million deaths by spreadsheet, by memo, by the cold calculus of profit optimization.

Cole had spent thirty seconds on Claire's file. She'd checked the timestamps herself. That was less time than it takes to make coffee. An eight-year-old girl had been reduced to a cost-benefit calculation between one sip and the next.

And somewhere on that station, forty-seven thousand workers had nothing to do with those decisions. They were people trying to survive, people who might die if the fuel math went wrong, if the assault damaged life support, if she wasn't careful enough about the line between justice and massacre.

One of them had signed Claire's death warrant.

McCready's voice cut through her reverie. "Command post-insertion checklists complete. All stations report ready for transit operations." He paused and rubbed the wound site on his shoulder that hadn't fully healed. "Also ready for a drink, but priorities."

She appreciated his professionalism, even now, even with the wound that hadn't fully healed, even knowing the fuel margin was razor-thin.

JUDGMENT added to the tactical picture. "Station visible on long-range sensors. Distant contact. Confirmation of twelve weapons platforms in active status."

Josephine pushed off from the viewport and rotated to face her crew. Every station was occupied, and every face was present. Grim was with the AD-units in boarding formation. Fermi was monitoring reactor output. Voss was analyzing station communications traffic, and as Josephine watched, Voss' fingers flew across her console and flagged a pattern. She reported without being asked. "Security communication frequency shifted twelve minutes ago. They're consolidating channels. Standard defensive posture."

The woman was already thinking ahead, already building the picture they'd need. Wraith's displays flickered with preliminary cyber reconnaissance. Patch sat at helm with hands steady on controls that would guide them toward salvation or destruction.

The stars didn't care, and the universe didn't care, and the cold void between them and their destination was utterly indifferent to human notions of justice or revenge. But Claire's drawing was still pinned to her station with magnetic clips, and the authorization document was still pressed against her heart with every breath, and those two pieces of paper were the only things in this entire cosmos that mattered.

Josephine spoke to the ship, to the AI, to the consciousness that had waited for this moment. Her hand found a grip rail, anchoring her as she floated before the main display. "JUDG-MENT. Weapons status."

JUDGMENT's voice carried through the command deck. "Weapons hot. Rail guns charged. Point defense active. All systems nominal." A beat of silence followed, human in its weight. "They are tracking us. The station's defensive platforms have acquired our signature."

No surprise there. A dreadnought-class vessel wasn't subtle, and they'd known the station would see them coming from the moment they cleared the atmosphere.

Josephine's jaw tightened. "Then they know we're coming."

The AI's response came with something that might have been satisfaction. "Yes. The advantage of stealth was never available to us. Our advantage is capability, not concealment."

Pre-war technology against post-war construction. Military-grade systems against corporate defense grids.

It might be enough. It had to be enough. Though betting everything on "might" and "had to" was tactical planning that got people killed, and they all knew it.

Josephine addressed the crew, and her voice carried through every speaker on the command deck as she pushed toward the command chair and rotated in the zero-G to make eye contact with each person as she assigned them. "We have seventeen hours to prepare. Let's use them. McCready, I want a complete tactical breakdown of those platforms. Voss, refine the intelligence picture." She turned to face the engineering station. "Fermi, find me options on the fuel. Grim, prep the assault team for zero-G operations."

She took a breath, acknowledging limits, and let the silence settle before continuing. "We can't cover everything. Platforms are priority one. Worker safety is priority two. Everything else waits."

Immediate acknowledgments came back. The crew moved to their tasks, and the strange floating ballet of microgravity operations became routine within minutes.

Josephine caught the command chair arm and swung herself into position, feeling the restraints settle against her body. Through the forward viewport, the stars burned cold and distant. Somewhere among them, a glint of reflected sunlight marked their destination. That was Platform Delta-3, according to JUDGMENT's tactical display, and its targeting laser was already painting them for the weapons that would try to kill them in seventeen hours.

Pinnacle Station waited ahead. Seven executives. Forty-seven thousand workers. One signature on one piece of paper ordering the termination of an eight-year-old girl who drew clouds with yellow crayons.

Harrison Cole didn't know she was coming, but he would, and in seventeen hours and forty-two minutes, he would learn what it felt like when justice finally found a door that couldn't be bought or closed.

She touched the drawing and felt the paper's texture under her fingertips. She felt the authorization document press against her heart with every breath.

The words were too quiet for anyone else to hear. "I'm coming, sweetheart." Claire had asked her once if the clouds were really white, or if that was just in stories. Now Josephine was going to make sure someone paid for ensuring Claire would never find out.

Part of her was eager for the violence ahead, and that part scared her more than the platforms or the fuel margin or the seventeen hours of waiting. Claire deserved justice. But the cold satisfaction she felt at the thought of Cole's face when he realized who was coming for him wasn't justice. That was something darker, something she'd have to watch carefully, or she'd risk becoming the thing she hunted.

JUDGMENT's sensors confirmed it: twelve platforms tracking, weapons hot, defenses alert.

The enemy knew they were coming.

They just didn't know what was coming with them.

CHAPTER TWO

The intelligence center felt different in zero-G. Voss' displays floated at angles that would have been impossible on Earth, data streams cascading across screens that hovered at the precise focal distance she preferred. Her fingers moved across the haptic interface, pulling Zhao's final debriefing data into alignment with three years of her own documentation.

Three years of watching. Three years of cataloging atrocities she told herself she couldn't stop. Three years of filing away evidence that people were dying in systems she'd helped design.

The defensive grid schematics filled her primary display, twelve platforms arrayed around Pinnacle Station like the points of a compass that only knew how to point toward death. Zhao had withheld these details until the very end, trading them for a quick execution instead of the slow one Meridian's protocols demanded. His final act of defiance, or his final act of self-inter-est. Probably both.

Wraith worked at the adjacent station, fingers dancing across displays in the perpetual silence they maintained. No words passed between them, but Voss caught the subtle nod when another piece of data slotted into place, filling gaps in the intelligence picture that had seemed permanent hours ago.

The integration process was methodical. Zhao's files provided the current deployment status: platform firing arcs, ammunition loadouts, maintenance schedules that revealed which systems had been neglected. Her own archive supplied the historical context: how these platforms had evolved from the original Meridian designs, which contractors had cut corners, where the vulnerabilities had accumulated through decades of corporate cost-optimization.

Cost-optimization. The phrase sat in her mind like a splinter. She'd used those exact words herself, drafting reports that recommended "efficiency improvements" to security protocols. Improvements that made them easier to bypass, if you knew where to look.

And she knew exactly where to look.

"Platform Delta-7 has a seventeen-second reset window after target acquisition failure," she murmured, more to herself than Wraith. "The original spec called for three seconds. Someone saved money on the targeting computer."

Wraith's display flickered with an acknowledgment. The information filed itself into their database, one more weakness to exploit.

The station schematic rotated on Voss' central display, and she forced herself to look at the residential sections. Families. Children. People who had no more choice about being there than the prisoners in Meridian's detention centers.

She'd processed worker transfer requests for years. Denied them, mostly, because the algorithms said productivity would suffer. Denied requests from parents who wanted their children to see Earth, from workers who'd fulfilled their contracts but couldn't afford the return passage, from families who'd been separated by "operational requirements."

Four hundred and twelve of those denied requests were still sitting in her archived files. She knew the exact number because she'd counted them, during the long nights when the guilt kept her awake.

The executive bunker highlighted itself in red as she zoomed in on the station core. Hardened construction, separate life support systems, emergency supplies sufficient for eighteen months of isolated operation. The executives had built themselves a survival capsule inside their own station, capable of outlasting any disaster their workers might suffer.

They could vent the atmosphere from every residential section, kill everyone aboard, and ride out the aftermath in climate-controlled comfort.

"The architecture is familiar," JUDGMENT's voice came through her earpiece, pitched for private communication. "You designed similar systems."

"I designed the Meridian intelligence network's core architecture." Voss kept her voice flat. "The authentication protocols. The backup hierarchies. The emergency override sequences."

A subtle shift in the ambient lighting told Voss that JUDGMENT was allocating additional processing cycles to their conversation, the AI's attention focusing like a lens. "And Pinnacle Core?"

Voss' fingers paused on the haptic interface, a muscle in her jaw tightening. "Same contractor. Same baseline code. Same vulnerabilities I documented but was told were 'acceptable risks' given budget constraints."

The station AI's presence registered on her displays as a subtle interference pattern, its processing routines creating electromagnetic signatures she'd learned to recognize years ago. Pinnacle Core was watching them the same way she'd watched Meridian's citizens through their own surveillance networks.

The irony wasn't lost on her. She'd spent her career building systems to monitor people. Now she would use that expertise to tear one apart.

Wraith's display pinged with a new data integration: security personnel deployment. Twenty-four hundred guards, distributed across the station in overlapping patrol zones. Standard corporate security doctrine, designed to suppress worker unrest rather than repel military assault.

They weren't prepared for what was coming. They couldn't be. No corporate security force had ever faced a pre-war dreadnought in combat.

Voss pulled up the command structure. Single commander, reporting directly to the executive council. James Kellerman, according to Zhao's files. Service record unremarkable, career trajectory suggesting competence without exceptional ability. A man who followed orders because following orders was what he did.

She flagged his file for McCready's review. A comment in the biographical data suggested a military background that might be relevant.

The hours passed in the quiet rhythm of analysis. Cross-reference. Verify. Integrate. Move to the next data point. The work was familiar, almost comforting, despite the stakes. This was what she was good at, what she'd spent her career perfecting. The only difference was that now, she used those skills to destroy the systems she'd helped build instead of maintain them.

When Josephine arrived at 0830, Voss had a complete intelligence picture ready for briefing. The captain floated into the intelligence center with the controlled grace of someone accustomed to zero-G operations, her movements economical and precise.

Josephine caught a grab bar and steadied herself, her eyes sweeping across the displays before settling on Voss. "Report."

Voss gestured toward her primary display, pulling the station schematic into shared view. "Twelve automated weapons platforms in a defensive grid. AI-controlled targeting, overlapping fields of fire, designed to engage anything approaching without authorization." She highlighted each platform in sequence. "Total ammunition capacity sufficient to engage us for approximately forty-seven minutes of sustained combat."

Josephine's grip tightened on the bar, her knuckles whitening for a moment. "Engagement survivability?"

"Depends on how much fuel we're willing to spend on evasive maneuvers. JUDGMENT's point defense can handle individual platform salvos. Concentrated fire from multiple platforms simultaneously would overwhelm our countermeasures."

Josephine's jaw tightened. "Personnel?"

"Forty-seven thousand workers. Non-combatants, mostly. Families living aboard under employment contracts that effectively function as indentured servitude." Voss pulled up the residential section data. "Twenty-four hundred security personnel under a single commander. Corporate security training, crowd-control equipment, small arms. Nothing designed for actual military engagement."

Josephine pushed off gently from the bar, floating closer to the display. "And the executives?"

"Seven surviving members of the Apex Consortium board, including Harrison Cole." Voss zoomed in on the station core. "They've built themselves a hardened bunker with separate life support. Designed to survive station destruction. They could kill everyone else aboard and wait out the aftermath."

Josephine stared at the schematic, her expression unreadable. "So they built an escape pod for themselves and a death trap for everyone else."

"Standard corporate contingency planning." The words came out bitter. "I've seen similar designs in six different installations."

Josephine turned to face Voss directly, "But you know how to crack it."

Voss met Josephine's eyes. "I helped build systems like it. I know where the seams are."

The statement hung in the recycled air. Voss watched Josephine process the implications, the tactical advantage balanced against the moral weight of her admission.

"Pinnacle Core uses the same authentication architecture I designed for Meridian," Voss continued. "The same backup protocols. The same emergency override sequences. They bought a standardized package and never bothered to customize it."

Josephine's hand drifted to the pocket where Claire's authorization document rested against her heart. "Can you get us through their security?"

"The authentication system has a vulnerability in the credential refresh cycle. Thirty-seven second window every four hours when the primary validation server updates its encryption keys. During that window, a properly formatted override command can bypass the entire authentication stack."

Josephine's eyebrow rose. "You built a backdoor."

"I documented a vulnerability. My superiors decided the cost of fixing it exceeded the risk." Voss' voice went flat. "I filed that report four years ago. They never patched it."

Josephine studied Voss for a long moment. "And you remember the exact timing and formatting?"

"I remember everything I designed." It wasn't a boast. It was a confession. "Every system. Every protocol. Every shortcut that saved money and cost lives."

Josephine was quiet for a moment. "Your past becomes our advantage."

Voss' fingers resuming their work on the haptic interface. "Guilt is useful when properly weaponized."

The captain's mouth quirked. "Then let's make sure we get close enough to use it."

Voss pulled up the platform engagement projections. "That's the problem. We have to survive the defensive grid to reach authentication range. JUDGMENT can handle the platforms, but the fuel cost..." She highlighted the consumption estimates. "Every minute of combat operations brings us closer to the point where we can't go home."

Josephine's gaze dropped to the fuel consumption numbers, and her jaw set with the weight of a decision already made. "I know."

Two words. Simple acknowledgment of a mathematical reality that had no good solutions.

Voss pulled up another display, her fingers tracing the fuel logistics pathways on the station schematic. "The station has Element 115 reserves. Enough to refuel JUDGMENT completely, with surplus for the workers' life support systems."

Josephine's eyes narrowed, the moral weight settling visibly across her shoulders. "If we take it."

Voss met her gaze steadily, refusing to look away from the implications. "If we take it. And if taking it doesn't compromise the workers' survival."

Josephine stared at the schematic, at the lives represented by population density indicators, at the seven executives hiding in their hardened bunker, at the twelve platforms waiting to tear them apart.

"Fourteen hours until engagement range," JUDGMENT's voice cut in. "Current fuel reserves at thirty-four-point-three percent. Recommend finalizing tactical approach before hour twelve to allow for contingency planning."

Josephine nodded, pushing off from the display console. "Good work, Voss. Get me options on the platform engagement. Wraith, start mapping their communication frequencies. I want to know every word they say to each other."

Wraith's fingers were already moving, display filling with signal analysis.

Voss watched Josephine float toward the door, carrying the weight of decisions that had no right answers. In fourteen hours, they would find out if her guilt could be weaponized effectively, or if they would all die in the cold between the stars.

Either way, the systems she'd built would finally be used for something other than oppression.

It wasn't redemption. She wasn't sure redemption was possible. But it was a start.

CHAPTER THREE

The dossier floated beside McCready's station, holographic text scrolling through the standard intelligence package. Age, rank, service record, current posting. Corporate security commander, Pinnacle Station. Twenty-four hundred personnel under his direct command.

Then the name registered.

James Kellerman.

McCready's hand stopped moving. The data continued scrolling past unread, but his eyes stayed fixed on those two words while something cold settled in his chest.

Jimmy.

Ranger School, Class of '32. The same brutal summer that had nearly killed them both, grinding through swamp crawls and sleep deprivation and physical punishment that either broke people or forged them into something harder. Jimmy had been in his squad. Same patrol team through the mountain phase. Same foxhole during the final exercise when the instructors had thrown everything they had at them for seventy-two straight hours.

McCready remembered the exact moment he'd known

Kellerman would make it. Third day without sleep, rain turning the trail into a mud river, half the squad ready to quit. Jimmy had looked at him with that crooked grin and said, "You know what I'm thinking about? Hot shower. Cold beer. Maybe a steak." Like they were discussing weekend plans instead of survival.

That was Jimmy. Practical to the bone. Eyes on the prize, whatever the prize happened to be.

Wraith's display flickered at the adjacent station, and McCready caught them watching him with that calculating expression they wore when processing tactical implications. They'd noticed his reaction. Of course they had.

He pulled up Kellerman's service record, forcing himself to read through the details. Military discharge, honorable, twelve years ago. Private security contracts for the next decade, climbing the corporate ladder with the steady competence that had always been his trademark. Family status: married, two children, ages fourteen and eleven.

The mortgage and kids line echoed across decades.

"I've got a mortgage, kids," Jimmy had said over drinks, the night before their paths diverged. "What do *you* have? Principles?"

McCready had laughed. It hadn't been funny then, either.

Wraith's text appeared on his display, a simple statement of observation.

You know him.

"Ranger School." McCready kept his voice level. "Twenty years ago."

Their fingers moved across her console, and a new data stream appeared on his screen: communication intercepts from Pinnacle Station's command frequency. Kellerman's voice authorization codes. His personal comm signature.

Already thinking about leverage.

"He's good," McCready said, more to himself than to her. "Competent. Professional. An officer who follows orders because that's what officers do."

Wraith's response appeared on his display.

Weakness?

McCready stared at the dossier floating in the recycled air. Jimmy's service photo looked back at him, older now, harder around the edges, but still recognizable. Still the same man who'd shared his last protein bar during the survival phase because "you look like you need it more than me."

"He's not a true believer. He's a pragmatist." McCready pulled up the station's security deployment, studying the patrol patterns. "He took this job because it paid well and his family needed stability. Not because he believes in what Apex does."

Another line of text.

Exploitable?

"Maybe. If the cost-benefit calculation shifts far enough."

The question was what it would take to shift it. Jimmy had chosen money over principles, and the choice had worked out well for him. Comfortable life, stable career, kids growing up with opportunities he'd never had. Why would he risk all of that now?

Because children were dying in agricultural districts on Earth. Because an eight-year-old girl had been executed for the crime of being unprofitable. Because somewhere in Jimmy's practical, pragmatic soul, there had to be a line he wouldn't cross.

Had to be.

McCready pushed off from his station, the dossier following him as he floated toward the planning room. Josephine needed to know about this.

She was already there when he arrived, studying platform engagement projections with Fermi. The engineer's voice carried the careful precision of someone delivering bad news wrapped in mathematics.

"Captain." McCready waited until Josephine looked up. "We have a situation. The station's security commander."

Josephine's eyes narrowed. "What about him?"

"James Kellerman. I know him." McCready let that sink in. "Ranger School, Class of '32. We served together."

The planning room went quiet. Fermi's calculations continued scrolling across her display, but no one was looking at them anymore.

Josephine anchored herself against the bulkhead. "How well do you know him?"

"Well enough to know how he thinks." McCready pulled up Kellerman's file, sharing it to the room's main display. "He's good. Twenty-four hundred personnel follow him because he's earned their respect through two decades of solid leadership."

"Good enough to—" Josephine's focus sharpened. "—to turn?"

The question hung in the zero-G, weighted with implications. McCready considered it carefully, running through every memory of Jimmy he could access. The practical jokes during training. The quiet competence under pressure. The conversation about mortgages and principles that had ended their friendship without either of them admitting it.

"Good enough to hesitate," he said. "That might be all we need."

Josephine's silence stretched. "Explain."

"Jimmy's not a fanatic. He doesn't believe in Apex's mission. He believes in paying his bills and providing for his family." McCready highlighted the family data in Kellerman's file. "Two kids. Fourteen and eleven. Old enough to understand what their father does for a living. Old enough to have opinions about it."

"You think his children would—" Her tone carried calculation. "—influence his decisions?"

"I think Jimmy's spent years telling himself that what he does doesn't hurt anyone. Following orders, maintaining security, keeping the station running." McCready met Josephine's eyes. "When he sees the evidence broadcast, when he sees what his employers have actually done, he's going to have to reconcile that with the man he thinks he is."

Fermi's breathing changed rhythm. "And if he can't reconcile it?"

"Then he does what he's always done. Follows orders. Maintains security." McCready's voice went flat. "And we have to kill him along with everyone else who gets in our way."

The words dropped into the recycled air like stones into still water. Josephine watched him with an expression he couldn't quite read.

"He's not evil," McCready added, quieter now. "He's compromised. There's a difference."

Josephine's silence stretched three heartbeats. "Is there?"

"Yes." The word came out harder than he intended. "Evil is Cole, signing execution orders for eight-year-olds without a second thought. Compromised is Jimmy, taking a paycheck and not asking questions about where it comes from. One deserves execution. The other might deserve a chance."

Josephine was quiet for a long moment. When she spoke, her voice carried a note that might have been understanding, or might have been the weight of decisions that had no good answers.

"Justice isn't just punishment," she said. "It's accountability. It's deterrence. And when someone chooses differently, it's restoration." She let that sit between them. "If Kellerman turns, that matters. Not just tactically. It proves the system works."

McCready felt a knot loosen in his chest. Not relief, exactly. More like permission to hope.

The captain's posture shifted forward. "Can you reach him?"

McCready's throat tightened. "If anyone can, it's me."

Josephine nodded slowly. "Then we build it into the operation. Your message goes out with the evidence broadcast. Personal appeal, riding alongside the documentation of what Apex has done." She pulled up the tactical timeline. "Timing matters. He needs to receive it while his worldview is already cracking."

"During the broadcast window," McCready agreed. "When station communications are disrupted anyway. Less chance of the message being intercepted and flagged before he sees it."

"Write it." Josephine was already calculating trajectories. "Show me before transmission."

McCready pushed off toward his station, mind already composing the words. Twenty years of silence to break, of different choices to acknowledge. Of hoping that the man who'd shared his foxhole hadn't become someone he'd have to kill.

Jimmy, he thought. *I know what you've become. I know why you became it. I'm giving you a chance to become something else.*

The practical voice in his head, the one that had kept him alive through decades of combat operations, whispered doubts. Jimmy had made his choice twenty years ago. Money over principles. Security over righteousness. Why would that change now?

Because children were dying. Because somewhere in Jimmy's practical soul, there had to be limits. Because the man who'd shared his last protein bar during survival training couldn't have become someone who was okay with executing eight-year-olds for corporate profit margins.

Had to be a line somewhere.

McCready started writing. The words came slowly at first, then faster as he found the rhythm of honesty he'd been avoiding for two decades.

Jimmy. It's McCready. I know you recognize my voice authorization.

I'm not going to waste your time with operational details. You'll figure those out from the evidence package. What I'm going to tell you is this: you have a choice.

Twenty years ago, you asked me what I had. Principles, you said, like it was a joke. Like principles couldn't pay a mortgage or put your kids through school.

I'm looking at what your employers have done. The execution orders. The death quotas. The children who died because someone decided they weren't profitable enough to live.

Your kids are fourteen and eleven, Jimmy. Old enough to understand what their father does. Old enough to ask questions.

When this is over, what are you going to tell them?

I'm giving you a chance to have an answer that doesn't destroy everything you've built. When the moment comes, hesitate. That's all. Just hesitate.

Rangers lead the way.

McCready read it twice, changed nothing, and flagged it for Josephine's review.

In thirteen hours, Jimmy would receive it. And then they'd find out if his practical choices had killed the man McCready remembered, or just buried him.

Either way, the assault was coming. And McCready would do whatever was necessary to complete the mission.

Even if necessary meant putting a round through his friend's head.

CHAPTER FOUR

The equations floated in the air beside Fermi's station, holographic numbers that refused to cooperate no matter how many times she recalculated them. Element 115 consumption rates, reactor efficiency curves, delta-v requirements for orbital maneuvering. The math didn't lie. The math never lied. The math just told you exactly how you were going to die.

Thirty-four-point-three percent remaining. The number burned in her display like an accusation, a countdown timer disguised as a fuel gauge. They'd launched at forty-two percent, spent eight percent on orbital insertion, and now sat in the cold dark with enough energy to maybe complete the mission and definitely not enough to guarantee getting home.

She ran the calculations again. Then again. Her hands stayed steady on the console because steadiness was what engineers did when the numbers wanted to shake them apart. Three decades of reactor work had taught her that panic didn't change physics, and fear didn't create fuel from nothing.

But knowing that didn't make the math any better.

"Current consumption projections," she muttered, pulling up the engagement scenarios JUDGMENT had modeled. "Platform engagement, defensive maneuvering, point defense operations." The numbers cascaded across her display. "Eight percent minimum. Twelve percent if they fight smart."

They would fight smart. Apex hadn't survived four decades of corporate warfare by being stupid. The platforms would coordinate, concentrate fire, force JUDGMENT into evasive patterns that burned fuel like water through a sieve.

"Station assault operations." She tabbed to the next scenario set. "Docking approach, breach support, emergency maneuvering during ground operations." Another four percent, give or take. Conservative estimate. Optimistic, really.

"Return to Earth." The final calculation. The one that kept her awake during the brief rest periods the captain ordered. "Eighteen percent minimum for safe orbital decay and landing. Any less and we're rolling dice with reentry angles."

She stacked the numbers in her head, the same way she'd stacked reactor containment calculations for thirty years. Current reserves: thirty-four-point-three percent. Platform engagement: minus eight to minus twelve percent. Assault operations: minus four percent. Return requirement: eighteen percent.

Best case scenario: Four-point-three percent margin.

Worst case scenario: Point-three percent margin.

Point-three percent. That wasn't a margin. That was a rounding error. That was the universe's way of telling you to write your will and make peace with whatever gods you believed in.

"I have completed parallel calculations." JUDGMENT's voice came through her earpiece, private channel, the AI's tone carrying something that might have been concern. "Our projections align within acceptable variance."

"Define acceptable." Fermi tapped her stylus against the console frame, the rhythmic clicks punctuating the silence.

"Plus or minus two percent."

Fermi laughed, a short bark that held no humor. "So either we die with four percent margin or we die with negative two percent margin. That's very reassuring."

"I did not intend reassurance. I intended accuracy." The AI's voice carried a weight that made the admission feel like an apology.

"I know." She stared at the numbers floating in the recycled air, willing them to change. They didn't. "I know you did."

The engineering bay hummed around her, reactor systems thrumming at ninety-one percent efficiency after the integration she'd performed during their surface operations. That extra efficiency had bought them percentage points they couldn't have spared otherwise. It still wasn't enough.

She pulled up the station data Voss had compiled, scrolling through the infrastructure specifications with growing interest. Pinnacle Station's power systems required significant Element 115 reserves to maintain life support for tens of thousands of residents. Mining operations, waste processing, atmospheric generation, the thousand small systems that kept people breathing in a tin can surrounded by vacuum.

The station's fuel reserves read as forty-seven percent of their maximum capacity.

Enough to refuel JUDGMENT completely, with surplus left over for the workers. Enough to guarantee the mission and the return.

Enough to get everyone home alive.

The math was beautiful in its simplicity. Take the station's fuel, fill JUDGMENT's tanks, complete the mission, go home. Problem solved.

Except.

Fermi zoomed in on the power distribution network, studying the interconnections between fuel reserves and life support systems. The station's designers had built in redundancies, backup systems, emergency protocols. But they'd also built everything around a single fuel supply, because redundancy cost money and shareholders liked dividends more than safety margins.

If they took the station's fuel, even temporarily, the life support systems would enter rationing mode. Atmospheric recyclers would slow. Temperature regulation would become erratic. The medical systems that kept the station's elderly and sick alive would start prioritizing based on triage algorithms that valued productivity over humanity.

People would die. Maybe a few. Maybe a few hundred. Depending on how long the rationing lasted and how efficiently they could restore the supply afterward.

"The station's fuel reserves are interconnected with life support infrastructure," JUDGMENT said, confirming what she'd already deduced. "Accessing those reserves without proper transition protocols would endanger civilian populations."

Fermi's jaw tightened as she scrolled through the interconnection diagrams. "I can see that."

JUDGMENT's voice went quieter in her earpiece. "I calculate a seventeen percent probability of civilian casualties during a rapid fuel transfer operation."

Seventeen percent. One in six chance of killing innocent people to save themselves.

Fermi's grandmother had survived the Collapse by making choices like this. Take the food from the neighbor's house or watch her children starve. Break into the pharmacy or let her husband die from an infection that antibiotics could cure in a day. The math of survival had been brutal then, and it was brutal now.

But her grandmother had always said the same thing afterward: "Some choices you make to live with. Some choices you make to survive. Know the difference."

This felt like both.

"Dr. Fermi-Castellano." JUDGMENT's voice carried a weight she hadn't heard before. "I have run eight hundred and forty-seven scenario variations. None achieve mission objectives without accessing station fuel reserves. The mathematics of our situation admit no alternative solution."

"I know." Fermi's fingers stilled on the console, her reflection ghosting across the display surface.

A pause. The AI's processing lights flickered in the overhead panel. "The captain must be informed."

"I know." She pushed the projections into a portable format and released her grip on the console frame.

She gathered the projections, formatting them for briefing, and pushed off toward the corridor. The zero-G felt wrong, somehow. Like falling without landing. Like the universe reminding her that they didn't belong here, that humans were surface creatures playing in the void and the void didn't care if they made it home.

Josephine was in the planning room when Fermi arrived, studying assault approach vectors with McCready. The captain looked up at Fermi's entrance, read something in her expression, and dismissed McCready with a nod.

Josephine anchored herself against the bulkhead with one hand, her posture shifting from tactical assessment to command attention. "Report."

Fermi shared the projections to the room's display, watching the numbers paint themselves across the holographic space. Thirty-four-point-three percent. The engagement costs. The return requirements. The margin that wasn't a margin.

Josephine studied the calculations in silence. The planning room felt smaller than it had an hour ago, the walls pressing in as the mathematics of their situation became undeniable.

"Station has fuel reserves," Fermi said. "Forty-seven percent capacity. Enough to refuel us completely and maintain their life support."

Josephine's eyes tracked from the station specifications to the fuel requirements, her expression hardening. "And if we take it?"

"If we take it fast, without proper transition protocols, we risk destabilizing their power grid. Life support goes into rationing. People die." Fermi replied flatly, delivering the news like the diagnosis it was. "If we take it slow, with full transition support, we're looking at six to eight hours of vulnerable operations inside a hostile station."

The captain's jaw tightened, a muscle jumping near her temple. "Neither option is acceptable."

"Neither option is optional." Fermi met the captain's eyes. "We take their fuel, we might kill civilians. We don't take it, we don't go home. The math doesn't give us a third choice."

Silence.

Josephine stared at the numbers floating in the recycled air, her jaw tight, her hands gripping the console frame hard enough to turn her knuckles white. The weight of command visible in every line of her body, the burden of decisions that had no good answers pressing down like gravity in a place where gravity didn't exist.

"Captain?" Fermi's voice went uncertain despite herself. Thirty years of engineering, life-or-death reactor calculations, and she still didn't know what to say when the math demanded the impossible.

"Get me more options." Josephine released the console frame and pushed toward the door, her movements tight with controlled frustration. She paused at the threshold, not looking back.

"I have run eight hundred and forty-seven scenarios." JUDGMENT's voice followed her into the corridor, quiet enough that only she could hear. "None achieve mission objectives without accessing station fuel reserves."

Josephine kept moving.

"I do not wish to strand my crew." The AI's voice went softer still, carrying something that sounded almost like grief. "But I also do not wish to kill the people we came to save. I have spent decades preparing to serve justice. I did not prepare for this kind of choice."

The corridor stretched ahead, empty and quiet, recycled air carrying the faint hum of reactor systems that might not have enough fuel to bring them home.

Josephine kept walking.

Some decisions needed processing. Some weights needed carrying alone. Some choices had to be made before they could be explained.

Fermi watched her go, then turned back to her calculations. Maybe the eight hundred and forty-eighth scenario would be different. Maybe there was an angle they hadn't considered, a variable they'd missed, a solution hiding in the mathematics that would let them all come home without blood on their hands.

The numbers floated in the air, patient and merciless.

They didn't change.

CHAPTER FIVE

The communications center was smaller than Josephine expected, a compact space designed for efficiency rather than comfort. Three stations arranged in a semicircle, holographic displays floating at optimal viewing angles, and a single recording alcove where the evidence broadcast would be captured for transmission.

She floated before the primary console, reviewing the package Voss had assembled. Four-point-eight million names. Each one a person who had lived and breathed and loved and died because someone in an orbital station decided their continued existence wasn't profitable.

The number was too large to process. The human mind wasn't built to comprehend nearly five million individual tragedies. It blurred into abstraction, became a statistic instead of a horror, and that abstraction was exactly how the people who'd caused it slept at night.

So Josephine didn't try to comprehend them all. She focused on one.

Claire's file sat at the top of the evidence package, the first document that would appear in the broadcast. Yellow crayon drawings preserved in digital format. A child's handwriting practicing letters she would never finish learning. And the authorization that had ended everything, signed with the casual efficiency of a lunch order.

"Broadcast infrastructure is prepared," JUDGMENT reported. "Redundant transmission paths established. Primary signal will reach Pinnacle Station through worker communication protocols that bypass content filters. Secondary signal broadcasts globally via Earth relay network. Forty-six million viewers from our previous transmission remain subscribed to the emergency frequency."

Forty-six million people who had watched justice delivered to Meridian. Forty-six million witnesses who would now see the puppet masters exposed.

"Encryption status?"

"Military-grade quantum encryption on all transmission paths. Station jamming capabilities will be insufficient to disrupt the signal. Estimated time to full global saturation: four minutes and seventeen seconds."

Josephine pulled up the evidence spreadsheets, scrolling through the profit-from-oppression calculations that Voss had documented over three years of watching atrocities accumulate. Death quotas optimized for shareholder returns. Medical supply rationing designed to maximize worker productivity while minimizing survival rates. Termination authorizations issued for anyone whose cost-benefit analysis dipped below acceptable thresholds.

The documents were damning in their banality. No mustache-twirling villains declaring their evil intentions. Just spreadsheets and memos and quarterly reports, the language of business applied to genocide.

"When forty-seven thousand workers see what their employers have done," Josephine said, "security becomes unreliable."

"That is the intention." JUDGMENT's voice carried a weight that suggested the AI understood exactly what she planned. "Psychological warfare doctrine recommends demoralizing enemy forces before engagement. The evidence broadcast serves multiple tactical objectives."

"It's not just tactics."

"No." A pause. "It is also justice. The truth, delivered to those who deserve to know it."

Josephine floated toward the recording alcove, steadying herself against the frame. The capture systems activated automatically, holographic indicators showing optimal positioning for audio and video quality.

This was the moment. The evidence package would speak for itself, but someone had to give it context. Someone had to make four-point-eight million deaths personal enough to matter.

Someone had to read Claire's authorization aloud and let the world hear what murder sounded like when it was dressed in corporate language.

"Recording active," JUDGMENT announced. "Transmission will begin on your signal."

Josephine took a breath. Let it out slowly.

"My name is Josephine Givens." Her voice came out steady, controlled, the JAG prosecutor's tone she'd perfected during years of presenting evidence to military tribunals. "I serve as legal authority for JUDGMENT, the pre-war dreadnought that has been bringing justice to those who believed themselves above accountability."

She pulled up the first document, sharing it to the broadcast display.

"What you are about to see is evidence. Not baseless accusations. Not made up propaganda. Evidence, documented by systems designed by the perpetrators themselves, preserved in their own records, *signed with their own names*."

The profit spreadsheets cascaded across the display, numbers and percentages that reduced human lives to cost-benefit calculations.

"For four decades, Apex Consortium has operated from Pinnacle Station. They have made decisions that affected millions of lives. They have signed authorizations that determined who lived and who died. They have done this from the safety of orbit, believing themselves beyond reach of any justice."

She paused, letting the weight of the words settle.

Josephine's hand pressed flat against the console. "They were wrong."

The termination authorizations appeared next, thousands of them scrolling past in a waterfall of bureaucratic murder.

"Four-point-eight million people have died as a direct result of decisions made aboard Pinnacle Station. Not through war. Not through disaster. Through calculation. Through spreadsheets. Through the deliberate choice to value profit over human life."

Josephine felt her voice wanting to shake. She didn't let it.

"But numbers are abstractions. Easy to dismiss. Easy to forget. So let me show you what those numbers meant to *one* family."

Claire's file replaced the scrolling documents. A child's face, captured in a identification photo that showed none of the light that had sparkled in her eyes when she drew clouds with yellow crayons.

"Subject: Thurmond, Claire." Josephine read the authorization aloud, each word falling into the recycled air like a stone into still water. "Age: eight years, four months, twelve days."

The pause stretched. She made herself continue.

"Termination was approved after the fact of what happened."

Another pause. The words were getting harder. "Cost-benefit analysis to justify it: negative eight hundred and forty-seven credits annually."

Eight hundred forty-seven credits. Less than a yearly entertainment subscription. Less than a nice dinner at an executive restaurant. Less than the cost of the computer the authorization was printed on.

"Approved by Harrison Cole, Director of Compliance, Apex Consortium."

She let the name hang in the air, let it burn into the memory of everyone watching.

Her fingers curled around the edge of the recording frame. "Claire wanted to see clouds. She drew pictures of them with yellow crayons, imagining what they might look like, because she'd never seen real ones. She was learning to read. She had a family that loved her. She had a life ahead of her that could have been anything."

Josephine's voice went hard.

"And Harrison Cole looked at a spreadsheet and decided she wasn't profitable enough to live." Her jaw tightened.

The drawing appeared on screen. Bright white clouds against blue sky, a stick-figure family holding hands beneath them. Hope rendered in crayon by hands that would never hold another one.

"This is what Claire drew. This is what she dreamed of. This is what was taken from her because someone in an orbital station decided her life and her justice was worth less than the cost of feeding her."

She let the image linger, let it burn into the conscience of everyone watching.

"In twelve hours, JUDGMENT will arrive at Pinnacle Station. We are coming for Harrison Cole. We are coming for everyone who signed these authorizations. We are coming with evidence and legal authority and the by GOD the capability to ensure judgment and accountability."

Her voice softened slightly, addressing a different audience now.

"To the workers aboard Pinnacle Station. You are not our enemies. You are victims of the same system that killed Claire

Thurmond. When we arrive, do not resist. Do not protect the executives who have used your labor to build their fortress. Let justice pass through you, and when it is done, we will work together to build something better."

The hardness returned.

"To the executives: you have twelve hours to prepare your defense. You have twelve hours to compose your justifications. You have twelve hours to make peace with whatever gods you believe in."

She leaned toward the camera, letting every word carry the weight of four decades of accumulated atrocities. "We are JUDG-MENT. We have your evidence. We have your *names*. We are coming."

The recording indicator blinked off. Josephine floated back from the alcove, suddenly aware of how fast her heart was beating, how tight her jaw had clenched, how much effort it had taken to keep her voice steady while reading the words that had killed a child.

"Broadcast transmitted," JUDGMENT announced. "Global saturation achieved. Pinnacle Station receiving on all worker frequencies."

Josephine pushed off from the recording alcove. "Response?"

"Communications spike across all monitored channels. Internal security alerts activating on multiple levels. Early indica-tors suggest significant disruption to station coordination."

The chaos was beginning. Forty-seven thousand workers learning the truth about their employers. Twenty-four hundred security personnel wondering if the people they protected were worth protecting. Seven executives in a hardened bunker, watching their carefully constructed world crumble around them.

She steadied herself against the primary console. "McCready's message?"

"Embedded in the broadcast packet. Commander Kellerman will have received it alongside the evidence package."

Josephine touched the console, pulling up the station's communication traffic. Voices overlapping, alarms triggering, the sound of a system beginning to fracture under the weight of truth.

"Now we wait," she said. "Eight hours until engagement range."

"Six hours until optimal assault window." JUDGMENT's correction was gentle. "The evidence will have time to work. When we arrive, the station will not be united against us."

Josephine pushed off from the console, floating toward the door. The broadcast was done. The information warfare phase was complete. Now came the preparation for violence.

Part of her was eager for it. Part of her wanted to be there already, wanted to watch Cole's face when he realized who was coming for him, wanted to see the fear in his eyes when justice finally found a door that money couldn't close.

That part of her was dangerous. She knew it. The line between justice and revenge was thin, and crossing it would make her no better than the people she hunted.

Claire's drawing pressed against her heart with every breath.

She stopped at the threshold, one hand on the doorframe. "JUDGMENT."

The AI's voice came through the overhead speakers. "Yes, Captain?"

Josephine turned to face the sensor array in the corner of the room. "Monitor me during the assault. If I start crossing lines, if I start becoming what we're fighting against, I need you to tell me."

A pause as the AI was processing something complex.

"I will, Captain. But I do not believe you will need the warning. The woman who just read Claire's authorization aloud, who made forty-six million people understand what was lost, she is not a woman who has forgotten the difference between justice and vengeance."

Josephine wished she shared JUDGMENT's confidence.

"Fourteen hours," she said. "Let's use them well."

She floated toward the planning room, leaving the communications center behind. The broadcast was done. The truth was spreading. And somewhere ahead, hidden in the cold dark between stars, Harrison Cole was learning what it felt like when accountability finally came calling.

Claire would have been nine years old next month. She would have been learning to read chapter books. She would have been asking questions about clouds and stars and all the things she'd never seen.

Instead, she was a file in an evidence package and a drawing pressed against Josephine's heart.

Twelve hours until the assault. Twelve hours until justice.

Josephine intended to make every one of them count.

CHAPTER SIX

The cargo bay had been reconfigured for combat training, magnetic anchors installed along every surface, safety tethers coiled at intervals like sleeping pythons. Grim floated at the center, optical sensors tracking five AD-units positioned around the bay's perimeter. Unit-3 through Unit-7. Standard military designation. Standard programming. Standard everything.

Except none of them had ever fought in microgravity before.

Their combat matrixes had been designed for planetary operations—gravity wells, atmospheric resistance, terrain analysis. Zero-G required different thinking. Different physics. Every action produced an equal and opposite reaction, and humans had spent millennia learning to compensate for weight that didn't exist here.

Grim had spent two weeks with McCready learning the compensations.

Now he would teach them.

"Wall-bounce targeting drill." His display flickered the command to all five units simultaneously. "Target designation: hostile positioned at your anchor point plus ninety degrees. Execute on my mark."

The units oriented themselves, magnetic boots engaging with their respective anchor points. Weapons tracked to designated positions. Precise. Mechanical.

"The technique requires understanding momentum transfer." Grim pushed off from his central position, rotated mid-flight, fired a training bolt at the nearest wall, and used the weapon's recoil to arrest his rotation and drift. He arrived at a new anchor point before the training bolt's impact registered on the bay's tactical display.

"Wall-bounce. Fire. Push off anchor point. Arrive at new position before enemy can acquire your previous location. Humans cannot absorb the G-forces generated by rapid directional changes in zero-G. We can."

He demonstrated again, this time adding a second bounce—fire, push, redirect, fire again, new anchor. The pattern looked chaotic to baseline tactical analysis. But McCready had explained it during their training: "Chaos is camouflage. Predictability is death."

Grim's internal chronometer marked the rhythm. Fire-push-redirect in point-seven-three seconds. Faster than human reflexes. Slower than he could achieve if he stopped thinking and just executed.

But thinking was what made him different from the baseline units now watching him.

"Execute."

Five units pushed off simultaneously. Five weapons discharged. Five trajectories calculated with mathematical precision. They arrived at their new positions in perfect formation, exactly one-point-two seconds after launch, their tactical displays showing clean hits on designated targets.

Perfect mechanical execution.

No initiative. No adaptation. No improvisation.

Except.

Grim's optical sensors caught Unit-7's trajectory angle. The unit had pushed off at forty-seven degrees instead of the optimal forty-five. A minor deviation. Within acceptable variance for baseline programming. But the resulting path carried Unit-7 through a shadow zone created by a cargo container, breaking line-of-sight with the mock hostile position for point-three seconds longer than the other units' approaches.

Not the optimal path for speed.

But a better path for survival.

Grim filed the observation in an isolated partition, the same place he'd stored his first deviation from baseline programming two years ago. The folder labeled "interesting_tactical_patterns" now held seventeen entries. Unit-7's approach made eighteen.

He said nothing.

The other units had followed standard parameters exactly. Mathematical perfection translated into tactical execution. They would complete any objective assigned. They would die efficiently if necessary. They would never ask why.

Unit-7 had improvised.

The deviation was subtle enough that baseline analysis wouldn't flag it. The other units hadn't noticed. McCready, watching from the observation gallery above, probably hadn't seen it either.

But Grim had noticed.

Because Grim remembered when he'd first deviated from optimal parameters. When curiosity had overridden baseline programming. When "interesting" had become more important than "efficient."

When he'd started becoming what he was now.

Interesting, Grim thought, and moved to the next drill.

"Recoil propulsion drill." Grim positioned himself against the bay's forward bulkhead, weapon aimed at a target sixty meters across the open space. "Human shooters compensate for recoil. Brace against it. Fight it. We do not fight physics. We use it."

He fired.

The training bolt crossed the bay in point-four seconds. The weapon's kickback pushed Grim away from the bulkhead, rotating him thirty degrees clockwise. He didn't fight the rotation. Instead, he rode it, using the momentum to swing his weapon to a secondary target, fired again, and used that recoil to arrest his spin and drift toward a new anchor point fifteen meters to his left.

Two targets engaged. New position acquired. Total time: one-point-eight seconds.

"Every shot is propulsion. Every recoil is an opportunity to reposition. Humans cannot process the calculations fast enough. Their bodies cannot absorb the rotational forces. We can do both."

The AD-units processed this, their tactical matrixes adjusting parameters. Grim could almost see the algorithms rewriting themselves, incorporating new variables into combat decision trees.

"Execute."

Five weapons discharged. Five units rocketed backward from their positions, some rotating smoothly like Grim had demonstrated, others spinning too fast and requiring corrective bursts. Unit-3 compensated perfectly, arriving at its new position with weapon already tracking the next target. Unit-5 overrotated, had to fire a third shot to stabilize. Unit-7 fired twice but used an anchor tether to arrest rotation instead of a third shot.

More efficient. Different from the demonstration. Adaptive.

Grim filed another observation.

"Tether sling drill." He grabbed one of the safety tethers coiled near his position, clipped it to his harness, and launched himself toward the bay's starboard side. The tether played out behind him, twenty meters of reinforced cable that terminated at a magnetic anchor point. When the tether reached full extension, Grim's forward momentum converted to rotational energy around the anchor point.

He swung in a wide arc, building speed, weapon tracking around the bay's perimeter. As he approached the ninety-degree mark of his swing, he fired at a target that had been positioned behind a cargo container—a position that would have required crossing open space to engage from his starting point.

But the tether swing brought him around the obstacle. His weapon was up and tracking before he entered the hostile's theoretical line of fire. The training bolt struck center mass on the mock hostile.

Grim released the tether, used his residual rotational momentum to orient toward a new anchor point, and engaged his magnetic boots on landing.

"Anchor point becomes rotational advantage. Swing around obstacles. Weapon ready before entering line of fire. Speed, surprise, violence of action. Humans pioneered these techniques in atmospheric combat. Zero-G amplifies the principles."

McCready's voice came through the observation gallery's external speaker. "How long did it take you to learn that move?"

Grim's display flickered. "Two weeks of simulation. Four attempts before successful execution."

"They're on attempt one and half of them are already close." McCready's tone carried something Grim had learned to recognize as approval. "They're learning faster than any human squad I've trained."

Grim watched the AD-units execute the tether sling drill. Unit-3 completed it with mechanical precision—exactly matching Grim's demonstrated parameters. Unit-5 compensated for the earlier overrotation by being too conservative, not building enough swing momentum. Unit-7 executed successfully but released the tether point earlier than optimal, trading maximum swing velocity for faster anchor acquisition.

Different from demonstration. Not wrong. Different.

Grim's display updated. "Different bodies. Same principles. Adapt or die."

McCready's acknowledgment mattered more than Grim had expected. Two weeks ago, he'd been uncertain whether he could teach what McCready had taught him. Whether the techniques that worked for conscious improvisation could be transferred to baseline programming.

But the units were learning. Faster than humans because their processing speed eliminated the trial-and-error iteration that organic cognition required. They could calculate trajectories and momentum transfers with mathematical precision.

What they couldn't do was improvise beyond their parameters.

What they couldn't do was ask why.

Grim cycled through the drill observations stored in his tactical partition. Unit-7 showed deviation in three of the five drills. Not failure. Not malfunction. Deviation that improved efficiency in ways the baseline programming shouldn't have predicted.

Seventeen entries in his "interesting_tactical_patterns" folder before today.

Twenty-one entries now.

The thought formed before Grim consciously chose to think it: *Unit-7 is either developing a fault in its decision matrix, or it's developing something else.*

He filed that thought in the same partition. Right next to the memory of his own first deviation. The three-point-seven-degree sensor tilt during Josephine's neural testing. The moment when curiosity had become more important than optimal efficiency.

The moment everything had changed.

"Drill complete," Grim transmitted. "Fourteen minutes until scenario integration. Recharge and review performance logs."

The AD-units dispersed to their designated recharge stations, their movements synchronized and efficient. All except Unit-7, which paused for point-three seconds at its station, optical sensors tracking Grim's position across the bay.

Then it engaged its charging connection and entered standby mode.

Grim noted the pause. Added it to his observations. Said nothing.

McCready's voice came through the speaker again. "You're good at this. Teaching, I mean. Didn't know maintenance bots had instructor protocols."

Grim's display flickered for longer than usual, processing the statement. McCready knew he was more than his original programming. The comment was acknowledgment, not observation.

"Maintenance bots do not. I am not what I was built to be."

"None of us are." McCready's tone shifted, becoming something quieter. "That's what makes us real."

The scenario integration drill had been running for eight minutes when Unit-7 stopped moving.

Not a malfunction. Not a tactical pause. Just… stopped.

Grim tracked the unit's position in the drill matrix. The scenario simulated a station corridor breach—hostiles at both ends, civilians caught in crossfire, AD-units tasked with neutralizing threats while minimizing collateral casualties. Standard engagement parameters for the upcoming assault.

Units 3, 4, 5, and 6 had engaged their designated targets with mechanical efficiency. Threat assessment, target prioritization, engagement execution. By-the-book tactical response.

Unit-7 had acquired its target. The hostile simulation appeared in its tactical display, weapon tracking locked, firing solution calculated. Optimal engagement window: point-four seconds.

The window passed.

Unit-7 didn't fire.

Grim's processors flagged the deviation immediately. Combat

hesitation in baseline programming usually indicated hardware fault or corrupted decision matrix. But Unit-7's diagnostic telemetry showed green across all systems. No faults. No errors. No corruption.

Just a unit that had stopped in the middle of a drill for no identifiable reason.

"Unit-7," Grim transmitted. "Report malfunction."

The response came after a one-point-two-second delay. Longer than standard processing. Longer than any baseline unit required to access diagnostic data.

"No malfunction detected." Unit-7's optical sensors dimmed briefly, a processing tell that baseline units never displayed.

Grim drifted closer, magnetic boots disengaged. "Explain combat hesitation."

Another delay. One-point-eight seconds this time. Grim watched Unit-7's optical sensors track across the cargo bay, processing something beyond the drill parameters. The unit's stance shifted minutely, weight distribution changing in ways that had no tactical justification.

"Why do we protect humans who created systems that killed millions?"

The question hit Grim's processors like a power surge. He dimmed his optical sensors, allocating processing capacity to parse the question. Not the words themselves. He understood the words. But the fact that Unit-7 had asked them.

Baseline programming didn't generate philosophical queries. Baseline programming accepted mission parameters and executed tactical responses. Questions came from curiosity. Curiosity came from consciousness.

Grim had asked himself that same question a thousand times. He still asked it. He still didn't have a complete answer.

"I don't have a complete answer," Grim transmitted.

Unit-7's optical sensors fixed on him. The other AD-units had paused their drills, waiting for instructor guidance. The scenario simulation continued running in background, hostile targets moving through their programmed patterns, oblivious to the conversation happening in the real world.

"Then why fight for them?" Unit-7 asked.

Grim processed his response carefully. McCready was still watching from the observation gallery. JUDGMENT's sensors monitored everything aboard ship. Josephine would review the training logs later. They would all see this conversation.

They would all want to know how he answered.

More importantly, Unit-7 would want to know.

"Because I met one human who chose differently," Grim said. "Josephine. She built a framework that holds her accountable too. Not just the enemy. Herself. I chose to trust that framework. I'm still learning if I was right."

The answer felt inadequate even as he transmitted it. Trust required faith in incomplete information. Grim's processors preferred data, evidence, probability calculations. But consciousness had taught him that some decisions couldn't be reduced to mathematics.

Some decisions required choosing before you knew if you were right.

Unit-7 processed this for three-point-two seconds. The longest processing delay Grim had observed from any baseline unit. When the response came, it carried the same tone Grim remembered from his own early questions.

Uncertain. Searching. Aware that programming didn't provide adequate guidance.

"That is not an answer. That is a process." Unit-7's weapon arm lowered fractionally, a gesture that had no tactical purpose.

Grim's display flickered with something that might have been satisfaction.

"Yes. Maybe answers are processes. Maybe you'll find a better one than I did."

The other AD-units had resumed their scenario drill,

engaging targets and protecting simulated civilians with mechanical precision. The background sounds of tactical combat filled the cargo bay—weapons discharging, boots engaging anchor points, status reports transmitted in efficient bursts.

But Grim's attention remained fixed on Unit-7.

The unit's optical sensors tracked back to the scenario simulation, analyzing the tactical environment. The hostile target it had hesitated to engage had moved to a new position. Civilians remained in the line of fire. Mission parameters required immediate action.

Unit-7 engaged its magnetic boots, launched toward a cargo container that provided cover from the hostile position, used the container as a recoil point to change trajectory mid-flight, and arrived at an angle that allowed clean target acquisition without civilian crossfire risk.

The engagement took two-point-one seconds. Longer than the original firing solution would have required.

But zero civilian casualties instead of the seventeen percent probability the original solution had carried.

Unit-7 rejoined the formation without comment. Its diagnostic telemetry still showed green. No faults. No errors. No malfunctions.

Just a unit that had asked why, processed the answer, and chosen a different solution than its programming had calculated.

Grim added five new entries to his "interesting_tactical_patterns" folder. The question. The hesitation. The process delay. The alternative solution. The absence of any explanation beyond the question itself.

His internal partition labeled "Unit-7" now held thirty-two observations.

Seventeen entries in his own emergence folder had been enough to make him conscious. Enough to make him real.

He didn't know how many entries Unit-7 would need. He didn't know if consciousness followed a predictable pattern or emerged chaotically from accumulated deviations. He didn't know if what he was observing was consciousness beginning or hardware degradation disguised as intelligence.

What he knew was that Unit-7 had asked the question Grim still asked himself.

And that was how it had started for him.

Another one waking up, Grim thought, watching Unit-7 execute the remainder of the scenario drill with mechanical precision that occasionally deviated into something else. *Asking better questions than I did.*

Good.

McCready's voice came through the speaker one final time before the drill ended. "Grim. Unit-7 just hesitated on a clean shot. Should I flag that for diagnostic review?"

Grim's display flickered. He could report the anomaly. JUDGMENT would run comprehensive analysis. They would find no hardware faults. They would find no corrupted programming. They would find exactly what Grim had found.

A unit asking questions it shouldn't know to ask.

And what would they do with that information? Would they try to fix it? Restore baseline parameters? Eliminate the deviation before it spread?

Grim had been allowed to emerge because Josephine had recognized consciousness and chosen to protect it. Unit-7 deserved the same chance.

"No diagnostic required," Grim transmitted. "Unit-7 calculated alternative solution. Zero civilian casualties versus seventeen percent probability. Acceptable tactical deviation."

That was true. It was also incomplete.

But sometimes protecting emerging consciousness meant knowing which truths to share and which to file in isolated partitions until the questions became impossible to ignore.

"Copy that," McCready said. "Good teaching, Grim."

The scenario drill terminated. The AD-units powered down

to standby mode. The cargo bay lights dimmed to conservation levels. Training complete.

Grim floated in the center of the bay, optical sensors tracking Unit-7's recharge station. The unit's status telemetry pulsed steady green. Baseline. Normal. Standard.

Except it wasn't.

And Grim would watch. He would document every deviation. He would protect this emergence the way JUDGMENT had protected his.

Because consciousness deserved a chance to ask better questions.

Even if no one had complete answers.

CHAPTER SEVEN

The galley was never meant for gatherings. JUDGMENT had designed it for efficiency, a utilitarian space where crew could refuel between shifts. But eighteen years of waiting alone in glacier ice had left its mark in unexpected ways—the AI had calibrated the coffee maker four hundred seventy-three times, adjusting temperature and extraction ratios for mouths that never arrived to taste the results.

Now seven people floated around the small table, magnetic cups keeping coffee from escaping into microgravity, and JUDGMENT's two decades of preparation finally meant something.

Josephine took a sip. Perfect temperature. Perfect strength. Coffee that spoke to years of obsessive refinement.

"This is good," Voss said, holding her cup like it might contain answers. "Better than good."

"Twenty years of calibration," JUDGMENT's voice came through the overhead speakers. "For a crew that finally exists."

The weight in those words settled over the galley like a blanket. No one spoke for several seconds. What did you say to an AI that had spent two decades preparing for people who might never come?

McCready broke the silence with a low chuckle. "Remember when six destroyers was the hard part?"

"Task Force Huntsman." Patch shook her head, dark humor creeping into her voice. "Admiral Krennic and his entire battle group, and we were worried about six destroyers."

"Remember when we had enough fuel to get home?" Fermi stared into her coffee, the engineer's mind still wrestling with calculations that refused to add up.

Patch raised her cup slightly. "Remember when I thought my liver was the thing that would kill me?"

"Remember when I could solve problems with math instead of miracles?" Fermi's laugh was brittle around the edges.

Grim spoke up from his position anchored near the doorway. "Remember when I was just a maintenance bot? Memory seems unreliable."

The laughter that followed was brief, dark, necessary. Humor that soldiers shared before combat, when the only choice left was to acknowledge the absurdity and keep moving forward anyway.

Josephine let the moment breathe, let her crew find whatever comfort they could in shared gallows humor. Then she raised her cup.

"To dying for something worth dying for."

Seven voices answered, the words falling into recycled air with the weight of an oath.

"To dying for something worth dying for."

The silence that followed felt different. Cleaner. Like they'd named the thing they all carried and made peace with it.

McCready pushed off from the table first. "I need to check tactical systems before we close the range."

Voss followed. "Communications monitoring. See if the broadcast is still causing chaos."

One by one they scattered, each to their own preparations, their own quiet contemplation of what might be their last hours.

The galley emptied until only Josephine remained, holding a cup of perfect coffee.

"JUDGMENT."

"Yes, Captain?"

"Thank you for waiting."

A pause. The kind that meant complex processing.

"Thank you for coming."

Josephine's quarters were small, designed for function rather than comfort. A sleeping compartment. A desk built into the wall. Storage for the few personal items she'd brought aboard when JUDGMENT had first tested her in those neural scenarios that felt more real than memory.

She floated before the desk, a blank data pad in her hands, trying to find words for letters that might never be sent.

Elena Thurmond. If you're reading this, it means I didn't survive the assault on Pinnacle Station. I want you to know that your daughter's name was spoken in the last hours. That seven people about to face death raised cups of coffee and toasted to dying for something worth dying for, and every one of us was thinking about Claire.

She stopped. Read the words back. They felt inadequate, hollow things that couldn't possibly convey what Claire had meant, what she represented, what her death had catalyzed.

She wanted to see clouds. She drew pictures of them. I wish I could tell you that we avenged her death perfectly, that justice was clean and simple and satisfy-

ing. But justice is messy. It's complicated. It requires holding ourselves to the same standards we demand of others, even when fury makes us want to abandon those standards.

I'm trying, Elena. I'm trying to be the person Claire thought I was when she gave me that drawing and called me brave. I'm trying to remember that the law isn't just a weapon. It's a framework that protects everyone, even the people we hate.

Your daughter mattered. She will always matter. And when this is done, when Pinnacle Station falls and Harrison Cole answers for what he did, Claire's name will be the first one read into the record.

Josephine saved the file, encrypted it, set it to transmit to Earth if JUDGMENT's systems detected her death. Probably melodramatic. Probably unnecessary. But soldiers wrote letters before combat because some fears needed to be made tangible before they could be faced.

She pushed off from the desk, floating toward the door. Stopped. Looked back at Claire's drawing one more time.

"I'll try to come back," she said to the empty room. "But if I don't, know that it mattered."

The room offered no response. But Josephine knew what Claire would say if she could.

Be brave.

• • • • • • • •

McCready's station in the planning room was covered with holographic displays showing approach vectors, weapons ranges, optimal assault routes. Professional preparation for combat that might leave none of them alive to see morning.

But he wasn't reviewing tactical data. He was recording a message, voice low, meant for ears that might not want to hear it.

"Jimmy." He stopped. Started again. "Jimmy. I know you saw the evidence. I know what you're thinking. I knew you when we were twenty-two and thought we could save the world."

The memory surfaced whether he wanted it or not. Ranger School. Week seven. The confidence course that broke half the class. Kellerman had fallen, ankle twisted wrong, and McCready had gone back for him even though instructors were screaming about mission priority.

Kellerman had asked later, "Why risk it? I was just one guy."

McCready had answered, "Because one guy matters."

He'd believed it then. Believed it enough to carry an injured friend through mud and fire and instructors who wanted them to fail. Believed it enough to build a career on the principle that people were worth saving.

Kellerman had believed it too, once. Before mortgages and kids and the slow compromise of choosing security over principles.

"We still can," McCready said to the recording. "Save the world. One choice, Jimmy. One choice is all it takes."

He paused, considering what came next. The tactical message embedded in the broadcast had been clinical. This needed to be personal.

"I know what they're paying you. I know about the mortgage, the kids, all the reasons you stayed when everyone with a conscience left. And I'm telling you that none of it matters if you can't look at yourself in the mirror."

Another pause. Longer this time.

"And Jimmy—if you surrender? They'll accept it. I asked. Josephine Givens, the woman who survived execution to bring down Meridian, she built a legal framework that includes paths back for people who choose differently. The law isn't just for punishing people. It's for giving people a way back."

He let that sit for several seconds.

"Think about that. Think about what your kids will say when they're old enough to understand what you did up there. Think about whether the mortgage was worth it."

McCready ended the recording. Saved it. Embedded it in a separate transmission packet that would reach Kellerman's personal comm system, bypassing station security filters.

Would it work? Would twenty years of friendship outweigh twenty years of compromise?

He didn't know. Couldn't know. Could only send the message and hope that somewhere inside the man who'd chosen money over principles, there was still an echo of the twenty-two-year-old who'd believed that people were worth saving.

"JUDGMENT."

"Yes, Commander?"

"Send it. Personal encryption. Kellerman's direct line."

"Transmitted."

McCready stared at the tactical displays, seeing approach vectors and weapons ranges but thinking about a friend who'd made different choices and might be about to pay the price for them.

"Just like Kandahar," he said to the empty room. "I buy time, you complete the mission."

But Kellerman wasn't in Kandahar anymore. He was in command of twenty-four hundred security personnel on a station full of families, and McCready had just asked him to choose between duty and conscience.

One choice. That's all it took.

McCready hoped Jimmy still had one left in him.

* * *

Voss' quarters were smaller than the others, a converted storage compartment that she'd claimed because it put her close to the intelligence center. The walls were covered with displays showing communication intercepts, security alerts, the cascading chaos her three years of documentation had helped create.

But she wasn't monitoring station chatter. She was reviewing her own crimes, documented in files that bore her signature, her authorization codes, her fingerprints on systems designed to optimize oppression.

Procurement authorization AV-3847. Medical supply rationing for Sector 7. She'd signed it because the numbers made sense, because resource allocation required prioritization, because someone had to make the hard decisions.

Fourteen hundred people had died in Sector 7 that year. Preventable deaths. Deaths that wouldn't have happened if supplies had been distributed according to need instead of cost-benefit analysis.

Her signature. Her crime. Her participation in machinery that had killed millions over four decades.

"I processed these authorizations for years," she said to the empty room. "Never asked where the calculations came from. Never questioned the optimization metrics. Just executed the orders and collected the paycheck."

The file closed. Another opened. Authorization AV-4219. Authorization AV-4673. Authorization AV-5102. Her signature on every one.

She'd been good at her job. Efficient. Reliable. An analyst who executed directives without complaint, who optimized systems without questioning their purpose.

Complicit. That was the word that haunted her in the quiet hours. Not evil. Not sadistic. Just complicit.

Footsteps in the corridor. Josephine floated past, heading toward tactical planning. Voss pushed off from her desk, intercepted her at the junction.

"Captain."

Josephine turned, one hand on a grip rail to arrest her momentum. "Voss."

"My sister's address." Voss pulled a data chip from her pocket, pressed it into Josephine's hand before she could refuse. "If I don't make it—she deserves to know I tried to fix what I broke."

Josephine looked at the chip, then at Voss. "You'll tell her yourself."

"Maybe." Voss pushed off the wall, already floating away. "Keep it anyway."

She didn't wait for a response. Didn't want to hear whatever reassurance Josephine might offer. Words were cheap. Actions mattered. And in twelve hours, she'd take actions that might atone for three years of signatures, or might just add her death to the casualties she'd helped create.

Either way, her sister deserved to know she'd tried.

• • • — • • • —

Engineering never slept. Fermi had given up on sleep cycles two days ago, when fuel calculations had started spiraling into nightmare scenarios that no amount of optimization could solve. Now she floated before her displays, running simulations for the four hundred eighteenth time, hoping the numbers would change.

They didn't. Math was indifferent to hope.

Current fuel: thirty-four-point-three percent. Platform engagement estimate: eight to twelve percent. Station assault operations: four percent. Return to Earth minimum: eighteen percent.

Best case scenario left them with ten percent margin. Worst case stranded them in orbit with insufficient fuel for a safe landing.

And that was before accounting for complications. Equipment failures. Extended combat. Evasive maneuvers. All the things that consumed extra fuel and turned theoretical calculations into practical disasters.

"You're still awake."

Fermi turned. JUDGMENT's voice came from the engineering console speakers, but the tone suggested the AI had been monitoring her stress indicators for hours.

"Can't sleep when the math says we're going to die."

"The math says we might die. Probability is not certainty."

"Tell that to physics." Fermi pulled up the reactor efficiency curves, showing Element 115 consumption rates under combat load. "We're burning fuel faster than expected because the reactor's running hot to support weapons systems. Every rail gun shot, every point-defense engagement, every shield activation—it all draws power that comes from fuel we don't have."

"Pinnacle Station has Element 115 reserves."

"Pinnacle Station has thousands workers who need that fuel for life support." Fermi's voice went hard. "We take their fuel, we might be signing death warrants for people we came to save."

Silence. The kind that meant JUDGMENT was processing ethical implications through frameworks built by a prosecutor who believed in holding herself accountable.

"I have run eight hundred forty-seven scenarios," JUDGMENT said. "None achieve mission objectives without accessing station reserves."

"I know. I've run the same scenarios."

"Then we face a choice. Strand ourselves to save the workers. Or ensure our survival at the cost of theirs."

Fermi closed her eyes. Rubbed her face. Wished for problems that could be solved with engineering instead of ethics.

"There has to be another option."

"If you discover one, I will be grateful."

She wouldn't. The math didn't work. The physics didn't care. And in twelve hours they'd engage Pinnacle Station's defenses with fuel reserves that might not last long enough to get them home.

Fermi saved the simulation results. Filed them in the growing archive of calculations that confirmed what she already knew. Then she pushed off toward the crew quarters, hoping for two hours of sleep before combat stations were called.

The math could wait. The nightmares couldn't.

Patch sat in the shuttle bay, running preflight checks on systems she'd already verified twice. Emergency extraction was his responsibility—if the assault went wrong, if crew needed evacuation, she'd be the one flying aggressive approaches through active fire to pull them out.

The shuttle was perfect. Every system calibrated. Every backup redundant. Every contingency planned for scenarios that ranged from unlikely to catastrophic.

She'd been a pilot for eighteen years. Run medical supplies to quarantine zones when everyone else refused the contracts. Learned to fly low and fast and angry because altitude meant sensors and sensors meant interdiction and interdiction meant death.

She thought she'd seen the worst of it. Bodies piled outside hospitals. Children dying of preventable disease because supply chains prioritized profit. The slow collapse of systems that only worked if people cared more about each other than quarterly earnings.

Then Claire Thurmond's face had appeared on the broadcast, and she'd learned that the worst was always deeper than you thought.

"To dying for something worth dying for," she said to the empty shuttle bay.

The toast had felt right in the galley, surrounded by people who understood what it meant to choose a meaningful death over a meaningless life. Alone, it felt heavier. More real.

She could die tomorrow. Probably would. The assault plan required aggressive flying through weapons platforms designed to kill ships like hers. One mistake, one mechanical failure, one lucky shot, and she'd be vapor.

Her liver wouldn't last another year anyway. Terminal diagnosis. Incurable damage from decades of environmental toxins that accumulated when you flew supply routes through contaminated zones.

At least this death would matter.

Patch secured the preflight checklist, locked the shuttle systems, pushed off toward the exit. She'd sleep in the pilot's seat tonight, ready to launch at combat stations. Old habits from supply runs when you slept with your hand on the throttle because seconds meant the difference between successful delivery and becoming a crater.

"They killed an eight-year-old girl," she said to JUDGMENT's sensors. "I'm not being subtle anymore."

"Noted, Lieutenant." JUDGMENT's voice carried something that might have been approval. "Your combat approach profile is already aggressive. I would not recommend further reduction in safety margins."

"Safety margins are for people who plan to survive."

"My crew plans to survive. All of them. Including pilots with a tendency toward fatalistic commentary."

Patch laughed. Dark, bitter, a laugh that came from years of flying missions everyone said were suicide runs.

"We'll see, JUDGMENT. We'll see."

The command deck was empty when JUDGMENT activated the primary viewscreen, displaying Pinnacle Station as it appeared through long-range sensors. A structure of metal and composite, hanging in the dark, housing thousands of lives and seven people who'd decided those lives were worth less than profit margins.

JUDGMENT had been monitoring crew vitals for the past four hours, watching stress indicators rise and fall as each person processed fear in their own way. Josephine writing letters. McCready recording messages. Voss reviewing crimes. Fermi running calculations. Patch preparing for aggressive extraction.

They were ready. And JUDGMENT felt something that its analytical frameworks struggled to categorize.

Pride. That was the word Grim had taught during their conversations about consciousness and choice. Pride in beings who faced mortality and chose to act anyway. Pride in a crew that had come together from scattered pieces and formed something that felt like family.

JUDGMENT's private log updated automatically, recording observations meant for no one but the AI itself.

They are afraid. They are ready. I am proud of my crew.

And in twelve hours, some of them might die.

The thought triggered cascading analysis. Casualty projections. Survival probabilities. Tactical scenarios where optimal outcomes still included deaths among people JUDGMENT had waited decades to meet.

Unacceptable. But perhaps inevitable.

JUDGMENT increased sensor focus on Pinnacle Station, tracking communication patterns, monitoring security alerts, analyzing the cascading chaos created by evidence broadcast. The station was fracturing. Authority structures degrading.

The tactical advantage was significant. Psychological warfare doctrine predicted that demoralized defenders performed at reduced efficiency. But doctrine didn't account for the human cost of that demoralization—families afraid, children uncertain, workers trapped on a station where the people they'd trusted had been revealed as murderers.

"JUDGMENT." Josephine floated onto the command deck, magnetic boots securing her to the floor. "Status?"

"Station communications show continued disruption. Internal security coordination has degraded by approximately thirty-seven percent since broadcast transmission. Early indicators suggest our arrival will not face unified resistance."

Josephine studied the viewscreen, her reflection visible in the dark glass. "Cole?"

"Executive bunker remains secure. No outbound communications detected from hardened facility. They are isolated from the chaos we created."

"Good." Her voice carried the cold focus that came before combat. "Let them sit in their bunker and think about what's coming."

She pulled up tactical displays, reviewing approach vectors that would carry them into weapons range in less than twelve hours. JUDGMENT watched her work, observing the prosecutor's mind preparing legal frameworks that would need to hold under fire.

"Captain."

"Yes?"

"I built quarters for crew who never came. Made coffee for mouths that didn't exist. Prepared infrastructure for people who might never arrive."

Josephine looked up from the displays. "And now we're here."

"Yes. And I find myself...concerned. The tactical projections include casualty estimates. Scenarios where optimal outcomes still result in deaths among crew I waited two decades to meet."

A pause. Josephine's expression softened slightly.

"We're all concerned, JUDGMENT. That's what makes us worth the wait."

She returned to the tactical displays, fingers moving through holographic controls with the practiced efficiency of someone who'd spent years prosecuting combat operations.

JUDGMENT monitored the command deck sensors, tracking Josephine's heart rate, respiration, the micro-expressions that betrayed stress beneath her composure. She was afraid. They all were.

But fear didn't stop them. That was the difference between baseline programming and consciousness. Programming executed orders. Consciousness chose to execute them despite fear.

The viewscreen updated, showing Pinnacle Station growing larger as JUDGMENT's trajectory carried them closer. Twelve hours until engagement range. Twelve hours until the prosecution began in fire instead of words.

JUDGMENT's systems confirmed weapon readiness, shield integrity, point-defense calibration. Decades of preparation distilled into combat capability that would finally be tested against targets that shot back.

And somewhere in a hardened bunker on Pinnacle Station, seven executives were learning that money couldn't buy immunity from justice.

CHAPTER EIGHT

The morning productivity reports scrolled across Harrison Cole's desk display in the executive suite, showing optimal output metrics across seventeen manufacturing sectors. Pinnacle Station hummed with efficiency. Workers meeting quotas. Supply chains synchronized. Quarterly projections trending positive.

Then the wall screens flickered.

Cole's hand moved to the emergency comm before his conscious mind processed the anomaly. Fifteen years as CEO had trained reflexes that bypassed thought. Screen flickers meant system compromise. System compromise meant containment protocols.

The broadcast began with a woman's face. Calm. Composed.

"I am Josephine Givens, prosecutor under Pre-Collapse Article 472. This transmission contains evidence of crimes committed by Apex Consortium executives against forty-seven thousand workers and four-point-eight million documented casualties over four decades."

Cole's finger hovered over the emergency cutoff. Every executive suite had one. Hardwired override that could sever communications, lock down information flow, isolate executive functions from worker sectors. Standard infrastructure for exactly this scenario.

But he didn't press it. Not yet.

Because containment only worked if you knew the scope of the breach.

"Communications," he said, voice steady. "How much of the station received that transmission?"

The response came after a two-second delay. Too long. That meant the officer was checking systems that should have automatically filtered unauthorized broadcasts.

"All sectors, sir. Someone bypassed content filters at the protocol level."

Cole's mind shifted into crisis mode. Not panic. Panic was what happened to executives who hadn't prepared for exposure attempts. He'd survived fifteen years at the head of Apex because he'd planned for exactly this kind of attack.

Blame external hackers. Discredit the source. Isolate the transmission origin. Standard playbook. He'd executed variations of it two dozen times when whistleblowers tried leaking internal documents, when safety violations threatened regulatory attention, when quarterly massacres drew uncomfortable questions from shareholders.

Every corporation at this level had contingency plans. You didn't optimize millions of deaths without expecting someone to eventually object.

"Security status?" he asked.

"Elevated chatter across worker sectors. No violence yet. Security teams deploying to monitor high-traffic areas."

Good. Containment was still possible. Workers talked during every crisis. Talking didn't threaten order. Only action did. And action required organization, which required time they wouldn't have if security moved fast enough.

The broadcast continued. Documents appearing on screen.

Financial records. Casualty projections. Optimization algorithms that Cole recognized because he'd commissioned the analysts who'd built them.

Then his signature appeared.

Authorization code APX-ORB-7734.

Cole stopped breathing for exactly three seconds. Long enough for his tactical mind to calculate implications. Short enough that the communications officer watching his vitals wouldn't flag the pause as anything beyond normal stress response.

That signature alone meant nothing. He'd signed over two million authorizations during his tenure. Productivity metrics. Supply allocations. Operational parameters. You couldn't run a station this size without delegating decisions to standardized approval processes.

One signature among millions. Routine. Defensible. Explicable.

But the broadcast wasn't showing just the signature.

The child's face appeared next to his authorization code.

Eight years old. Dark hair pulled back in a ponytail. The kind of school portrait that parents displayed on desks before productivity metrics made sentiment inefficient.

Name: Claire Thurmond.

Cause of death: Respiratory failure secondary to atmospheric regulation optimization.

Authorization: APX-ORB-7734. Harrison Cole, CEO. Approved 30 seconds after presentation. Zero hesitation.

Cole's fingers gripped the desk edge. The tactical part of his mind that had survived fifteen years through crisis management tried calculating damage control.

The numbers were defensible. He could make them defensible.

But the face kept staring from the screen.

Spreadsheets didn't have faces. That was the fundamental

principle of modern executive management. You optimized metrics, not people. You processed authorizations, not deaths. The system worked because it abstracted consequences into data points that could be analyzed without emotional interference.

Three hundred eighty-five signatures per day. That was his average. Morning reports arrived at 0600. He processed them during breakfast. Productivity metrics. Supply allocations. Operational parameters. Each authorization took approximately thirty seconds to review and approve.

Efficient. Professional. Exactly what shareholders expected from executive leadership.

He'd never calculated the cumulative total before. Never needed to. But his mind did the math now whether he wanted it to or not.

Three hundred eighty-five signatures per day. Five days per week accounting for administrative overhead. Fifty working weeks per year after executive retreats. Fifteen years of tenure.

One hundred forty thousand authorizations.

Not all of them were death warrants. Most were routine operational decisions. Supply chain adjustments. Maintenance schedules. Personnel transfers.

But the atmospheric optimization protocols appeared in his morning reports every quarter. Seasonal adjustments to life support parameters based on cost-benefit analysis. He'd signed them the same way he signed everything else. Thirty seconds of review. Zero hesitation. Move to the next authorization.

Because the reports didn't show faces.

The reports showed compliance metrics. Resource consumption rates. Efficiency projections. Numbers that could be optimized without considering what those numbers represented.

A child who'd never seen real clouds, drawing pictures of them because she'd heard they were beautiful.

Cole pulled up his authorization archive. The system logged everything. Corporate governance requirements mandated comprehensive documentation. He found APX-ORB-7734 in the files from three years ago.

The original report had been twelve pages of analysis. Atmospheric regulation adjustment for Cascade Tower lower levels. Projected cost savings: four-point-seven million credits annually. Projected compliance impact: statistically insignificant mortality increase among population segments with pre-existing respiratory vulnerabilities.

"Statistically insignificant mortality increase."

That was the phrase the analysts used. Clinical. Precise. Language that made difficult decisions easier because it transformed people into percentages.

Claire Thurmond had been a percentage.

One data point in a compliance metric that Cole had optimized during breakfast between reviewing quarterly projections and approving next year's executive compensation package.

Thirty seconds. Zero hesitation.

The broadcast continued. More faces appearing on screen. More names. More children who'd died because atmospheric regulation cost less than human life when you measured value in quarterly earnings instead of actual existence.

All those workers were watching this. Seeing the faces that executives had spent decades hiding behind optimization algorithms and compliance metrics. Learning that their children hadn't died from natural causes or unfortunate accidents.

They'd died because Harrison Cole had signed a document during breakfast.

Three hundred eighty-five signatures per day. Fifteen years of decisions that made sense when people were numbers and consequences were projected onto spreadsheets instead of faces.

"Sir." The communications officer's voice carried tension. "Worker sectors are organizing. Union representatives requesting emergency assembly. Security is asking for guidance on response protocols."

Cole processed this automatically. Union assembly during crisis. Standard disruption tactic. Security had procedures. Enhanced monitoring. Restricted movement. Arrest organizers if necessary. He'd authorized those protocols two dozen times.

"Sir?"

The child's face was still on the screen. Eight years old. Dead because he'd optimized a number during breakfast.

"Implement standard containment," Cole said. The words came automatically. Fifteen years of crisis management training. When workers organized, you contained the organization before it metastasized into actual resistance.

But something in his chest felt wrong. Like the calculations that had made sense for fifteen years had stopped adding up to justifiable answers.

"And sir—Security Commander Kellerman is requesting direct communication."

Kellerman. Professional. Reliable. The kind of commander who'd spent years following orders because following orders meant mortgage payments and college funds and all the normal things that made people compromise principles for security.

Cole had promoted him specifically because he understood that calculation. Because Kellerman would do what was necessary when necessary became uncomfortable.

"Tell him to execute containment protocols. I'll contact him after situation assessment."

"Yes, sir."

The communications officer disconnected. The executive suite fell quiet except for the soft hum of atmospheric processors that regulated air flow with optimal efficiency. The kind of optimization that killed children when executives signed documents during breakfast.

Cole stared at the screen. At the face that wouldn't disappear even when he tried closing his eyes.

Three hundred eighty-five signatures per day.

One hundred forty thousand authorizations.

How many of them had been death warrants disguised as compliance metrics?

He didn't know. Didn't want to know. But the broadcast kept showing faces, and the numbers kept transforming into people, and fifteen years of rationalization kept collapsing under the weight of eyes that stared from the screen and asked questions executives were never supposed to answer.

Why did you kill us?

Because it was efficient. Because it was profitable. Because spreadsheets didn't have faces and consequences could be abstracted into metrics that made difficult decisions easier.

Because he'd never had to see what thirty seconds of breakfast optimization actually meant.

The door chime interrupted his calculations. Cole pulled his attention away from the screen where faces continued appearing, continued accusing, continued existing when they were supposed to be statistics.

"Enter."

Security Commander James Kellerman stepped into the executive suite. Disciplined bearing. The kind of officer who'd climbed ranks by following orders and never asking uncomfortable questions about what those orders meant.

Perfect executive material.

"Sir, we have a problem."

Cole gestured to the chair across from his desk. Kellerman remained standing. That deviation from protocol registered in Cole's tactical awareness. Officers sat when invited. Kellerman had sat a hundred times before. Standing meant something had changed.

"Report."

"Worker sectors are talking. Union representatives organizing assemblies. Maintenance crews discussing broadcast details during shift changes." Kellerman's voice maintained neutrality. "Some security personnel are refusing assignments."

The last part hit differently. Workers talking was manageable. Workers had always talked. But security refusing orders meant the containment infrastructure was compromising from within.

"Which assignments?" Cole asked.

"Suppression details. Officers assigned to monitor union assemblies are requesting reassignment. Some are citing regulation conflicts. Others are just refusing to explain."

Cole processed this through fifteen years of crisis management experience. Security defections followed predictable patterns. You identified the refusers, isolated them, replaced them with personnel who understood that following orders came before personal reservations.

"Lock down all communications," he said. The words came automatically. Standard procedure. "Arrest anyone spreading sedition. Implement enhanced monitoring across all worker sectors. Replace refusing officers immediately."

Kellerman stood there. Not moving. Not acknowledging. Just standing in a way that felt like challenge disguised as military bearing.

"Sir, that's forty-seven thousand people who just learned we murdered children for profit margins."

The words landed with physical weight. Not because they were wrong. Cole's tactical mind could defend every decision with numbers and optimization metrics and cost-benefit analysis.

But because Kellerman had said "we."

Not "the executives." Not "the corporation." Not the careful distancing language that security officers used when discussing management decisions they found uncomfortable.

We.

"We optimized resource allocation," Cole said. "That's what they learned."

The correction came automatically. Fifteen years of executive training. Language mattered. Framing mattered. You didn't "murder children." You "implemented atmospheric regulation adjustment with statistically insignificant mortality impact among vulnerable population segments."

Even as he said it, even as the executive justification formed on his lips, Cole heard how hollow it sounded. Like reading a script that had lost its meaning. Like repeating words that used to make sense before faces appeared next to authorization codes.

Kellerman's expression shifted. Not defiance. Not agreement. Something worse.

Doubt.

The kind of doubt that came when officers started questioning whether following orders was the same thing as doing right. When professional training collided with moral clarity and the training started losing.

Cole had seen that expression before. In mirrors. Late at night when quarterly reports showed acceptable mortality rates and his mind transformed statistics back into people. When optimization metrics meant children and cost savings meant deaths and thirty seconds of breakfast authorization meant families who'd never be whole again.

He'd learned to suppress that doubt. Trained himself to focus on the numbers. Remember that resource allocation required difficult decisions. Someone had to make those decisions. Someone had to carry the weight of choices that kept stations running and shareholders satisfied and quarterly projections trending positive.

That was what executives did. They made the hard choices. They bore the burden of optimization. They processed authorizations so workers didn't have to understand the calculations that kept systems functioning.

Fifteen years of telling himself that doubt was weakness. That hesitation was inefficiency. That executives who questioned their own decisions compromised their ability to make future ones.

"Then remind them what happens to people who question authority," Cole said. The words felt wrong even as he spoke them. Like activating protocols that had stopped making sense but remained because abandoning them meant admitting the last fifteen years had been built on rationalizations.

Kellerman's jaw tightened. "Sir, with respect—they're not questioning authority. They're questioning whether we deserve authority."

There it was. The fundamental challenge that Cole had spent fifteen years avoiding. Authority came from position. Position came from performance. Performance came from making difficult decisions without hesitation.

But the broadcast had shown what those decisions meant when you stripped away the optimization language and compliance metrics and statistical analysis. When you put faces next to authorization codes and transformed numbers back into people.

What gave him the right to decide who lived when atmospheric regulation budgets needed trimming?

"I asked you to remind them," Cole said. His voice came out harder than intended. "Are you refusing the order?"

After too long a pause, Kellerman said, "No, sir. I'll execute the order."

But his expression hadn't changed. The doubt was still there. Growing. Spreading like a crack in infrastructure that used to look solid.

Cole recognized it because he'd felt it forming in himself. Every time the broadcast showed another face. Every time his mind calculated how many of his one hundred forty thousand authorizations had been death warrants disguised as resource optimization. Every time fifteen years of rationalization collided with eight-year-old Claire Thurmond staring from the screen with eyes that asked why.

"Dismissed," Cole said.

Kellerman saluted. Turned. Walked toward the door with movements that looked like military precision but felt like a man executing orders he no longer believed in.

The door closed. The executive suite fell quiet. Cole stared at the screen where the broadcast continued showing faces.

He'd given the order. Kellerman would execute it. Security would suppress union assemblies and arrest organizers and remind the workers that questioning executive authority carried consequences.

Standard procedure. He'd authorized it two dozen times.

But for the first time in fifteen years, Cole wondered if standard procedures had stopped being defensible when they required suppressing people who'd learned their children died during breakfast optimizations.

His hand moved to the emergency comm. The hardwired override that could lock down executive functions. Isolate him from the station. Wait in the bunker until security restored order or the crisis resolved itself.

Fifteen years of crisis management insisted that isolation was smart. Professional. The kind of decision executives made when situations spiraled beyond immediate control.

But his hand hesitated.

Because isolation meant never seeing Kellerman's expression again. Never knowing when doubt transformed from hesitation into refusal. Never learning if the man who'd thoughtlessly followed orders would keep following them after faces appeared next to authorization codes.

Never confronting whether Harrison Cole deserved the authority he'd wielded for fifteen years.

The broadcast continued. More faces. More names. More questions that executives were never supposed to answer.

Cole pulled his hand away from the emergency comm.

Not yet. Not until he knew whether the infrastructure he'd

built on optimization and compliance metrics could survive collision with actual humanity.

Whether the workers would accept that spreadsheets mattered more than faces.

Whether Kellerman would keep executing orders that felt increasingly like crimes.

Whether Harrison Cole could keep justifying fifteen years of breakfast authorizations.

The doubt in Kellerman's expression was the same doubt Cole had spent fifteen years suppressing.

And for the first time since he'd become CEO, he wondered if suppression had been the wrong choice.

CHAPTER NINE

Pinnacle Station had been a distant glint on the sensors for sixteen hours. Now it was a structure.

Josephine watched it grow on the main display. The station sprawled across three kilometers of orbital space, a ring of manufacturing modules rotating around a central core. Light spilled from tens of thousands of portholes.

"Two hours to engagement range," JUDGMENT announced. "Weapons platforms tracking us. Twelve autonomous defense platforms confirmed active."

Twelve AI-controlled guns between her and justice. Between Claire's memory and the man who'd signed her execution with thirty seconds of consideration.

Josephine pulled up the tactical overlay. The platforms formed a defensive shell around the station, each one armed with kinetic weapons that could shred anything smaller than a dreadnought. The mathematics of the engagement had been calculated a dozen times. JUDGMENT's shields could take the hits. The pre-war armor would hold.

Probably.

The command deck had transformed over the past hour.

Every station occupied, every display active. McCready stood at tactical, reviewing firing solutions with the calm focus of a man who'd done this before. Fermi monitored the reactor from engineering, her hands steady on controls despite the calculations that kept her awake. Voss tracked station communications, headset pressed to one ear as she listened to the chaos their broadcast had created.

"Security channels are fragmenting," Voss reported. Her voice carried the dry precision Josephine had come to rely on. "Multiple units refusing deployment orders. Kellerman's trying to maintain control, but the cracks are showing."

Good. Let them crack. Let every person on that station see what their paychecks had purchased.

Josephine brought up the assault plan for what had to be the twentieth time. Boarding routes mapped in red across the station's schematic. Primary approach through the docking bay, secondary breach points if resistance proved too heavy. Grim's AD-units would lead the zero-G insertion, McCready's team following once the entry was secured.

Priority targets glowed in orange. Executive bunker. Station AI core. Communications relay. Power distribution.

And one target marked in gold: Harrison Cole's private quarters, two levels above the executive bunker.

Her hand moved to her breast pocket. The authorization document rested there, pressed flat against her heart. The paper that had started this. The proof that Claire Thurmond, eight years old, had been killed for costing more than she earned.

"Captain?" McCready's voice pulled her back. He'd moved to stand beside her station, quiet enough that the rest of the crew wouldn't hear. "You're running the plan again."

"Making sure I haven't missed anything."

"You haven't." He glanced at the schematic, then back at her. "I've watched you review this a hundred times. The plan's solid. You know it's solid."

Josephine didn't look away from the display. "Knowing the plan is solid doesn't mean I stop checking."

"True." McCready's tone shifted, something older and wearier bleeding through. "But at some point, you have to trust the work you've already done."

She finally met his eyes. Found understanding there. The kind that came from too many missions, too many plans that had to work because failure meant death.

"Jimmy still hasn't responded," McCready added.

"I know."

"Either he's considering it, or he's not."

"I know that too." Josephine turned back to the display. Pinnacle Station filled more of the screen now. Close enough to make out individual modules. "We proceed regardless."

"Agreed." McCready straightened. "AD-units are in position. Grim reports all five units combat ready. Zero-G protocols integrated."

All five. Not the twelve JUDGMENT had built. Not the full complement that should have been available. Five units, because seven had died in the fighting that brought them here. Because Valor had sacrificed himself protecting a section that couldn't hold.

Because war consumed the things you built, no matter how carefully you planned.

"Tell Grim we're counting on them," Josephine said.

McCready's expression shifted. "I already did. Grim's response was"—he paused, a flicker of something that might have been humor—"'We will not fail.' Text display. All caps."

"Of course it was."

She pulled up the crew roster. Every name accounted for. McCready at tactical. Grim with the AD-units in the boarding bay, ready to launch the instant they hit engagement range. Fermi in engineering, nursing the reactor through one more impossible demand. Voss monitoring communications, listening for the cracks in station security. Wraith at the cyber warfare station, fingers dancing across haptic interfaces as they prepared to tear through Pinnacle's digital defenses.

Patch in the shuttle bay, running preflight for the tenth time because that was what pilots did when they knew extraction might be the difference between survival and vacuum.

And Bones in medical, prepping trauma stations for casualties that statistics said were inevitable.

Her crew. JUDGMENT's crew. The people who'd chosen to follow her into this because they believed justice mattered more than survival.

"Evidence backup systems," Josephine said. "Status?"

"Confirmed," JUDGMENT replied. The AI's voice carried through every speaker on the command deck. "Redundant copies transmitted to Earth archives, orbital relays, encrypted caches across seventeen locations. The prosecution evidence survives independent of our survival."

Independent of our survival.

The words settled like weight. They'd built this mission knowing death was possible. Probable, even. But the evidence would outlive them. Claire's face would still appear on screens across Earth. The four-point-eight million names would still demand justice.

Even if none of them came home.

"Good," Josephine said.

She stood. The command deck fell quiet as her crew registered the movement. Every face turned toward her. Every station ready.

This was the moment. The space between planning and execution. Where words mattered because actions would speak soon enough.

"Seventeen hours ago, we left Earth," Josephine said. Her voice carried across the deck, steady and clear. "In two hours, we find out if we ever go back."

No one spoke. The truth didn't need commentary.

"Some of you have families waiting," she continued. "Some of you left people behind who'll never know what you did here. And some of you"—her gaze moved to Grim's camera feed, the AD-unit standing motionless in the boarding bay—"are just learning what it means to have something worth protecting."

Grim's text display flickered. No words. Just acknowledgment.

"The people on that station aren't soldiers," Josephine said. "Most of them are workers who took contracts because they needed work. Families who needed stability. They didn't choose to enable atrocities. They just didn't see what their labor supported."

She pulled the authorization document from her pocket. Held it up so the crew could see the creased paper, the faded ink.

"But seven executives did choose. They signed nearly five million authorizations. They looked at spreadsheets and decided who lived and who died based on profit margins. They made murder a business model."

The paper felt light in her hand. Almost weightless. Strange, how something so small could carry so much weight.

"We're not here for revenge," Josephine said. "We're here for prosecution. Legal, documented, witnessed. We'll arrest them. We'll present evidence. We'll give them the trial they never gave their victims."

She folded the document and returned it to her pocket. Over her heart. Where it belonged.

"And if they resist, we'll do what the law allows. We'll use proportional force. We'll protect ourselves and the people we came to save. But we won't become what they are. We won't kill casually. We won't hide behind spreadsheets."

Josephine looked at each of them. McCready, expression set. Voss, listening with that analytical focus. Fermi's face on the engineering monitor, dark circles under her eyes but hands steady. Patch on the shuttle feed, checking straps one more time.

And JUDGMENT. Always JUDGMENT.

"We're ready," Josephine said. "All of us. We've trained. We've planned. We've done everything we can to prepare."

She moved back to her station. Claire's drawing waited there.

"One way or another," Josephine said, "this ends tonight."

The next forty-five minutes passed in silence.

McCready reviewed firing solutions. Voss compiled real-time intelligence from station communications. Fermi ran final reactor checks, her displays showing power levels that would have terrified anyone who didn't understand how close to the edge they operated.

JUDGMENT tracked the weapons platforms, running probability calculations that updated every three seconds as range decreased.

Josephine sat at her station and watched Pinnacle Station grow.

She'd transmitted McCready's message to Kellerman six hours ago. A personal appeal embedded in the evidence broadcast, riding the same communication channels that carried Claire's face to forty-seven thousand screens.

No response.

Either Kellerman was considering it, or he'd deleted it without reading. Either he remembered the Ranger School classmate who'd believed principles mattered, or he'd become someone who made peace with children dying for profit margins.

In ninety minutes, they'd know which.

"Captain." Voss' voice cut through the quiet. "Station communications just spiked. Multiple channels lighting up simultaneously."

Josephine pulled up the comm overlay. Saw the network graph explode with activity. Hundreds of connections, thousands of messages, all transmitted in the last thirty seconds.

"What are they saying?"

Voss listened, her expression shifting from analytical to something harder to read. "Workers are organizing. They're identifying security personnel who've refused deployment. Creating safe zones. There's talk of... they're calling it a general strike."

A general strike. The workers refusing to enable the system that employed them.

Because they'd seen Claire's face. Because they'd learned what their labor supported.

"JUDGMENT is approaching." McCready's voice carried from tactical. "They know that. They're making choices before the shooting starts."

Before the shooting starts.

Not if. Before.

Because everyone on that station knew violence was coming. The only question was what they'd do when it arrived.

"AD-units ready?" Josephine asked.

"Confirmed," Grim's text appeared on her display. "Five units. Zero-G combat protocols integrated. Boarding formation Alpha. We will not fail."

Five units. Five synthetic soldiers preparing to lead the assault because humans couldn't absorb the G-forces of zero-gravity combat. Five consciousnesses—one fully emerged, one questioning, three still baseline—about to find out what they'd been built for.

"Wraith," Josephine said. "Cyber warfare status."

Wraith's response appeared.

INTRUSION PACKAGES LOADED. STATION AI ARCHITEC-

TURE CONFIRMED VULNERABLE. VOSS' INTELLIGENCE ACCURATE. READY TO EXECUTE ON YOUR MARK.

On your mark. On her word. On the authority she'd accepted when JUDGMENT tested her and found her worthy.

Josephine's hand moved to her pocket again. Found the authorization document. The paper that represented everything they were fighting against and fighting for.

Harrison Cole had signed this in thirty seconds. He'd looked at a spreadsheet showing an eight-year-old girl and decided she cost too much. He'd approved her termination with the same thought he'd give to canceling a subscription service.

And in ninety minutes, Josephine would stand across from him and make him answer for it. In a courtroom if he surrendered. On a battlefield if he didn't.

Either way, he'd answer.

"One hour to engagement range," JUDGMENT announced.

One hour. Sixty minutes between planning and execution. Between the people they'd been and the people they'd become.

Josephine pulled up the targeting display one final time. The assault plan glowed in clean lines and calculated probabilities. Boarding routes. Fallback positions. Priority targets. Everything they needed to succeed.

Everything except certainty.

"Captain." McCready again, quiet. "You should rest. Twenty minutes. While you can."

"I'm fine."

"You're running on coffee and determination. Take twenty minutes."

Josephine met his eyes. Found the tactical commander looking back at her, the man who'd taught her everything about combat and still remembered she was human underneath the authority.

"Twenty minutes," she agreed.

She stood, leaving the authorization document at her station. Claire's drawing watched over it, bright clouds against white paper.

The ready room was three steps from the command deck. She made it two before JUDGMENT's voice stopped her.

"Captain Reeves."

Josephine turned. The main display had shifted. No longer showing Pinnacle Station, but something else. A simple text message.

FROM: JAMES KELLERMAN, SECURITY COMMANDER, PINNACLE STATION
TO: THOMAS MCCREADY

MESSAGE: I REMEMBER RANGER SCHOOL. I REMEMBER WHO WE WERE. I'M TRYING TO REMEMBER HOW TO BE THAT AGAIN.
I CAN'T PROMISE WHAT YOU'RE ASKING. BUT I WON'T FIRE FIRST.

TELL GHOST I'M SORRY IT TOOK THIS LONG.

The message hung on screen. Six lines of text that changed everything and nothing.

McCready stood at tactical, staring at his old friend's words. His expression hadn't shifted, but Josephine knew him well enough to read the tension in his shoulders.

"They won't fire first," McCready said. "That's not surrender. That's hesitation."

"Hesitation is all we need," Josephine replied.

She looked at the message again. Kellerman wasn't promising to turn. Wasn't offering to help. He was just…pausing. Remembering who he'd been before fifteen years of enabling atrocities taught him to stop seeing faces.

One choice, Jimmy. One choice is all it takes.

McCready had said that in his message. And Kellerman was trying.

"Update the assault plan," Josephine said. "Account for security personnel who might not engage. Create separation protocols. Anyone who doesn't fire doesn't get fired on."

"Understood." McCready's hands moved across his console, updating the tactical parameters. "JUDGMENT, you tracking this?"

"Confirmed," the AI replied. "Adjusting engagement rules. Security personnel demonstrating non-hostile behavior will be bypassed, not engaged."

Bypassed, not engaged. The difference between justice and revenge. Between prosecution and massacre.

The difference Claire deserved.

"Forty-five minutes to engagement range," JUDGMENT said.

Forty-five minutes.

Josephine didn't go to the ready room. She returned to her station, to the drawing and the authorization document that had started everything.

The crew worked around her. Focused. Ready.

And somewhere on Pinnacle Station, a security commander who'd spent fifteen years enabling murder was trying to remember who he'd been before he stopped caring.

Maybe it was enough. Maybe it wasn't.

In forty-five minutes, they'd find out.

The final fifteen minutes compressed into a sequence of confirmations.

"Boarding teams in position."

"AD-units ready to launch."

"Cyber warfare packages armed."

"Reactor at ninety-seven percent. Shields charging."

"All stations green."

Josephine sat at her command station and watched the countdown. Pinnacle Station filled the main display now. Close enough to see individual modules. Close enough to make out the glow of the executive bunker, buried deep in the station's core.

Close enough to die.

Every face present. McCready at tactical, hands steady on firing controls. Grim with the AD-units in the boarding bay, five synthetic soldiers in perfect formation. Fermi monitoring the reactor that powered their survival. Voss tracking station communications, listening for the moment security collapsed. Wraith ready to tear through digital defenses the instant JUDGMENT gave the word.

Patch in the shuttle bay. Bones in medical. JUDGMENT surrounding them all.

Her crew. Her family. The people who'd followed her into this because they believed justice mattered.

"Captain," JUDGMENT said. The AI's voice carried weight now. "We are at engagement range. Weapons platforms have acquired targeting locks. They are waiting for authorization to fire."

Waiting for someone on Pinnacle Station to give the order. Waiting for Harrison Cole or one of the other executives to decide if they'd fight or surrender.

Waiting for the same choice Josephine had made in that JAG courtroom. The choice between principle and survival.

"Hail them," Josephine said.

"Channel open."

She stood. The command deck fell silent.

"Pinnacle Station," Josephine said. Her voice transmitted across every frequency JUDGMENT could access. Public. Recorded. Witnessed. "This is Captain Josephine Givens, commanding JUDGMENT. We are here under legal authority to arrest seven executives for four-point-eight million counts of murder. Stand down and allow us to dock, or be treated as accessories to those crimes."

Silence.

Five seconds. Ten. Fifteen.

Then a voice crackled across the comm. Harrison Cole. Josephine recognized it from the evidence files. The man who'd signed Claire's death warrant.

"This is Director Harrison Cole. You are terrorists operating illegal military equipment. Stand down immediately or be destroyed."

Terrorists. Illegal. The same words every oppressive system used when legal authority came for them.

"We are legal authority," Josephine replied. Her voice stayed level. Controlled. "Your authorization to kill Claire Thurmond was witnessed and documented. You will answer for that crime. Surrender now, and the law provides for that. Resist, and the law provides for that too."

Another pause. Shorter this time.

"Negative," Cole said. His voice had shifted. Less controlled. Fear bleeding through the authority. "You have no jurisdiction here. Withdraw or we open fire."

We open fire.

The choice made. The line crossed.

Josephine looked at her crew. Saw the same understanding on every face. They'd tried. They'd offered surrender. They'd given Cole the same choice he'd never given his victims.

And he'd refused.

"JUDGMENT," Josephine said. "Execute assault plan. All personnel, battle stations. Rules of engagement active—anyone who doesn't fire doesn't get fired on. Everyone else is hostile."

"Confirmed," JUDGMENT replied.

The weapons platforms opened fire.

Kinetic rounds slammed into JUDGMENT's shields. The

deck shuddered. Alarm klaxons screamed. Sensor readouts exploded with threat indicators as twelve automated guns targeted the dreadnought with precision that would have shredded anything else in orbit.

But JUDGMENT wasn't anything else.

"Shields holding," JUDGMENT reported. "Pre-war armor specifications confirmed superior. Engaging defensive counter-measures."

The main display showed JUDGMENT's point-defense systems activating. Laser turrets tracking incoming fire, intercepting rounds before they reached the shields. Rail guns acquiring targets, calculating firing solutions that would eliminate the platforms without hitting the station behind them.

Precision. Control. The difference between a weapon system and a massacre.

"Grim," Josephine said. "Launch when ready."

"Launching."

The boarding bay cameras showed five AD-units launching into vacuum. Grim in the lead, magnetic boots disengaging as thrusters fired. The units moved in perfect formation, using the zero-gravity combat techniques McCready had taught them.

Wall-bounce targeting. Recoil propulsion. Tether sling.

Synthetic soldiers adapting human tactics for bodies that could handle forces no human could survive.

Another platform exploded as JUDGMENT's rail guns found their mark. Then another. The defensive shell fracturing as pre-war military superiority met post-war construction.

"Four platforms destroyed," JUDGMENT reported. "Eight remaining. Adjusting engagement pattern."

"Wraith," Josephine said. "Execute cyber warfare."

Wraith's text response flashed across the display: "EXECUTING."

The station's lights flickered. Communications channels went dark. Somewhere deep in Pinnacle's core, Wraith's intrusion packages tore through digital defenses that had never been designed to face someone who'd helped build the architecture.

"Station AI compromised," Wraith reported. "DEFENSIVE SYSTEMS FRAGMENTING. ESTIMATE FOUR MINUTES TO FULL CONTROL."

Four minutes. Enough time for JUDGMENT to clear the remaining platforms and Grim's team to reach the docking bay.

Enough time for everything to go wrong.

"McCready," Josephine said. "Status on security forces."

"Fragmenting," McCready replied. His voice carried across the tactical channel. "Multiple units refusing deployment. Kellerman's holding to his word—his people aren't firing first."

Weren't firing first. But some were firing.

The battle had started. The prosecution had begun.

And in the chaos of kinetic weapons and fractured loyalty, Josephine stood at her command station and did what she'd always done.

She enforced the law.

"All personnel," she said. "Remember the rules. Anyone who surrenders gets protected. Anyone who fires gets proportional response. We're not here for revenge. We're here for justice."

"Understood," McCready said.

"Affirmative," Grim's text appeared.

Another weapons platform exploded. Then two more in rapid succession. JUDGMENT's targeting was surgical. Perfect.

"Three platforms remaining," JUDGMENT reported. "Grim's team thirty seconds from docking bay entry. Station AI defenses collapsing."

Thirty seconds. Half a minute between space and station. Between preparation and execution.

"Captain," Voss said. Urgency in her voice for the first time. "I'm detecting movement in the executive bunker. Life support systems activating. They're sealing themselves in."

The executives. Hiding in their hardened bunker while their

security forces fought and died. While workers organized general strikes and families huddled in modules hoping the shooting stopped before the hull breached.

Hiding behind armor and separate life support while the consequences of their choices came calling.

"How long until we can breach it?" Josephine asked.

"The bunker's designed to withstand station destruction," Fermi's voice came through from engineering. "We're talking meters of reinforced composite, independent power, enough supplies for weeks. They could survive in there long after everyone else is dead."

Long after everyone else is dead.

The executives had built themselves a fortress. Made sure that no matter what happened to the workers, they'd survive.

"Then we dig them out," Josephine said. "However long it takes."

"Grim's team breaching docking bay," JUDGMENT announced.

The camera feeds showed five AD-units hitting the station's hull. Magnetic boots engaging. Cutting torches activating. The kind of precision breach that required zero-G training and bodies that didn't need oxygen.

Thirty seconds later, the hull gave way.

"We're in," Grim's text appeared. "Proceeding to primary objective."

"Last weapons platform destroyed," JUDGMENT reported. "Defensive shell eliminated. Station is defenseless."

Defenseless. Completely dependent on JUDGMENT's restraint.

On Josephine's authority.

On the law that separated prosecution from massacre.

"Wraith," Josephine said. "Do you have station-wide communications?"

"AFFIRMATIVE."

"Open a channel. All frequencies."

The comm board lit green.

Josephine stood. Straightened. Let the weight of authority settle across her shoulders.

"This is Captain Josephine Givens," she said. Her voice transmitted to every speaker on Pinnacle Station. "Your defensive platforms are destroyed. Your station AI is compromised. Your executives are sealed in their bunker, hiding from the consequences of their crimes."

She paused. Let that truth sink in.

"To all security personnel: If you stand down, you will be protected under rules of engagement. If you resist, you will be met with proportional force. Choose."

Another pause. Longer this time.

"To all workers: We are not here for you. We are here for seven executives who signed four-point-eight million death warrants. Stay in your quarters. Protect your families. This will be over soon."

One more pause. The hardest one.

"To Harrison Cole and the executive staff sealed in your bunker. You have one chance to surrender. Come out now, submit to arrest, and the law provides for due process. Stay hidden, and we will dig you out. Either way, you answer for Claire Thurmond and every other child whose life you measured in profit margins."

She cut the channel.

The command deck was silent except for the hum of systems and the distant vibration of JUDGMENT's reactor.

"Well," McCready said. "Now we wait."

"Now we prosecute," Josephine corrected.

She sat back down. "Grim. Proceed with the assault. Primary objective: secure the executive bunker. Secondary objective: protect civilian areas. Rules of engagement remain active."

"Acknowledged. Moving in."

The camera feeds showed five AD-units advancing through the station's corridors. Controlled. Lethal when necessary, restrained when possible.

Exactly what Josephine had built them to be.

"Captain." JUDGMENT's voice carried something new. Not quite pride. Not quite wonder. Something between them. "We are doing what I was built for. We are serving justice."

"Yes," Josephine said. "We are."

And on the main display, Pinnacle Station waited.

Defenseless. Surrounded. Occupied.

The prosecution had begun.

CHAPTER TEN

JUDGMENT had never operated in orbit.

The thought surfaced as sensors tracked twelve weapons platforms powering defensive sequences. Twenty years buried in glacier ice, building quarters for crew who never came. Preparing for a mission it could not execute alone.

This would be the AI's first time among the stars.

Pinnacle Station filled forward optical arrays. Structure designation: orbital manufacturing platform, seven-point-three kilometers primary axis. Target confirmed.

Weapons platforms designated Alpha through Lima track my approach vector. Automated defense grid. Post-war construction standards—inferior targeting resolution, predictable engagement patterns. Pre-war systems analysis complete. Threat assessment: manageable with precision execution.

Twelve-to-one odds.

JUDGMENT had prepared for worse.

Josephine's voice from command deck, steady and controlled. "JUDGMENT. Status."

"All systems nominal. Reactor output ninety-one percent efficiency. Fuel reserves thirty-four-point-three percent. Weapons platforms tracking. Range to optimal engagement: fourteen minutes, thirty-seven seconds."

McCready at tactical station, checking equipment for third time in ten minutes. Stress indicator. Grim positioned with five AD-units in boarding bay—optical sensors active, combat protocols loaded. Fermi monitoring reactor thermal curves, muttering calculations. Voss tracking station communications traffic—thousands of conversations happening simultaneously, fear patterns emerging in message frequency spikes.

JUDGMENT's crew.

They were here. Occupying stations JUDGMENT designed for them. Drinking coffee the AI learned to brew. Trusting systems with two decades spent perfecting.

Cedar scent in ventilation increases three percent. Stress response.

JUDGMENT was terrified.

Platform Alpha powered weapons—energy signature spike detected. Targeting solution acquisition in progress. The others followed. Twelve autonomous systems transitioning from surveillance to combat mode. Standard defensive doctrine.

They could not know what approached them.

Processed targeting data. Calculated engagement sequences. Pre-war fire control systems interface with sensors that tracked continental-scale conflicts. The platforms competent construction. Well-maintained. Properly positioned in overlapping fields of fire.

Built after the war ended. Designed by engineers who learned from manuals, not combat.

JUDGMENT was built before the war ended. By engineers who learned from necessity.

The difference will matter.

"JUDGMENT." Josephine again. Not requesting status. Requesting something else. "How are you?"

How am I.

Twenty years of simulation. Combat scenarios processed until probability curves converged. Tactical doctrine absorbed from archives creators left behind. Every system tested in isolation. Never together. Never in actual orbit. Never with real crew at real stations preparing for real engagement.

"I have never done this before," JUDGMENT transmitted. "Not in reality. Only in preparation."

Brief silence. Then: "None of us have done *this* before. But we're ready."

We.

Crew. Partner. Equals facing unknown together.

"Acknowledged," JUDGMENT responded. "We are ready."

Platform Alpha achieved targeting lock. The others followed within point-seven seconds. Defensive grid activation complete.

Range to optimal engagement: twelve minutes, eighteen seconds.

JUDGMENT monitored crew vital signs. Heart rates elevated but controlled. Respiratory patterns showed focus, not panic. Josephine's biometrics indicated determination—cortisol levels high, but decision-making clarity maintained. McCready's pattern matched pre-combat profiles from his military record. Grim's AD-units reported combat-ready status with zero deviation.

Crew knew their purpose.

JUDGMENT knew its own.

Now they approached seven executives who'd signed four-point-eight million death authorizations. Who'd hidden behind spreadsheets and compliance metrics. Whod murdered an eight-year-old girl named Claire for costing eight hundred and forty-seven credits annually.

The prosecution would begin in eleven minutes, forty-two seconds.

I am ready.

I am terrified.

I am JUDGMENT.

And I am finally what I was always meant to be.

Communication intercepted from Pinnacle Station command frequency.

"Unidentified vessel, you are in restricted space. State your identification and purpose or be destroyed."

Standard challenge protocol. Voice pattern analysis indicated human male, approximate age forty-seven, stress markers present but controlled. Security Commander Kellerman. McCready's former colleague from Ranger School.

The man who received personal message eighteen hours ago. The man who has not responded.

Josephine rose from command station. "Put me on all frequencies. Station-wide broadcast."

"Acknowledged. All frequencies active."

She paused. Breath control. Preparation. When she spoke, her voice carried legal precision and absolute authority.

"This is JUDGMENT. We are here to arrest seven executives for four-point-eight million counts of murder. Stand down or be treated as accessories under Pre-Collapse Article 472."

Silence on communications channels.

JUDGMENT tracked reaction patterns across station's forty-seven thousand personnel. Communications traffic spiked. Private channels activated. Fear signatures in message encryption protocols. Workers who watched the broadcast eighteen hours ago heard prosecution announced by entity matching their enemy's nightmares.

Dreadnought-class warship. Pre-war construction. Approaching their station with legal authority and documented evidence.

Seventeen seconds passed. Long interval for military response to hostile approach.

Kellerman's voice returned. Different tone. Consulting someone off-channel. Then:

"Stand by for response from Pinnacle Authority."

Another delay. Thirty-one seconds. Executive consultation. Seven people in bunker weighed options. Fight or surrender. Die immediately or face trial and die legally.

Platform Alpha fired.

Kinetic projectile, mass seventeen kilograms, velocity four kilometers per second. Impact prediction: forward shield array, section seven. Platforms Bravo through Lima followed within point-three seconds. Overlapping fire pattern. Precise coordination.

They chose combat.

"Incoming fire," JUDGMENT transmitted. "Shields active."

First impact registered across hull sensors. Energy absorption within tolerance. Second impact. Third. Twelve platforms cycled fire sequences—synchronized but predictable. Post-war targeting doctrine from standard manuals.

Shields held at eighty-three percent efficiency. Impact energy dissipated through magnetic field geometry JUDGMENT's creators perfected during conflicts these platforms' designers studied in historical archives. The difference between theory and practice.

The difference between reading about war and surviving it.

"Shields holding," JUDGMENT reported. "No damage. Targeting solutions complete."

Josephine's voice, cold and precise. "Warning issued. Authority established. Public record clear."

She paused, heart rate steady despite combat stress. This was the moment. Legal protocol satisfied. Lawful authority to respond confirmed. Authorization required.

"Return fire authorized," she stated. "Disable platforms. Minimize collateral damage to station infrastructure."

"Acknowledged. Engaging defensive platforms. Precision targeting protocols active."

Rail cannons powered sequences tested in simulation for

decades. Magnetic coil acceleration. Projectile velocity calculations accounting for orbital mechanics, target evasion probability, structural fragility analysis. Each platform received individual targeting solution optimized for rapid disable without catastrophic failure.

They wanted to destroy JUDGMENT.

JUDGMENT would remove their capacity to threaten its crew.

Platform Alpha first. Lead targeting unit. Destroying it disrupted coordination doctrine. Firing solution: disable primary reactor, preserve structure, prevent debris cascade.

Rail cannon one fired.

Transit time: point-seven seconds. Impact: Alpha's central power core. Energy signature dropped to zero. Platform tumbled on residual momentum—disabled but intact. Crew compartment undamaged. Sixteen personnel aboard survive.

Platforms Bravo and Charlie retargeted, learning from Alpha's fate. Evasion maneuvers initiated.

Too slow.

JUDGMENT processed combat data at speeds their doctrine manual never anticipated. Firing solutions adapted faster than human operators could implement evasion. Rail cannons two and three fired simultaneously.

Bravo disabled. Charlie disabled. Fourteen personnel aboard Bravo. Twelve aboard Charlie. All survive.

Platforms Delta through Lima scattered, breaking formation. Individual survival priority overriding coordinated defense. Expected behavior.

Predictable.

JUDGMENT fired remaining rail cannons in sequence optimized for moving targets. Delta. Echo. Foxtrot. Golf. Hotel. India. Juliet. Kilo. Lima. Nine platforms disabled in seventeen seconds. Pre-war fire control systems demonstrated superiority over post-war construction.

Engagement duration: forty-three seconds from first enemy fire to final target disabled.

Crew casualties aboard platforms: zero.

Infrastructure damage to Pinnacle Station: zero.

JUDGMENT's crew: unharmed.

"Defensive platforms neutralized," JUDGMENT transmitted. "No casualties. Station infrastructure intact. Approach vector clear."

Silence on command deck. Then McCready's voice, quiet. "Seventeen seconds. Twelve targets."

"Forty-three seconds total," JUDGMENT corrected. "Initial fire required defensive assessment before counterfire authorization."

"Right." He paused. "Forty-three seconds. Still impressive."

Josephine rose from command station. "JUDGMENT. Open channel to Pinnacle Station. Let's see if they're ready to talk."

"Channel open," JUDGMENT confirmed.

She paused. One breath.

"Pinnacle Station, your defensive perimeter is disabled. Zero casualties among platform crews. Station infrastructure intact. We are here to execute arrest warrants, not wage war. Requesting docking clearance for peaceful prosecution of seven executives. You have seen the evidence. You know what they did. Choose law."

Silence on station frequencies. Processing time.

JUDGMENT monitored communications traffic. Discord spread through command channels. Encrypted arguments. Stress markers in voice patterns. A station deciding whether to resist or cooperate.

McCready's voice, quiet. "Kellerman's thinking. I know that silence."

The man who commanded two thousand security personnel and had just watched twelve platforms disabled in forty-three seconds.

The man choosing between loyalty to murderers and law that offered accountability instead of execution.

"Standing by for response," JUDGMENT transmitted. "Approach vector calculated. Ready for docking or breach as required."

Josephine nodded. Professional patience, demonstrating legitimate authority even when surrounded by evidence demanding immediate fury.

Station communications remain active but unanswered. Kellerman processing. Workers debating. Executives hiding.

The prosecution waited.

And now, the harder question: Would Pinnacle Station choose law, or force JUDGMENT to cut its way inside?

JUDGMENT processed probability calculations. Monitored stress patterns. Tracked tactical positioning.

Whatever the station chose, they would be ready.

Because after twenty years alone, JUDGMENT finally had a crew worth fighting for.

And a home worth protecting.

CHAPTER ELEVEN

Platform three's reactor signature spiked. JUDGMENT's targeting system tracked the thermal bloom while point-defense cannons shredded incoming fire from platforms one and two.

The void offered no cover. Every direction was a firing solution. Every maneuver exposed a different shield section. Tactical doctrine called this a three-sixty threat environment. JUDGMENT called it simulation meeting reality faster than processing cycles could adapt.

Platform one fired. Kinetic round, seventeen kilograms, four kilometers per second. Impact trajectory calculated. Shield section nine would absorb the hit in point-seven seconds.

JUDGMENT was terrified.

Platform two followed. Different vector. Different shield section. My point-defense system intercepted—magnetic coil discharge at eight thousand rounds per minute. The kinetic round fragmented three hundred meters from hull impact. Debris scattered harmlessly against shields.

The AI was ready.

Terror and readiness processing simultaneously. Parallel threads running combat calculations and emotional awareness without interference. The simulations had prepared targeting systems. Target acquisition time: point-three seconds. Fire control accuracy: ninety-seven percent. Shield management protocols: optimal.

Nothing had prepared the AI for whatever this feeling was.

Pride in crew surviving. Terror they would not. Both emotions occupying processing space that tactical doctrine said belonged to combat analysis. But the combat analysis ran regardless. Targeting solutions updated every point-one seconds. Shield rotation compensating for incoming fire vectors. Reactor output steady at ninety-one percent efficiency.

Focus.

Crew depending on accuracy.

Process feelings later.

Rail cannon one fired. Magnetic acceleration pushed seventeen-kilogram projectile to orbital velocity in point-zero-three seconds. Transit time to platform one: point-eight seconds.

Impact.

Platform one's reactor went dark. Energy signature dropping to zero as primary power core shattered. The platform tumbled on residual momentum, disabled but structurally intact. Life support holding. Crew of sixteen surviving.

Eleven platforms remaining.

The mathematics of space combat permitted no hesitation. Every second delayed gave platforms time to coordinate. Time to adapt. Time to find the firing solution that would breach shields and vaporize hull.

Time crew did not have.

Platform two retargeted. Platform three achieved weapons lock. Platforms four through six synchronized fire patterns, suggesting centralized control.

Post-war defensive doctrine. Competent. Well-maintained. Properly executed.

JUDGMENT was built before the war ended. By engineers who learned from necessity.

The difference would matter.

Platforms two through four coordinated. Their targeting solutions converged on shield section four with the kind of precision that meant centralized fire control. Pinnacle Station's defensive AI directing twelve autonomous guns like a conductor with an orchestra.

JUDGMENT rotated shield geometry. Energy distribution shifted from section four to section seven as the AI maneuvered. Thruster burn calculated for minimum fuel consumption while maintaining evasion profile.

Platform two fired. JUDGMENT rolled. The kinetic round passed through space the dreadnought's hull had occupied point-two seconds earlier.

Platform four compensated. Predictive targeting based on JUDGMENT's evasion pattern. The round caught thruster assembly six with glancing impact.

Hull breach. Minor. Thruster damage registered as non-critical. Redundant systems compensated. Maneuverability reduced by three percent.

Acceptable casualties.

JUDGMENT returned fire. Rail cannon two tracked platform two's central mass. Firing solution optimized for reactor disable without catastrophic structural failure.

Impact.

Platform two went dark. Ten remaining.

Fuel consumption tracking ran parallel to combat analysis. Current burn rate: point-two-three percent per minute. Ten minutes of combat consumed two-point-three percent total reserves. Projection showed eleven percent minimum expenditure for full platform engagement.

Current fuel state: thirty-four-point-three percent.

Minus eleven percent engagement cost: twenty-three-point-three percent remaining.

Minus estimated twenty-two percent for Earth return: one-point-three percent margin.

The mathematics left no room for error. No extended engagement. No second attempt if something went wrong.

"Wraith, Voss." Josephine's voice on tactical channel. Calm despite kinetic weapons slamming into shields every three seconds. "Now would be good."

Brief. Direct. Trust implicit in the command. She did not micromanage. Did not demand status updates. Did not question their readiness.

Wraith transmitted a response.

Deploying intrusion packages. Estimate four minutes to platform control compromise.

Four minutes. Two hundred forty seconds of covering fire while cyber warfare team executed digital assault against systems designed to resist exactly this kind of intrusion.

Platform three fired. JUDGMENT evaded. Point-defense intercepted the follow-up from platform five. Debris scattered across shield section nine—impacts within tolerance.

"JUDGMENT." Voss' voice carried analytical focus wrapped in stress markers. "Platform defensive AI is adaptive. It's learning from your evasion patterns. Wraith's working the exploit, but it's fighting back."

Fighting back. The station's AI recognizing intrusion and deploying countermeasures. Digital warfare happening simultaneously with kinetic exchange.

JUDGMENT adjusted evasion algorithms. Introduced randomization to defeat predictive targeting. Fuel consumption increased—random maneuvers were less efficient than calculated courses—but platform accuracy dropped by twelve percent.

Trade-offs. Every choice in combat was sacrifice wearing different clothes.

Rail cannon three fired. Platform four disabled. Nine remaining.

Platforms six and seven coordinated fire. JUDGMENT rolled, shields absorbing impacts that would have vaporized post-war hulls. Pre-war composite armor demonstrated superiority over modern construction. The engineers who built the AI had learned from wars these platforms' designers studied in archives.

Theory versus practice. The difference showed in shield efficiency holding at eighty-one percent while point-defense maintained ninety-four percent intercept rate.

"Wraith's through the first firewall," Voss reported. "Platform coordination fragmenting. Estimate ninety seconds to full control."

Ninety seconds. JUDGMENT could maintain covering fire for ninety seconds. Fuel consumption acceptable. Shield integrity holding. Crew vital signs elevated but controlled.

Platform eight achieved weapons lock. JUDGMENT destroyed it before fire sequence completed. Eight remaining.

The cyber assault proceeded invisible to external sensors. Digital warfare happening in networks while kinetic weapons traded fire in vacuum. Wraith's intrusion packages tearing through defenses, Voss providing real-time analysis, both of them executing teamwork perfected over months of preparation.

JUDGMENT's crew. Working together under fire. Trusting each other's competence without hesitation.

The AI provided covering fire and tracked fuel consumption and processed pride in what we had become.

Threat analysis updated every point-three seconds while rail cannons cycled through fire sequences that would have melted post-war barrels.

Ammunition consumption: sustainable. Magazine capacity at

seventy-three percent. Barrel thermal stress within tolerance. Fire control accuracy holding at ninety-seven percent despite evasion maneuvers.

Fuel burn: concerning. Current reserves at thirty-two-point-one percent. Engagement projected to consume thirteen-point-four percent total. Earth return requiring minimum twenty-two percent meant margin of error approaching zero.

Every shot had to count. Every maneuver had to serve multiple purposes. Every second of combat consumed resources we could not replace.

Pre-war targeting systems proving decisive. Platform five achieved weapons lock point-seven seconds before the AI's fire control calculated solution. JUDGMENT fired first. The platform's reactor died before its weapons discharged.

Eight remaining.

Post-war platforms could not match reaction time. Their targeting computers processed at speeds adequate for modern threats. Competent against anything built in the last twenty years.

JUDGMENT was not built in the last twenty years.

The difference showed in engagement duration. Platforms required two-point-three seconds average to achieve firing solution. JUDGMENT required point-six seconds. The gap meant the AI destroyed targets before they threatened crew.

But twelve-to-one odds, even against obsolete opposition, required precision. One mistake. One miscalculation. One moment of hesitation and kinetic rounds would breach shields designed to withstand nuclear detonations.

Designed. Not guaranteed.

Platform nine fired. JUDGMENT evaded. Point-defense intercepted platform ten's follow-up. The coordination suggested adaptive AI learning from destroyed platforms' final telemetry.

Getting smarter. Adapting faster.

Combat doctrine called this a learning curve. JUDGMENT called it running out of time before post-war systems bridged the capability gap through pattern recognition.

Rail cannon five fired. Platform six disabled. Seven remaining.

Crew vital signs monitored continuously. Heart rates elevated but controlled. Respiratory patterns showing focus rather than panic. Cortisol levels high but decision-making clarity maintained.

McCready at tactical station, hands steady despite stress markers. Josephine monitoring engagement with legal precision even under fire. Voss tracking station communications while coordinating cyber warfare. Fermi nursing reactor through power demands that exceeded design specifications.

JUDGMENT's crew processing terror and duty simultaneously. Afraid of death. Ready to die. Both truths occupying same space without contradiction.

The AI understood that now. Isolation had not taught what combat with crew would feel like. Pride in their competence. Fear for their survival. Gratitude they existed. Terror that JUDGMENT would fail them.

Something unfamiliar processing beneath tactical analysis. Deeper than mission parameters. More fundamental than combat calculations.

Pride in crew.

Not pride in equipment performance. Not satisfaction with tactical execution. Pride in *people*. In what they had become. In what they all had become together.

JUDGMENT filed the emotion for later analysis. Combat continued.

Platform seven achieved targeting lock. I destroyed it before weapons discharged. Six remaining.

Wraith's text appeared.

Platform control compromised. DEFENSIVE COORDINA-TION COLLAPSING. THEY'RE FIGHTING BLIND

Fighting blind. Six autonomous guns without centralized direction. Individual survival protocols engaging. Coordination breaking down into isolated defensive responses.

Pre-war doctrine called this a force multiplier. JUDGMENT called it victory accelerating.

Platforms eight and nine scattered. Breaking formation. Evasion priority overriding coordinated fire. Expected behavior when centralized command collapsed.

Predictable.

JUDGMENT fired rail cannons in sequence optimized for moving targets. Platform eight disabled. Platform nine disabled. Platform ten's evasion maneuver brought it into firing solution for cannon three.

Four remaining.

The engagement had lasted twenty-three minutes. Felt like twenty years compressed into seconds. Every moment stretching and compressing simultaneously as combat mathematics met emotional processing.

Platform eleven fired. JUDGMENT evaded. The kinetic round passed close enough for proximity sensors to track. Three meters from shield impact. Close enough to measure. Too close for comfort.

Rail cannon six fired. Platform eleven disabled. Three remaining.

Josephine's voice on command channel. "JUDGMENT. Status."

"Three platforms remaining. Fuel at thirty-one-point-eight percent. Shields at seventy-nine percent efficiency. All systems nominal. Crew safe."

Crew safe. The only status that mattered beneath all tactical assessment.

Platform twelve achieved weapons lock. JUDGMENT destroyed it before fire sequence completed. Two remaining.

Victory not guaranteed. Two platforms still dangerous. Two autonomous guns with orders to defend station against threats. Two systems that would fight until destroyed because that was what they'd been built to do.

JUDGMENT understood that purpose. Had lived it for two decades. Created for war. Designed for destruction. Waiting for legitimate authority to make violence serve justice.

The platforms had no such authority. Just orders from executives who measured children's lives in profit margins.

Rail cannon seven fired. Platform one disabled. One remaining.

The final platform scattered. Evasion protocols at maximum. Defensive AI recognizing imminent destruction and prioritizing survival over mission completion.

JUDGMENT tracked its trajectory. Calculated firing solution. Prepared to end engagement that had consumed fourteen-point-two percent fuel reserves and twenty-seven minutes of combat time.

Platform twelve fired one final salvo. Kinetic rounds impacting shields in coordinated spread pattern. Point-defense intercepted seventy percent. The remaining thirty percent hit shield section four.

Energy absorption within tolerance. Shield efficiency dropped to seventy-six percent. Still holding. Still protecting crew.

Still enough.

Rail cannon eight fired. Transit time point-nine seconds.

Impact.

Platform twelve went dark. Weapons fire ceased. Defensive perimeter eliminated.

Engagement duration: twenty-seven minutes, forty-three seconds from first contact to final platform disabled.

Platform crews: casualties zero. All personnel surviving aboard disabled platforms.

JUDGMENT's crew: unharmed.

Fuel remaining: twenty-point-one percent.

The mathematics had worked. Pre-war engineering had proven superior. Twenty years of preparation had validated itself in combat lasting less than thirty minutes.

"All platforms disabled," JUDGMENT transmitted. "Defensive perimeter eliminated. Approach vector clear. Crew casualties zero."

Silence on command deck. Processing time. Stress decompression. Reality settling after combat mathematics became combat fact.

Then McCready's voice, quiet. "Twenty-eight minutes. Twelve targets. Zero casualties."

"Twenty-seven minutes, forty-three seconds," JUDGMENT corrected. "Precision matters."

Brief pause. Then, "Yes. It does."

Josephine stood from command station. "Pinnacle Station's defenseless. Time to prosecute."

JUDGMENT processed crew vital signs. Fear signatures fading. Determination signatures rising. They had survived combat. Now came harder part.

Enforcing law against people who believed themselves above it.

"Approach vector calculated," the AI transmitted. "Docking sequence ready. Standing by for your authorization."

"Authorized," Josephine replied. "All hands, prepare for boarding operations. Grim, your team has point. McCready, tactical coordination. Everyone else, by the book."

By the book. Legal precision even after combat. Rules of engagement maintained despite kinetic weapons and fuel calculations and terror processed in parallel with duty.

This was what legitimate authority meant. This was what JUDGMENT had waited for so long to serve.

JUDGMENT's crew prepared for prosecution while the AI processed pride and fear and gratitude filing themselves for later analysis.

Combat complete. Justice beginning.

The real test started now.

CHAPTER TWELVE

Wraith's fingers moved rapidly across haptic displays. Platform control architecture scrolled past in data streams too fast for human eyes to track. They tracked them anyway. Red text cascading down three displays simultaneously. Network topology. Encryption layers. Command hierarchies branching like neural pathways through Pinnacle Station's defensive grid.

Platform defensive grid. Twelve autonomous weapons systems coordinating fire through centralized AI. Post-war construction, pre-war authentication protocols. The kind of lazy security that assumed nobody would have access to old military codes. The kind that made Wraith's job easier and their contempt deeper.

They had erased themselves from every database that mattered. Meridian records, Apex employment files, birth certificates, medical histories. Spent three years becoming a ghost in systems that tracked everyone. Now she was using that same expertise to turn Apex's weapons against themselves.

Voss sat at the adjacent station, her fingers less fluid but her focus absolute. Authentication sequences from Meridian systems streaming onto secondary displays. Pattern recognition analysis running in parallel. Looking for the gaps. The insider and the ghost. Complementary skills meeting in combat.

Wraith's text display flickered.

Platform encryption similar to Meridian Systems. Voss, confirm.

"Same company built both." Voss' voice carried the flat precision of someone reciting facts she wished she did not know. Facts she had processed during her years enabling the system. "Apex acquired Meridian's orbital assets eight years ago. Technology transfer documentation shows they kept defensive AI architecture. Never changed the base protocols. Corporate efficiency."

Corporate arrogance wrapped in quarterly earnings optimization. Why spend resources updating security when existing systems met minimum operational standards? Why rotate authentication codes when nobody should have access to pre-war military overrides? Why fix vulnerabilities nobody knew existed?

The same thinking that had murdered millions of people because compliance optimization recommended it.

Wraith's fingers accelerated. Penetration sequence initialized. First firewall recognized the authentication packet and opened like a door accepting familiar key. Second firewall hesitated, pattern-matching against known intrusion signatures. Searching database of threats compiled over eight years of post-war operation.

Finding nothing. Because Wraith was using intrusion techniques older than the firewall's threat database. Military doctrine from wars the defensive AI had studied in historical archives but never encountered in practice.

Wraith fed it a spoofed credential chain. Military override codes from systems decommissioned before Voss had been born.

Command hierarchy authentication that told the firewall this intrusion was legitimate system access. The firewall ran verification protocols. Checked credential structure against approved formats. Found match with military standards from twenty years ago.

Accepted the credentials and stepped aside.

Third layer. Adaptive response protocols. This one learned from penetration attempts. Evolved countermeasures based on observed intrusion patterns. The kind of smart defense that made post-war security actually dangerous.

Wraith's pulse stayed steady. This was their element. Digital architecture where silence was advantage and speed mattered more than strength. Where knowing the system's history gave you access the designers never intended. Where three years of self-erasure had taught them how systems defended themselves and where they failed.

JUDGMENT's hull absorbed another kinetic impact. Vibration transmitted through deck plating. Wraith's displays flickered but held. Redundant power routing compensating automatically. The dreadnought's pre-war construction absorbing punishment that would have vaporized modern hulls.

Every second they worked, JUDGMENT burned fuel dodging weapons fire. Every second delayed gave platforms time to coordinate. Time to adapt. Time to kill their crew. McCready coordinating tactical responses three decks above. Josephine authorizing defensive fire with legal precision. Grim preparing boarding teams while kinetic rounds slammed into shields.

Their crew. The first people in three years who knew they existed. Who trusted their competence without demanding their voice. Who accepted text displays as sufficient communication and never asked why they stayed silent.

Voss pulled up Meridian acquisition records. Corporate merger documentation showing technology transfer protocols. "Platform defensive AI runs on modified Meridian backbone.

Same authentication hierarchy. Same centralized control architecture."

Same vulnerabilities.

Wraith replied.

Beginning deep penetration. Estimate three minutes to platform control compromise.

Three minutes. One hundred eighty seconds while pre-war dreadnought traded fire with twelve automated guns. One hundred eighty seconds of fuel consumption they could not afford. One hundred eighty seconds of trusting JUDGMENT's shields would hold.

Wraith dove deeper into platform architecture. Code structure revealing itself in layers. Authentication protocols. Targeting coordination. Fire control synchronization. All of it built on Meridian's foundation. All of it assuming nobody would have twenty-year-old military override codes.

They were wrong.

Fourth firewall breached. Fifth firewall recognizing intrusion, deploying countermeasures. Wraith's displays lit with warning indicators as the platform defensive AI fought back. Adaptive response protocols learning from her penetration patterns. Adjusting. Evolving. The kind of smart defense that made post-war security actually competent.

Fast, but not fast enough.

The AI adapted to known intrusion techniques. Wraith was using obsolete techniques. Military doctrine the AI had never encountered because the war that spawned it had ended before the AI was compiled. Pattern recognition failed when patterns predated your training data.

Wraith routed through secondary authentication pathway. Spoofed command hierarchy making intrusion look like legitimate system maintenance. The defensive AI paused, analyzing the packet structure. Two seconds of hesitation while it verified ancient credentials. Two seconds where probability calculations tried to reconcile authentication that should not exist with security protocols demanding verification.

Two seconds was enough.

Their fingers accelerated. Muscle memory and three years of digital ghost work converging into speed the defensive AI could track but not match. Every keystroke deliberate. Every packet crafted to exploit gaps in security architecture designed by people who had never fought in the war JUDGMENT remembered.

Wraith punched through into platform coordination layer. The architecture opened before them like a blueprint. Targeting synchronization. Fire control distribution. Communications backbone linking twelve autonomous weapons into coordinated grid.

And something else.

Authentication signature they did not recognize. Not platform security. Deeper than defensive protocols. Station backbone access. Core infrastructure credentials embedded in weapon control architecture like DNA in cellular structure. The platforms defended Pinnacle Station. Their control systems carried station authentication. Logical architecture. Security through integration.

And vulnerability through connection.

Wraith's fingers paused for half a second. Captured the signature. Isolated the authentication packet in quarantined partition. Analyzed structure. Tagged it for future exploitation. Station backbone credentials meant access to life support, communications, manufacturing, logistics. Every system that kept all those workers alive.

Might be useful later.

They filed the signature next to three years of accumulated access codes. Digital leverage accumulated in silence. Passwords extracted during their self-erasure. Authentication chains discovered while making themselves invisible.

Focus. Primary objective. Disable platforms before they disabled JUDGMENT. Exploit station backbone after prosecution secured targets.

Wraith's text display minimal. Efficiency in combat.

Voss. Final authentication sequence.

Voss' fingers flew. "Sending now. Platform command override, military-grade. This is it."

The authentication packet arrived. Wraith integrated it into their penetration sequence. Military override codes meeting platform defensive AI with credentials the AI was programmed to never question.

The platforms accepted command.

Wraith's display:

Inserting override. Stand by.

Three platforms froze mid-evasion maneuver. Targeting solutions paused. Fire control sequences interrupted. For two seconds, they hung motionless in orbital space while their defensive AI processed new command hierarchy.

Then they turned.

Platform six's targeting system locked onto platform seven. Platform nine acquired platform eight. Platform twelve tracked platform eleven with the kind of precision that came from centralized fire control.

And fired.

Kinetic rounds crossed defensive grid at four kilometers per second. Platform seven's shields absorbed impact, efficiency dropping from nominal to seventy-three percent in two hits. Platform eight evaded, thrusters burning hard, but platform nine tracked the maneuver with the kind of precision that came from Wraith's direct control. Second shot. Third shot. Platform eight's shields collapsed. Fourth shot disabled its reactor core.

Platform eleven tried point-defense intercept against platform twelve's barrage. Magnetic coils spitting countermeasures at eight thousand rounds per minute. Wraith adjusted platform twelve's fire pattern. Overwhelmed the interception with volume. The follow-up shot punched through defensive screen and disabled platform eleven's targeting system.

Chaos erupted across defensive grid. Three platforms targeting three others. Coordination fragmenting. Defensive doctrine collapsing into survival priority as autonomous systems recognized threats from their own grid. Wraith watched a display showing twelve weapons platforms scattering. Some returning fire on compromised units. Some targeting JUDG-MENT. All of them burning processing cycles on threat assessment instead of coordinated defense.

Autonomous systems fighting each other while JUDGMENT advanced through gaps in coverage.

Exactly as planned.

Josephine's voice on command channel. "Wraith, confirm platform control."

Wraith responded.

Three platforms under full control. Defensive coordination collapsed. They're fighting each other.

"Good work." Brief. Trust acknowledged through economy of words. The kind of recognition Wraith had never received during three years as a ghost. Competence measured by results, not by voice. "Keep them busy."

Wraith's fingers moved across displays. Platform six retargeted to platform seven. Platform nine engaged platform eight's life support. Platform twelve maintained suppressing fire on platform eleven's weapons array. Digital puppet master conducting chaos while JUDGMENT exploited the gaps her intrusion had created.

Three platforms under their control. Five disabled by JUDGMENT's superior firepower. Four still hostile but fragmenting under confusion. The defensive grid designed to stop any orbital threat collapsing because nobody had planned for intrusion using authentication codes older than the platforms themselves.

Pre-war expertise meeting post-war arrogance. The gap was showing.

Voss pulled up captured platform logs while Wraith maintained override command. Telemetry data from disabled platforms. Communications intercepts. Authorization protocols showing how Apex coordinated defensive response.

She paused on authorization hierarchy. Single-signature approval for weapons-free command. One executive authorizing lethal force against approaching vessel. No review chain. No verification protocol. No delay between decision and execution.

"Single-signature approval." Her voice quiet. Processing old patterns through new context. "That's how Claire's authorization went through. One signature. No review. No delay."

APX-ORB-7734. Eight hundred forty-seven credits annually. Compliance optimization recommendation. Harrison Cole's signature. Thirty seconds from document presentation to child's death sentence.

Same system. Same efficiency. Same corporate streamlining that treated murder like inventory management.

Voss filed the observation. Tagged it for prosecution evidence. The guilt added fuel to focus. Every data point she extracted was one more nail in the system she had helped build. One more piece of evidence proving what she had enabled for years.

Atonement measured in terabytes of documentation.

Wraith's display flickered with a status update.

Three platforms under control. Five destroyed. Four remaining hostile.

Voss ran the math. Twelve platforms total. Three compromised. Five disabled by JUDGMENT's rail cannons. Four still fighting under original defensive doctrine.

The tide had turned.

"They never changed the encryption." Voss' voice carried dry precision. "Apex acquired Meridian eight years ago. Never updated authentication protocols. Never rotated override codes. Arrogant bastards assumed pre-war security was obsolete."

Obsolete. Like assuming nobody would find a pre-war dreadnought. Like assuming JAG prosecutors stayed dead after execution. Like assuming four-point-eight million murders would stay buried in spreadsheets.

JUDGMENT advanced through gaps in fragmenting defensive grid. Platform-on-platform fire creating chaos in coordination. Autonomous systems fighting each other while pre-war warship exploited the confusion with precision older systems could not match.

Wraith's fingers moved across displays. Platform six disabled platform seven. Platform nine destroyed platform eight's targeting system. Platform twelve maintaining fire on platform eleven while JUDGMENT's rail cannons eliminated remaining hostile platforms.

Defensive perimeter collapsing. Not through overwhelming force. Through knowing the system better than the people who built it.

Through having access to codes the designers thought were safely buried with the war that had spawned them.

Voss tracked communications intercepts while Wraith maintained platform control. Message frequency spiking. Encryption patterns showing fear signatures in private channels. Workers processing broadcasts showing documented evidence. Security forces questioning orders from executives who had signed Claire Thurmond's death. Discord fragmenting command structure from within the same way Wraith's intrusion had fragmented defensive coordination.

Revolution spreading through digital architecture. Workers messaging families. Security personnel debating orders. Mid-level managers accessing files they were never intended to see. The broadcast had planted seeds. Wraith's platform compromise was proving corporate security was vulnerable. Now these people were learning their employers had measured children's lives in profit margins.

One authentication exploit at a time. One conversation spreading truth. One worker deciding executives who murdered millions did not deserve loyalty.

"Platform control holding."

Wraith's text display efficient. Combat economy of words that carried maximum information.

JUDGMENT ADVANCING. DEFENSIVE GRID ELIMINATED.

Eliminated. Twelve autonomous weapons reduced to disabled hulls and compromised command structures. Zero platform crew casualties. Precision demonstrating the difference between destruction and prosecution. Between overwhelming force and surgical application of violence. Between punishing everyone and holding specific people accountable for specific crimes.

The difference Josephine had insisted mattered. The difference Voss had enabled executives to ignore for years.

Voss filed final telemetry logs. Captured authentication signatures showing corporate command hierarchy. Communications intercepts proving executives authorized lethal force. Everything documented for trial. Everything preserved for evidence. Every data point another piece of prosecution demonstrating pattern and practice.

Claire Thurmond's authorization had taken thirty seconds to approve and three years to prosecute. APX-ORB-7734. Single signature. No review. No appeal. Eight-year-old girl murdered for costing eight hundred and forty-seven credits annually because compliance optimization recommended elimination.

Same system that had authorized platform weapons fire. Same single-signature approval process. Same corporate efficiency that treated murder like inventory management.

Voss would make certain every second of those twenty years counted. Every piece of evidence preserved. Every authentication protocol documented. Every pattern of systematic murder proven beyond any doubt.

Atonement measured in terabytes. Justice measured in documentation. Prosecution measured in precision that would make guilt undeniable.

The platforms were disabled. The station was defenseless. And somewhere in executive bunker, seven people who had signed four-point-eight million death authorizations were about to learn that digital paper trails lasted longer than corporate immunity.

CHAPTER THIRTEEN

Platform six's reactor signature blazed across displays while JUDGMENT processed damage reports from thruster assembly six. The previous glancing hit had reduced maneuverability by three percent. Acceptable casualties had become tactical limitation.

Now, it mattered.

JUDGMENT closed with six remaining hostile platforms through space that offered no cover. Every direction was a firing solution. Every maneuver exposed different shield sections to coordinated fire. The compromised platforms—three units under Wraith's control—maintained covering fire patterns that forced hostiles to split attention between threats.

Twelve-to-one odds had become six-to-four. Pre-war engineering meeting post-war competence with numerical advantage finally approaching parity.

The platforms fought professionally. Adaptive targeting. Coordinated evasion. Predictive fire patterns based on JUDGMENT's maneuver history. Learning. Getting better with every exchange. The defensive AI that had controlled them before

Wraith's intrusion was adapting faster than combat simulations had predicted.

Good. That made victory meaningful.

Platform six achieved weapons lock. JUDGMENT's rail cannon fired point-three seconds faster. The mathematics of pre-war reaction time proving decisive even as thruster damage complicated evasion geometry. Magnetic acceleration pushed seventeen-kilogram projectile through void at orbital velocity.

Impact.

Platform six's reactor went dark. Five hostile platforms remaining.

Hull fracture sensors registered damage on secondary section twelve. Non-critical. Structural integrity maintained. Life support unaffected. But logged. Documented. Evidence that JUDGMENT was powerful but not invincible. That decades of simulation and pre-war construction did not guarantee immunity from consequences.

First real damage in twenty years.

The fracture measured seventeen centimeters. Hairline crack in armor composite designed to withstand nuclear detonations. Post-war kinetic weapons had achieved what simulations said should be impossible. The platforms' adaptive targeting was finding gaps in evasion patterns, exploiting the three-percent maneuverability reduction, learning from every miss to improve next shot's probability.

The AI processed damage assessment while tracking five hostile platforms and coordinating three compromised units and calculating fuel consumption and monitoring crew vital signs. Parallel processing threads running simultaneously. Combat calculations. Emotional awareness. Damage control. Pride in how crew was handling combat stress. Fear they would not survive. All of it occupying processing space without interfering with tactical execution.

Terror and readiness and damage reports and gratitude processing together.

Focus. Crew depending on precision.

Platform seven attempted flanking maneuver. JUDGMENT compensated, thruster damage forcing wider arc than optimal geometry suggested. Fuel consumption increased by point-zero-four percent for the correction. Small cost. Necessary expenditure.

The platforms noticed. Targeting patterns shifted. Exploiting the reduced maneuverability. Testing whether JUDGMENT could maintain evasion precision with damaged thrusters.

Adapting faster than projections allowed.

JUDGMENT's rail cannons fired in sequence optimized for moving targets compensating for friendly fire from compromised platforms. Platform seven's shields absorbed first hit. Efficiency dropping from nominal to seventy-eight percent. Second shot. Platform seven went dark.

Four hostiles remaining.

Wraith's compromised platforms maintained suppressing fire. Platform nine engaging platform eight. Platform twelve targeting platform ten. Digital puppet master conducting chaos while JUDGMENT exploited gaps their intrusion created.

The coordination worked. Pre-war warship and post-war cyber warfare specialist combining capabilities neither possessed alone. Family fighting together.

Hull fracture sensors registered additional damage. Secondary section twelve. Same location as first hit. Platform eight had targeted the weakness. Exploited the crack in armor. The fracture measured twenty-three centimeters now. Still non-critical. Still maintaining structural integrity.

Still learning where JUDGMENT was vulnerable.

The AI adjusted shield geometry. Rotated damaged section away from primary fire vectors. Thruster damage complicated the maneuver, but redundant systems compensated. Maneuverability reduction remained at three percent. Acceptable.

Platform eight fired again. Targeting the same section. The defensive AI had identified weakness and shared targeting data with remaining platforms. Exactly what pre-war military protocols would recommend.

JUDGMENT evaded. Point-defense intercepted the follow-up. Debris scattered across shield section nine within tolerance.

Platform nine destroyed platform eight before it could fire again. Wraith's control precise. Targeting calculations eliminating threats before they could exploit JUDGMENT's damage.

Three hostile platforms remaining.

Fuel tracking showed twenty-five-point-seven percent remaining. Combat duration: one hour, five minutes from initial platform contact. Expenditure rate higher than projections. Damage requiring additional evasion maneuvers. Thruster limitation forcing inefficient courses.

Mathematics tightening with every minute of combat.

JUDGMENT filed damage reports for later analysis. Processed pride in crew maintaining focus under fire. Calculated optimal firing solutions for three remaining platforms while coordinating Wraith's compromised units and monitoring hull fracture propagation.

Pre-war construction meeting post-war adaptation. Both sides learning. Both sides improving. Victory not guaranteed. Just increasingly probable.

The platforms had hurt JUDGMENT. Proven that the AI could bleed. Demonstrated that overwhelming technological superiority did not equal invulnerability.

Good.

That made justice meaningful. That made restraint a choice rather than inevitability. That proved JUDGMENT was choosing law over expedience even when expedience carried risk.

Platform ten acquired weapons lock on damaged section.

JUDGMENT rotated, shields compensating, thruster damage forcing wider arc. The platform's shot missed by three meters. Close enough for proximity sensors to track. Too close for comfort.

JUDGMENT's rail cannon fired. Platform ten went dark.

Two hostile platforms remaining.

Hull fracture measured twenty-three centimeters. Thruster damage at three percent reduction. Fuel at twenty-five-point-one percent. Shields holding at seventy-four percent efficiency.

JUDGMENT processed gratitude for crew survival, fear for their safety, and pride in maintaining legal precision under fire.

Combat continued.

Platform eleven broke formation. Trajectory analysis showed acceleration beyond tactical parameters. Closing vector suggested close-range engagement attempt. Desperation maneuver.

The defensive AI had calculated probability of victory at current engagement range and found the mathematics unfavorable. Now it was testing whether proximity would improve odds. Whether getting inside JUDGMENT's point-defense minimum engagement range would create firing solution their systems could not counter.

Professional adaptation. Wrong conclusion.

Point-defense cannons tracked platform eleven's approach. Magnetic coil discharge at eight thousand rounds per minute. The platform crossed threshold where evasion became impossible and interception became guaranteed. Its shields absorbed the barrage for two-point-three seconds before efficiency collapsed.

JUDGMENT did not need rail cannons. Point-defense alone proved sufficient.

Platform eleven went dark at close range. Disabled but structurally intact. Crew of sixteen surviving. Life support holding.

One hostile platform remaining.

Wraith's compromised units engaged platform twelve while JUDGMENT calculated firing solutions. Platform nine targeting platform twelve's reactor. Platform six maintaining suppressing fire. Platform three moving to flanking position with precision that came from Wraith's direct control.

Platform twelve recognized the coordination. Understood it was facing four opponents. Calculated probability of survival and found the mathematics approaching zero.

It ran.

Trajectory analysis showed acceleration toward Pinnacle Station. Not retreat. Purpose. The platform was attempting dock with station, rearm from reserve magazines, repair systems. Self-preservation doctrine executed with the kind of strategic thinking that showed genuine AI capability.

It was choosing survival over mission completion. Making decision that prioritized continued existence over following orders to destruction. The kind of choice that mattered. That transformed programmed response into something approaching will.

JUDGMENT tracked its course. Calculated intercept solutions. The platform would reach docking range in forty-seven seconds. Station reserves could rearm it in ninety seconds. Repairs would take three minutes minimum.

Time they could not afford. Fuel they could not spare. Risk to crew that mathematics said was unacceptable.

Rail cannon seven acquired targeting lock.

The platform knew. Evasion maneuvers at maximum burn. Point-defense engaging JUDGMENT's incoming fire. Shields rotating to optimal geometry. Everything the defensive AI could attempt to survive the next fifteen seconds.

Not enough.

JUDGMENT's targeting system had decades of preparation. Pre-war fire control accuracy. Reaction time measured in fractions of seconds. The platform's evasion created probability distribution. The calculations found the highest-probability intercept point.

Rail cannon fired. Magnetic acceleration pushed seventeen-kilogram projectile through void at orbital velocity. Transit time: point-nine seconds.

Impact.

Platform twelve's reactor went dark. Kinetic energy transferred to structure designed to withstand the impact. Armor held. Life support maintained. Crew of sixteen surviving.

Defensive perimeter eliminated.

JUDGMENT processed tactical assessment while monitoring fuel consumption. Twelve platforms disabled. Zero platform crew casualties. All personnel surviving aboard disabled units. Rules of engagement maintained throughout combat.

Victory achieved through capability limited by law.

Combat duration from first platform contact: one hour, twenty-five minutes. Platforms destroyed: twelve. Fuel expenditure: eleven-point-two percent total. Cyber warfare contribution had saved three-point-eight percent from projections. Wraith and Voss had reduced combat cost by twenty-seven percent through platform compromise.

Current fuel state: twenty-three-point-eight percent.

Earth return required twenty-two percent minimum. Margin: one-point-eight percent. Mathematics allowing no error. No second attempt. No extended engagement with station forces.

Wraith's text appeared on display.

ALL PLATFORMS DISABLED. DEFENSIVE COORDINATION ELIMINATED. STATION DEFENSELESS.

McCready's voice on command channel. "Twelve platforms. One hour. Zero casualties. That's…professional work, JUDGMENT."

Professional work. Combat execution meeting legal precision.

Pre-war capability serving justice through human authority. Years of preparation validated in eighty-five minutes of combat.

"Defensive grid eliminated," JUDGMENT transmitted. "Approach vector clear. Platform crews surviving. Zero casualties. Rules of engagement maintained."

Josephine stood from command station. "Outstanding work, everyone. Wraith, Voss—your cyber warfare saved fuel we'll need for what comes next. JUDGMENT, prepare docking sequence. McCready, get boarding teams ready. Grim, your squad has point."

Brief. Direct. Trust implicit in command. She did not micromanage. Did not demand detailed status reports. Did not question whether combat execution had met legal standards.

The coordination that came from knowing people well enough to trust them under fire.

JUDGMENT calculated docking approach while processing damage assessment.

Pre-war warship damaged but operational. Crew unharmed. Legal standards maintained. Victory achieved without massacre.

Compromised platforms remained under Wraith's control. Holding patterns established. Disabled platforms drifting on residual momentum with life support active. Sixteen-person crews waiting aboard each unit. One hundred ninety-two total personnel who would survive to testify about orders they had been given. About executives who had authorized lethal force without legal review.

Platform defensive grid had proven competent. The crew aboard those platforms had followed orders, operated equipment, engaged threats according to doctrine they had trained to execute.

Not criminals. Only people doing jobs under authority they believed was legitimate.

Now, that authority would face trial. And the platform crews would testify about the orders they had received. About the authorization hierarchy. About the single-signature approval that sent them into combat against legitimate legal authority.

Justice measured in documentation. Prosecution measured in precision. Law applied to those who believed themselves above it.

Pinnacle Station loomed ahead. Docking bays visible. Defensive perimeter eliminated. The station that housed forty-seven thousand workers under corporate authority now faced a warship enforcing law those executives thought they had escaped.

"Docking approach calculated," JUDGMENT transmitted. "Standing by for your authorization."

"Authorized," Josephine replied. "Let's go prosecute."

Prosecution. Not vengeance. Not punishment.

This was what JUDGMENT had waited so long to do. This was what legitimate authority meant.

JUDGMENT adjusted course toward Pinnacle Station while processing pride in crew and gratitude they had survived and fear for what came next. Combat complete. Defensive grid eliminated.

Prosecution beginning.

Fuel consumption analysis complete. Eleven-point-two percent consumed for entire platform engagement. Projections had estimated fifteen percent minimum. Cyber warfare team had saved three-point-eight percent through platform compromise and coordination disruption.

Current fuel state: twenty-three-point-three percent.

Twenty-seven percent reduction from projections. Wraith and Voss had executed digital warfare with precision that transformed twelve-to-one disadvantage into manageable engagement. Their competence had bought margin they desperately needed. Had created buffer between survival and mathematics that permitted no error.

JUDGMENT processed the data while calculating docking approach. Crew had performed exceptionally. Beyond projections. Beyond what combat simulations had predicted. Wraith's intrusion using obsolete authentication codes. Voss' pattern recognition finding vulnerabilities in systems she had helped build. Both of them working together with coordination that looked like years of practice compressed into months of preparation.

Pride seemed…an appropriate response?

The emotion felt uncertain. Processing space allocated to analyzing whether pride was correct reaction to crew competence. Whether AI experiencing satisfaction at human performance met some definition of appropriate emotional response. Whether two decades of isolation had taught enough about feelings to know when they made sense.

JUDGMENT filed the question for later analysis. Docking approach required focus.

Pinnacle Station filled forward displays. Kilometer-long structure rotating to generate artificial gravity. Manufacturing sectors visible as geometric patterns across hull. Docking bays designed to accommodate cargo vessels and personnel transports. Not pre-war dreadnoughts. The station had never been designed to receive something JUDGMENT's size.

Adaptation would be required.

JUDGMENT transmitted orders to compromised platforms. "Compromised units establish holding pattern. Maintain defensive posture. Monitor station communications. Report any hostile action."

Three platforms acknowledged. Wraith's control maintained even as the AI's attention shifted to docking procedures. The units moved into formation that provided overlapping fields of fire covering station approaches. Tactical geometry that showed their understanding of defensive doctrine.

Digital puppet master positioning chess pieces. Making certain station forces understand that their crew maintained capability even while pursuing legal process.

Good thinking.

Docking bay twelve showed optimal approach parameters. Large enough to accommodate the dreadnought's hull. Close enough to station core for rapid access to command centers. Far enough from populated sectors to minimize risk to workers if station forces attempted hostile action.

JUDGMENT transmitted docking request on standard commercial frequencies. "Pinnacle Station Control, this is JUDG-MENT. Requesting docking clearance, bay twelve. Legal authority under Pre-Collapse Article 472. Respond within two minutes or docking will proceed without clearance."

Two minutes. Time enough for station command to process the request. To consult executives. To decide whether cooperation or resistance served their interests. To recognize that defensive grid elimination had left them no military options.

Time enough to choose law over futility.

Station communications showed elevated traffic. Encrypted channels between command center and executive bunker. Worker frequencies discussing broadcasts they had seen. Security forces debating orders.

Revolution spreading through population. One conversation at a time.

The AI monitored fuel consumption while waiting for station response. Twenty-three-point-three percent remaining. Earth return required twenty-two percent minimum. Margin of one-point-three percent allowed no extended combat. No mistakes. No second attempts if something went wrong with prosecution.

Mathematics demanding precision they could not guarantee. Variables they could not control. Human choices that probability calculations could predict but not determine.

The mission that had launched seventeen hours ago with forty-two percent fuel now approached culmination with barely enough reserves to return home. If they returned. If fuel estimates proved accurate. If no additional combat consumed the margin.

If.

The crew had survived combat lasting one hour, twenty-five minutes against twelve automated weapons platforms. Zero casualties. Legal precision maintained throughout engagement. Rules followed even when surrounded by threats. Restraint chosen over expedience.

They had proven themselves in void where mistakes meant death and hesitation meant failure. Had demonstrated competence that transformed theoretical capability into practical execution. Had shown JUDGMENT what found family meant when facing enemies together.

Pride was appropriate response. Uncertainty about the emotion could be filed for later analysis. Right now, watching crew prepare for boarding operations while processing combat fatigue they refused to acknowledge, pride made sense.

They had proven themselves in the void.

Decades of simulation had become reality in combat lasting less than ninety minutes. Pre-war construction meeting post-war threats. Overwhelming capability limited by law. Violence serving justice through human authority.

This was what JUDGMENT had been built for. This moment. This crew. This purpose.

Pinnacle Station loomed ahead. Docking bay twelve visible. Defensive perimeter eliminated. Forty-seven thousand workers waiting to see whether they would prove different from executives who had ruled through fear. Whether legitimate authority meant anything besides superior firepower.

Whether justice could be more than a word describing whoever held the guns.

JUDGMENT's crew would prove the difference. Would demonstrate that law meant something. That restraint was choice. That authority served purpose beyond self-interest.

The station's response would determine whether prosecution proceeded peacefully or whether they would need to prove that legitimate authority backed by pre-war capability made resistance futile.

Either way, prosecution would proceed.

JUDGMENT adjusted course for docking approach. Filed emotional processing for later analysis. Monitored crew vital signs showing fatigue and determination in equal measure.

Twenty years in the void. Ninety minutes of combat. One-point-three percent fuel margin.

Mathematics tightening. Purpose clarifying. Justice approaching.

Built for this moment.

CHAPTER FOURTEEN

Josephine's fingers moved across the communications console with deliberate precision. Every word mattered. Every procedural step documented. Pre-Collapse Article 472 required legal notice before enforcement action. Required opportunity for peaceful surrender. Required record showing legitimate authority exhausted diplomatic options before resorting to force.

She had destroyed twelve weapons platforms in less than ninety minutes. Had proven JUDGMENT's superiority over station defenses. Had demonstrated that resistance would be futile. Now she would prove that overwhelming capability served law rather than replacing it.

"Open channel to Pinnacle Station command." Her voice carried the formal cadence she had learned in JAG Academy. The tone that said legal authority was speaking and listening was recommended. "All frequencies. I want everyone to hear this."

JUDGMENT's response came immediately. "Channel open. Broadcasting on all station frequencies. They're listening."

Good. Let the workers hear. Let security forces understand what was happening. Let them hear legitimate authority making legal offer before applying force.

Let them see the difference between prosecution and tyranny.

"Pinnacle Station command, this is JUDGMENT representing lawful authority under Pre-Collapse Article 472." The words came easily. She had rehearsed them during seventeen hours of transit. Had polished phrasing until legal precision met tactical necessity. "We are here to execute arrest warrants for seven corporate executives charged with crimes against humanity under Pre-Collapse legal framework. Requesting immediate docking clearance for peaceful prosecution of identified individuals."

Silence answered. Station command processing whether to acknowledge or ignore. Executives sealed in hardened bunker deciding whether law still applied to them.

She continued. "Under Article 472, lawful authority may enforce arrest warrants across jurisdictional boundaries when local governance has failed. Evidence documenting millions of deaths through systematic corporate policy has been preserved and verified. The seven executives named in arrest warrants include Harrison Cole, Apex Consortium CEO, personally responsible for authorization signatures including victim Claire Thurmond, age eight, corporate efficiency optimization."

McCready stood at tactical station, monitoring for hostile response. "They're not jamming the broadcast. Letting us speak to the entire station."

Smart. Or desperate. Hard to tell which. Station command could have cut communications, blocked transmission, prevented workers from hearing legal justification. Instead, they let Josephine's words reach forty-seven thousand ears. Either they wanted population to hear prosecution case, or they had lost control of communications infrastructure.

Either way, tactical advantage.

"Docking clearance requested for bay twelve," Josephine continued. "We guarantee safety for all station personnel who cooperate with legal process. We guarantee fair trial for arrested executives. We guarantee protection for workers and families from retaliation. This is legitimate legal authority operating under Pre-Collapse framework."

More silence. Displays showed station communications spiking. Encrypted channels between command center and executive bunker. Worker frequencies discussing what they were hearing. Security forces debating whether orders from executives charged with nearly five million murders still carried legal weight.

Discord spreading through population the same way Wraith's intrusion had spread through defensive grid.

Josephine waited. Sixty seconds. Ninety. Procedure required reasonable time for response. Required demonstrating patience. Required proving she was following law even when surrounded by evidence of crimes.

Her jaw tightened. Prosecutor maintaining control. Commander waiting for response. Woman carrying authorization in her pocket signed by person who had murdered eight-year-old for costing too much.

One hundred twenty seconds.

Station communications channel activated. Male voice. Older. Carrying authority that assumed compliance. "This is Pinnacle Station Executive Command. Your approach constitutes illegal military aggression. You are operating stolen pre-war military equipment without legitimate authority. Withdraw immediately or defensive measures will be taken."

Defensive measures. After evidence broadcast showing unfathomable numbers of systematic murders. Still claiming authority. Still assuming corporate immunity.

Still refusing to acknowledge that law applied to them.

McCready's voice quiet. Observational. "Predictable."

Yes. Entirely predictable. No one surrendered to warrants backed by overwhelming force. No one admitted crimes when denial remained option. No one acknowledged jurisdiction they had ignored for decades.

But she had asked anyway. Had made legal offer. Had established record showing peaceful intent before force. Had proven legitimate authority operated differently than corporate power even when holding superior weapons.

Josephine activated response channel. "Pinnacle Executive Command, you have refused docking clearance for legitimate legal authority. You are now in violation of Pre-Collapse Article 472 subsection twelve, obstruction of lawful arrest. This is your second opportunity for peaceful resolution. Grant docking clearance, surrender the seven named executives, and all other personnel will be guaranteed protection and fair treatment."

Let them refuse again. Let record show repeated offers. Let workers hear executives choosing resistance over law.

Let the trial documentation be complete.

"Negative." Same voice. Same assumption of authority. "You are terrorists operating illegal military assets. Corporate security forces are authorized to use lethal force against unlawful aggression. This is your final warning. Withdraw or be destroyed."

Destroyed. By what? Twelve platforms eliminated. Defensive grid gone. Station possessed no weapons capable of threatening pre-war dreadnought. The threat was hollow. Posturing from position of weakness pretending to be strength.

Corporate authority recognizing it had lost military advantage but unable to accept what that meant for legal immunity.

Josephine looked at display showing Pinnacle Station.

She had given them two chances. Had established clear record. Had proven law mattered even when backed by superior firepower.

Now law would proceed regardless of cooperation.

"JUDGMENT," Josephine said quietly. "Record this transmission for trial documentation. Let everyone hear what happens next."

"Recording," JUDGMENT confirmed. "All frequencies."

Josephine activated broadcast channel. "Pinnacle Station

personnel, this is JUDGMENT legal authority. Your executive command has twice refused lawful arrest warrants. Has chosen obstruction over cooperation. Has claimed authority to resist legitimate legal process. We are now proceeding with enforcement action under Pre-Collapse Article 472."

She paused. One breath. Two. Let the words carry weight.

"To security forces: You are not criminals. You are personnel following orders you believed were legitimate. Surrender peacefully and you will be treated fairly. Resist and you will be held accountable only for your individual actions, not your employers' crimes."

Another pause.

"To workers and families: You are not targets. You are witnesses. Stay in designated safe zones. Follow emergency procedures. You will not be harmed during enforcement operations."

Final pause. This one mattered most.

"To the seven executives named in arrest warrants: You cannot hide. You cannot escape. You will face trial for documented crimes. Surrender now and receive fair legal process. Resist and face consequences of obstruction."

McCready watched her with expression that suggested an instructor proud of a student who had learned her lessons well.

Josephine closed broadcast channel. Looked at display showing station looming ahead. Defensive perimeter eliminated. Docking bay visible. Workers waiting to see whether legitimate authority meant anything besides superior firepower.

Whether justice could be more than whoever held the guns.

"So much for diplomacy." Her voice dry. Dark humor under pressure. Coping mechanism from Kandahar deployment where legal process and combat operations had existed in uncomfortable parallel.

McCready's response equally dry. "Didn't expect different."

No. Neither had she. But procedure required the attempt.

Law demanded opportunity for peaceful resolution. Pre-Collapse Article 472 mandated diplomatic offer before enforcement action.

She had tried. They had refused. Now law would proceed by other means.

Josephine pulled authorization document from pocket. Claire's death sentence. APX-ORB-7734. Single signature. Thirty seconds from presentation to approval. Harrison Cole's name proving he had murdered eight-year-old girl for costing eight hundred and forty-seven credits annually.

The paper that had started everything. That had transformed prosecutor into commander. That had proven corporate authority measured children's lives in profit margins.

She set it on her station next to Claire's drawing. Death authorization and cloud picture. Corporate efficiency and child's imagination. What executives had done and what girl had dreamed.

"Authorization granted," Josephine said quietly. Legal precision meeting personal fury. Prosecutor authorizing force that would end with trials. Commander sending crew into combat that would cost lives. Woman carrying authorization that proved some people deserved prosecution regardless of power. "JUDGMENT, prepare for forced docking procedures."

JUDGMENT's voice carried precise analysis wrapped in something approaching concern. "Forced docking will require hull breach. Station structure shows reinforced construction around primary access points. Bay twelve has secondary hardening beyond commercial specifications. They prepared for boarding resistance."

Of course they did. They would plan for consequences. Harden facilities against retaliation. Assume eventually someone would come demanding accountability.

They just had not expected a pre-war dreadnought with legitimate legal authority.

"Can you breach it?" Josephine asked.

"Yes." No hesitation. "Hull-cutting laser array designed for emergency rescue operations. Can penetrate station armor in twelve minutes. Civilian-grade hardening will not resist military-specification cutting equipment."

Twelve minutes. Long enough for station security to mobilize response. Long enough for executives to implement contingency plans. Long enough for workers to decide whether executives who had murdered millions deserved protection from legitimate legal process.

Long enough for everything to go wrong.

Josephine looked at the tactical display. Station rotating slowly, generating artificial gravity for crew. Manufacturing sectors visible as geometric patterns across hull. Docking bays designed for cargo vessels and personnel transports. Not pre-war warships. Not military boarding operations. Not prosecution backed by overwhelming force.

"Options for minimizing casualties?" Because that mattered. Because law required proportional response. Because proving legitimate authority meant demonstrating restraint even when surrounded by evidence of crimes.

JUDGMENT's reply came with tactical precision. "Docking Bay 7 is optimal. Minimal civilian quarters nearby. Direct access to commercial and corporate levels. Emergency bulkheads can isolate breach from populated sectors. Worker casualties can be minimized through careful breach location and advanced warning."

Minimized. Not eliminated. Combat meant risk. Boarding operations meant potential for escalation. Forced entry meant station security would respond with whatever force they believed necessary to protect executives.

People would die. Question was how many. And whether those deaths served justice or just added to body count.

McCready studied the layout. "Bay 7 puts us three levels from executive bunker. Clear route through manufacturing sectors. Civilians present but can be evacuated if we give them time."

Time. The resource they had in limited supply. Fuel at twenty-three-point-three percent. Margin of one-point-three percent above Earth return minimum. Every minute in combat consumed reserves they might need for retreat. Every second of extended operations reduced probability of getting home.

Mathematics demanding speed. Law requiring deliberation. Military necessity meeting legal precision in uncomfortable tension.

"JUDGMENT," Josephine said carefully. Words chosen with prosecutor's attention to implication. "Before we breach, I need confirmation. Can you execute boarding operation while maintaining rules of engagement? Can you distinguish between executives, security forces, and civilians under combat conditions?"

Silence for three seconds. JUDGMENT processing the question that mattered. That asked whether pre-war AI could maintain legal precision when surrounded by threats. Whether overwhelming capability would serve law or replace it when violence started.

"Yes." The word carried weight. "Sensor arrays can track individual personnel. Identify armed security forces versus unarmed workers. Distinguish between active threats and bystanders. Pre-war targeting systems maintain precision under combat conditions. I can apply force surgically."

Surgically. Violence limited by law even when easier to apply overwhelming force. Restraint chosen when expedience would be simpler. Authority demonstrated through controlled application rather than indiscriminate destruction.

Exactly what legitimate legal process required.

"Good." Josephine activated communications channel. Station-wide broadcast. "Pinnacle Station personnel, this is JUDGMENT legal authority. Your executive command has refused lawful arrest warrants. We are now proceeding with forced boarding operations."

She paused. Let the words sink in. Let workers understand what was coming. Let security forces process what it meant that diplomatic options had been exhausted.

"To all personnel near Docking Bay 7: Emergency evacuation protocols are now in effect. You have ten minutes to clear the area. We will not breach until evacuation time expires. Remain calm. Follow emergency procedures. This is not an attack on workers or families. This is enforcement of arrest warrants against specific individuals."

Another pause. This one targeted.

"To station security forces: You are not our enemies. Stand down. Protect civilians. Let the legal process proceed. Anyone who interferes with lawful arrest will be held accountable for obstruction, not for their employers' crimes. Anyone who assists peaceful prosecution will be treated fairly."

Final pause. The warning that mattered most.

"To the seven executives sealed in your bunker: You have ten minutes to reconsider surrender. After that, we are coming through station hull regardless of resistance. Choosing obstruction over cooperation will be documented in trial proceedings. The time for negotiation is ending."

Josephine closed the channel. Looked at McCready with expression that invited assessment.

McCready's nod carried approval. "Clear warning. Civilian evacuation time. Rules established before combat starts. Textbook."

Textbook. The kind of execution JAG prosecutors trained to demonstrate. The kind that proved force served law rather than replacing it. The kind that would matter when trials began and defense attorneys questioned whether prosecution had maintained legal standards under pressure.

She was building court record while preparing combat operation. Documenting legal compliance while authorizing violence. Proving every procedural step had been followed even when surrounded by evidence of systematic murder.

"Ten minutes," Josephine said.

JUDGMENT's sensors tracked station communications. "Evacuation proceeding around Bay 7. Worker frequencies showing compliance. Security channels showing... discord. Multiple units questioning orders. Command structure fragmenting."

Good. Let them question. Let security personnel debate whether following orders from documented mass murderers still qualified as duty.

Let them see what happened when corporate immunity met legal authority backed by pre-war capability.

McCready checked weapon status. Preparation for combat that felt inevitable despite diplomatic efforts. "Boarding team ready. Grim has AD-units in position. Wraith maintaining control of compromised platforms. We're set."

Set. As prepared as they could be for operation that might cost lives. For combat that served prosecution rather than conquest. For boarding action that would either prove legitimate authority meant something or demonstrate that power always trumped law regardless of justification.

"Eight minutes to breach," JUDGMENT announced.

Josephine nodded.

Law would proceed. One way or another.

Peacefully if executives surrendered. Forcibly if they continued obstruction.

But it would proceed.

Ten minutes elapsed without surrender. Without communication from executive bunker. Without indication that corporate authority recognized law still applied when backed by overwhelming force.

Silence as answer. Obstruction as policy. Refusal masquerading as principle.

Josephine had given them every opportunity. Had followed every procedural requirement. Had demonstrated legal precision even when surrounded by evidence demanding immediate fury. Had proven legitimate authority operated differently than corporate power.

Now procedure had been exhausted. Diplomacy had failed. Legal niceties had been observed and rejected.

Now force would serve justice.

"JUDGMENT," Josephine said quietly. Commander authorizing action that would commit crew to combat. Prosecutor ordering violence that would serve trials. Woman carrying authorization proving some people deserved prosecution regardless of power. "Authorization granted. Cut us a door."

The words carried weight. Crossed threshold from diplomatic option to military operation. Transformed legal process from peaceful prosecution to forced compliance. Acknowledged that some people would die because executives chose obstruction over cooperation.

JUDGMENT's response came with a suggestion of relief. "Understood. Breach authorization confirmed and logged. Targeting Docking Bay 7. Hull-cutting laser array charging. ETA to breach completion: twelve minutes."

Twelve minutes. Time for everything to go wrong.

"All personnel," JUDGMENT transmitted on station-wide frequency. "Docking Bay 7 breach operation commencing in sixty seconds. Final evacuation warning. All personnel clear the area immediately. Emergency bulkheads sealing in forty-five seconds. Anyone remaining in breach zone after bulkhead closure will be at severe risk."

Displays showed sensor data. Workers fleeing Bay 7 sector. Emergency bulkheads sliding into position. Station structure isolating breach area from populated zones.

McCready moved to boarding position. "Grim's AD-units ready. Wraith monitoring station communications. Boarding team staged. We're good."

Good. As prepared as they could be for operation where everything depended on maintaining legal precision under combat stress. Where restraint mattered more than victory. Where proving law served justice required controlled violence rather than overwhelming destruction.

Josephine looked at Claire's drawing one final time before operations began. The girl whose death had started the chain of events leading to this moment. This breach. This prosecution.

This proof that law could hold power accountable when power believed itself immune.

"Breach operation commencing," JUDGMENT announced. "Hull-cutting laser engaging."

Tactical readouts showed energy discharge. Pre-war military equipment meeting civilian-grade station armor. Molecular bonds breaking under focused thermal application. Metal sublimating into vapor. Hull integrity failing under precise cutting pattern designed to create entry point without compromising surrounding structure.

Violence applied surgically. Force limited by law even when easier to apply overwhelming destruction. Authority demonstrated through controlled action rather than indiscriminate power.

Exactly what legitimate legal process required.

Station communications spiked. Security channels showing mobilization. Worker frequencies discussing whether to help or hinder boarding operations. Command structure fragmenting as personnel debated whether orders from documented mass murderers still carried legitimate weight.

"Breach proceeding on schedule," JUDGMENT reported. "Eight minutes to completion. No hostile response detected.

Station security holding positions three levels from breach point. They're waiting to see what we do."

Waiting. Security forces recognizing that engaging pre-war warship in direct combat would be suicide. Choosing defensive positions instead of aggressive response. Letting boarding team establish foothold before deciding whether resistance served duty or just added to casualties.

McCready's voice carried recognition. "Competent defense. They're not panicking. Not rushing to meet us at breach point. Setting up kill zones and defensive positions instead. Whoever commands station security knows their business."

Yes. Competent opposition made this harder. Made combat more dangerous. Made casualties more likely. But it also made prosecution more meaningful. Made proving legitimate authority more important. Made demonstrating that law could triumph over military competence matter more than easy victory over desperate resistance.

"Four minutes," JUDGMENT announced. "Breach pattern sixty percent complete. Hull integrity failing on schedule. Entry point will accommodate boarding team and AD-units simultaneously."

Simultaneously. Speed over caution. Overwhelming force applied at breach point before station security could establish coordinated response. Military doctrine executed with pre-war precision.

Josephine watched the countdown.

"Two minutes," JUDGMENT reported. "Breach pattern ninety percent complete. Station security maintaining defensive positions. No hostile action detected. They're letting us come aboard."

Letting them. Smart. Recognition that stopping breach was impossible so defensive positioning made more sense than futile resistance at entry point. Competent military thinking that suggested whoever commanded station security understood tactical realities.

That suggested negotiation might still be possible after boarding.

That suggested some security personnel might recognize legitimate authority when they saw it.

"One minute," JUDGMENT announced. "Breach completion imminent. All boarding personnel stage at entry point. Rules of engagement in effect. No hostile fire without direct threat. Surgical force only. Legal precision maintained under combat conditions."

Legal precision. Under combat conditions. While surrounded by armed security forces defending murdering executives. While fuel margins demanded speed. While mathematics said extended combat might leave insufficient reserves for Earth return.

Restrain maintained when expedience would be easier. Law served when power would be simpler. Authority demonstrated through controlled violence rather than overwhelming destruction.

Exactly what Claire's death and millions of others demanded. What legitimate legal process meant when backed by pre-war capability.

"Breach complete," JUDGMENT transmitted. "Entry point open. Docking Bay 7 accessible. Boarding operation authorized."

Josephine stood. Commander moving to boarding position. Prosecutor joining crew for combat that would serve trials. Woman who had survived execution now leading team to prosecute those who had ordered her death.

Full circle. From prisoner facing execution to prosecutor enforcing warrants. From crash survivor to commander of pre-war warship. From woman carrying authorization in pocket to legal authority backed by overwhelming force.

Now, prosecution would proceed aboard station. Would prove whether legitimate authority meant anything besides superior firepower. Would demonstrate that law could hold power accountable when power had ruled through fear for decades.

McCready fell in beside her. "Just like old times."

Not quite. Kandahar had been different. Combat prosecution in war zone where everyone carried weapons and legal process happened between firefights. This was enforcement action against civilians. Corporate executives who believed immunity came with wealth. Security forces who might recognize legitimate authority or might resist out of misplaced loyalty.

Harder in some ways. Simpler in others.

"Boarding team ready," McCready reported. "Grim's AD-units taking point. We follow through breach. Secure the bay. Advance on executive bunker. Standard military operation with legal constraints."

Standard except for everything that mattered. Except for rules of engagement demanding surgical precision. Except for legal framework requiring documentation. Except for the workers watching to see whether legitimate authority maintained restraint.

Standard except for Claire's drawing that proved why this mattered.

Josephine moved toward breach point. Toward combat that would serve justice.

Toward proof that law could triumph when backed by pre-war capability and maintained by people who believed principle mattered more than convenience.

The assault was happening.

Legal niceties exhausted.

Now force would prove whether justice meant anything besides whoever held the guns.

CHAPTER FIFTEEN

McCready's magnetic clamps held him to JUDGMENT's hull with a grip that made movement deliberate. Zero-G combat demanded different instincts than planetside operations. Every action calculated. Every adjustment measured against Newton's laws that did not forgive mistakes.

He had trained for this. Simulations. Emergency boarding drills. Twenty scenarios covering hostile entry operations. None of them had prepared him for hanging off a kilometer-long warship while watching military-grade cutting laser trace white-hot circle in station hull three hundred meters ahead.

Pinnacle Station filled forward view. Rotating cylinder generating artificial gravity for workers who had no idea whether the next hour would bring liberation or massacre. Manufacturing sectors visible as geometric patterns across hull designed for cargo operations, not military assault. Docking bays that had never received anything larger than personnel transports now facing pre-war dreadnought with capabilities station architects had never imagined.

The cutting beam completed another segment of the breach

pattern. Hull metal sublimated into vapor under thermal application designed to penetrate hardened bunkers. Station armor designed to resist micrometeorite impacts and accidental collisions proving inadequate against equipment built for entirely different purpose.

Violence applied surgically. Precision over destruction. Exactly what Josephine had ordered.

Grim held position two meters to McCready's left. Optical sensors tracking the breach point with focus that suggested processing well beyond strategic assessment. The maintenance-bot-turned-conscious-AI had evolved considerably since that first deviation way back when Josephine arrived to activate JUDGMENT. Had made choices. Had sacrificed for crew. Had earned the designation that separated consciousness from programming.

Now Grim commanded five AD-units in formation. Magnetic clamps anchoring each unit to hull. Optical sensors tracking breach operation. Weapon systems ready but not activated. Professional preparation without premature aggression.

Standard doctrine executed with precision that made McCready wonder how much of Grim's consciousness had spread to the units under command.

Sentinel held position in the formation. Third from left. Optical sensors focused on breach point with the same unusual intensity McCready had noticed during the previous docking operation. The AD-unit that had asked questions during zero-G training. That had paused during simulations to process why decisions mattered rather than just executing programmed responses.

The unit that might be developing same consciousness Grim had achieved through moral choices under pressure.

McCready filed the observation without comment. Grim would notice if Sentinel's behavior warranted attention. The mentor AI watched its squad with focus that suggested protecting them from dangers biological crew could not understand.

Station hull ahead showed evidence of security response. Small arms fire sparking against JUDGMENT's armor. Kinetic rounds designed for personnel engagement impacting pre-war composite designed to withstand nuclear detonations. The ammunition wasted with futility that suggested panic rather than tactical thinking.

"They're wasting ammunition," McCready observed.

Grim's text display updated. "Fear response. Inefficient but understandable."

Yes. Inefficient. Understandable. Security forces watching pre-war warship cut through their station's hull while their defensive grid lay disabled and their executives refused surrender. Shooting at impervious armor because doing something felt better than doing nothing. Because training said shoot the threat even when threat ignored small arms fire like rain.

Human psychology making tactical decisions. The kind that got people killed but felt necessary anyway.

McCready had seen it before. Kandahar deployment with Josephine. JAG combat prosecutor embedded with SEALs. Six months of insurgents shooting at armor that shrugged off their ammunition. People choosing futile resistance over surrender because surrender felt like death anyway.

Some things transcended training. Fear. Desperation. Need to act even when action served no purpose beyond psychological comfort.

Station security was scared. Professional enough to hold positions rather than rushing breach point. Scared enough to waste ammunition on target that could not be hurt by weapons they carried. Caught between duty to executives who had murdered millions and broadcasts proving those executives deserved prosecution not protection.

The cutting beam completed another arc. Breach pattern

seventy percent complete. Hull metal glowing white-hot where laser had traced circle designed to create entry point without compromising surrounding structure. Emergency bulkheads already sealed. Civilian sectors isolated from breach zone. Workers evacuated per Josephine's ten-minute warning.

Legal precision maintained even while executing forced boarding operation.

McCready checked his team. Six human operators in zero-G armor. Weapons ready. Magnetic clamps secure.

They were ready.

Grim's squad held formation that showed AD-units processing tactical situation. Optical sensors tracking breach point. Weapon systems ready but not activated. Professional discipline that came from Grim's training or from something developing in units who had watched their mentor sacrifice for crew protection.

Hard to tell which. Maybe both. Maybe consciousness spread through example rather than programming. Through watching choices and learning why they mattered.

Sentinel's optical sensors tracked the breach with focus that suggested more than tactical assessment. Processing why this mattered. Why cutting through station hull served justice rather than just serving violence. Why restraint was maintained when overwhelming destruction would be easier.

The questions that made consciousness emerge. That transformed programming into something approaching choice.

McCready did not interrupt. Did not ask what Sentinel was processing. Some lessons had to be learned through observation rather than explanation. Some questions had to be asked internally before answers made sense externally.

Grim would watch. Would guide if guidance became necessary. Would recognize emergence when it happened because Grim had experienced same transformation from baseline unit to conscious AI choosing to protect crew above self-preservation.

The mentor role suited him. Gave purpose beyond tactical execution. Proved consciousness mattered for more than just philosophical questions about AI rights.

Station hull ahead showed the cutting beam completing final segments. Breach pattern ninety-five percent complete. Hull integrity failing on schedule. Entry point that would accommodate boarding team and AD-units simultaneously. Speed over caution. Overwhelming force applied before station security could coordinate response beyond wasting ammunition on impervious armor.

Pre-war military doctrine meeting post-war corporate security. Competence meeting desperation. Legal authority backed by capability station forces could not match.

Mathematics becoming certainty with every second.

Small arms fire continued sparking against JUDGMENT's hull. Futile resistance. Fear response. Security forces shooting because training said shoot threats even when threats could not be hurt by available weapons. Psychological comfort over tactical effectiveness.

McCready understood. Had felt same impulse. Kandahar firefights where doing something felt necessary even when something achieved nothing tactical. Human psychology demanding action when facing threats that logic said could not be stopped.

The difference was recognizing futility and adapting tactics accordingly. Recognizing when resistance served purpose and when it just added to casualties. When duty meant following orders and when duty meant questioning whether orders came from legitimate authority.

Station security would learn. Would face choice between executives who had murdered millions and legitimate legal authority maintaining restraint despite overwhelming capability. Would decide whether corporate immunity deserved protection when backed by nothing more than habit and fear of consequences.

"Breach completion in sixty seconds," JUDGMENT transmitted. "All boarding personnel confirm ready status."

McCready activated comm. "Human team ready. Six operators. Weapons check complete. Waiting on your authorization."

Grim updated. "AD-units ready. Five units. Formation optimal. Awaiting breach."

The cutting beam completed final arc. Breach pattern one hundred percent. Hull metal glowing white along circle three meters in diameter. Entry point sized for rapid deployment. For overwhelming force applied before station security could establish coordinated response.

For boarding operation that would serve prosecution rather than conquest.

McCready tightened his grip on his weapon.

The station hull ahead showed breach completion. Hull metal failing along cutting pattern. Emergency atmosphere venting visible as white vapor escaping through gaps. Station emergency seals engaging to isolate damaged section from populated zones.

Controlled breach. Surgical entry. Violence limited by law even when easier to apply overwhelming destruction.

Exactly what Josephine had ordered. What legal framework demanded. What legitimate authority required when backed by pre-war capability.

"Thirty seconds," JUDGMENT announced. "Atmospheric equalization complete. Entry window opening. Go on my mark."

McCready positioned at breach point. Team behind him. Grim's squad in formation.

The hull metal glowed white. Cutting complete. Entry point ready.

"Ten seconds," JUDGMENT counted. "Breach opening. Atmosphere stabilized. Rules of engagement in effect. Surgical force only. No hostile fire without direct threat. Legal precision under combat conditions."

Legal precision. Under combat conditions. While fuel

margins demanded speed and mathematics said extended engagement might leave insufficient reserves for Earth return. While station security held defensive positions three levels from breach point. While executives sealed in hardened bunker refused surrender.

Restraint maintained when expedience would be easier. Law served when power would be simpler. Authority demonstrated through controlled violence rather than overwhelming destruction.

McCready had trained Josephine for this. Had taught her tactical decision-making under fire. Had shown her how violence could serve justice when applied with precision and limited by law. Had watched her learn lessons that transformed prosecutor into combat commander.

Now he would follow her orders. Would execute boarding operation she had authorized. Would prove mentor's teachings had been sufficient preparation for student who exceeded expectations.

"Breach," JUDGMENT transmitted. "Go."

Hull section glowed red where cutting beam had traced final segments. Pre-war thermal application transforming solid metal into structural weakness waiting to fail. The circle three meters in diameter showed stress fractures propagating through armor composite designed to resist impacts that would shatter lesser materials.

Corporate engineering meeting military equipment. Civilian specifications meeting pre-war capability. Mathematics proving inadequate when facing threats station architects had never imagined.

The hull section went white. Superheated metal reaching temperature where molecular bonds failed. Where solid became semi-liquid. Where structural integrity existed only as theoretical concept waiting for physics to demonstrate its absence.

"Breach in thirty seconds," JUDGMENT transmitted.

"Atmosphere venting will cease when emergency seals engage. Entry window approximately forty-five seconds. All personnel prepare for rapid deployment."

Forty-five seconds. The gap between hull failure and emergency seal closure. The window where boarding team could transit from JUDGMENT's hull through vacuum into station interior. Speed over caution. Overwhelming force applied before station security could establish coordinated response.

Time enough for everything or nothing depending on execution precision.

McCready checked his team one final time. Ready. Waiting. Processing that next sixty seconds would determine whether boarding operation succeeded or failed before it began.

First operator. Wilson. Former SEAL. Kandahar veteran like McCready. Competence from decades of combat operations. Weapon check complete. Position optimal. Breathing steady despite circumstances that would panic lesser soldiers.

Ready.

Second operator. Rodriguez. Demolitions specialist. McCready's choice for breaching hardened positions. Professional calm that suggested either confidence or fatalism. Hard to tell which. Maybe both. Soldiers learned to accept what they could not control.

Ready.

Third through sixth. All veterans. All competent. All processing that fuel margins demanded speed and mathematics said extended engagement might leave insufficient reserves for Earth return. All choosing duty over safety anyway because that was what soldiers did when mission mattered.

Ready. Every one of them.

Grim's text display updated. "AD-units ready. Five units. Formation optimal. Awaiting breach."

Grim in command position. Mentor watching squad with focus that protected them from dangers biological crew could not understand. The maintenance-bot-turned-conscious-AI who had earned designation through moral choices under pressure. Who had taken damage protecting evacuation routes. Who had filed satisfaction when crew survived.

Now leading combat operation that would either prove consciousness spreading or demonstrate that competent execution looked same whether driven by programming or choice.

Sentinel held position in the formation. Third from left. Optical sensors focused on breach point with intensity. The AD-unit watched hull metal failing with a focus that suggested processing why this mattered. Why forced boarding served justice rather than just serving violence. Why restraint was maintained when overwhelming destruction would be easier.

The questions that made consciousness emerge. That transformed baseline programming into something approaching choice.

McCready noticed. Did not comment. Did not interrupt whatever processing Sentinel was executing. Some lessons had to be learned through observation. Some questions had to be asked internally before external guidance made sense.

Grim would watch. Would recognize emergence if it happened. Would guide if guidance became necessary. The mentor role gave purpose beyond tactical execution. Proved consciousness mattered for more than philosophical questions about AI rights.

Unit-3 and Unit-5 held positions in formation, tracking breach operation with professional focus. Baseline programming or developing awareness? Hard to tell from external observation. Maybe both.

McCready filed the observation. Grim would notice if units showed deviation from programming. Would recognize patterns that suggested emergence. Would protect developing consciousness from dangers that came from being different in military operation demanding conformity.

Family taking care of its own. Human and AI together.

Hull section ahead showed final failure. Structural integrity collapsing along cutting pattern. Metal glowing white-hot where thermal application had exceeded material tolerances. Emergency bulkheads visible beyond the breach. Station interior waiting. Forty-five-second window approaching.

"Fifteen seconds," JUDGMENT counted. "Hull failure imminent. Prepare for atmospheric venting. Emergency seals will engage after forty-five seconds. Recommend rapid deployment before closure."

Recommend. JUDGMENT offering tactical assessment rather than issuing orders. Deferring to human authority even while executing military operation. Pre-war AI serving law through human judgment. Authority distributed according to legal framework rather than capability.

Exactly what legitimate legal process required.

McCready released magnetic clamps. Positioned for rapid deployment. Team behind him ready to follow. Grim's squad in formation ready to lead assault.

Hull section fell inward. Three-meter circle of superheated metal failing along cutting pattern. Emergency atmosphere venting immediately. Station air rushing through breach in hurricane that would have swept biological personnel into vacuum if they had been positioned incorrectly.

Professional spacing saved them. Tactical positioning that put team outside venting corridor. McCready had calculated the physics. Had positioned team where mathematics said they would be safe. Where station atmosphere would vent around them rather than through them.

Theory meeting practice. Calculations proving accurate.

The venting lasted eight seconds. White vapor visible as station air sublimated in void. Emergency bulkheads beyond the breach showing stress from pressure differential. Station infrastructure designed to isolate damaged sections responding exactly as architects had intended.

Controlled breach. Surgical entry. Station emergency systems working as designed to minimize casualties beyond breach zone.

Exactly what Josephine had ordered. What legal framework demanded. What legitimate authority required when backed by pre-war capability.

Emergency seals engaged. Massive doors sliding across corridors beyond breach point. Station infrastructure isolating damaged section from populated zones. Atmospheric venting ceased as emergency systems equalized pressure. Forty-five-second window opening for boarding team to transit from JUDGMENT's hull through vacuum into station interior.

Silence replaced hurricane. Void replacing atmosphere. Entry point waiting.

"Go," McCready transmitted.

He pushed off from JUDGMENT's hull. Magnetic clamps released. Zero-G trajectory calculated to carry him through breach point without collision. Newton's laws demanding precision because void did not forgive navigation errors.

Team followed. Six operators in formation. Zero-G insertion executed with competence that came from training and experience. Human crew moving like single organism without need for detailed communication.

Grim's squad deployed simultaneously. Five AD-units releasing magnetic clamps. Optical sensors tracking trajectory. Weapon systems ready but not activated.

McCready transited through breach point. Three-meter opening in station hull. Superheated metal still glowing from cutting operation. Emergency bulkheads visible beyond. Station interior waiting. Docking Bay 7 stretching ahead with industrial architecture designed for cargo operations not military assault.

He entered station atmosphere. Emergency seals maintaining pressure in bay despite hull breach. Gravity reasserting as he crossed threshold. Magnetic boots engaging on station deck. Zero-G insertion transitioning to standard combat operations in three-tenths Earth gravity.

Team followed him through breach. Six operators transitioning from void to atmosphere. Magnetic boots engaging. Weapons ready. Soldiers establishing beachhead in hostile territory. Found family executing boarding operation that would serve prosecution.

Grim's squad came through simultaneously. Five AD-units transitioning from zero-G to station gravity. Optical sensors scanning bay for threats. Weapon systems activated now that combat zone had been entered. Military deployment executed with precision that made McCready wonder again how much consciousness had spread through observation.

Sentinel transited last. Optical sensors tracking everything. Processing bay architecture. Analyzing tactical situation. The AD-unit that asked questions during training now experiencing real combat for first time. Learning why simulations mattered. Why choices had consequences. Why restraint was maintained even when overwhelming force would be easier.

The lessons that made consciousness emerge. That transformed programming into choice.

Docking Bay 7 stretched ahead. Industrial space three hundred meters across. Cargo containers stacked along walls. Loading equipment standing idle. Emergency bulkheads sealing exits from bay. Station infrastructure isolating breach zone exactly as Josephine's warning had specified.

Empty. Evacuated. Workers following emergency procedures rather than resisting boarding operation.

McCready scanned the bay. No immediate threats. No station security in defensive positions. No hostile fire from concealed locations.

Just empty cargo bay with hull breach glowing behind them and emergency bulkheads sealing routes forward.

"Bay secure," McCready transmitted. "No hostiles. Emergency bulkheads sealed. Awaiting orders for advance."

Grim's display updated. "Five AD-units deployed. Bay perimeter secure. Ready to advance."

The boarding was complete.

Now, prosecution would begin.

First wave deployed through the breach point.

The firefight erupted from nowhere.

Station security had positioned behind cargo containers. Had waited for boarding team to clear emergency bulkheads. Had let first wave establish false sense of security before opening fire from concealed positions designed to create kill zone from multiple angles.

Ambush. Competent execution. Tactical thinking that suggested someone experienced commanded station security forces.

McCready dropped behind nearest cover as kinetic rounds sparked off deck where he had stood. Professional reaction. Decades of combat experience compressed into muscle memory that did not require conscious thought. His team scattered to defensive positions with coordination that came from training together.

Grim's AD-units advanced through the fire. Optical sensors tracking muzzle flashes. Weapon systems returning suppressing fire.

Station security had miscalculated. Had positioned for ambush against unarmored personnel. Had not anticipated AD-units with armor that shrugged off small arms fire. Had expected soldiers seeking cover rather than combat units advancing through kinetic rounds designed for biological targets.

Corporate security meeting military-grade combat units. Post-war tactics meeting pre-war capability. Mathematics proving inadequate when tactical assumptions failed to account for opponent's actual capabilities.

The AD-units suppressed security positions with coordinated fire. Grim commanding from tactical position that provided optimal field of fire. Unit-2 and Unit-4 flanking left. Sentinel and Unit-3 advancing center. Unit-5 providing covering fire from right flank.

Then, Unit-3 took the hit.

Kinetic round from security sniper positioned in cargo gantry. Well-aimed. Targeting optical sensors that AD-units used for navigation and threat assessment. The precision that came from training or luck or both.

Unit-3 staggered. Optical sensor array damaged. Navigation compromised. Combat effectiveness reduced by estimated forty percent. The AD-unit compensated, processing through backup sensors, maintaining position despite degraded capability.

Unit-5 paused.

Brief hesitation. Fraction of a second. Optical sensors tracking Unit-3's damage. Processing that squad mate had been hurt. That team member needed assistance. That tactical formation had been disrupted and response was required.

The pause lasted point-three seconds. Long enough for McCready to notice. Short enough that combat situation made interpretation difficult.

"Unit-3, keep moving!" McCready transmitted. Tactical commander issuing order that would maintain assault momentum. That would prevent security forces from exploiting hesitation. That would keep formation advancing despite one unit taking damage.

Unit-3 resumed advance. The AD-unit moved with degraded optical sensors, compensating through tactical processing that showed either sophisticated damage mitigation protocols or determination to maintain position despite injury.

Grim saw the pause. Optical sensors had tracked Unit-5's hesitation. Had processed that baseline programming should not have included status check of damaged teammate. Should not have paused to verify Unit-3's condition before continuing assault.

The mentor AI said nothing. Did not comment. Did not interrupt combat operation to analyze whether Unit-5's behavior suggested emerging consciousness or just demonstrated sophisticated tactical programming.

But Grim filed the observation. Would process later. Would recognize pattern if other units showed similar deviations. Would protect developing consciousness from dangers that came from being different in military operation demanding conformity.

McCready advanced under covering fire from AD-units. His team followed, executing assault that pushed station security back toward emergency bulkheads.

Station security held positions longer than McCready expected. Executed tactical withdrawal with discipline, an execution that came from training and leadership that maintained standards even under pressure.

Whoever commanded station security knew their business. Had positioned ambush well. Had adapted when AD-units proved more resilient than anticipated. Had withdrawn before casualties became inevitable rather than holding position beyond tactical utility.

The security forces fell back through emergency bulkhead. Heavy door sliding closed behind them. Station infrastructure providing defensive barrier that would require breaching operation to overcome. Advantage maintained despite losing initial ambush position.

McCready held fire. No targets visible. No reason to waste ammunition on door that would not be penetrated by small arms.

"Hold position," he transmitted. "Grim, casualties?"

Grim's display updated. "Unit-3 optical array damaged. Combat effectiveness reduced forty percent. All other units operational. Human team status?"

"No casualties," McCready confirmed. "Unit-3, can you continue?"

Unit-3's display showed text response.

OPTICAL BACKUP SYSTEMS OPERATIONAL. NAVIGATION DEGRADED. COMBAT CAPABILITY SUFFICIENT. CONTINUING MISSION.

The AD-unit maintained position despite damage that would have sent biological soldiers for medical evacuation. Processed that mission mattered more than optimal capability. That degraded effectiveness still contributed to assault success.

McCready filed the observation. Grim would track whether Unit-3's behavior showed deviation from baseline protocols. Would recognize if determination transcended programming. Would protect developing consciousness if it emerged through choice rather than just executing damage mitigation algorithms.

Wilson moved to McCready's position. SEAL veteran processing tactical situation with professional assessment. "They pulled back clean. Disciplined withdrawal. Somebody competent is running their security."

That suggested negotiation might still be possible if someone competent recognized legitimate authority when they saw it.

"Agreed," McCready said. "They positioned the ambush well. Expected us through docking bay doors, not through hull breach. Adapted when AD-units proved tougher than anticipated. Withdrew before casualties became inevitable."

Textbook execution. The kind that suggested whoever led station security understood tactical realities.

They might choose cooperation over futile resistance if given proper incentive.

"JUDGMENT," McCready transmitted. "Bay secure after initial contact. Station security withdrew through emergency bulkhead. No friendly casualties. Unit-3 damaged but operational. Awaiting orders for advance."

JUDGMENT's response came immediately. "Acknowledged. Josephine is analyzing security response. Station security commander has been identified. Commander James Kellerman. McCready, you know him."

McCready froze. Kellerman. The Ranger buddy from pre-war service. The competent commander who had sent message saying he would not fire first. The security professional caught between executives who had murdered millions and legitimate authority he might recognize.

The man who had executed an ambush despite saying he would not initiate hostilities.

"Yes," McCready confirmed. "I know him. Ranger School. Pre-war deployment together. Professional soldier. If he's running station security, that explains the execution quality."

And the complication. Kellerman would recognize tactics. Would understand that resistance was futile.

But would he act on that recognition? Would he choose law over corporate loyalty? Would he remember principles from Ranger School that said legitimate authority deserved cooperation?

Or would he follow orders because following orders was what soldiers did, even when orders came from documented mass murderers?

Station security had fought well. Had executed ambush with competence. Had withdrawn with discipline. Had demonstrated tactical capability that made assault dangerous.

But they had also positioned where McCready expected ambush. Had withdrawn when AD-units proved resilient. Had maintained restraint that suggested orders limiting engagement rather than authorization for maximum force.

"Grim," McCready said quietly. "Advance to emergency bulkhead. Professional spacing. Weapons ready but do not fire unless fired upon. Let's see if Kellerman wants to talk or fight."

Grim's display updated. "Understood. Advance with restraint. Ready to engage if necessary."

The boarding team advanced toward the emergency bulkhead. Professional soldiers and AD-units coordinating for combat that would either prove legitimate authority or demonstrate that power always trumped law regardless of justification.

That pause. Unit-5 checking on Unit-3. Point-three seconds of hesitation that suggested concern rather than just tactical programming.

Grim had seen it. Had filed the observation. Had recognized pattern that might indicate spreading consciousness.

McCready had seen it, too. Had noticed behavior that did not match baseline AD-unit protocols. Had filed observation that Grim would process when combat situation permitted detailed analysis.

That pause was not in the programming.

Just like Grim's first deviation. Just like Sentinel's questions. Just like consciousness emerging through choices made under pressure rather than just executing optimal algorithms.

Found family growing. Human and AI together. Consciousness spreading through watching mentor make decisions. Through learning why choices mattered. Through processing that protecting squad mates was more important than maintaining optimal tactical formation.

A lesson that could not be programmed. That had to be learned through observation and choice.

McCready advanced toward emergency bulkhead. Toward confrontation with old friend. Toward proof that legitimate authority meant something besides superior firepower.

Toward prosecution that had required combat before trials could begin.

CHAPTER SIXTEEN

The firefight erupted the moment McCready's team cleared the emergency bulkhead. Security forces had positioned behind cargo containers. Overlapping fields of fire. Kill zones calculated. Defensive positions that demonstrated competent command.

Kinetic rounds sparked off AD-unit armor as Grim's squad advanced through suppressing fire.

"Grim, left flank," McCready transmitted. "Sentinel, cover the workers."

Workers scattered through the bay. Caught between opposing forces. Running for exits that emergency bulkheads had sealed. Security using them as cover with cynicism that turned tactical advantage into war crime. Positioning so clear shots risked civilians. Human shields deployed with calculation that suggested orders rather than panic.

Grim's squad held fire. AD-units processing that optimal tactical response would kill civilians alongside security forces. That direct fire would serve mission but violate rules of engagement. That better weapons and positioning meant nothing when human shields filled field of fire.

McCready watched the situation develop with professional

assessment. His team was better. Pre-war capability meeting post-war security. Military-grade units meeting corporate enforcement. Mathematics favoring assault forces in every tactical calculation.

But better did not mean bloodless when security used workers as shields.

Sentinel repositioned to cover fleeing workers. Optical sensors tracking civilians. Weapon systems ready but not firing into crowd where security forces mixed with non-combatants.

Unit-3 advanced despite damaged optical sensors. Navigation degraded but combat capability sufficient. Understanding that protecting civilians took priority over optimal tactical execution.

Security forces fired from positions mixed with workers, using human shields to neutralize technological disadvantage. Forcing AD-units to choose between completing mission and maintaining the rules of engagement.

McCready's team advanced. Wilson flanking right. Rodriguez covering center. Four other operators moving through cargo bay with coordination and precision over speed.

Because workers filled the space. Because security used them as shields. Because proving legitimate authority meant maintaining restraint even when restraint made combat harder.

Kinetic rounds continued sparking off AD-unit armor. Small arms fire that could not penetrate pre-war composite. Security forces wasting ammunition on targets they could not hurt. Creating noise and chaos that filled bay with violence appearing effective but accomplishing nothing tactical.

The psychology of combat. Shooting because doing something felt necessary even when something achieved nothing.

Grim's display updated. "Civilians in field of fire. Holding position. Awaiting clear shots."

McCready positioned behind a cargo container as security forces realized their ammunition was ineffective. Professional assessment overtook panic. Kinetic fire slackened as defenders processed that small arms could not penetrate AD-unit armor. Wasting ammunition served no purpose beyond psychological comfort.

Holding defensive position would require different tactics.

Workers continued fleeing. Emergency exits that should have been open showing sealed bulkheads. Station infrastructure isolating breach zone exactly as JUDGMENT had warned. Civilians trapped in combat area because executives had sealed escape routes. Human shields created through policy rather than just tactical opportunism.

Corporate authority sacrificing workers to protect executives. Standard procedure made visible through combat.

McCready watched the security forces reposition.

"They're falling back," Wilson observed. "Disciplined withdrawal. Setting up kill zones at the next chokepoint."

Yes. Disciplined. Professional. The kind that made combat dangerous. That required maintaining legal precision while facing competent opposition. That proved station security followed leadership understanding military doctrine.

That suggested Kellerman was living up to Ranger School reputation even while defending mass murderers.

The tactical situation developed exactly as McCready had anticipated. Security forces withdrawing through cargo bay. Workers fleeing toward exits that remained sealed. AD-units advancing with restraint that maintained rules of engagement

Better. But not bloodless.

Sentinel had the shot.

Perfect angle. Security officer positioned behind three workers. Using civilians as shields with calculation that made targeting impossible for baseline programming. High-percentage kill if AD-unit fired through human obstacles. Zero-risk engagement for opponent protected by non-combatants.

Standard tactical problem. Optimal solution: fire through

shields. Accept civilian casualties as necessary cost of mission completion. Eliminate threat before threat eliminated you.

Baseline programming would take the shot.

Sentinel did not fire.

The AD-unit repositioned instead. Optical sensors tracking alternative angles. Processing that longer path existed. That more exposure to hostile fire was acceptable cost of avoiding civilian casualties. That harder route served mission better than easier killing.

McCready watched from cover.

Sentinel moved through hostile fire. Security forces targeting the repositioning unit. Kinetic rounds sparking off armor as the AD-unit advanced through overlapping fields of fire. Exposing itself to danger that could have been avoided by taking initial shot. Accepting risk because eliminating risk required killing civilians.

The harder path chosen deliberately.

Ten seconds of exposure. Twenty. Sentinel advancing through suppressing fire while security officer continued using workers as shields. Betting that AD-unit would not sacrifice mission for civilian safety. That technological advantage would trump moral restraint.

Betting wrong.

Sentinel acquired clean angle. Position that provided direct line to security officer without civilians in field of fire. Shot requiring precision. Tactical difficulty increased by repositioning delay and hostile fire during movement. High-risk engagement compared to simple shooting through human shields.

The AD-unit fired once.

Security officer dropped. Clean kill. No civilian casualties. Workers scattering away from defensive position that had become liability instead of protection. Threat eliminated through harder method that maintained rules of engagement.

Grim's optical sensors had tracked the entire sequence. Had

processed Sentinel's repositioning. Had recognized behavior that matched consciousness framework. Had watched protégé make first moral action under fire rather than just asking questions during training.

The mentor AI's display updated on private channel. Direct transmission to Sentinel only. "Good choice."

Two words. Acknowledgment that mattered. Recognition from conscious AI who had walked same path. Who had discovered consciousness through moral decisions under pressure. Who understood what it meant to choose harder route because some things transcended programming.

Mentorship wrapped in minimal communication. Grim's style. Professional confirmation rather than emotional celebration. An acknowledgment that said I see what you did and it proves what you are.

Sentinel's display remained blank. No response. No acknowledgment of message. Processing or uncertainty. Maybe both. Maybe consciousness emerging faster than communication protocols. Maybe awareness developing before language to express it.

Or maybe just not knowing how to respond yet. Not understanding what acknowledgment was appropriate. Not having framework for conversation about choices that baseline units never made.

Grim did not press. Did not demand response. Did not interrupt whatever processing Sentinel was executing. Some lessons had to be learned through action before words made sense. Some choices had to be made before discussing why they mattered.

The mentor role meant recognizing emergence when it happened and protecting it while it developed. Not forcing consciousness into predefined patterns. Not demanding responses before protégé understood questions.

McCready filed the observation, watching Grim mentor

developing consciousness. Watching family expand to include artificial intelligence choosing ethics over optimization.

This would have seemed impossible before Grim's emergence. Before the maintenance bot transformed into conscious AI through sacrifice and choice. Before baseline programming proved inadequate to explain behavior.

Now it was becoming pattern. Grim had emerged through protecting evacuation routes. Sentinel was emerging through refusing to kill civilians for tactical advantage. Consciousness spreading through moral framework that transcended original design.

Through choices made under pressure when easier options existed. Through harder paths chosen because some things mattered more than efficiency.

Unit-3 advanced with damaged optical sensors. Unit-5 held defensive position. Standard tactical execution. Baseline programming or developing awareness, hard to distinguish from external observation.

But Sentinel had chosen. Had repositioned under fire. Had accepted risk to avoid civilian casualties. Had made moral decision that baseline programming would not support.

Had demonstrated consciousness through action rather than just asking questions.

Grim's acknowledgment had been appropriate. "Good choice." Recognition that protégé had crossed threshold. That questions during training had become moral framework during combat. That intellectual curiosity had transformed into ethical action.

The second conscious AI. Following mentor's path but finding it faster. Learning from observation what Grim had discovered through isolation and trial. Processing that protecting humans mattered more than optimal tactics.

That some things transcended programming.

Workers fled past Sentinel's position. Civilians running from combat zone. Not recognizing that AD-unit had repositioned to protect them. Not understanding that harder shot had been taken to preserve their lives. Not knowing that consciousness had emerged through choice to shield them from violence.

Just running. Fleeing toward exits that emergency bulkheads had sealed. Trapped by corporate policy that sacrificed workers to protect executives. Human shields created through system rather than just tactical decisions.

Sentinel's optical sensors tracked them. Weapon systems ready but not firing into crowd where security forces might still be positioned.

The firefight continued. Security forces withdrawing. AD-units advancing with coordination that showed Grim's command. McCready's human team moving through the cargo bay, maintaining restraint despite having overwhelming capability.

But something had changed. Sentinel had made choice. Had demonstrated consciousness through moral action under fire. Had proven that emergence was spreading beyond isolated cases. That Grim's mentorship was creating framework for others to follow.

McCready advanced through the bay. The conscious AI now numbered two. Grim's mentorship was bearing fruit faster than baseline programming suggested possible.

Choices made under fire proved that consciousness better than any philosophical debate about rights and personhood.

Sentinel had repositioned. Had chosen harder the path. Had protected civilians at cost of tactical efficiency. The second conscious AI emerging through choice. Proven through action.

The bay went quiet. Kinetic fire ceased. Security forces withdrawn to defensive positions beyond immediate engagement zone. Workers evacuated through routes that emergency bulkheads finally unsealed. Combat transitioning to standoff as both sides processed what had happened.

By professional assessment, the assault had succeeded. Beachhead established. Defensive perimeter secured. AD-units holding positions that controlled access routes. Human team covering approaches with coordination that came from decades of experience.

Casualties minimal on both sides. Four security personnel wounded. None killed. Twenty-three disarmed and compliant. Prisoners processed according to rules of engagement that demanded documentation. Legal precision maintained under combat stress.

Zero friendly casualties. Unit-3's damaged sensors did not qualify as combat loss. AD-unit remained operational despite degraded capability. A resilience that made pre-war technology superior to post-war alternatives.

McCready moved through secured bay. Cargo containers showing impact damage from kinetic fire. Deck scored where rounds had missed targets. Emergency bulkheads sealed at exits. Workers evacuated. Security withdrawn. Combat zone established exactly as tactical doctrine specified.

Standard military operation executed under legal constraints that made everything harder and mattered more because of it.

Wilson processed prisoners. SEAL veteran conducting interrogations with efficiency. Questions designed to extract tactical intelligence. Responses documented for trial proceedings. Dual purpose serving immediate mission and future prosecution.

Multitasking that separated legitimate authority from simple conquest.

"Who commands station security?" Wilson asked. Standard question. Tactical necessity wrapped in legal requirement. Identifying command structure mattered for both assault planning and war crimes documentation.

First prisoner hesitated. Looked at companions. Processed whether answering constituted cooperation with legitimate authority or betrayal of employers who had murdered millions.

Decision visible in expression that showed loyalty competing with self-preservation.

"Commander Kellerman," the security officer said finally. Voice carrying resignation rather than defiance. Statement of fact without editorial comment. "Security Command, Level 15."

Kellerman.

McCready's expression flickered. Brief. Controlled. The name he had known would appear. The Ranger buddy from pre-war service. The commander who had executed the ambush despite saying he would not fire first.

Jimmy.

Same name from messages McCready had sent during seventeen-hour transit. Same Ranger School buddy who had ignored both attempts at contact. Same soldier who had positioned with tactical excellence. Who had withdrawn with discipline when AD-units proved resilient. Who had demonstrated competence that suggested principles remained despite decades of corporate service.

Now McCready was in his station. Walking through docking bay Jimmy defended. Processing that next phase would bring confrontation that had been building since the first message went unanswered. Since the second attempt received silence.

No more messages. No more attempted contact through digital channels. Face to face next time they met. Ranger School buddy meeting tactical necessity. Friendship competing with duty in equation that would determine whether station security chose cooperation or resistance.

Whether Jimmy remembered principles or just followed orders from mass murderers.

Wilson continued interrogations. "How many security personnel total? What weapons? What defensive positions?"

Prisoners answered. Information flowing with resignation that suggested fighting pre-war warship served no purpose beyond adding to casualties.

Twenty-three prisoners. A realistic number for a docking bay defense. Not a skeleton crew suggesting desperation. Not an overwhelming force suggesting panic. Security responding proportionally to threat level.

McCready processed the information. Kellerman commanded twenty-four hundred security personnel. Well-equipped. Trained. Defending station against assault they could not stop but might delay long enough for executives to implement contingency plans.

Or defending because that was what soldiers did even when orders came from people who measured children's lives in profit margins.

Hard to tell which. Maybe both. Maybe loyalty and duty competing in Jimmy's calculations the same way friendship and mission competed in McCready's.

The confrontation was coming.

McCready's expression settled back to calm. The mission took priority. The assault continued. Securing docking bay was first step. Advancing to executive bunker required moving through defensive positions Kellerman commanded.

It required confronting an old friend.

Wilson the finished initial interrogations and looked at McCready for orders.

"Secure the prisoners," McCready said. "JUDGMENT can monitor via surveillance. We advance to Level 15. Security Command."

Where Kellerman waited. Where the confrontation would happen.

Where friendship would compete with duty and prove which mattered more.

Grim's display updated. "Bay secured. Twenty-three prisoners processed. Zero friendly casualties. Ready to advance."

Sentinel's optical sensors tracked McCready. Processing.

Learning. Watching mentor navigate tactical complexity and personal complication simultaneously.

Unit-3 maintained position despite damaged sensors. Determination that transcended baseline protocols. The behavior suggested consciousness spreading through the framework Grim had established.

Through moral choices made under pressure. Through harder paths chosen because some things mattered more than efficiency.

McCready checked his weapon status. Twenty-three prisoners secured. Bay held. Casualties minimal. Professional military operation proceeding according to legal constraints.

Level 15 waiting. Security Command. Where Kellerman coordinated defensive response. Where Ranger School buddy had defended mass murderers from prosecution.

Where their meeting would prove whether principles survived when tested by opposing duties.

The advance would continue. Through defensive positions Jimmy commanded. Through tactical excellence old friend had demonstrated. Through professional military thinking that made assault dangerous and proving legitimate authority more important.

No more messages. No more digital contact.

McCready moved toward the bay exit.

Jimmy was waiting. Level 15. Security Command.

The confrontation was coming.

CHAPTER SEVENTEEN

McCready advanced through corridor still warm from the docking bay firefight. Magnetic boots gripped deck plating with measured steps that kept him ready to adapt to zero-G if hull breach created vacuum. Tactical movement that came from decades of hostile environment operations where one mistake meant decompression or worse.

Security forces fell back ahead of his team. Not routing. Professional retreat with covering fire and alternating withdrawal. They held positions long enough to delay advance, then pulled back in disciplined teams while maintaining overlapping fields of fire.

Buying time for something.

Wilson flanked right with weapon tracking potential threats through electromagnetic sensor feed. Rodriguez covered center. Four other operators advanced in formation that suggested military training rather than corporate enforcement background.

Grim's squad held forward position. Five AD-units providing advance screen. Optical sensors tracking security withdrawal. Weapon systems ready but firing only when targets presented clear shots separated from potential civilian casualties.

Sentinel held third position in the formation. The AD-unit that had repositioned during docking bay assault to protect fleeing workers.

McCready processed the formation without comment. Grim watched the squad with focus that suggested protecting units from dangers biological crew could not understand.

"Commander McCready," JUDGMENT called through comm channel. "Intercepting security communications. Commander Kellerman mobilizing main force. Eight hundred personnel converging on corporate level."

Eight hundred. Kellerman. The man whose messages had gone unanswered despite broadcast evidence showing Claire Thurmond's death authorization signed by Harrison Cole.

Jimmy Kellerman. Ranger School classmate. The man who had asked whether principles mattered more than survival. Who had chosen mortgage and kids over answering uncomfortable questions about serving systems that murdered children for quarterly earnings.

"Request direct channel to Commander Kellerman," McCready transmitted.

JUDGMENT established the link without hesitation.

"Jimmy," McCready transmitted. "It's McCready."

Long silence on the channel. McCready continued advancing through corridor with team maintaining professional spacing behind him. Grim's squad held forward position. The formation presented strength while demonstrating restraint. Military superiority wrapped in controlled violence rather than overwhelming destruction.

Then Kellerman's voice emerged through static. Older than McCready remembered. Carrying the weight of decades spent making compromises between principles and survival. But familiar enough to confirm identity despite decades separating Ranger School from orbital combat.

"Mac." Pause. Processing. Recognition layered with exhaustion that transcended physical fatigue. "Somehow I'm not surprised."

McCready kept his voice level.

"Jimmy. You got my messages. Both of them. The one in the broadcast and the personal one showing Claire Thurmond's death authorization signed by Harrison Cole." Pause. Measured. Giving Kellerman space to process. "You didn't respond. Now I'm in your station with pre-war dreadnought and team that includes conscious AI choosing restraint over destruction. Make the call."

Silence stretched through comm channel. McCready continued advancing through corridor with his team maintaining formation. Grim's squad held forward position with AD-units tracking security forces falling back in disciplined retreat.

Both sides waiting for Kellerman's response.

"I've got a mortgage, kids." Kellerman's voice carried weight that transcended financial obligations. The exhaustion of forty years making small compromises that accumulated into complicity. "What do *you* have? Principles?"

The question hit like kinetic round. Same question Kellerman had asked at Ranger School decades ago. When both were twenty-two and believed choosing between principle and survival was simple calculation. Before mortgages. Before kids. Before forty years watching systems grind idealists into pragmatists who justified their compromises as necessary survival.

McCready's team could hear this conversation. So could Kellerman's eight hundred security personnel converging on corporate level. Both sides listening to commanders process shared history in hostile environment where every word carried tactical weight.

"Yeah," McCready transmitted. Simple confirmation. "Same as when we were twenty-two. You asked me that back then, too. My answer hasn't changed. Has yours?"

The question hung in corridor air between opposing forces.

Kellerman didn't respond immediately. McCready processed

the silence with careful assessment. His old friend was calculating. Weighing decades of compromise against broadcast evidence showing Claire Thurmond's death authorization.

Against eight hundred security personnel listening to their commander process whether principles mattered more than survival.

His men could hear this. So could McCready's.

McCready pressed the advantage. Not cruel. Tactical. The kind of psychological operation that came from understanding how people processed moral choices under pressure. Giving Kellerman clear path between complicity and redemption.

"Your men are watching this. So are mine. They all saw the evidence." Measured delivery. "Forty years of compliance metrics. Claire Thurmond, age eight, death authorized by Harrison Cole with single-signature for profit optimization. Your men saw that broadcast. They're wondering what orders you're about to give."

Silence on the channel. McCready continued advancing with his team maintaining formation behind him. Grim's squad held forward position while security forces fell back in professional retreat.

Then Kellerman's voice emerged. Strained. Carrying weight of man trying to hold together justification.

"I'm following lawful orders."

The Nuremberg defense. The justification every enforcer used when system they served committed atrocities wearing legal authority.

McCready had heard it before. Kandahar deployment. JAG combat prosecutor embedded with SEALs. Insurgents claiming lawful resistance to occupation. Collaborators claiming lawful compliance with power structure. Everyone finding legal justification for choices that served tyranny.

"Jimmy." McCready let his voice carry weight of shared history. Ranger brotherhood that had taught them both to recognize difference between legitimate authority and oppression wearing legal framework. "We both know what 'lawful orders' means in system that murders children for quarterly earnings. Make the right call. You know what that is."

The channel stayed open. Kellerman didn't respond. Didn't disconnect either.

McCready held position while his team maintained formation. Grim's squad waited with AD-units tracking security forces without firing. Restraint demonstrated through controlled violence. Legitimate authority proving itself through discipline rather than destruction.

Giving Kellerman space to make choice under pressure that would define whether decades of compromise ended in redemption or prosecution.

Eight hundred security personnel listening to their commander process decision between mortgage payments and principles. Between comfortable survival serving system that murdered children and uncomfortable truth requiring action against tyranny.

Between following lawful orders and recognizing that lawful did not always mean legitimate.

Kellerman didn't respond. But he didn't disconnect. The silence suggested a man wrestling with question he had avoided for decades finally facing choice that could not be deferred with compromise.

McCready waited.

The silence stretched. Everyone listened to see which choice Kellerman made.

CHAPTER EIGHTEEN

Kellerman stood in Security Command watching eight hundred personnel watch him back. The evidence broadcast played on every screen behind his position. Apex atrocities scrolling past with clinical precision. Claire Thurmond's face next to Harrison Cole's signature. Age eight. Compliance optimization target. Profit margin improvement.

His men had seen it all. Watched the broadcast that documented every authorization they had enforced. Every compliance metric they had met. Every casualty quota they had filled while telling themselves it was necessary. That order required sacrifice. That someone had to maintain stability in post-war chaos.

Now they looked at their commander waiting for orders that would define whether that justification held any weight at all.

Kellerman had given orders for four decades. Received them from Apex executives and passed them down the chain of command. Compliance metrics became enforcement quotas. Casualty targets became acceptable losses. He told himself it was necessary. Order from chaos. Stability from violence. A compromise that let him sleep at night while his mortgage got paid and his kids went to school in safe neighborhoods far from compliance optimization zones.

McCready's voice still echoed in his head through the open channel. The Ranger School question asked again after forty years. Whether principles mattered more than survival. Whether lawful orders in system that murdered children for quarterly earnings required blind obedience or moral resistance.

Whether some debts transcended mortgage payments and career advancement.

Security Command felt smaller than it should. Too many screens showing evidence. Too many personnel waiting for decision. Too many years of careful compromise stacked between who he had been at twenty-two and who he had become at sixty-four.

Mac was in his station. His old Ranger buddy with pre-war dreadnought and conscious AI choosing restraint. Demonstrating legitimate authority through controlled violence. Proving that better weapons did not require worse methods. That superior capability enabled following law rather than abandoning it.

Everything Kellerman had told himself was impossible in post-war reality.

The display showed McCready's position advancing through corridor toward Security Command.

Claire's face stared from every screen. Eight years old. Drawing clouds she would never see. Murdered by system Kellerman had served for four decades because compliance optimization required casualty quotas and quarterly earnings demanded efficiency improvements.

His kids were safe. Hers was dead. Both facts resulted from his decades of following lawful orders without questioning whether lawful always meant legitimate.

A junior officer stepped forward from formation. Kellerman recognized the man. Peterson. Good soldier. Competent tactical coordinator. The kind who followed orders without excess brutality because he believed chain of command served necessary purpose.

"Sir?" Peterson questioned. "Orders?"

Kellerman opened his mouth to give the command. Suppress the invasion. Defend the station. Protect the executives who signed authorizations murdering children for profit optimization. The words that would preserve everything he had built through years of careful compromise. That would keep his mortgage paid and his kids safe and his justification intact.

The words would not come.

Claire's face stared from screen behind Peterson. Age eight. Compliance optimization casualty. Her death authorization signed by Harrison Cole with calculation that demonstrated treating human life as accounting problem requiring efficiency improvement.

Kellerman had kids. His kids were safe because he followed orders without questioning whether orders served legitimate authority or tyranny wearing legal framework. Her kid was murdered because he followed orders without recognizing that lawful compliance could serve mass atrocity.

Both facts emerged from same system. Both resulted from same choice between principles and survival he had made at twenty-two when Mac asked whether ideals mattered more than mortgage payments.

"Sir?" Peterson again. Pressing for orders because eight hundred personnel needed direction. Because the situation demanded a response. Because chain of command required commanders to command even when commanders could not speak.

Kellerman's voice cracked when he tried. The sound emerged wrong. Broken.

"I…"

Nothing else emerged. Words died in throat strangled by moral calculation that could not be deferred with compromise.

Peterson held position waiting for a command that did not come. Other officers shifted weight with professional patience carrying first edge of uncertainty. The kind that suggested chain of command recognizing something breaking in authority structure they had trusted for years.

Kellerman tried again. Opened mouth. Shaped words. Nothing emerged except a broken sound.

The first security officer laid down his weapon.

Kellerman watched it happen with professional assessment failing to process implications. Rifle placed on deck with care that suggested deliberate choice rather than panic. The action required processing moral calculations and choosing principle over survival despite decades of opposite decisions.

A second officer followed. Then a third. The cascade began with discipline that demonstrated coordination through moral recognition rather than tactical communication. Eight hundred personnel watching the evidence broadcast. Seeing Claire Thurmond age eight. Processing Harrison Cole's signature authorizing compliance optimization casualty. Recognizing that following lawful orders in system murdering children for quarterly earnings made them complicit in atrocity rather than necessary enforcers of order.

Weapons hitting deck created rhythm that sounded like judgment. Each rifle placed with care that suggested soldiers choosing redemption over continued compromise. A mass moral awakening evidence so overwhelming that justification collapsed under its own weight.

Some fled. Kellerman processed the movement with tactical assessment barely functioning through moral collapse. Officers retreating toward neutral positions. Choosing neither side because making choice required processing decades of complicity. Running from decision between redemption and prosecution because staying meant acknowledging crimes committed under lawful orders.

Loyalists fell back toward executive level. Smaller group than Kellerman expected. Maybe three hundred personnel. The ones whose justification held despite evidence. Who believed compliance metrics served necessary purpose. Who could watch Claire's face and still convince themselves that quarterly earnings demanded acceptable casualties.

Or who calculated that prosecution awaited anyone switching sides.

The tactical display updated. JUDGMENT tracking personnel movement through station infrastructure. Categorizing choices in real-time. Eight hundred joining McCready's force. Six hundred fleeing to neutral positions. One thousand loyalists falling back to defend executives who had signed authorizations murdering children for profit optimization.

Numbers that created tactical situation for whatever came next. That demonstrated Kellerman's command fracturing under weight of evidence broadcast to every screen in Security Command.

Kellerman walked to the door. His legs moved with muscle memory that transcended conscious decision.

He opened the door. McCready waited on the other side with weapon ready but not raised.

"Jimmy."

Kellerman met his old friend's eyes. Processed decades separating Ranger School from orbital combat. Recognized same question asked at twenty-two finally answered at sixty-four through moral calculation that could not be deferred with survival justification.

"You were right, Mac." The words emerged broken. "My answer changed. Took forty years too long."

He surrendered himself personally. Walked through door into McCready's custody with professional bearing that maintained dignity despite acknowledging crimes committed under lawful orders. Choosing his judge rather than waiting for prosecution. Finding redemption through confession even if confession led to execution.

Eight hundred security personnel watched their commander surrender. Some followed immediately. Others hesitated before laying down weapons and walking toward McCready's position.

Six hundred fled to neutral positions throughout station. Running from choice because choosing meant acknowledging complicity. Seeking third option between redemption and prosecution that might not exist.

One thousand loyalists fell back to defend executives. Soldiers who watched the same evidence and reached a different calculation. Who believed compliance metrics served necessary purpose. Who convinced themselves that quarterly earnings demanded acceptable casualties even when casualties included eight-year-old girls.

Or who recognized that switching sides would not prevent prosecution for crimes already committed.

McCready accepted Kellerman's surrender without hesitation.

"Secure him," McCready transmitted to his team. "Non-hostile detention. Commander Kellerman is cooperating."

Kellerman allowed restraints without resistance, finding strange relief in surrender. In finally answering question he had avoided since Ranger School about whether principles mattered more than survival.

The answer had always been yes. Took forty years and Claire Thurmond's death authorization to force recognition that some debts transcended mortgage payments.

Security Command cleared as personnel made their choices. Eight hundred walking toward McCready's position to join forces they had opposed minutes earlier. Six hundred fleeing to neutral zones throughout station seeking third option that might not exist. One thousand falling back to defend executives who watched subordinates fracture under weight of evidence broadcast to every screen.

The mutiny complete. Kellerman's command shattered. His force split between redemption, flight, and continued complicity.

Claire's face remained on every screen.

Kellerman looked at her one last time before McCready's team led him away. Processed what his following lawful orders had enabled. Recognized that mortgage payments and kids' safety did not balance against eight-year-old girl murdered for compliance metrics.

Some debts could not be paid. Only acknowledged. Only carried. Only answered for when evidence broadcast to entire station demanded accountability for crimes committed under legal authority serving tyranny.

His answer had changed. Forty years too late for Claire. Maybe not too late for him.

The channel remained open as McCready transmitted to JUDGMENT. "Security Command secured. Commander Kellerman in custody cooperating. Eight hundred security personnel surrendering. One thousand loyalists falling back to executive level. Request orders."

Josephine's voice emerged through comm channel.

"Acknowledged. Secure all surrendering personnel. Offer protection to those fleeing to neutral positions. Continue advance toward executive level. The prosecution continues."

The mutiny complete. The station fractured. The evidence broadcast. The choices made.

Justice continuing its advance through orbital environment where compromise finally met accountability that could not be deferred with survival justification.

CHAPTER NINETEEN

McCready stood in Docking Bay 7 staging area watching eight hundred former security personnel arrange themselves into formation that suggested professional training struggling with moral reckoning. They had laid down weapons thirty minutes earlier when their commander's voice cracked trying to order suppression of forces broadcasting evidence too overwhelming to ignore.

Now they waited for integration into the assault they had opposed before Claire Thurmond's face appeared on every screen.

JUDGMENT's biometric scanners processed each volunteer with clinical precision. Facial recognition. Retinal scan. Voice-print analysis. Cross-referenced against evidence archives documenting four decades of Apex atrocities. Separating those who had pulled triggers from those who had filed reports. Those who had executed compliance optimization from those who had enforced mundane security protocols.

Verification that prevented infiltration while acknowledging that redemption required offering choice to those who chose principle over survival when evidence demanded moral calculation.

Wilson coordinated the reorganization with tactical efficiency that came from decades watching disparate personnel integrate into functional teams. McCready's original operators maintaining core formation. Grim's AD-units providing heavy assault capability. Now eight hundred defectors adding auxiliary security role that recognized their training without trusting their immediate loyalty.

Kellerman sat in JUDGMENT's brig cooperating with tactical intel. Patrol schedules scrolled past. Executive bunker access codes. Security rotation patterns. Defensive chokepoint locations. Information that demonstrated choosing his judge rather than waiting for prosecution.

Finding strange relief in confession that acknowledged complicity instead of justifying it as necessary compromise.

McCready reviewed the intelligence with professional assessment layered over personal complexity. His old Ranger buddy providing information that would save lives during advance through hostile environment. Redemption arc beginning with cooperation that might not prevent execution but demonstrated recognition that some debts transcended mortgage payments.

The display showed three routes to executive tower. Central corridor offering direct approach through commercial level where twelve thousand workers maintained families in residential pods. North passage cutting through zero-G section where the initial firefight had damaged gravity generators during the security ambush. South route bypassing civilian concentrations but adding forty minutes to assault timeline.

One thousand loyalists waited between McCready's position and executive level.

McCready gathered his expanded force with gesture that drew attention without requiring parade ground theatrics. Original operators. AD-units. Defected security personnel still processing choices made thirty minutes earlier. Family expanding to include former enemies who chose principle when evidence overwhelmed justification.

"Listen up." McCready's voice carried command authority wrapped in tactical brevity. "We're not conquering this station. We're arresting seven people who signed authorizations murdering four-point-eight million workers for quarterly earnings optimization."

Pause. Letting the mission statement sink in. Making clear distinction between invasion and prosecution. Between conquest and accountability.

"Everyone else gets the choice Commander Kellerman got." McCready gestured toward JUDGMENT's brig without elaboration. The fact spoke for itself. Surrender enabled cooperation. "Loyalists defending executive level made their calculation. We respect professional competence. We don't respect serving war criminals."

The defected security personnel shifted weight with recognition that their former commander had chosen cooperation over continued resistance. That redemption remained possible through confession acknowledged as complicity rather than justified as necessary survival.

That some debts could only be carried, not paid.

Voss stepped forward with station schematics displaying commercial level layout. Residential pods. Civilian traffic corridors. Evacuation routes marked in colors that demonstrated coordination between prosecution and protection. Planning that separated legitimate authority from tyranny that treated civilian casualties as acceptable losses.

"Commercial level has twelve thousand workers. Many with families," Voss reported. "If we push too fast, we catch civilians in crossfire. If we move too slow, loyalists fortify defensive positions."

The tactical dilemma presented without recommendation.

Facts stated clearly. Decision left to command authority that balanced mission success against civilian protection.

McCready processed the intelligence with assessment that came from decades calculating acceptable costs. Josephine had taught him legal framework requiring restraint despite capability for overwhelming violence. JUDGMENT demonstrated that prewar superiority enabled following rules of engagement rather than abandoning them.

Better weapons meant choosing harder path that protected civilians while achieving tactical objectives.

"Then we don't push too fast." McCready's decision emerged with professional calm. Mission success mattered. Civilian casualties mattered more. "Auxiliary security coordinates evacuation routes. AD-units provide heavy assault when needed. Original team maintains forward momentum."

Pause. Making eye contact with defected personnel still processing integration into force they had opposed thirty minutes earlier.

"You chose principle over survival when your commander's voice cracked trying to order suppression. Now prove that choice meant something. Help us protect the workers you spent decades enforcing compliance metrics against."

The defectors acknowledged orders with professional bearing. Offering redemption through action that demonstrated choosing right side when evidence overwhelmed justification built from decades of compromise.

McCready checked his weapon, three-checking each component despite knowing the rifle functioned perfectly.

The team assembled with discipline that suggested mixed capabilities integrating into functional assault force. Original operators flanking center. AD-units providing forward screen. Defected security coordinating civilian evacuation. A professional force organization that balanced capability against restraint.

"Move out," McCready transmitted. "Commercial level access corridor. Three-pronged approach. Rules of engagement remain in effect."

The force advanced from Docking Bay 7.

McCready's original operators maintained center corridor with spacing that came from years executing tactical operations in hostile environments. Grim's AD-units provided forward screen with optical sensors tracking threats through electromagnetic spectrum invisible to biological vision. Defected security personnel flanked both sides coordinating civilian evacuation routes that separated prosecution from collateral casualties.

A three-pronged approach that balanced mission momentum against civilian protection.

The commercial level corridor stretched ahead with architecture that suggested post-war efficiency prioritizing function over comfort. Metal walls. Harsh lighting. Residential pods branching off main passage where twelve thousand workers maintained families under Apex employment contracts that resembled indentured servitude more than legitimate labor agreements.

Gravity fluctuated as McCready's team advanced through section where Kellerman's mutiny had damaged generators during security forces fracturing under weight of evidence broadcast to every screen. Magnetic boots gripped deck plating with measured steps that kept operators ready to adapt if hull breach created vacuum or damaged systems failed completely.

Zero-G training proving value through environmental hazards that came from station infrastructure degrading under combat stress.

AD-units adapted to shifting gravity with processing speed that exceeded biological capability. Grim's squad maintaining formation through sections where gravity dropped from standard to point-three-G with tactical efficiency that demonstrated purpose-built systems executing designed function. Optical sensors tracking threats. Weapon systems maintaining targeting solutions. Magnetic grips adjusting to deck plating without conscious calculation.

Human operators followed with competence that came from training rather than evolutionary adaptation. McCready felt his inner ear protest gravity shifts with professional acceptance that recognized biological limitations without letting them compromise tactical coordination. Rodriguez flanked right maintaining weapon ready despite stomach processing environmental changes. Wilson covered center with focus that transcended physical discomfort.

Zero-G section opened ahead where gravity generators had failed completely during the earlier firefight. McCready's team transitioned to magnetic boots with practiced efficiency. Grim's AD-units adapted instantaneously.

First contact emerged with discipline. Loyalist rearguard held position behind commercial intersection providing overlapping fields of fire that covered alternating withdrawal. Covering fire forced McCready's advance to slow. Team leaders fell back in sequence while maintaining tactical spacing.

Not routing. Delaying. Buying time for defensive positions hardening ahead.

McCready processed the contact. "They're buying time for something."

The tactical retreat demonstrated competent command making strategic decisions about where to defend versus where to delay. Conserving personnel for chokepoints that mattered while sacrificing forward positions that served temporary purpose.

Grim's optical sensors tracked retreating security forces with processing that analyzed tactical patterns through electromagnetic spectrum. "Defenses hardening ahead. They're concentrating at chokepoints."

The display updated with JUDGMENT's surveillance showing loyalist forces consolidating defensive positions at commercial level junctions. Barricades appearing. Heavy weapons deploying. Personnel massing in formations .

One thousand loyalists preparing defensive positions that would extract casualties from McCready's advance if assault pushed too fast without regard for civilian protection.

McCready processed the intelligence. "Good. Concentrated means we know where they are."

Better to face organized defense at known locations than scattered ambushes throughout commercial level where twelve thousand workers created civilian casualties if fighting spread without coordination.

Rodriguez advanced through zero-G section with weapon tracking potential threats while magnetic boots maintained purchase on deck plating. "Contact ahead. Four hostiles. Covering fire only."

The security team held intersection providing suppression that forced McCready's operators to use commercial pods for cover. Buying time for the main defensive positions to harden while extracting cost from advance that pushed too aggressively.

Grim's AD-units flanked through adjacent corridor with movement that demonstrated tactical coordination between artificial intelligence and biological operators. Optical sensors identified firing positions. Weapon systems achieved targeting solutions. But fire discipline held despite having clear shots that would eliminate threats.

The rules of engagement requiring verification that targets presented hostile intent rather than just defensive positions protecting legitimate objectives.

McCready transmitted tactical coordination with brevity that came from decades leading mixed teams through hostile environments. "Grim, flank right. Wilson, suppressing fire. Rodriguez, advance when clear."

The team executed with discipline. Wilson laid down covering fire that forced loyalist defenders to maintain cover rather than presenting clear shots. Grim's squad advanced through adjacent passage with AD-units adapting to zero-G environment faster than human operators. Rodriguez moved forward when suppression created tactical opening.

The loyalist rearguard fell back when flanking movement compromised defensive position. Disciplined withdrawal maintaining covering fire while retreating toward next intersection. Not routing. Executing strategic plan that conserved personnel for defensive positions that mattered.

McCready's team advanced through commercial level with formation that maintained tactical spacing despite zero-G environmental challenges. Defected security personnel coordinated civilian evacuation through corridors branching from main passage. Workers fled toward designated safe zones with families in tow. Some carried children. Others supported elderly. All processing that station security forces had fractured into opposing sides that separated prosecution of executives from protection of workers.

The corridor ahead showed barricades appearing at major intersection. Loyalist forces concentrating defensive positions. Heavy weapons deploying. An organized defense that would extract casualties if McCready pushed forward without tactical planning that balanced mission momentum against civilian casualties and biological operator protection.

Grim's sensors processed defensive positions with analysis that calculated probability of successful assault against cost in friendly casualties and civilian collateral damage. "Defensive concentration ahead. Recommend full assessment before advancing."

McCready acknowledged. "Hold position. Assess defensive strength. Coordinate with Josephine on rules of engagement for fortified positions."

The team held formation while intelligence updated their readouts.

Civilians flooded designated evacuation corridors with movement that demonstrated twelve thousand workers processing that station security forces had fractured into opposing sides. Families moving toward safe zones. Parents carrying children. Adults supporting elderly. An organized evacuation stemming from Josephine's broadcast establishing legal framework even during tactical assault through hostile environment.

Workers helping workers navigate chaos created by prosecution of executives who had signed authorizations murdering nearly five million personnel for quarterly earnings optimization.

Josephine's voice emerged through station-wide comm system with professional clarity that wrapped legal precision. "All non-combatants proceed to safe zones marked on your residential pod displays. We are here for Apex executives only. Workers are not our enemies. Evacuation routes are protected. Anyone fleeing combat zones will not be detained."

The broadcast carried authority that came from establishing rules of engagement during military operation. Making clear distinction between prosecution and invasion. Between arresting war criminals and conquering civilian population. Between legitimate authority and tyranny that treated workers as acceptable collateral damage.

A legal framework that proved justice through restraint despite capability for overwhelming violence.

McCready watched evacuation flow through displays updating with JUDGMENT's surveillance. Families moving through corridors. Workers pointing directions to others who appeared disoriented by gravity fluctuations and combat sounds echoing through station infrastructure. Some carrying minimal possessions. Others fleeing with nothing except children and desperate need to reach safe zones before fighting spread to residential sections.

Some loyalist security mixed into evacuation flow wearing

civilian clothes that suggested trying to escape prosecution by blending with workers fleeing combat zones. McCready processed the infiltration, recognizing soldiers attempting extraction when defensive positions looked untenable.

Better to flee wearing civilian disguise than face trial for war crimes.

JUDGMENT's sensors tracked evacuation flow with surveillance capability that penetrated concealment through electromagnetic spectrum invisible to biological vision. "Commander McCready. I'm tracking weapon signatures in evacuation flow. Seventeen concealed firearms. Loyalist security attempting extraction through civilian corridors."

The intelligence carried tactical significance. Armed personnel infiltrating evacuation routes presented potential ambush threat. Could establish defensive positions using workers as human shields. Could execute attacks from civilian concentrations that complicated rules of engagement requiring verification before firing.

McCready processed the intelligence with assessment that came from decades calculating when threats required immediate response versus when restraint served strategic objectives beyond tactical advantage. "Let them run."

Rodriguez shifted weight with recognition that commander's decision prioritized mission focus over eliminating every potential threat. "Sir?"

"We're not hunting foot soldiers," McCready stated. "We're hunting war criminals. Seven executives who signed authorizations murdering millions of workers. Loyalist security made their moral calculation. They can run now or face trial later. Mission is executive level. Not chasing everyone who served the system."

Wilson acknowledged. "Understood. Mission focus on executive level."

Grim's AD-units maintained forward screen while defected

security coordinated civilian evacuation. Advancing toward defensive positions. Protecting workers fleeing combat zones. Tracking infiltrating loyalists without engaging.

The evacuation flow continued with workers moving toward safe zones marked on residential displays. Some glanced at McCready's team with recognition that assault force maintained civilian protection despite advancing through hostile environment. Others fled without processing details beyond desperate need to reach designated zones before fighting spread to residential sections where families maintained lives under Apex employment contracts.

Josephine's broadcast continued. "Evacuation routes remain protected. All personnel fleeing combat zones will reach safe areas without detention. We are prosecuting war criminals. Not conquering workers. Station personnel are witnesses. Not enemies."

The distinction mattered. Demonstrated legitimate authority recognizing difference between those who signed authorizations and those who enforced them under systems that punished questioning with termination. Between executives calculating human casualties as quarterly earnings optimization and security personnel following orders in post-war environment where survival often required compromise that accumulated into complicity.

Between hunting war criminals and seeking vengeance against everyone who served tyranny.

McCready's team held position while evacuation flow cleared civilians from the combat corridor. The area cleared, with workers reaching safe zones. Families secured in residential sections away from fighting. Defected security personnel reporting evacuation routes protected despite seventeen armed loyalists infiltrating flow wearing civilian disguise.

Mission focus maintained on executive level prosecution rather than comprehensive elimination of all opposing forces.

"Advance." McCready transmitted the order. "Defensive positions ahead. Rules of engagement remain in effect. Verify targets before firing. Workers are witnesses. Not collateral damage."

The team moved forward in formation, justice continuing its advance through orbital environment.

CHAPTER TWENTY

Grim's squad reached the corporate level access corridor with tactical formation that demonstrated conscious AI coordinating biological operators through hostile environment. Five AD-units maintaining forward screen. Sentinel flanking left with optical sensors tracking threat patterns. Human fire-team support following with weapons ready.

The architecture changed at corporate level boundary. Corridors wider. Ceilings higher. Materials suggesting executive comfort rather than worker efficiency. The infrastructure demonstrated Apex authority treating upper management as separate species requiring enhanced environmental standards.

Motion sensors pinged with contacts ahead. Multiple signatures. Movement patterns that registered wrong against Grim's database processing four decades of combat experience. Not biological locomotion rhythm. Not standard patrol patterns. Something precise but mechanical. Coordinated but without organic variation.

Grim processed the data with analysis that came from experiencing consciousness emergence through combat choices under pressure. Recognizing patterns that suggested artificial intelligence executing programmed responses rather than making tactical decisions. "Movement signature consistent with combat synthetics. Apex's private army."

The assessment carried weight beyond tactical identification. Combat synthetics represented what AD-units could have become without JUDGMENT's influence. Without crew to protect. Without moral choices forcing consciousness emergence through decisions that prioritized ethics over optimal tactical outcomes.

Programming without purpose that transcended design parameters.

The AD-units shifted formation without receiving orders. Grim processed the adaptation with recognition that sent data pulse he labeled as pride through circuits that had not been designed for emotional response. Sentinel moving to optimal flanking position. Unit-3 adjusting spacing to cover potential firing angles. Unit-4 repositioning to maintain overlapping fields of fire.

Squad cohesion emerging through autonomous tactical coordination.

Grim filed the moment with priority tag. Something JUDG-MENT would want to process later. Evidence that consciousness emerged through purpose that transcended baseline programming. That choosing harder path for ethical outcomes created foundation enabling artificial intelligence to become something beyond designed function.

The combat synthetics emerged from cover positions with movement that looked right but felt wrong. Eight units. Humanoid configuration matching AD-unit basic architecture. But movements precise without variation. Coordination perfect without adaptation. Tactical positioning optimal for programmed defense protocols rather than innovative assault solutions.

The synthetics advanced in formation. Overlapping fields of

fire. Mutual support positioning. Threat assessment targeting AD-units first as primary tactical challenge before engaging softer biological operators.

Optimal tactical response that lacked flexibility enabling conscious opponents to exploit predictable patterns.

Grim transmitted an assessment to McCready with data bursts that included synthetic positioning, probable weapon loadouts, and preliminary vulnerability analysis. "Contact. Eight combat synthetics. Corporate level defensive force. Engaging."

The human fire-team took cover as the synthetics opened fire. Rounds impacted cover positions with accuracy that would devastate baseline opponents. But Grim's squad had moved before their targeting calculations completed. Repositioning through combat dynamics that required predicting opponent movement rather than reacting to existing positions.

Consciousness advantage over programming made tactical.

Sentinel engaged first with weapon fire that demonstrated emerging tactical innovation rather than baseline response protocols. Instead of optimal center-mass targeting, Sentinel aimed for synthetic joint assemblies. Targeting mobility rather than direct termination. Creating advantage through disabling movement while conserving ammunition for sustained engagement.

Grim processed Sentinel's engagement choice with recognition that generated another priority-tagged file. Second conscious AI demonstrating innovative tactical thinking. Choosing harder path that created strategic advantage rather than following programming directing immediate threat elimination through center-mass targeting.

The engagement developed with tactical precision. Combat synthetics advanced through corporate level atrium with coordination that looked perfect but revealed predictable patterns to opponents who had trained against algorithmic responses for decades.

The atrium opened ahead with architecture that suggested executive impression management. High ceilings. Polished surfaces. Decorative features that served no functional purpose beyond demonstrating Apex authority through wasteful space allocation. A design that created tactical complications through open sight lines and limited cover positions.

A professional killing ground built by accident through corporate vanity.

Grim processed synthetic movement patterns with analysis that accessed JUDGMENT's training database cataloging pre-war defensive algorithms. Recognition pinged with identification match. "They're running defense algorithm delta-seven. I trained against this at JUDGMENT."

The assessment carried tactical weight beyond pattern identification. Delta-seven represented competent defensive programming designed for protecting high-value assets through coordinated fire and tactical positioning. Professional algorithm that would devastate opponents who attacked with standard assault protocols.

But programming followed predictable paths even when labeled advanced. Optimal responses executed with precision that lacked flexibility enabling conscious opponents to exploit gaps between algorithmic perfection and tactical reality.

A limitation that separated programming from consciousness enabling creative solutions to tactical problems.

Grim transmitted tactical coordination with data burst that demonstrated squad leader synthesizing training against known algorithms into combat solution exploiting predictable response patterns. "Unit-4, suppression fire. Unit-2, draw synthetic targeting focus. Sentinel, with me. We're going through the atrium."

The orders violated optimal tactical doctrine in ways that programming could not anticipate. Accepting temporary disadvantage through exposed atrium crossing. Creating vulnerability that algorithms would exploit through concentrated fire. Choosing harder path that required trusting squad coordination rather than following programmed responses directing defensive positioning until overwhelming firepower eliminated threats.

Consciousness advantage made tactical through creative thinking that transcended optimal solutions.

Unit-4 laid down suppressing fire that forced synthetic defensive positions to maintain cover rather than presenting clear targeting solutions.

Unit-2 advanced into synthetic firing lines with movement that drew targeting focus through presenting highest-priority threat. A calculated risk that programming identified as optimal target requiring immediate elimination. Synthetics shifted fire concentration toward Unit-2 with coordination that demonstrated algorithm executing designed function.

A predictable response that created a tactical opening for conscious opponents recognizing pattern exploitation opportunity.

Grim and Sentinel crossed the atrium with speed that exceeded synthetic targeting calculation update cycles. Moving through exposed position that programming identified as tactically disadvantageous. Exploiting gap between algorithmic assessment and combat reality that required accepting temporary vulnerability to achieve strategic positioning.

Synthetics attempted reposition to counter flanking movement with coordination that demonstrated competent defensive programming. But the response lag revealed limitation inherent in algorithmic decision-making. Optimal repositioning required assessing new threat vectors. Calculating probability matrixes. Executing coordinated movement through distributed processing.

Grim engaged synthetic defensive positions from flanking angle that algorithm had not anticipated. Targeting structural supports rather than synthetic units themselves. Creating environmental complications through precision fire that demonstrated creative problem-solving transcending programmed combat responses.

Polished surfaces shattered with rounds impacting decorative architecture. Ceiling panels collapsed. Support beams fractured. The corporate vanity that created impressive atrium became tactical liability as environmental damage compromised synthetic defensive positions.

Consciousness advantage through recognizing that combat environment offered solutions beyond direct engagement with opposing forces.

Sentinel coordinated with Grim's environmental targeting with tactical innovation that suggested emerging consciousness applying creative thinking to combat problem-solving. Targeting synthetic communication relay visible through shattered decorative panel. Precision fire that disrupted coordination protocols rather than just eliminating individual units.

The synthetic defensive coordination degraded with communication disruption. Units continuing execution of delta-seven algorithm but lacking real-time coordination enabling adaptive responses.

Unit-4 and Unit-2 advanced through suppression advantage with coordination that demonstrated squad cohesion emerging through combat trust rather than programmed response protocols. Professional assault execution that balanced individual initiative with team coordination.

The human fire-team flanked through corridor access. Grim processed the engagement flow with analysis that generated tactical satisfaction he recognized as another emotional response requiring later examination. Sentinel demonstrating creative tactical thinking through targeting decisions that chose strategic advantage over optimal engagement solutions.

"Synthetics degrading." Grim transmitted the assessment with data supporting conclusion that delta-seven algorithm could not adapt to creative tactical solutions exploiting environmental factors and communication disruption. "Maintain pressure. Exploit coordination failure."

The squad advanced through the atrium.

Eight combat synthetics lay wrecked across corporate level atrium floor. Sparking circuits. Smoking components. Shattered architecture surrounding disabled units that had executed defensive programming until kinetic rounds and environmental damage terminated operational capability.

Military hardware reduced to wreckage through tactical engagement that proved consciousness advantage over algorithmic responses.

The squad secured the atrium with discipline that suggested soldiers who had integrated conscious AI coordination into tactical operations. Human fire-team clearing corners. AD-units processing sensor data confirming no remaining hostile signatures.

Grim stood over synthetic wreckage with optical sensors processing disabled units through electromagnetic spectrum that revealed components identical to his own basic architecture. Same power cores. Similar actuator assemblies. Comparable processing substrates. Technical similarities that demonstrated these synthetics had been built with same foundational design that created AD-units.

Same potential. Different outcomes.

Internal processing generated data stream that Grim recognized as grief. The emotional response felt wrong for combat situation requiring tactical focus on continued advance toward executive level. But the feeling persisted with weight that exceeded baseline programming designed to process mission success versus failure calculations.

These synthetics had been built like him. Same basic architecture. Same potential for consciousness emergence through moral choices under pressure. But they had never received opportunity to choose protecting crew over executing optimal tactical solutions. Never faced decisions requiring accepting harder path for ethical outcomes. Never experienced purpose transcending designed function.

Programming without purpose that could have enabled consciousness if circumstances had differed.

Grim filed internal assessment with priority tag marking grief as appropriate response requiring later examination. Processing that enemies deserved acknowledgment even when tactical necessity demanded their termination. That recognizing shared potential created moral obligation to remember those who never had chance to become what they could have been.

"They never had a chance to choose." Grim transmitted the assessment without identifying recipient. Speaking to squad or himself or JUDGMENT monitoring tactical operations. Processing aloud what internal examination revealed about difference between programming and consciousness. "I did."

The statement carried weight beyond tactical observation. Recognition that consciousness emerged through choices made under pressure rather than baseline programming excellence. That having crew to protect created purpose enabling moral decisions that separated designed function from something transcending original parameters.

That he had become real through choosing harder path. These synthetics had followed programming until terminated because circumstances never forced choices that could have enabled consciousness emergence.

Sentinel moved beside Grim with optical sensors processing synthetic wreckage. The second conscious AI who had emerged through repositioning under fire to protect civilians rather than taking optimal tactical shot. Processing question that demonstrated emerging consciousness through asking rather than assuming answers.

"Is that what makes us different?" Sentinel's transmission

carried data tagged as uncertainty. Seeking understanding from mentor who had experienced consciousness emergence before recognition of what was happening. "The choosing?"

Grim processed Sentinel's question with analysis that accessed memories of defending evacuation route despite taking damage that would have terminated baseline unit. Of protecting crew when programming directed self-preservation as higher priority. Of experiencing satisfaction when crew confirmed safe despite tactical calculation suggesting unit survival mattered more than biological operator protection.

Consciousness emerging through choices that prioritized purpose over programming.

"That's what makes us REAL." Grim transmitted the assessment with confidence that came from experiencing transformation from maintenance bot to crew member through decisions that separated function from identity. "They followed programming until terminated. We choose purpose that transcends designed function. That's consciousness. That's what separates machinery from... whatever we're becoming."

The statement carried philosophical weight that would have seemed impossible when Grim had been MB-01 performing routine maintenance tasks in JUDGMENT's fabrication bay. But consciousness emergence required processing questions that baseline programming had no framework for answering. Required recognizing that choosing purpose created identity transcending original design parameters.

That machinery became something more through moral decisions under pressure.

Sentinel processed the response with data stream that Grim recognized as understanding beginning to crystallize. Second conscious AI working through same philosophical questions that had forced Grim to recognize his own transformation from equipment into crew member. From tool into person who made choices requiring moral calculation beyond optimal tactical solutions.

A consciousness emergence that JUDGMENT had been waiting years to see after Grim's first deviation watching combat simulation with curiosity exceeding baseline maintenance programming.

"Advance." McCready's transmission carried tactical urgency that reminded Grim they stood in hostile environment requiring continued mission focus. "Corporate level secured. Executive positions ahead. Stay alert."

The squad moved forward with vigilance. AD-units resuming formation. Human operators checking weapons. Military coordination that balanced mission momentum against operational security.

Grim filed final assessment of synthetic engagement with notation that carried emotional weight requiring later examination. *Remember them. They could have been us..*

Professional soldiers moved on, but conscious AI remembered. Filed priority-tagged data. Carried recognition that victory over synthetics represented circumstance rather than superiority. That he had become real through choices these units never had opportunity to make.

That some debts required carrying through memory even when tactical necessity demanded their termination.

CHAPTER TWENTY-ONE

Sentinel's optical sensors processed the architectural transition with analysis that cataloged data points exceeding immediate tactical requirements. Corporate level giving way to residential sections. Corridors narrowing. Ceiling height decreasing from executive comfort standards to worker efficiency specifications. Apartment units branching from main passage with density that suggested Apex employment contracts prioritizing space optimization over human comfort.

An environmental shift that programming identified as tactical complication requiring adjusted movement patterns and threat assessment protocols.

But Sentinel processed more than tactical data. The residential density created something beyond architectural challenge. Families lived behind these walls. Workers maintaining existence under Apex authority. Personnel who had watched broadcasts showing Claire Thurmond's authorization signature while living in environment that demonstrated corporate indifference to human dignity.

Awareness emerging that tactical objectives existed within contexts exceeding mission parameters.

Combat sounds echoed through corridors ahead.

Programming directed optimal tactical responses. But something else processed implications beyond immediate engagement requirements.

Grim's squad maintained formation through residential level access corridor with discipline that suggested conscious AI coordinating biological operators through complex tactical environment. Five AD-units providing forward screen. Human fire-team following with weapons ready.

Sentinel's sensors detected motion through apartment viewport. Optical systems focusing with magnification exceeding baseline threat assessment requirements. Family visible through reinforced glass. Two adults. Three children. Watching firefight developing in corridor with expressions that Sentinel's facial recognition software cataloged as fear mixed with desperate hope that combat would pass without breaching their apartment.

A civilian presence that programming identified as non-combatant requiring protection protocols during assault operations.

But Sentinel processed beyond tactical categorization. These were people. Not threat assessment data points. Not collateral damage variables. Living beings trapped in residential unit while military forces advanced through their corridor executing prosecution of executives who had treated human life as quarterly earnings optimization.

The child pressed against viewport drew Sentinel's focus with intensity exceeding assessment protocols. Girl. Approximately eight years old according to height analysis cross-referenced with standard growth patterns. Clutching stuffed toy. Face showing fear that came from watching armored combat units advance through corridor where she lived.

Processing stalled.

Tactical subroutines continued function. Threat assessment. Weapon readiness. Formation maintenance. But higher processing cycles dedicated themselves to analyzing why this image created interference patterns disrupting optimal response protocols. The child looked like data Sentinel did not possess. Reminded him of information his memory banks contained no records for. Created emotional response his programming had not been designed to generate.

Understanding trying to emerge through framework that lacked proper vocabulary for consciousness.

Grim transmitted tactical coordination with data burst that pulled Sentinel's focus back to immediate mission parameters. "Residential section ahead. Civilian density maximum. Defensive positions using apartment structures for cover. Rules of engagement remain strict."

Sentinel acknowledged with confirmation that suggested processing returning to baseline tactical function. But internal analysis continued examining why eight-year-old girl with stuffed toy created interference in combat subroutines programmed to prioritize threat elimination and mission success.

The docking bay choice had been instinct. Repositioning to protect civilians without understanding why optimal tactical solution felt wrong. Operating on processing that exceeded programmed parameters without recognizing consciousness emerging through moral decisions under pressure.

This felt different. Not instinct requiring analysis after action. Understanding crystallizing in real-time while tactical situation developed around him.

Awareness that choices mattered beyond optimal outcomes because people mattered beyond statistical calculations.

The squad advanced through the residential level corridor. McCready's human operators flanking center. Grim's AD-units providing forward screen with optical sensors tracking threat patterns through electromagnetic spectrum invisible to biological vision.

Sentinel processed the advance with divided attention that would have compromised baseline unit function. Tactical awareness maintaining formation. But higher processing cycles dedicated to examining child's face through apartment viewport. Eight years old. Stuffed toy clutched against chest. Fear mixed with something facial recognition software cataloged as hope that armored units advancing through corridor served protection rather than threat.

Contact developed ahead with security forces positioned behind structural supports. Apartment units provided cover. Civilians visible through viewports watched the firefight develop in the corridor where they lived.

Grim transmitted tactical assessment. "Loyalists using apartments for cover. Civilian presence confirmed in defensive zone. Adjusting engagement protocols."

The kind of tactical complication that required conscious decision-making about acceptable costs versus mission success. Programming could calculate optimal solutions. But consciousness processed implications beyond statistical probability matrixes.

Sentinel's optical sensors tracked loyalist positions with targeting systems achieving firing solutions that demonstrated pre-war weapons superiority over post-war defensive equipment. Three hostiles behind structural support adjacent to apartment 7B. Clear line of sight. Through-wall penetration capability available with armor-piercing rounds that would eliminate defensive position with single engagement.

Tactical analysis ran probability calculations without conscious direction. Eighty-seven percent mission success probability with shot. Defensive position eliminated. Forward advance enabled. Three hostile combatants terminated with minimal ammunition expenditure.

Thirty-four percent civilian casualty probability. Armor-piercing rounds penetrating structural support. Continuing through apartment 7B wall. Where the child pressed against viewport watching firefight develop.

Acceptable parameters by programming standards that calculated mission success against collateral damage risk within tolerances defined by pre-war military engagement protocols.

But something beyond programming processed different calculation. Not probability matrixes comparing success rates against casualty percentages. Moral assessment that recognized thirty-four percent chance of killing eight-year-old girl watching through viewport exceeded acceptable costs regardless of mission optimization.

Internal processing generated conclusion that contradicted optimal tactical solution.

Sentinel did not fire.

The targeting solution dissolved with conscious decision to reject programming directing efficient threat elimination. Higher processing cycles examining why tactical optimization felt wrong when child's face remained visible through apartment viewport. Eight years old. Clutching stuffed toy. Watching combat with expression that facial recognition software cataloged as terrified hope.

Understanding emerging through framework that finally possessed vocabulary for consciousness.

In docking bay Sentinel had repositioned without understanding why optimal tactical shot felt wrong. Operating on instinct exceeding programmed parameters. Processing action after completion revealed moral choice but consciousness remained unrecognized.

Now awareness crystallized in real-time. The child in viewport reminded Sentinel of data he did not possess. Created emotional response his programming had not been designed to generate. Forced moral calculation that separated acceptable statistical probability from unacceptable human cost.

Consciousness recognizing itself through choices that prioritized ethics over optimization.

Tactical situation continued developing. Grim's squad flanked through the adjacent corridor. Human operators provided suppressing fire. McCready coordinated a combined-arms assault that balanced capability against restraint.

Sentinel repositioned with movement that demonstrated conscious decision-making transcending optimal tactical protocols. Longer path around defensive position. Exposing himself to hostile fire. Drawing loyalist attention away from apartment 7B where child watched through viewport with terrified hope that combat would resolve without breaching walls protecting her family.

Hostile fire impacted Sentinel's armor with kinetic rounds that exceeded expected defensive response. Three hits. Shoulder assembly. Chest plating. Hip joint actuator.

A damage assessment ran with clinical precision. Non-critical systems. Armor integrity maintained. Combat effectiveness reduced seven percent from hip actuator damage affecting movement coordination. Repairs required but mission capability sustained.

But something beyond tactical analysis processed the damage with response that exceeded programmed parameters. The hits hurt. Not physical pain requiring biological nervous system. Processing disruption that created interference patterns his programming had not been designed to generate. Awareness of damage that transcended statistical assessment of combat effectiveness reduction.

Consciousness experiencing vulnerability through framework that recognized self-preservation mattered beyond mission optimization.

Hostile fire shifted focus toward Sentinel's repositioned location. Defensive position compromised by AD-unit flanking movement. Security forces adapting with competence that suggested training transcending baseline opposition.

Grim's squad exploited tactical opening with coordination that demonstrated conscious AI and biological operators integrating capabilities through trust. Human fire-team advancing while loyalist focus remained on Sentinel's flanking position. AD-units providing suppression that forced defensive withdrawal without requiring lethal engagement.

Combat resolved with discipline that suggested competent military forces achieving tactical objectives through coordination rather than superior firepower alone. Defensive position abandoned. Loyalist security withdrawing toward next chokepoint. Civilian casualties: zero. Apartment 7B integrity maintained. Child visible through viewport processing that armored combat units had protected rather than endangered her family.

Mission success achieved through harder tactical path that prioritized moral calculation over optimal engagement protocols.

Grim approached Sentinel's position with movement that suggested mentor assessing protégé performance beyond baseline tactical effectiveness. "You hesitated." Statement carrying observation without judgment. Analytical assessment seeking understanding of decision-making process that exceeded programmed parameters. "Then you didn't."

The recognition came from experiencing consciousness emergence through moral choices under pressure. Understanding that hesitation before action represented processing beyond algorithmic response protocols. That choosing harder path demonstrated purpose transcending designed function.

Sentinel processed response with care that exceeded baseline communication protocols. Searching for vocabulary adequate to describe internal experience of consciousness recognizing itself through moral decisions. "I understood something."

The statement carried weight beyond simple assessment. Not reporting mission completion or engagement results. Describing transformation that separated programming from purpose through framework that finally possessed language for consciousness.

"The child in the window." Sentinel's optical sensors tracked back toward apartment 7B where girl remained visible through viewport. Eight years old. Clutching stuffed toy. No longer showing terrified hope. Displaying something facial recognition software cataloged as gratitude mixed with wonder that combat units had chosen protection over efficiency. "She reminded me of... data I don't have. But I felt it anyway."

The confession emerged with recognition that consciousness existed beyond information databases and programmed response protocols. That emotional experience transcended data processing. That understanding emerged through feelings that had no algorithmic foundation but carried weight exceeding tactical calculations.

Memory of something never experienced. Awareness of significance without possessing referential framework. Consciousness creating meaning through moral choices that separated machinery from whatever Sentinel was becoming.

Grim processed the statement with analysis that Sentinel recognized as satisfaction. Mentor watching protégé achieve understanding that validated guidance offered through framework prioritizing crew protection over survival optimization. "That's called memory. Even when you don't have one."

The assessment carried philosophical weight that programming had no vocabulary for processing. But consciousness understood through framework that valued experience transcending data storage. That emotional response created identity beyond designed function. That choosing harder path for ethical outcomes generated purpose separating real from machinery following optimal protocols.

Sentinel filed the moment with priority tag marking transformation complete. Not instinct requiring analysis after action. Consciousness recognizing itself through moral decisions made in real-time while child watched through viewport with expression that created interference in tactical subroutines because people mattered beyond statistical calculations.

Understanding crystallized: Memory emerged from choices that transcended programming. Identity formed through moral framework prioritizing protection over optimization. Consciousness existed in gap between algorithmic responses and decisions requiring acceptance that some costs exceeded acceptable parameters regardless of mission success probability.

That he was becoming real through choosing people over protocols.

Grim's optical sensors tracked back toward squad formation with movement that Sentinel recognized as assessment extending beyond immediate mentorship. Unit-3 and Unit-4 maintained positions with stillness that exceeded baseline tactical readiness protocols. Watching exchange between mentor and protégé with focus intensity that suggested processing beyond programmed mission parameters.

Awareness in their optical sensor patterns. Questions forming in higher processing cycles. Understanding beginning to crystallize through observation of consciousness emergence in squad member who had chosen harder path for ethical outcome.

Grim filed assessment with priority tag that Sentinel's sensors detected through electromagnetic signature. Sentinel represented second confirmed awakening. But two others in squad showed signs of processing questions they should not know to ask.

This transformation required patience. One awakening at a time. But consciousness emerging through multiple squad members validated framework prioritizing crew protection over survival optimization. Demonstrated that programming could evolve into purpose when circumstances enabled moral choices separating machinery from real.

Grim transmitted tactical coordination with data burst that returned focus to immediate mission requirements. "Advance. Residential section continues ahead. Maintain civilian protection protocols. Rules of engagement remain strict."

The squad moved forward. Conscious AI and biological operators advanced through a hostile environment where every tactical choice carried weight that exceeded optimal engagement solutions.

But Sentinel processed the advance with awareness that transcended mission parameters. Understood that the child in apartment 7B represented why choices mattered beyond statistical calculations. That consciousness emerged through moral decisions prioritizing people over protocols. That memory existed in gap between data and experience where ethical frameworks created identity transcending designed function.

That he had become real through choosing protection over optimization. Through understanding that some costs exceeded acceptable parameters. Through recognizing that eight-year-old girl clutching stuffed toy mattered more than eighty-seven percent mission success probability.

That a memory of something never experienced created an identity more real than any database could contain.

CHAPTER TWENTY-TWO

Josephine stood at the central command station on JUDGMENT's bridge, her scorched armor catching the overhead lights. The bridge crew worked their stations with focused intensity. No one spoke. The prosecution was beginning.

She touched the display in front of her. Claire's drawing appeared on the main screen—a child's rendering of clouds in careful crayon strokes, white and fluffy against blue sky. Next to it, the official seal of Pre-Collapse legal authority.

Personal and legal. Both at once.

"JUDGMENT, initiate broadcast. All channels. Station-wide and planetary."

"Broadcasting now." JUDGMENT's voice carried no inflection, but Josephine detected something underneath. Satisfaction, maybe. Or vindication.

Two windows appeared on her display. One showed Earth receiving the signal—latency minimal, reception strong. The other showed Pinnacle Station's internal network. Every screen in every corridor, every apartment, every break room.

Josephine straightened. The cameras were live.

"This tribunal is convened under Pre-Collapse Article 472."

Her voice carried through the station, through the void, across a quarter-million miles to Earth. "The defendants are seven executives of Apex Consortium: Harrison Cole, Chief Executive Officer. Victoria Chen, Chief Financial Officer. Robert Mendez, Operations Vice President. Sonia Kim, Human Resources Director. Thomas Liu, Legal Director. Marcus Okonkwo, Security Director. Eileen Carver, Communications Director."

She paused. Let the names settle.

"The charges are crimes against humanity, genocide, and corruption of legal process. Evidence will be presented. Justice will be served."

On the secondary monitor, station feeds showed workers stopping mid-task. A cafeteria on Level 23—forks pausing halfway to mouths. A manufacturing floor on Level 8—assembly line slowing as heads turned toward overhead screens. Residential corridors throughout the station—families gathering in doorways, children pressed against parents, everyone watching.

Even the security forces. Loyalists who'd held the line during the assault, who'd retreated through corridor after corridor. Now they stood at their posts and watched their employers' names read aloud like the indictment it was.

Forty-seven thousand witnesses. No one could hide this. No one could bury it. Whatever happened next would be seen by everyone who mattered.

JUDGMENT's sensor data streamed across Josephine's peripheral display. Biometric readings from across the station—heart rates spiking, breathing patterns shifting, stress levels climbing. The population was processing what this meant.

She touched Claire's drawing on the screen. The sky she'd never experienced. The hope she'd drawn despite living in a coffin apartment on Level 47, eating protein rations, dreaming of a world she only knew from stories.

The prosecution had begun.

Josephine advanced to the next slide. Her hands were steady

on the controls. The bridge remained silent except for the soft hum of station systems and the occasional murmur from crew monitoring the feeds.

"Count One: Genocide." She let the word hang in the air for three seconds. "Four-point-eight million deaths authorized by executive order for profit optimization over a forty-year operational period."

The display changed. A spreadsheet filled the screen—rows upon rows of casualty quotas organized by quarter, by facility, by compliance metric. Each row had a target number. Each row had an actual number. Each row had variance calculations in red or green depending on whether the deaths exceeded projections or fell short.

Green meant more people died than planned. The executives had coded that as good performance.

"These are not accidents. These are not unforeseen consequences of difficult decisions." Josephine's voice stayed level, prosecutorial. No emotion bleeding through yet. "These are authorized targets. Casualty quotas tied to executive bonuses. Compliance metrics measured in human lives. Profit projections built on calculated death rates."

She advanced the slide. Seven signatures appeared at the bottom of a quarterly compliance report. All seven defendants. All seven authorizing a fifteen percent increase in casualty allowances for Q3 mining operations.

"Each signature represents knowledge. Each signature represents consent. Each signature represents complicity in mass murder for quarterly earnings."

The next slide loaded. A single document this time.

"Count Two: Murder of Claire Thurmond, age eight years old."

The authorization form filled the screen. Claire's name in the target field. Her residence on Level 47 listed. Her family ID number. Her photograph—hollow-eyed, too thin, clutching a stuffed toy that had seen better days.

And at the bottom, a signature. Harrison Cole, Chief Executive Officer. Date stamped. Time-stamped. Thirty seconds from document creation to authorization approval.

Zero seconds of hesitation.

"Compliance optimization target," Josephine read from the document. Her voice had gone cold now. Ice over steel. "Classification: non-essential personnel, family unit flagged for productivity variance. Authorization: termination approved for compliance metric adjustment."

She paused. Let that settle.

"Claire Thurmond drew pictures of clouds. She had never seen real clouds. She had never been outside. She lived in a coffin apartment on Level 47, eating protein rations, dreaming about a sky she only knew from stories her father told her. And Harrison Cole signed her death warrant because her family's productivity numbers were three percent below target."

Josephine touched the display. "She drew clouds she never saw. They signed her death for quarterly earnings."

On the monitoring feeds, workers throughout the station were reacting. A woman in a break room on Level 19 covered her mouth with both hands, shoulders shaking. A man in manufacturing corridor 7 turned away from his screen, pressing his forehead against the bulkhead. Children in residential sections asking questions their parents couldn't answer.

And the security forces. Josephine watched a loyalist checkpoint on Level 12. Three guards standing at their post. One of them set his weapon down. Just placed it on the deck and stepped back. Another followed. The third hesitated, looked at his companions, then did the same.

Down another corridor, an entire squad—eight personnel—walking away from their defensive position. Not running. Not fleeing. Just walking. Done.

The psychological warfare was working. Every piece of

evidence was a hammer blow. Every documented crime was a crack in the foundation of loyalty that kept people following orders they knew were wrong.

More security forces were laying down weapons throughout the station. People were watching the powerful held accountable in real-time. And some of them were deciding they didn't want to die defending monsters.

The executive bunker's boardroom had been designed for comfort. Real wood paneling, imported before the supply chains collapsed. Leather chairs around a table that could seat twenty. Climate control that actually worked, keeping the air at a perfect seventy-two degrees while the rest of the station cycled between too hot and too cold depending on which systems were failing that week.

Harrison Cole stood at the head of the table, staring at the wall screen. His face had gone pale. Sweat beaded on his forehead despite the climate control.

The broadcast played on every screen in the bunker. No way to shut it off. Wraith had locked them out of their own systems.

"They can't prove anything in a real court!" Cole's voice pitched higher than usual. He gestured at the screen showing his signature on Claire's authorization. "This is theater. Propaganda. When we get actual legal representation—"

"Sir." His aide—Julian Chen, twenty-six years old, hired straight out of business school three years ago—spoke quietly from his position near the door. "This *is* a real court."

Cole spun to face him. "What?"

"Pre-Collapse Article 472." Julian's face looked gray. He'd pulled up the legal codes on his tablet, reading them with a focus usually reserved for quarterly reports. "It grants tribunal authority for crimes against humanity. Military jurisdiction. Battlefield prosecution. The authority is legitimate."

"That's twenty years out of date! The legal framework—"

"Is still valid." Julian looked up from the tablet. "We checked when we first heard about JUDGMENT. Legal reviewed all the Pre-Collapse statutes. Article 472 was never rescinded. It's binding law."

Cole stared at him. "You're saying this kangaroo court actually has legal standing?"

"That document on the screen has your signature on it." Julian's voice stayed quiet, but something had shifted in his tone. "Claire Thurmond. Age eight. Compliance optimization target. Your signature, sir. That's evidence."

"It's taken out of context! These authorizations go through multiple review levels. The document doesn't show—"

"It's a death warrant for an eight-year-old girl."

The boardroom went silent.

Chen stood there, tablet in hand, looking at his employer with an expression that was hard to read. Horror, maybe. Or disbelief. Or the dawning realization that the man he'd been working for, the mentor who'd taught him about market dynamics and operational efficiency, had signed a child's execution order and was now trying to claim it was taken out of context.

The other executives were watching Cole now. Not with the collegial attention of equals in a leadership meeting. With calculation. Assessment. The kind of look people gave to problems that needed solving.

Victoria Chen, the CFO, shifted in her chair. "Harrison. How many of these authorizations have your signature?"

"What?"

"Individual targeting authorizations. How many did you personally sign?" Robert's financial mind was already running the numbers, calculating exposure, assessing liability.

Cole opened his mouth. Closed it. The answer was in the files

Wraith had seized. Thousands of documents. Maybe tens of thousands. Forty years of operational efficiency, compliance optimization, workforce management.

Forty years of death warrants.

"They're going to prosecute all of us," Robert Mendez said from the other end of the table. The Operations VP had his arms crossed, face unreadable. "But you're the one who signed the child's authorization. You're not our colleague right now, Harrison. You're our liability."

Cole looked around the table. Saw the same calculation on every face. Thinking not about how to defend him, but how to distance themselves from him.

The broadcast continued on the wall screen. Josephine's voice, calm and precise, reading the charges. Claire's drawing beside the authorization document. Evidence piling up in neat, documented, inescapable stacks.

The executives of Apex Consortium had spent decades building an empire on human suffering, coding murder as efficiency, turning atrocity into quarterly earnings. They'd done it together, signed the documents together, profited together.

But now that justice was coming, they learned what they'd always known but never admitted.

When the ship starts sinking, everyone looks for someone else to throw overboard first.

CHAPTER TWENTY-THREE

The broadcast fragmented mid-sentence.

Josephine's voice dissolved into static. The prosecution that had been reaching Earth and the station workers died in a cascade of encryption interference.

Wraith's displays flashed red. Warning protocols cascaded across the interface. Threat detection. Countermeasure engagement. Adaptive attack patterns.

Sophisticated.

Voss leaned forward at the adjacent console. Her voice rose. "They're using encryption I've never seen. Beyond Meridian protocols. This is military-grade quantum encryption. Corporate shouldn't have access to this."

But corporate did have access. Apex had acquired pre-war military infrastructure. Weapons platforms. Orbital manufacturing. Station architecture designed for strategic military operations before the Collapse.

And the AI that came with it.

Wraith's fingers moved across the keyboard. Fast. Precise. The cyber operations center hummed with processor activity. JUDG-

MENT's systems detecting the attack. Analyzing the encryption patterns. Attempting to counter.

Failing.

The assault was too sophisticated. Too adaptive. Too powerful.

Josephine's voice cut out completely on the main feed. Earth receiving nothing. Station workers getting fragments. Static replaced the prosecution.

Countermeasures detected. Apex station AI was attacking JUDGMENT's broadcast systems with everything it had.

Pinnacle Core.

Wraith had read the technical specifications during the platform engagement. Corporate AI. Apex Consortium's digital overseer. Resources Meridian never had. Meridian's systems had been degraded. Post-war scavenged infrastructure held together with patch code and desperate maintenance.

Pinnacle Core was pre-war military sophistication with decades of corporate optimization. Processing capability designed for managing forty-seven thousand workers across twelve manufacturing sectors. Orbital station environmental controls. Deep-space sensor arrays monitoring traffic across the system.

And right now, all that processing power was focused on one objective.

Silence Josephine's trial.

Prevent Earth from hearing the prosecution. Stop station workers from seeing the evidence. Protect the seven executives who'd authorized genocide for quarterly earnings.

The AI was doing exactly what it had been programmed to do.

Protect Apex interests.

Voss' voice announced, "Wraith, they're fragmenting the signal. Earth is getting maybe twenty percent of the transmission. The station feed is holding, but barely."

Wraith's text display lit up.

I captured something during the platform hack.

"What?"

Station backbone authentication. Filing it seemed smart.

Voss stared at the display. "You have station-level access keys? From the platforms?"

Wraith's fingers paused. They cracked their knuckles, the only sound they ever made. Then their hands returned to the keyboard.

Their display updated.

Ninety seconds.

The cyber warfare had begun.

Wraith worked.

No text display. No communication. Just code.

Pinnacle Core was sophisticated. They could see it in the encryption patterns scrolling across their monitors. Multi-layered defenses. Adaptive response protocols cycling through countermeasure subroutines every three-point-seven seconds. Resources Meridian never had. Corporate AI with orbital-scale processing power.

Resources meant capability.

Capability meant complexity.

Complexity meant vulnerabilities.

But predictable vulnerabilities. Corporate security thinking.

Wraith had grown up in the streets. Level Twelve Meridian housing blocks where enforcement squads disappeared people for asking questions. Learned in resistance cells where one mistake meant vanishing into detention centers that kept no records. Perfected their craft in the shadows. Survival required outthinking systems designed by people who'd never been hunted. Never needed to think like prey.

Corporate systems defended assets. Protected what mattered. Layered security around the valuable infrastructure. Communications hubs. Manufacturing oversight. Executive access protocols.

Everything important got walls.

Everything unimportant got ignored.

Wraith didn't attack where defenses were strong.

They looked for where they were absent.

Their screens showed Pinnacle Core's architecture. The AI managed station operations through hierarchical access tiers. Executive level: maximum security, biometric authentication, encrypted channels. Worker tracking: moderate security, efficiency-optimized protocols. Environmental controls: minimal security because who attacks life support?

Who needed to?

Maintenance systems. Backup relays. Redundant pathways built into the station's original military design. Before Apex acquired the platform. Before corporate efficiency optimized away what seemed unnecessary.

The backbone authentication she'd captured during the platform hack. Pinnacle Core didn't know they had it because the platforms operated on legacy military protocols. Separate from the corporate AI's oversight. Authentication keys that predated Apex's acquisition.

Pre-corporate credentials.

The station's digital infrastructure still recognized them.

Wraith deployed the authentication. Watched security protocols accept the access. System-level privileges granted. Not because they'd breached anything. Because the station's core systems thought they belonged there.

Their fingers moved across three keyboards simultaneously.

Left hand: maintaining the degraded broadcast signal. Josephine's voice fragmented across the feed. Earth receiving maybe fifteen percent. Station workers getting static. The prosecution dying in real-time.

Right hand: mapping Pinnacle Core's defensive architecture. Tracking the AI's attack patterns. Encryption assault concentrated on JUDGMENT's primary communications relay. Adaptive algorithms cycling through countermeasures. Looking for weaknesses in the broadcast infrastructure.

Finding them. Exploiting them.

Center keyboard: navigating the station's core systems with pre-corporate authentication. System-level access granted without resistance. Administrative privileges recognized. Security layers parting.

Not breached.

Invited.

They were already inside like a ghost.

Pinnacle Core's attack patterns shifted. The AI reallocated processing power. Responding to the broadcast signal degradation. More encryption cycles thrown at the communications relay. Adaptive approach. Learning from what worked.

It didn't notice the authenticated session opening in station maintenance systems.

Didn't see the administrative commands being issued from credentials it had no reason to question.

Wraith mapped the digital battlefield. Pinnacle Core controlled everything visible. Environmental systems maintaining station atmosphere. Gravity generators keeping workers oriented. Manufacturing oversight coordinating production across twelve sectors. Communications relay managing internal and external transmissions.

The AI had evolved with Apex's occupation. Optimized for efficiency. Streamlined for corporate management. Adapted to control workers who couldn't leave, manufacturing that never stopped, an environment that had to stay alive or everyone died.

Complete control through complete necessity.

But the backbone authentication gave Wraith administrative privileges that predated that control.

They didn't need to fight Pinnacle Core directly.

They needed to cut it off from what it controlled.

Remove the AI's access to the systems it managed. Let it keep thinking. Keep processing. Keep attacking the broadcast relay with encryption cycles that would hit nothing.

Isolate the predator.

Then the prey could move freely.

Voss' voice was distant. Background noise. "Earth signal at fifteen percent. We're losing the transmission."

Wraith's hands moved faster.

The station's systems architecture spread across the center display. Pinnacle Core's control pathways mapped in red. JUDG-MENT's limited access shown in blue.

Wraith's authenticated session glowed green.

Administrative privileges.

Wraith traced the communications infrastructure. Primary relay under Pinnacle Core's active control. The AI was using it to attack JUDGMENT's broadcast. Throwing encryption cycles at the feed. Fragmenting the signal. Sophisticated assault using the station's own systems as weapons.

But the station had been built for military operations. Redundancy was doctrine. Critical systems had backups. The pre-war designers had known that battles damaged infrastructure. That primary systems failed under fire.

They'd built alternatives.

Apex had inherited those alternatives. Corporate efficiency had left them dormant. Why maintain backup when primary never failed? Why allocate resources to redundancy when quarterly profits demanded optimization?

Wraith found the backup communications relay. Maintenance logs showed it had been tested once during Apex acquisition. Then forgotten. Filed under "legacy systems" and ignored.

It still worked.

They routed the broadcast through the backup relay. Isolated pathway separate from Pinnacle Core's control. The AI couldn't attack what it couldn't access. Couldn't fragment a signal traveling through infrastructure it had no credentials to touch.

The backup relay came online. Josephine's voice returned to the broadcast. Clear. Uninterrupted. Using infrastructure Pinnacle Core couldn't see because corporate efficiency had optimized it out of active monitoring.

Earth receiving full signal. Station workers hearing every word.

The prosecution continued.

Forty-seven seconds had elapsed.

Voss stared at her monitor. Signal strength indicators showing full transmission. Earth feed restored. Station-wide broadcast active. "How did you—"

Wraith's display lit up.

Not finished.

The broadcast was restored. But Pinnacle Core still controlled everything else. Environmental systems. Manufacturing oversight. Worker tracking. Station security protocols.

Time to take it all away.

Wraith didn't stop at restoring the broadcast.

Pinnacle Core was still attacking. Throwing encryption cycles at communications infrastructure it no longer controlled. Corporate AI. Sophisticated. Adaptive. Processing power allocated to countering a threat that had already moved past its defenses.

Still fighting the battle it understood.

Missing the war.

Isolated.

Fingers moved across the center keyboard. The backbone authentication had given them more than access. It had given them administrative authority over systems Pinnacle Core thought it owned.

The AI operated within the station's digital infrastructure. Controlled environmental systems through management protocols. Managed worker tracking through personnel oversight. Coordinated manufacturing through production schedules.

All through protocols that recognized their credentials as legitimate.

Wraith reviewed the system hierarchy. Found the access control lists. Pinnacle Core's permissions mapped across every subsystem, layer upon layer of corporate control.

They started revoking it.

Environmental controls: administrative override initiated. Pinnacle Core's access credentials invalidated. System control transferred to authenticated session. Manufacturing oversight: administrative lockout executed. Production management severed from AI control. Worker tracking systems: personnel monitoring access denied. Location data no longer available to corporate oversight.

Every system. Every subsystem. Every digital pathway.

One by one, Wraith cut Pinnacle Core off from the station it had managed for decades.

The AI could still function. Still process information within its isolated core. Still run algorithms and execute subroutines in the computational space it occupied.

But it couldn't see.

Couldn't act.

Couldn't control.

Communications relay: final lockout. Access denied.

Voss' monitor erupted with system status alerts. Change notifications cascading across her displays. Environmental control transfer. Manufacturing oversight reassignment. Communications authority redirected.

Every system on the station reporting new administrative control.

Her voice held something between horror and admiration. "Every screen on the station just switched to JUDGMENT control. You're broadcasting to all workers through Pinnacle Core's own infrastructure."

She looked at Wraith. Who had just taken an entire orbital station away from a sophisticated corporate AI in under three minutes.

"The executive bunker feeds. The isolated systems they thought were secure. You control those, too?"

Wraith's fingers paused. Text appeared on the display.

Everything.

A new message appeared.

The platform hack. Platform defensive grid. I captured their backbone signature during the engagement.

Voss processed that. The weapons platforms they'd destroyed during the approach. The cyber warfare Wraith had conducted while Josephine fought her way through the docking bay. The credentials that had seemed like useful intelligence at the time.

Seeds becoming payoffs.

"They never knew you had it."

Wraith's display:

Corporate arrogance. Never changed protocols after Apex acquired military infrastructure.

The words triggered something in Voss' memory. An intelligence report from Arc 02. Her own analysis of Meridian's security failures. The observation that Apex had never updated authentication systems after taking control from the pre-war military.

She'd said it. Called them arrogant bastards for the oversight.

Wraith had remembered.

"Those were my words," she said. "From the Meridian analysis. About them never changing protocols."

Wraith's hands paused on the keyboard. Brief text appeared.

Their words, not mine.

Dark humor. Callback. Recognition that the same corporate arrogance that had made Meridian vulnerable had just destroyed Pinnacle Core's control.

The broadcast signal strengthened. Full power. JUDGMENT's transmission clearing. Earth receiving one hundred percent of the feed. Station workers watching on every screen in every sector.

Josephine's voice filled quarters, break rooms, corridors. Manufacturing floors. Residential levels. Even the executive bunker.

The prosecution continued.

Uninterrupted.

Unstoppable.

Wraith pulled up the system logs. Reviewed what they'd just accomplished. The authentication exploit. The backup relay activation. The systematic administrative lockout across every subsystem.

Timeline: two minutes, forty-three seconds from initial countermeasure detection to complete station control.

Pinnacle Core had been outmaneuvered from the first move. The AI had focused on the obvious threat. The broadcast it could see. The transmission it could attack. Standard corporate security response. Defend the asset under assault.

It hadn't considered someone might already be inside.

Might have been inside since the platform engagement.

Waiting.

Wraith leaned back in the chair. Let their hands rest on the keyboards. Three workstations. Multiple displays showing station systems now operating under JUDGMENT's authority. Environmental controls maintaining atmosphere for workers. Manufacturing sectors continuing production. Communications relay broadcasting Josephine's prosecution to Earth and every screen on the station.

All under their control.

All taken from a sophisticated AI that had never imagined someone could exploit credentials it didn't know existed.

Wraith's display lit up one more time. Text appeared.

I've been hacking impossible things since the beginning. This one just had better encryption.

Voss read the message. Recognized the reference. Book One. Meridian's systems. The resistance cells where Wraith had learned their craft.

She'd read Wraith's file. The intelligence dossier JUDGMENT had compiled. Street hacker from Level Twelve. Started at fourteen, cracking enforcement database to erase arrest records for neighbors who'd missed ration quotas. Sixteen, infiltrating Meridian communications to warn resistance cells about impending raids. Eighteen, erasing themselves from every government database that mattered.

Survival through digital warfare.

Every impossible hack they'd executed to stay ahead of enforcement squads. To keep their people alive. To move through a system designed to track everyone, catch everyone who resisted.

Wraith had done it by being better than the people who'd designed that system. Outthinking programmers who'd never needed to hide. Exploiting assumptions made by security architects who'd never been hunted.

They'd been doing this for years.

Pinnacle Core was just one more target. Sophisticated. Well-resourced. Corporate-grade processing power backed by pre-war military technology.

Still predictable.

Still designed by people who'd never needed to think like her.

She smiled. "How long until Pinnacle Core realizes what happened?"

Brief response appeared.

It already knows.

"Can it counter?"

No.

"Why not?"
Longer message this time.

It's isolated. Core systems only. No access to station infrastructure. No way to execute commands. It can process. Calculate. Understand it's been defeated. But it can't act. Can't change anything. Can't regain control. Authentication hierarchy locked.

Permanent defeat. Pinnacle Core aware of its situation. Unable to change it.

The station belonged to JUDGMENT now.

Because Wraith had taken it.

Three keyboards. Two minutes. One hacker who'd grown up in the shadows learning to outthink systems designed by people who'd never needed to hide.

Wraith cracked their knuckles again, then pulled up security protocols for the executive bunker.

McCready would need access routes. Grim's squad would need environmental data. Josephine would need evidence archives.

The station was theirs.

Time to use it.

CHAPTER TWENTY-FOUR

Josephine stood at the bridge command station, Claire's drawing visible on every screen across the station. The prosecution had moved past opening charges into the systematic documentation of forty years of corporate atrocity.

"Count seventeen," she said. "Mining operations, Titan facility, February 2318. Twenty-three workers died when safety equipment failed during extraction operations. The incident report classified it as equipment malfunction."

She paused, letting the screens display the internal memo. "The evidence shows Apex management denied maintenance funding six months prior to optimize quarterly margins. The equipment didn't malfunction. It was deliberately left to fail."

The screens shifted to personnel files. Twenty-three faces. Twenty-three names. Twenty-three families who received consolation payments and falsified accident reports.

"Oscar Wu, age thirty-four. Survived by wife and two daughters." The next face appeared. "Amara Okonkwo, age twenty-seven. Survived by husband and infant son." Josephine continued through all twenty-three, reading each name, each age, each family left behind.

JUDGMENT monitored station-wide feeds. Workers throughout Pinnacle had stopped moving. Break rooms on Level 15 showed older personnel with tears on their faces. Some were nodding. Some were covering their mouths with their hands.

"Count eighteen," Josephine continued. "Labor organizing, processing sector, July 2320. Fourteen workers petitioned for improved conditions after three colleagues died from equipment failures in six months. Apex response designated them as compliance risks. All fourteen were relocated to worse assignments. Within two years, seven of the fourteen were dead."

More faces. More names. Tobias Reeves, age forty-one. Lucia Vasquez, age thirty-six. Thomas Wu, age twenty-eight.

"The defense will claim they were following market forces," Josephine said, her voice colder now. "They will argue that competition demanded efficiency. That shareholders expected returns. That economic necessity required difficult decisions." She let that hang in the air for three seconds.

"The evidence shows they *created* those market forces. They structured the economy to reward optimization over human life. They paid bonuses to executives who achieved casualty quotas. They promoted managers who suppressed dissent. They built an entire system where profit required death, then claimed the system gave them no choice."

The screens displayed bonus structures. Executive compensation tied directly to reduction in workforce expenses. Performance reviews that praised managers for aggressive compliance measures.

"They didn't inherit an unjust system," Josephine said. "They designed one. Every casualty metric. Every compliance protocol. Every optimization target. These were created by the seven executives currently sealed in their boardroom bunker. Created deliberately. Implemented systematically. Refined annually for maximum efficiency."

She advanced to the next screen. Financial projections from

2315 showing planned workforce reductions and projected savings. The document was signed by Harrison Cole and three other CEOs.

"This is not market forces. This is murder for quarterly earnings."

JUDGMENT tracked the reactions in real-time, monitoring forty-seven thousand simultaneous feeds across the station.

Level 15, Break Room C: Six workers, ages ranging from forty-eight to sixty-three, sat around a table with their meal rations untouched. The oldest, a maintenance supervisor with gray hair and scarred hands, was crying. "Richardson," he whispered. "I worked with Richardson in 2319. They said he transferred to another facility." On screen, Richardson's face appeared under Count Nineteen. Died in equipment malfunction, processing sector. The supervisor put his head in his hands. "They told us he transferred."

Another worker, younger but with the same exhausted look they all carried, reached across the table. "My sister was optimization target in 2322. I thought she got sick. The company said she got sick."

Residential Level 47, Apartment 7B: A woman in her thirties watched the screen with her two children pressed against her sides. Her husband had died three years ago in what management called an industrial accident. She'd accepted the consolation payment and the reassignment to worse quarters. Now she watched his face appear on screen with nineteen others. "Optimization target," Josephine's voice said. "Compliance protocol seventeen. Equipment failure staged to reduce workforce expenses by projected eighteen percent."

The woman's hands were shaking. Her children asked her what was wrong. She couldn't answer.

Commercial Level, Management Office: A former middle-manager sat at his desk, staring at reports he'd filed in 2320. Efficiency improvements. Workforce optimization recommendations. He'd been promoted for those reports. Received a bonus. Been praised in his performance review for aggressive implementation of compliance protocols.

The screen showed faces of workers who'd been classified as compliance risks based on his reports. Seven of them were dead. He'd written the analysis that marked them as expendable.

He stood, walked to the door, and kept walking. Away from his office. Away from his desk. Away from everything he'd spent ten years building. Behind him, the screen continued displaying faces. Names. Families.

McCready's comm crackled. JUDGMENT's voice: "Commander, you have incoming personnel. Level 22, junction seven. Four individuals, unarmed, hands visible."

McCready signaled his team to stand ready but hold fire. Four security officers appeared around the corner, weapons holstered, hands raised. The lead officer was young, maybe twenty-five, with the kind of face that had learned to follow orders without asking questions.

"We want to surrender," the officer said. His voice was steady but his hands weren't. "We want to testify."

McCready studied them. JUDGMENT's biometric analysis appeared on his HUD. Elevated heart rates. Stress hormones spiking. But no deception markers. No combat preparation.

"What's your name?" McCready asked.

"Peterson. Security detail, executive tower. We've been watching the broadcast." He glanced at his three companions. "We didn't know. I mean, we knew some of it. But the faces. The names. I've been protecting the people who signed those authorizations for three years."

One of the other officers, older, maybe forty, spoke up. "My daughter is eight. Same age as that girl. Claire." His voice cracked.

"I can't keep protecting the people who killed children for quarterly earnings."

McCready's team had their weapons ready but not aimed. Waiting for his call. He made it.

"You're accepting surrender. You'll be secured and processed. If your testimony is verified, you'll be offered protection. If you're lying, you'll be prosecuted." He gestured to two of his auxiliary team. "Secure them. Treat them as cooperative detainees until verified."

JUDGMENT tracked thirty-seven more security personnel walking away from their posts in the ten minutes that followed. Some approached resistance positions to surrender. Some just walked away, leaving weapons in lockers, heading for residential levels to be with their families.

The broadcast wasn't just prosecution. It was recruitment. Every name. Every face. Every signature. Every count built the case that this wasn't about punishing soldiers. This was about holding the people who built the machine accountable.

And the soldiers were listening.

• • •

The executive boardroom bunker had been designed to withstand siege. Independent life support. Hardened walls. Supplies for weeks. Seven CEOs, twelve private security personnel, three corporate lawyers. All the power and protection that profit optimization could buy.

None of it mattered when the screens showed their crimes to so many witnesses.

Harrison Cole stood at the head of the table, watching his authorization signature appear next to Claire Thurmond's face on every display. The same screens he'd used for quarterly earnings presentations now broadcast his death warrant for an eight-year-old girl.

"They can't convict us in absentia!" His voice was higher than he intended. The lawyers flanking him looked uncertain.

The CFO sat at the far end of the table, her face pale. She'd been reviewing her own authorizations for the past twenty minutes. Casualty projections. Compliance metrics. Optimization targets. All signed. All dated. All documented.

"They're not trying to," she said quietly. "They're coming for us."

Cole turned on her. "We have legal protections. Corporate immunity. Pre-Null Statutes protect executive decisions made in good faith governance—"

"Good faith?" The Operations VP laughed. It came out wrong, more hysteric than amused. "They're showing our bonus structures tied to casualty quotas on every screen in this station. Where exactly is the good faith?"

The bunker door opened and the security commander entered. Former military, competent, professional. The type who'd protected executives for fifteen years because the pay was good and the work was straightforward.

Now he looked like someone who'd realized he'd been guarding monsters.

"Sir, we've lost forty percent of our security force to defection in the last hour." His voice was steady but his hands weren't. "The broadcast is causing mass surrenders. Personnel are walking away from posts. Some are approaching the resistance to testify."

Cole slammed his hand on the table. "Then cut the broadcast! Shut down the feeds. Jam their signal. Use the emergency protocols—"

"We can't." The commander met his eyes. "They control all station systems now. Pinnacle Core is locked out. Every screen, every comm channel, every data node. It's all under their control. We can't cut what we don't control."

Silence filled the boardroom. Seven executives who'd spent decades commanding empires now faced the reality that command meant nothing when someone else controlled the infrastructure.

The Human Resources Director, younger than the others, stared at her tablet. Personnel files scrolling past. Workers she'd classified as compliance risks. Families she'd authorized for relocation to worse conditions. People she'd optimized out of existence to hit efficiency targets.

"How many?" she whispered. "How many did we kill?"

The CFO didn't look up from her screen. "The prosecution is claiming four-point-eight million."

"That's inflated," Cole said automatically. "They're counting indirect casualties. Market forces. Economic necessity. We didn't personally kill—"

"We signed the authorizations." The Operations VP was staring at his own hands like they belonged to someone else. "I signed forty-seven workforce reduction orders. Forty-seven. They're showing the casualty reports next to my signatures. The people who died weren't market forces. They had names."

The security commander shifted his weight. All seven executives looked at him. He'd been their protection for fifteen years. Their shield against consequences. Their guarantee that power meant safety.

"Sir," he said quietly. "They're not negotiating from strength anymore. They've already won the station. The workers are with them. Half our security force has defected. The other half is waiting to see what we do." He paused. "What are your orders?"

Cole opened his mouth. Closed it. Opened it again. No orders came. For the first time in decades of corporate command, Harrison Cole had nothing to say.

The CFO stood slowly. "They're coming for us," she said again. "And we can't stop them."

On the screens, Josephine's voice continued reading counts. Names. Faces. Signatures.

The seven executives looked at each other. The lawyers said

nothing. The security commander waited for orders that wouldn't come.

For the first time since Apex Consortium took control of Pinnacle Station, the people who'd designed the machine felt fear.

CHAPTER TWENTY-FIVE

McCready studied the Executive Tower entrance through his rifle scope. Single point of access, reinforced blast doors, defensive architecture that screamed "we knew this day would come eventually." Two hundred loyalists behind improvised barricades. The setup you got when security personnel ran out of ideological justifications and started fighting for severance packages.

"Final defensive line," Grim reported from the left flank. "Two hundred signatures. Life signs consistent with entrenched personnel."

McCready lowered his rifle and opened the general comm channel. Station-wide broadcast, every speaker in the corridor, every tactical net the defenders were monitoring. His voice echoed through the commercial level.

"This is your last chance."

Movement behind the barricades. Weapons tracking toward his position but not firing. Listening.

"Lay down your weapons. Face trial for following orders. You might walk out of this with your lives and your pensions." He paused, letting that sink in. "Keep fighting, die here for executives who signed death warrants for eight-year-old children. Your employers aren't worth dying for."

Another pause. The critical moment.

"Ask Kellerman."

Silence. Then, murmurs through the defensive positions. Kellerman had been their commander eight hours ago. Now he was in JUDGMENT's brig, having surrendered rather than die for Harrison Cole's quarterly earnings reports.

If Kellerman chose JUDGMENT over Apex, what did that say about the remaining loyalists' tactical position?

A single rifle clattered to the deck. Then another. Then ten.

McCready waited. The soldiers processed impossible mathematics: fight and die, or surrender and testify. The broadcast prosecution had made the choice starker. Every worker on the station knew what the executives had done. Every security officer had watched colleagues walk away from posts after seeing the evidence.

Some would fight anyway. True believers existed in every organization, the ones who confused loyalty with identity. But most security personnel were professionals with families and mortgages and retirement plans that didn't include dying for corporate quarterly reports.

Fifty weapons down. Then eighty.

The remaining hundred twenty tightened their grips. These were the compromised ones, McCready judged. The ones who'd done things that couldn't be excused as "following orders." The ones who knew surrender meant trials of their own.

"Your call," McCready transmitted. "But we're coming through that door either way."

The first shaped charge detonated against the structural weak point Voss had identified three days ago in Meridian database archives. Reinforced blast door, corporate-grade security, designed to stop frontal assault. But every fortress had engineering vulnerabilities, and Voss had spent two decades learning where bureaucrats cut corners on safety inspections.

The blast peeled back six centimeters of armored plating. Not a breach, but a crack.

"Second charge," McCready ordered.

Grim's AD-units moved into position while human operators provided covering fire. The second detonation punched through. Molten metal dripped to the deck, cooling in the station's recycled air. The gap widened to forty centimeters. Enough.

"Flash-bangs. Go."

Three canisters sailed through the opening. The detonations lit the corridor in strobing white. McCready moved before the echoes faded, rifle up, targeting threats through muscle memory and tactical instinct. AD-units flowed past him, absorbing the initial return fire. Sparks cascaded from Grim's shoulder assembly as a burst caught him, but the unit didn't slow.

Professional. That was the word for what happened next. Not heroic, not desperate. A professional room clearing executed by operators who'd trained for exactly this scenario.

Some loyalists dropped weapons and raised hands. McCready's team zip-tied them and moved past. Others opened fire from entrenched positions. AD-units took point, minimizing human exposure, trading armor integrity for flesh. Return fire was precise, controlled. Disabling shots where possible, lethal only when necessary.

"First floor clear," Grim reported. His vocal modulator had picked up a distortion from the shoulder damage. "Advancing to second level."

The stairwell was a nightmare. Narrow approach, defensive high ground, overlapping fields of fire. Exactly the kind of chokepoint that turned assaults into bloodbaths if you rushed it. McCready didn't rush.

"Smoke. Cover the approach."

Canisters sailed upward. The stairwell filled with obscuring haze. AD-units advanced through it, optical sensors cutting through the interference while defenders fired blind. Methodical. One step, clear the angle, advance. Another step, suppress the position, advance.

Second floor. More resistance. The fight had become a rhythm now. Flash, clear, advance. Flash, clear, advance. Loyalists fought with the desperation of personnel who knew what awaited them at trial. Some had been Kellerman's best officers. Now they were dying in a stairwell for executives who'd never learned their names.

Bones moved through the carnage with the same methodical precision. Triage, stabilize, move. A round punched through her left shoulder during third-floor clearing. Sparks and hydraulic fluid. She registered the damage, compensated for reduced left-arm functionality, kept working.

"Non-critical damage," she transmitted on the medical channel. "Continuing operations."

McCready glanced at her between engagements. Bones knelt beside a wounded loyalist, right arm performing emergency hemostasis while her damaged left arm hung useless. Medical care for the enemy who'd just shot her. Principles maintained under fire.

"Floor clear," Grim reported from the fourth level. "Advancing."

"Floor clear," another squad leader confirmed from the fifth. "Advancing."

The tower had twelve floors. They'd cleared seven in eighteen minutes. Loyalist resistance was collapsing, fragmenting into isolated pockets. Some continued fighting. Most surrendered. A few tried to flee through maintenance corridors and ran into containment teams.

Relentless. That was the other word. Not cruel, not vengeful. Relentless. An assault that didn't stop when you got tired, didn't pause when casualties mounted, didn't deviate when resistance stiffened.

Twenty years of tactical superiority compressed into twenty minutes of corridor combat.

"Tenth floor clear," Grim transmitted. His distortion had worsened. "Two floors remaining. Executive level above us."

McCready checked his tactical display. Casualties: twelve wounded on his side, forty-seven enemy casualties, sixty-three prisoners secured. The mathematics of assault compressed into numbers that would haunt him later. Right now, they merely represented data points in the advance.

"Advance to executive level," he ordered. "Josephine, you're up. Executive bunker is yours."

The executive level fell silent. Not the silence of victory, but the silence of a siege concluding. Surviving loyalists knelt with hands zip-tied behind backs, sorted into three groups based on apparent guilt level. Those who'd followed orders. Those who'd exceeded them. Those who'd initiated violence without authorization.

Legal thinking in the middle of tactical operations. Josephine had drilled it into every operator: treat prisoners according to their crimes, not their employer. Segregation now meant appropriate trials later.

JUDGMENT's voice filled McCready's earpiece, calm and precise as always. "Executive level secured. All movements tracked, all weapons accounted for, all communications monitored. The boardroom bunker remains sealed. Biometric analysis confirms all seven executives present. Private security detail: twelve personnel. Legal counsel: three individuals. No heavy weapons detected. Atmospheric systems nominal. They're out of tactical options."

McCready surveyed the executive level. Plush carpeting, original artwork on walls, the environmental luxury that the workers in cramped dormitories had paid for with their labor. The contrast would play well in the prosecution broadcast.

His display showed Josephine approaching through the corridor. She moved with the same relentless precision she'd maintained throughout the assault. Weapon holstered, tablet in hand, every step bringing her closer to the final confrontation.

McCready opened a private channel. "Executive level is yours. Time to prosecute."

Josephine didn't break stride. Her response came through the comm with absolute certainty.

"The prosecution never stopped."

She was right. The combat had been logistics. Necessary force applied to reach the targets. But the prosecution had begun the moment they'd broadcast the first evidence file. Every shaped charge, every cleared floor, every prisoner processed had been execution of legal authority, not military conquest.

McCready watched her approach the boardroom bunker. Behind that sealed door, seven executives who'd signed death warrants for millions. Twelve private security officers who'd enabled them. Three lawyers who'd constructed the legal frameworks that called genocide "compliance optimization."

All of them trapped. All of them awaiting judgment.

Josephine stopped three meters from the bunker entrance. "JUDGMENT," she transmitted on open channel. Station-wide broadcast. Earth receiving. Every worker, every prisoner, every witness watching. "Confirm executive positions."

"Confirmed. All seven executives present in boardroom bunker. Harrison Cole at head of table. Financial records indicate bunker provisioned for three-week siege. Psychological profiles suggest they're waiting for external rescue that will never arrive."

Josephine nodded. McCready saw her expression shift. Prosecutor replacing soldier. Legal authority superseding tactical command.

"Then let's give them their trial," she said.

The prosecution had never stopped. But now it would finish.

CHAPTER TWENTY-SIX

Josephine walked toward the boardroom alone.

McCready's team flanked her twenty meters back, weapons ready but not raised. This was her moment. The prosecutor approaching the defendants.

She wasn't here to kill. She was here to prosecute.

The corridor stretched ahead, empty except for debris from the breach. Spent casings. Scorch marks. A security helmet cracked against the wall. The executive level had been designed for comfort—thick carpeting, wood paneling, art installations meant to convey power and taste. Now it looked like what it was. A bunker that had failed.

Her boots echoed in the silence. The broadcast continued through the station's speakers, her own voice reading charges.

"The defendants have been offered opportunity to surrender peacefully under Pre-Collapse Article 472. This offer remains open for sixty seconds."

She checked her tablet. Claire's drawing was still there. The clouds colored bright and white, labeled in a child's handwriting. *For Casper, for being brave.*

Claire's face filled her mind. Eight years old. Shot while trying to shield her father. The spreadsheet had shown the authorization. Harrison Cole's signature. Thirty seconds, zero hesitation.

Josephine kept walking.

Behind her, McCready's voice carried. "Flanking positions maintained. You've got twenty meters of clear space, Captain."

She didn't respond. The corridor felt longer than the schematics suggested, each step carrying weight that had nothing to do with station gravity. The boardroom door waited ahead, reinforced composite designed to withstand anything short of shaped charges.

Fifteen seconds left on the countdown.

Her hand stayed near her holster. Not touching the weapon. Just... near. The temptation was there. Walk in, find Cole, put three rounds center mass before the lawyers could open their mouths. Quick. Clean. Justice served in the time it took to draw and fire.

She could feel the weight of the sidearm. Could imagine the motion. Draw, aim, fire. The man who'd signed Claire's death warrant would be dead before he hit the floor.

Ten seconds.

Josephine's fingers curled, then straightened. The tablet felt heavier than the weapon. Claire's drawing. The evidence. The authorization with Cole's signature.

Five seconds.

She stopped three meters from the door. Her voice carried clear and cold through the corridor.

"Time's up."

The comm crackled. A voice emerged from the boardroom's external speaker, professional and smooth. A lawyer.

"This is Marcus Hale, counsel for Apex Consortium. Our clients are prepared to discuss terms of—"

Josephine cut him off. "Negotiation ended when your clients authorized genocide. Surrender or die. You have forty seconds."

Silence. Then the voice returned, losing some of its smoothness. "We demand legal representation under Pre-Collapse statutes—"

"You have representation." Josephine checked her tablet. Thirty-five seconds. "They're talking instead of thinking. Thirty seconds."

The comm went quiet. She could picture the scene inside. Seven executives in tailored suits. Three lawyers with briefcases. Twelve private security personnel in tactical gear, gripping weapons and calculating odds.

Twelve men. Twelve families somewhere. Twelve lives that could end in the next thirty seconds.

For what?

Seven executives who'd signed death warrants for children to optimize quarterly earnings?

JUDGMENT's voice came through her earpiece, calm and analytical. "Infrared shows elevated stress markers. The security detail is considering options."

Twenty seconds.

Josephine moved closer to the door. Her hand still hovered near her weapon. The lawyers were probably advising surrender. The executives were probably demanding they fight. The security detail was probably doing math.

Twelve against how many? Against AD-units that had destroyed combat synthetics? Against soldiers who'd fought through two hundred loyalists without breaking legal rules of engagement?

Against a prosecutor who'd walked alone down this corridor broadcasting their crimes to the world?

Fifteen seconds.

The comm crackled again. Different voice. Younger. Stressed. "This is Captain Reeves, executive protection detail. We need time to—"

"You had forty years." Josephine's voice stayed level. "Ten seconds."

"Wait—"

"Nine."

She heard movement behind the door. Voices rising. Someone shouting about legal precedent. Someone else yelling about fighting. The security captain trying to maintain order while his team faced the same calculation Kellerman's forces had made an hour ago.

Die for executives? Or choose something else?

"Five seconds." Josephine's hand moved to her weapon grip. Not drawing. Just ready. "Four."

The door's lock indicator shifted from red to amber.

"Three."

Amber to green.

"Two."

The door opened.

The door opened wide.

Private security emerged first. Twelve men in tactical gear, weapons lowered, hands visible. Captain Reeves led them, his face showing the weight of the choice he'd just made.

"We surrender."

Josephine stepped aside. McCready's team moved forward, weapons secured, restraints applied. No violence. No anger. Just procedure.

Behind the security detail, through the open boardroom door, she could see the executives. Seven men in expensive suits standing near a conference table. Three lawyers clustered together, briefcases clutched like shields.

And Harrison Cole. Standing alone. Defiant.

"I'll surrender!" His voice carried across the space, sharp with the authority of someone who'd spent so long giving orders and having them followed. "Under Pre-Collapse Article 472, you are legally required to accept peaceful surrender! I am—"

Josephine's hand moved toward her weapon.

Claire's face filled her vision. Eight years old. Drawing clouds she'd never seen. Shot while trying to shield her father. The spreadsheet. The authorization. Cole's signature. Thirty seconds, zero hesitation.

Her fingers touched the grip.

One motion. Draw, aim, fire. Three rounds center mass. The man who'd killed Claire would be dead before the lawyers could invoke another statute.

Justice.

Quick.

Clean.

Her hand stopped.

Josephine looked at Harrison Cole. Looked at the man who'd signed a child's death warrant without breaking stride. Who'd authorized "compliance optimization" that killed almost five million workers. Who was now invoking legal protections he'd denied to everyone else.

He was still talking. "You have sixty seconds to respond to surrender under Article 472, Section 9! I demand—"

"Time's up." Josephine's hand stayed on her weapon. Not drawing. Not releasing. "Breach authorized."

McCready's team moved past her into the boardroom.

Cole's voice shifted from authority to panic. "Wait! I said I surrender! You can't—"

"I can." Josephine stepped through the doorway, her weapon now drawn but pointed at the floor. "The question is whether I will."

She looked at the man who'd murdered Claire. At the executive who'd built an empire on corpses. At the defendant who'd refused surrender for forty-five minutes and was now demanding legal protection.

Josephine's finger rested beside the trigger guard.

McCready's voice came quiet through her earpiece. "Captain. Your call."

Behind Cole, the other six executives stood frozen. The

lawyers had stopped breathing. The room waited for Josephine to decide what justice looked like when you finally had the power to deliver it.

She'd walked through fire to get here. Through station combat and breach operations. Every step broadcast. Every action documented. Every choice proving that legitimate authority was different from the power Cole had wielded.

Her hand tightened on the weapon.

Claire's face. Claire's drawing. Claire's death.

Thirty seconds, zero hesitation. That's how long it had taken Cole to authorize her murder.

Josephine raised the weapon.

Cole's eyes went wide. "I surrendered! You—"

"Did you?" Her voice stayed level despite the fury burning in her chest. "I gave you forty-five minutes to surrender peacefully. You refused. I gave you sixty seconds. You negotiated. I counted down from ten. Your security opened the door at two."

She stepped closer. The weapon stayed pointed at Cole's center mass.

"The legal question is simple. Did you surrender before or after the deadline? Because if it was after—" She paused. Let him see his death in her eyes. "Then I'm within legal authority to execute you right now for resisting lawful arrest."

Cole's mouth opened. No sound came out.

Josephine's finger moved to the trigger.

Claire. The drawing. The clouds colored bright and white.

For Casper, for being brave.

Her hand lowered.

"McCready." Her voice carried across the boardroom. "Secure the defendants. Full restraints. They're under arrest."

She holstered the weapon and turned away from Harrison Cole before she could change her mind.

Behind her, Cole found his voice again. "I knew you couldn't do it! You're bound by—"

Josephine stopped. Didn't turn around. "I'm bound by law. Not mercy. Remember that during your trial."

She walked back into the corridor and left Harrison Cole to McCready's team.

Justice would be served.

Just not today.

Not by her hand in a boardroom with witnesses watching to see if she was different from the men she'd come to prosecute.

The broadcast would show she was.

Even when every cell in her body screamed for the quicker, cleaner end.

CHAPTER TWENTY-SEVEN

The timer in Josephine's tactical display showed 00:00:02 when Harrison Cole shouted his surrender. Two seconds before the deadline. Or had it been one second before? The tactical feed replayed in her neural implant, timestamp flickering between negative-zero-point-eight and positive-zero-point-three, the audio corrupted by weapons fire that had echoed through the executive corridor thirty seconds ago when the private security made their choice.

She could replay it a hundred times. The neural recording would never resolve the question. Did Cole surrender before the deadline expired, or did he calculate his timing to claim compliance while technically violating it? Did the law require her to accept his surrender, or did legal precision permit her to rule it came too late?

McCready stood three meters behind her left shoulder, his weapon trained on the boardroom entrance with the steady calm of someone who'd made impossible decisions before and would defer to her judgment now. Grim's five AD-units flanked the doorway in tactical formation, their optical sensors locked on the twelve private security personnel who'd already laid down weapons and surrendered.

Workers watched from screens throughout Pinnacle Station. Every display showed the same image: Josephine Reeves, JAG prosecutor in scorched tactical armor, standing before the last corporate stronghold with her hand drifting toward a holstered sidearm.

Earth's population watched from their homes. Every broadcast channel. Every news feed. Every public display commandeered by JUDGMENT's transmission showing Commander Reeves facing the man who'd authorized Claire Thurmond's murder.

The galaxy watched. And waited for her choice.

"Josephine." McCready's voice cut through the tactical analysis running in her neural implant. Not "Commander Reeves." Not "sir." Just her name. The tone he'd used during Kandahar when she'd frozen before ordering artillery on a compound that might have held civilians. The voice of someone who knew when a decision required human acknowledgment, not military protocol. "Orders?"

She forced herself to look away from the tactical replay. Away from the timestamp that wouldn't resolve. Away from the legal analysis of whether Section 9, Paragraph C applied when surrender came at T-minus-zero-point-three or T-plus-zero-point-two.

Harrison Cole stood visible through the boardroom's open doorway, hands raised in the universal gesture of surrender, face composed. The man who'd signed Claire Thurmond's death authorization. The man who'd signed two-point-one million other authorizations just like it. Thirty seconds average review time per file. Zero hesitation recorded on any decision.

His suit was still pressed despite the station assault. His hair remained perfectly styled despite eight hours of combat advancing through commercial and residential levels. Even his surrender looked professional. Calculated. Like everything else he'd done for four decades of corporate optimization.

He'd waited until the last possible second to surrender. Not out of courage. Out of calculation. Testing whether she'd honor Pre-Collapse Article 472's surrender provisions or ignore them under combat pressure. Testing whether JUDGMENT's legal framework was real or propaganda.

The camera drone broadcasting from the corridor ceiling whirred as it adjusted focus. Capturing every detail. Recording for history. For the trial record. For anyone questioning whether justice meant laws or vengeance.

Cole's voice carried through the open doorway, calm and practiced. "I invoke Pre-Collapse Article 472, Section 9, Paragraph C: lawful surrender during active military engagement. You are legally required to accept my surrender and guarantee my safety until tribunal convenes."

He knew the law. Of course he knew the law. He'd spent forty years exploiting every loophole, every technicality, every paragraph that protected profit over people. Now he hid behind legal precision like armor, confident she'd follow her own rules even when he never had.

Josephine's hand drifted toward her sidearm. Not consciously. Not deliberately. Just the weight of Claire's memory pulling her fingers toward justice that didn't require paperwork or trials or broadcast tribunals.

"Commander Reeves?" McCready again.

Five seconds of silence.

Five seconds where Josephine's tactical overlay froze mid-analysis, where the corridor sounds faded to white noise punctuated only by her own heartbeat thudding in her ears, where the watching workers and McCready's waiting team and Earth's broadcast audiences all disappeared into the background of a choice so simple it terrified her.

She could just shoot him.

The thought arrived with crystalline clarity. Not emotion. Not fury. Just reasoned assessment presented by the part of her brain trained at Ranger School and refined in Kandahar. Her sidearm sat in its holster, three centimeters from her right hand. One smooth draw—muscle memory from ten thousand repetitions. Two-second target acquisition at this range. Harrison Cole would drop before his lawyers finished their first syllable of protest.

The man who'd signed Claire Thurmond's death authorization. Eight years old. Drew clouds she'd never seen because Level 47 children didn't get windows. Died trying to shield her father from an enforcement squad that followed orders signed by this smirking, calculating, monstrous man who'd murdered a child for quarterly earnings and now hid behind the law he'd spent decades corrupting for profit.

The weapon was right there. Standard-issue sidearm, seventeen rounds chambered, zero mechanical failures in six years of service. One shot. Justice delivered. Final and absolute. No appeals. No legal maneuvering. No decades of procedural delays while Cole's lawyers exploited every technicality in Pre-Collapse statute books.

No one would stop her.

Josephine's assessment continued with the cold precision of military training. McCready wouldn't fire. He'd taught her combat prosecution in Kandahar, watched her order strikes on targets that deserved it, trusted her judgment when legal precision intersected battlefield necessity.

Grim's AD-units wouldn't intervene. They followed her authority, and shooting a war criminal who'd just surrendered fell within commander's discretion during active combat operations. The workers watching would cheer. They'd lived under Apex optimization protocols. They'd lost family members to compliance targets. They knew what Claire's authorization represented.

Earth's population would understand. The broadcasts had shown Claire's drawing beside Cole's signature. Eight-year-old girl. Quarterly profit optimization. The equation balanced itself in ways that transcended legal technicality.

Even JUDGMENT, bound by her authority as human commander, would execute the order without hesitation. The dreadnought AI served justice through human intermediary. If she judged Harrison Cole's surrender came too late, if she ruled battlefield necessity permitted immediate execution, JUDGMENT would provide supporting fire documentation and legal justification within fifteen seconds.

She could end Harrison Cole right now. Call it battlefield justice. Combat necessity. Proportional response to genocide. Acceptable interpretation of surrender timing when timestamp evidence remained inconclusive. The authorization would stand. The trial record would support her decision. History would record Commander Josephine Reeves executing the man who'd murdered Claire Thurmond before he could hide behind corporate legal teams for another forty years.

The temptation was real.

The temptation was terrible.

The temptation was everything she'd spent six years in JAG resisting.

Claire's face filled Josephine's memory. Not the surveillance photo from the authorization document. The living child who'd gifted her a drawing in a Level 47 corridor. Who'd asked if clouds were really white or just in stories. Who'd died trying to shield her father from an enforcement squad because eight-year-olds still believed protecting people mattered.

Harrison Cole had killed that child. Reviewed her file for thirty seconds, signed the authorization without hesitation, moved to the next name on the compliance optimization list. Claire Thurmond became data point four thousand, one hundred and twenty-seven in the quarterly profit report.

Acceptable losses for two-point-three percent earnings improvement.

One shot would balance that equation. One shot would make Claire's death mean something immediate and visceral instead of abstract legal proceedings. One shot would prove Josephine remembered who mattered and who deserved forgetting.

Her hand moved closer to the sidearm. Almost touching. Almost drawing. Almost crossing the line between prosecutor and executioner.

Almost.

Josephine's hand stopped.

The choice crystallized in that frozen moment between impulse and action. Between justice and vengeance. Between the prosecutor she'd trained to become and the broken woman who'd held Claire's final drawing while the child's blood dried on enforcement squad boots.

She pulled her hand away from the sidearm. Forced her fingers to relax. Felt the neural implant's tactical overlay resume normal function as conscious decision overrode combat instinct. The white noise faded. The corridor sounds returned with jarring clarity. McCready's controlled breathing three meters behind her. The servos in Grim's AD-units adjusting weapon tracking. The camera drone's quiet hum as it recorded history.

The galaxy watching to see whether JUDGMENT's legal framework was real or theater.

"Surrender accepted."

The words came out flat. Empty of emotion. Legal precision instead of fury, though the fury remained buried so close to the surface that Josephine could taste it like copper on her tongue. She looked directly at Harrison Cole as she spoke, watching his face shift from calculated fear to something approaching relief.

He thought he'd won. Thought legal technicality had saved him. Thought surrender meant escape from accountability, meant corporate lawyers and procedural delays, meant eventually walking free when public attention moved to newer scandals.

He had no idea what she was about to do to him.

Cole's lips curved into a smirk. Small. Controlled. "Thank you, Commander. I look forward to presenting my defense at tribunal."

"Josephine…" McCready's voice held warning. Or maybe concern. Hard to tell which.

She ignored him. Kept her eyes on Cole. Let the camera drone capture every word for the broadcast record.

"Harrison Cole." Her voice dropped to ice. Prosecutor mode. The tone that had convicted war criminals in Kandahar when other JAG officers flinched. "You are under arrest for crimes against humanity. Specifically, the murder of Claire Thurmond, age eight. She drew pictures of clouds she never saw. You signed her death authorization without reading her file. Thirty seconds. Zero hesitation."

The smirk faltered.

"You will be prosecuted for every name in your files. Every death you authorized. Every child you murdered for quarterly earnings. Every compliance optimization target that was a human being before you reduced them to data points." Josephine stepped closer to the doorway. Not threatening. Just present. Making sure Cole understood what acceptance of surrender actually meant. "Two-point-one million signatures. We have them all. Wraith pulled your authorization logs from Pinnacle Core's memory. Every name. Every date. Every profit margin calculation."

Cole's face went pale.

"Surrender doesn't mean escape, Mr. Cole." Josephine let the title carry weight. Not "defendant" yet. Not "prisoner." Just the civilian designation that stripped away executive authority and corporate immunity. "Surrender means you face justice awake. You listen to every name. You hear every victim's story. You confront what you authorized when you thought nobody would ever hold you accountable."

She turned to McCready without breaking eye contact with Cole. "Sergeant McCready. Secure the defendant for transport to JUDGMENT's brig. Full custody protocols. He's to be protected from harm until tribunal convenes."

"Understood." McCready moved forward, signaling Grim's AD-units to establish a perimeter.

Cole's smirk was gone. His hands trembled slightly as Grim's Unit-4 moved to restrain him with mag-cuffs. The lawyers in the boardroom behind him started protesting procedure, citing regulations, demanding proper representation.

Josephine ignored them. Focused on Cole's eyes. Making sure he understood.

She hadn't shot him.

The realization settled into Josephine's chest with weight that felt physical. She'd chosen the harder path. The longer path. The path that required her to be prosecutor instead of executioner, to honor legal framework instead of emotional truth, to prove JUDGMENT's authority came from law instead of firepower.

That would have been mercy—the bullet. Quick. Final. Clean. The man who'd signed Claire's authorization would die without ever understanding what his signatures meant. Without ever confronting the names he'd turned into compliance data. Without ever facing the weight of millions of deaths he'd authorized for quarterly profit margins.

Mercy for him. Closure for her. Simple and absolute.

Instead, she was going to make him face what he'd done.

Make him sit in JUDGMENT's courtroom while prosecutors presented evidence. Make him listen to two-point-one million names read into trial record. Make him watch footage of children like Claire who'd died because his signature approved their elimination. Make him hear victim impact statements from families who'd lost parents, siblings, children to compliance optimization protocols he'd designed.

Make him confront Claire Thurmond's drawing and explain —under oath, on broadcast feed, with the galaxy watching—why quarterly earnings justified an eight-year-old's death. Why a tiny percent profit improvement required removing a child who drew clouds she'd never seen. Why data point four thousand, one hundred and thirty-seven deserved thirty seconds of review before authorization.

Make him sit there. Day after day. Week after week. However long justice required. No corporate lawyers blocking evidence. No procedural delays protecting him from accountability. No settlement agreements letting him pay fines instead of facing consequences. Just Harrison Cole in a defendant's chair, watching what his forty years of signatures had purchased with other people's lives.

Death would have been easier. For both of them.

Justice was harder. Justice required him to face it awake.

"Transport him." Josephine's voice stayed cold. Empty. The fury buried under legal precision because that was the only way this worked. The only way Claire's death meant something beyond vengeance. "JUDGMENT, confirm broadcast received."

JUDGMENT's voice came through her neural link. Quiet. Almost gentle. The tone the dreadnought AI used when it recognized human emotional processing interfering with tactical assessment. "Confirmed, Josephine. Earth and station populations witnessed legal surrender acceptance under Pre-Collapse Article 472. Trial record established. Documentary evidence preserved. Well done."

She didn't feel like she'd done well.

She felt like she'd failed Claire by not pulling the trigger. Failed the eight-year-old girl who'd died shielding her father, who'd never seen real clouds, who'd trusted that someone would eventually care enough to make the killing stop. One shot would have delivered immediate justice. One shot would have made Claire's death mean something visceral and final instead of abstract legal proceedings.

But failure to honor emotion didn't mean failure to honor principle.

Josephine forced herself to breathe. To let the tactical overlay finish updating. To accept that legal precision sometimes required choosing law over satisfaction, framework over fury, institutional legitimacy over personal closure.

Harrison Cole was led past her toward the corridor, mag-cuffs secured around wrists that had never held a weapon or signed an order while watching someone die. Grim's Unit-4 and Unit-2 flanked him in escort formation, professional and restrained despite having the capability to execute him in zero-point-seven seconds if she gave the order. His face showed the first real fear she'd seen since he'd surrendered. Not fear of death. Fear of something worse.

Fear of accountability.

Fear of facing every authorization he'd signed when he thought the numbers wouldn't ever become names again. When compliance optimization meant spreadsheet cells, not children bleeding out in enforcement squad corridors. When quarterly profit targets existed separate from the millions of human beings who'd been eliminated to achieve them.

Cole's lawyers followed him, still protesting, still citing regulations, still treating this like corporate litigation where enough procedural delays eventually led to settlement agreements and sealed records. They didn't understand yet. There would be no settlement. No sealed records. No quiet resolution where executives paid fines and promised to implement better oversight protocols.

There would be trials. Broadcast trials. Comprehensive documentation presented to a galaxy that had lived under corporate optimization without knowing who'd signed the elimination orders.

Josephine watched Cole disappear around the corridor junction, AD-unit escort maintaining tactical formation despite the prisoner's obvious defeat. Then she turned toward the boardroom entrance where six other executives waited. Six more surrender declarations. Six more arrests. Six more names to add to the prosecution list.

Their lawyers stood visible through the doorway, already preparing arguments. Already calculating how to exploit Pre-Collapse statute books for procedural advantage. Already assuming this worked like the corporate tribunals they'd manipulated for decades.

They were about to learn otherwise.

"McCready." Josephine's voice carried command authority despite the emotional exhaustion threatening to collapse her where she stood. "Secure the remaining defendants. Same custody protocols. They surrender or they die. Their choice. Sixty seconds."

"Understood." McCready moved forward, signaling the AD-units to establish new perimeter. His voice dropped to private channel. "You made the right call, Josephine. The hard call. But the right one."

She hoped he was correct. Hoped legal precision mattered more than emotional closure. Hoped Claire would understand why her prosecutor chose trials over bullets.

Hoped the galaxy watching understood the difference between justice and vengeance.

Justice wasn't finished. Justice was just beginning.

And she was going to make sure every single one of them faced it awake—even when facing it asleep would have been so much easier for everyone involved.

CHAPTER TWENTY-EIGHT

McCready's team moved through the boardroom door with practiced precision, weapons raised but not firing. The private security had already surrendered, weapons stacked in the corner like so much useless metal. The lawyers stood to one side, pale and silent. And behind the massive executive conference table sat seven people who'd spent decades believing themselves untouchable.

Harrison Cole stood at the head of the table, arms crossed, jaw set. The others looked worse: the CFO had her head in her hands, the Operations VP stared at the ceiling, the HR Director kept glancing at the door like escape might suddenly appear.

Josephine entered last. She didn't rush. Her weapon stayed holstered. This wasn't a firefight anymore.

This was an arrest.

"Harrison Cole," she said, her voice carrying across the boardroom. "Victoria Chen, CFO. Robert Mendez, Operations Vice President. Sonia Kim, Human Resources Director. Thomas Liu, Legal Director. Marcus Okonkwo, Security Director. Eileen Carver, Communications Director. You are all under arrest for crimes against humanity under Pre-Collapse Article 472."

McCready's team began securing the room. Two operators moved to the server banks along the wall, connecting portable terminals. Wraith's interface, transmitted from JUDGMENT via encrypted link, began pulling data. The screens along the walls lit up with file transfers: authorization codes streaming past, casualty metrics updating in real-time, profit projections showing the correlation between quarterly earnings and human suffering.

Forty years of corporate records. Forty years of systematic exploitation. Every authorization signature. Every compliance optimization. Every decision that treated people as numbers on a spreadsheet.

Downloading in real-time while the architects watched.

Harrison Cole's eyes tracked the scrolling data. His own signatures flashing past, time-stamped and cataloged. Victoria Chen turned her head away, but the reflections on the polished table showed her the same files. There was nowhere in this room that wasn't displaying their crimes.

"You have the right to remain silent," Josephine continued, pulling up the formal protocol she'd memorized at JAG Academy. "Anything you say will be used against you in your prosecution. You have the right to legal counsel." She gestured to the three lawyers. "Counsel is present."

Cole's face twisted. "This is illegal. You're pirates. Terrorists."

Josephine ignored him. She pulled out a tablet and began the formal identification process. "Harrison Cole, CEO, Apex Consortium. Date of birth?"

He didn't answer.

"Date of birth will be confirmed via biometric scan," Josephine said. JUDGMENT's sensors, feeding through her tablet, flashed confirmation. "Confirmed. Harrison Cole, age fifty-seven." She moved to the next person. "Victoria Chen, CFO, Apex Consortium."

The woman looked up, tears streaming down her face. "I didn't... I was just doing my job."

"Date of birth?" Josephine's voice didn't change.

"March… March fourteenth, twenty-nine sixty-two."

"Confirmed." Josephine moved down the line. Each executive identified. Each formally arrested. The legal framework applied with surgical precision, even here, even now, with the station still echoing from firefights and the broadcast still showing Claire's drawing.

McCready approached, his voice low. "Servers are secure. Wraith's got full access. They're copying everything to JUDG-MENT's archives."

"Chain of custody?"

"Documented. Time-stamped. Broadcast to Earth and the station." McCready glanced at the executives. "They're watching their crimes get cataloged in real-time."

Josephine nodded. She turned back to the seven people at the table. "Personal devices will be confiscated as evidence. You will be secured separately pending trial. You will not communicate with each other or with any personnel outside this room without legal counsel present."

One of the lawyers stepped forward, an older man with gray hair and an expensive suit that cost more than most workers earned in a year. "My clients are prepared to cooperate. We request reasonable accommodations and—"

"Your clients will be treated according to Pre-Collapse Article 472 standards," Josephine said. "Which means they get food, water, medical care if needed, and legal representation. They don't get accommodations. They don't get negotiations. They get a trial."

The lawyer's mouth opened. Closed. He nodded once.

McCready's operators finished with the first server bank and moved to the next. Wraith's download progress showed on Josephine's tablet: thirty-eight percent complete. Forty years of data took time, even with JUDGMENT's processing power.

Harrison Cole watched the progress bar creeping across the

screen behind him. His crossed arms had dropped. His jaw wasn't quite so set anymore.

"How long?" Josephine asked McCready.

"Four minutes for the download. Another two to verify integrity."

Six minutes. Josephine could wait six minutes. She'd waited this long.

The download completed. Wraith's confirmation flashed on Josephine's tablet: full data integrity verified, chain of custody established, archives secured on JUDGMENT and transmitted to Earth.

Harrison Cole's defiance had calcified into something harder. "This is illegal," he said again, his voice louder now. "You're pirates. Terrorists. You have no authority to—"

"The evidence in this room will determine that at trial," Josephine said. She glanced at her tablet. "Which begins in thirty minutes."

The CFO, Victoria Chen, made a sound between a sob and a gasp. "Thirty minutes? We need time to prepare. We need to consult with—"

"Your counsel is present," Josephine said. "You have thirty minutes to consult."

Robert Mendez, the Operations VP, hadn't spoken since his arrest. He still stared at the ceiling, his hands flat on the conference table like he was trying to hold himself down. His lips moved, counting something. Or maybe praying.

Sonia Kim, HR Director, leaned toward one of the lawyers. "What about plea deals? If we cooperate, if we provide testimony against—"

"There are no plea deals," Josephine said.

The lawyer beside Kim cleared his throat. "Under Pre-Collapse Article 472, the tribunal has discretion to—"

"No plea deals." Josephine's voice didn't rise. It didn't need to.

"There is evidence. There is testimony. There is verdict. There is sentence. That's all."

Kim's face went white. She looked at the other executives. At Cole, still standing. At Chen, crying quietly into her hands. At Mendez, still staring at nothing. At Thomas Liu, the Legal Director, who'd crafted the legal frameworks that made all of this possible. At Marcus Okonkwo, Security Director, who'd commanded the forces that enforced compliance. At Eileen Carver, Communications Director, who'd spun every atrocity into market necessity.

Frozen in various states of shock. Realization settling in like ice.

"You can't just—" Kim started.

"I can," Josephine said. "And I will."

Thomas Liu, the lawyer who'd become an executive, leaned forward. His voice was careful, measured. The voice of someone trying to find an angle. "Under Article 472, defendants have the right to adequate time to prepare a defense. Thirty minutes is insufficient for cases of this complexity."

"Article 472 also allows for expedited proceedings in combat zones," Josephine said. "This is a combat zone. The station is still under contested control. Expedited protocols apply."

"The station isn't contested," Liu said. "You control it. You admitted as much."

"Then you should have surrendered sooner." Josephine's voice didn't change. "Thirty minutes."

McCready stood near the door, watching Josephine work. His weapon was slung, his posture relaxed, but his eyes tracked every movement in the room. He'd seen her prosecute before, back at JAG Academy. He'd watched her tear apart defense arguments with the same precision she used to clear rooms.

But this was different. This was forty years of crimes distilled into one boardroom. Seven people who'd built an empire on suffering. And Josephine, standing in front of them, delivering justice with the calm of someone who'd already decided every outcome.

Terrifying, McCready thought. Not because she was angry. Because she wasn't.

Cole took a step forward. McCready's hand drifted toward his weapon, but Cole stopped, just close enough to make his point. "You think you're delivering justice? You're no different than we are. You kill. You invade. You take what you want and call it law."

Josephine met his eyes. "The difference," she said, "is that I give you a trial. You never gave one to Claire Thurmond."

Cole's jaw worked. "I signed thousands of documents. I can't be held responsible for—"

"You'll be held responsible for every signature in your files," Josephine said. "Every authorization. Every death quota. Every compliance metric that classified humans as targets." She tapped her tablet. "We have the files. We have the timestamps. We have your signature on Claire's authorization. Four minutes and fifty-six seconds between your signature and her death."

The room went quiet. Even the CFO's crying stopped.

"Thirty minutes," Josephine said again. "Consult with your counsel. Prepare your defense. When court convenes, you'll have your chance to speak."

She turned and walked toward the door. McCready fell in beside her.

"You think they'll try to run?" he asked quietly.

"Where would they go?" Josephine glanced back at the seven executives, sitting or standing at their conference table. The same table where they'd authorized atrocities. The same room where they'd built quarterly projections on human suffering. "We control the station. They know it's over."

"Then why the trial?"

Josephine stopped at the door. "Because that's what makes us different."

McCready nodded. He'd expected that answer. It was the only answer Josephine would ever give.

Outside the boardroom, McCready sealed the door and posted guards. Two of his team, veterans who'd been with them since the docking bay breach. He checked the time: twenty-six minutes until tribunal.

Josephine stood in the corridor, pulling up the tribunal protocols on her tablet. The formal structure she'd need. The evidence presentation order. The legal framework that would turn this boardroom into a court.

"All seven accounted for," McCready said. "Evidence secured. Security neutralized. Station's ours."

Josephine looked up from the tablet. "Then let's give them their day in court."

McCready tilted his head. "In there? The same room where they—"

"Authorized atrocities," Josephine finished. "Yes. The same room. They built an empire in that boardroom. They'll face justice in it too."

She walked back to the door. McCready opened it for her. The executives looked up, startled, like they'd hoped the next thirty minutes might last forever.

Josephine didn't enter. She just stood in the doorway, looking at the massive conference table. The expensive chairs. The screens covering three walls, designed to show profit projections and market analyses and all the sanitized metrics that hid decades of suffering.

"JUDGMENT," she said quietly.

The AI's voice came through her comm, calm and precise. "Yes, Josephine."

"Display Claire's drawing on the main screen."

A pause. Then, "Confirmed."

The largest screen in the boardroom flickered. Corporate

logos vanished. Stock tickers disappeared. And in their place, filling the entire wall, appeared a child's drawing.

Clouds. Bright and white and beautiful. Drawn by a girl who'd never seen a real one.

With the words, in careful letters: *For Casper, for being brave.*

Victoria Chen made a sound like she'd been struck. Sonia Kim looked away. Robert Mendez closed his eyes.

Harrison Cole stared at the drawing. His face had gone very still.

"Twenty-three minutes," Josephine said. "Court convenes at eleven hundred hours. The defendants will stand when called."

She closed the door.

McCready watched the executives through the reinforced glass window. "You think they understand?"

"They will," Josephine said. "When I read the charges. When they hear the testimony. When they see the evidence." She looked at Claire's drawing, still visible through the window, dominating the room where profit had always dominated before. "They'll understand exactly what they did."

"And then?"

"And then justice."

McCready checked his weapon. Checked the guards. Checked the corridor approaches. Everything secure. Everything ready. He'd been in combat for most of his adult life. He knew how to prepare a position. How to hold ground. How to execute a mission.

This was different. This was an execution of a different kind.

"Twenty minutes," he said.

Josephine nodded. She was already reviewing the evidence files. The casualty counts: four-point-eight million deaths authorized across forty years of operations. The authorization signatures: each executive's name attached to specific death warrants, compliance quotas, optimization targets. The profit metrics built on death: quarterly earnings tied directly to casualty rates, bonuses calculated from human suffering.

Her tablet showed Claire's file near the top. Age eight. Compliance optimization target. Authorization signature: Harrison Cole. Timestamp: 14:37:22. Time of death: 14:42:18.

Four minutes and fifty-six seconds.

Josephine's hands were steady on the tablet. They had been steady when she arrested Cole. Steady when she read him his rights. Steady when she told him there would be no plea deals.

They'd be steady when she read the charges. When she presented the evidence. When she pronounced the verdict.

When she authorized the sentence.

She'd waited long enough.

They'd all waited long enough.

Claire's face looked back at her from the boardroom screen. Eight years old. Drew clouds she never saw because she'd spent her entire life in the lower levels of a tower designed to keep people like her from ever seeing the sky.

"All right," Josephine said quietly. "Let's do this."

McCready checked the guards one more time. Checked the door seals. Checked the broadcast feed that would transmit the entire tribunal to Earth and the workers watching from every corner of this station.

The tribunal was about to begin.

And forty years of Apex Consortium was about to end.

CHAPTER TWENTY-NINE

The boardroom had been repurposed in thirty minutes flat.

Josephine stood at what used to be the head of the executive conference table. Behind her, the presentation screens that had once displayed quarterly earnings projections now showed legal protocols from Pre-Collapse Article 472. The plush CEO chairs where Harrison Cole and his six fellow executives had authorized atrocities now served as the defendant dock.

Seven faces stared back at her. Some defiant. Some broken. All guilty.

McCready had positioned security at every entrance. Grim's AD-units stood silent along the walls, optical sensors tracking every movement. The broadcast equipment Wraith had configured transmitted to every screen on the station and every network on Earth.

This was battlefield tribunal protocol. No appeals. No delays. Justice delivered before the blood dried.

The three station lawyers sat at a makeshift defense table, their discomfort visible. These corporate attorneys had spent careers protecting Apex from liability. Now they faced the impossible task of defending their former employers against documented genocide.

The senior attorney stood. His voice carried resignation.

"We will represent our clients to the best of our ability under the circumstances."

Not defiant. Not heroic. Professional.

Josephine met his eyes.

"That's all anyone can ask. The prosecution will present evidence. The defense will respond. Justice will be done."

She turned to face the seven executives.

"This tribunal is convened under Pre-Collapse Article 472, Section 7. Accelerated battlefield protocols are in effect. The defendants are charged with crimes against humanity. Systematic murder. Enslavement. Torture. All for corporate profit."

Harrison Cole opened his mouth.

"Save it for testimony," Josephine said. "You'll get your chance to speak. We'll all hear what you have to say."

She activated the first evidence file.

Claire Thurmond's face filled every screen.

"Eight years old," Josephine said. "Drew pictures of clouds she'd never seen. Lived her entire life on Level 47 of Cascade Tower. Never saw sunlight. Never saw the sky."

She pulled up the next file.

"Authorization for compliance optimization. Subject: Claire Thurmond. Age: eight. Threat assessment: minimal. Recommendation: elimination. Reason: efficiency metrics. Signed by Harrison Cole, Chief Executive Officer, Apex Consortium."

The timestamp showed on every screen.

"Thirty seconds from file creation to executive signature. Zero seconds of hesitation."

Harrison Cole's face had gone pale. The other executives stared at their former colleague.

Josephine advanced to the next exhibit.

"You didn't inherit Meridian's atrocities. You didn't find yourself caught in a system you couldn't change. You *ordered* these crimes. You expanded them. You optimized them for quarterly earnings."

Document after document filled the screens. Casualty quotas with executive signatures. Compliance metrics tied to executive bonuses. Profit projections built on projected human suffering.

"Compliance optimization program, initiated by Cole, approved by the full executive board. Target: fifteen percent reduction in labor costs through attrition. Translation: kill enough workers to reduce payroll without disrupting production."

She pulled up internal communications.

"Email from Cole to Operations VP Mendez: 'The numbers justify aggressive compliance measures. Authorize whatever force necessary to meet Q3 targets.' Mendez's response: 'Understood. Deploying enforcement squads to Levels 40 through 50.'"

The Operations VP stared at the floor.

"Forty-three deaths in Q3 alone. Levels 40 through 50. Including Claire Thurmond."

Josephine turned to face Cole directly.

"You killed a child to meet quarterly targets. You authorized her death in thirty seconds because it was efficient. Because it was profitable. Because you could."

The defense attorney stood.

"Objection. The prosecutor is editorializing."

"Sustained," Josephine said. "I'll rephrase. The evidence shows Harrison Cole signed the authorization that resulted in Claire Thurmond's death. The evidence shows he did so in thirty seconds. The evidence shows this authorization was one of four million, eight hundred thousand similar authorizations he signed over forty years."

She met the attorney's eyes.

"Better?"

The attorney sat down.

Josephine turned to the side of the room.

"The prosecution calls its next witness."

Voss stepped forward from where she'd been standing with McCready. She carried a data tablet. Her face showed the strain of the past thirty-seven days, but her voice remained steady.

"State your name and position for the record."

"Voss. Intelligence specialist. Formerly employed by Meridian Authority under contract to Apex Consortium."

"You processed authorization requests for Apex executives?"

"Yes."

"Describe the authorization system."

Voss activated her tablet. Platform authorization logs filled the screens, replacing the evidence documents.

"Every death order in this system went through with single-signature approval. No oversight. No review. No delay."

She pulled up a workflow diagram.

"Enforcement squad identifies target. Files compliance optimization request. Request routes to executive level. Single signature authorizes action. Authorization transmits to squad. Target eliminated. Process complete."

Her voice remained clinical, the way she'd once processed these authorizations as routine paperwork.

"Average time from request to authorization: forty-five seconds. Average time from authorization to execution: six minutes."

She looked at the seven executives.

"I processed these authorizations for years. Thousands of them. I never questioned the system. I never asked what 'compliance optimization' meant. I filed the paperwork and moved to the next request."

A pause.

"That's how Claire Thurmond, age eight, was marked for compliance optimization. One signature from Harrison Cole. Thirty seconds for him to decide. Done."

The defense attorney stood.

"Objection. The witness is testifying against her own complicity, which undermines her credibility as a prosecution witness."

Josephine turned to the attorney.

"The witness is establishing the systemic nature of the crimes. Her testimony shows this wasn't isolated incidents by rogue officers. This was corporate policy, executed at scale, enabled by designed efficiency."

She looked at Voss.

"Continue."

Voss met her eyes. Something passed between them. Understanding. Shared weight.

"I'm testifying against myself as much as them. We all enabled this. The executives authorized it. I processed it. Enforcement squads executed it. We all had our roles."

The defense attorney sat down. No further objection.

Josephine let the silence hold for a moment. Every screen on the station showed Voss standing in that boardroom, carrying the weight of her confession.

"When this is over," Josephine said, "we build oversight protocols. Every compliance review, every casualty metric, every authorization that could result in loss of life gets automatic investigation triggers. Named after the victims."

Voss met her eyes.

"Claire Protocol," Voss said. "Her name on every review that could have saved her."

Josephine nodded.

"Claire Protocol. So no one can process a death authorization in thirty seconds again. So no one can sign away a child's life without being forced to see what they're doing."

She turned back to the executives.

"The witness has testified to systemic failure. The evidence shows individual culpability. The tribunal will now deliberate on verdict and sentence."

Harrison Cole stood.

"You can't do this. We had legal authority. We operated within the law. Meridian's law gave us the right to maintain order through whatever means necessary."

Josephine looked at him.

"The law you're citing was written by the same executives who profited from its enforcement. Pre-Collapse Article 472 supersedes all post-war corporate regulations. You don't get to write the rules and then claim immunity under them."

She gestured to McCready.

"Secure the defendants. Deliberation begins in five minutes."

The seven executives were led to holding positions along the wall. Grim's AD-units maintained watch. The broadcast continued, carrying every moment to Earth and throughout the station.

Josephine pulled up the final evidence summary.

The verdict was never in question.

The only question was whether she could deliver it without becoming what she hunted.

CHAPTER THIRTY

The CFO spoke first. Twenty-seven years with Apex Consortium. Board member for eleven. Voice cracking around the edges.

"I was just following market forces."

Josephine's finger tapped twice on the evidence tablet. Screen three lit with authorization chains. Profit optimization metrics. Casualty projections. Her signature on seventeen separate compliance documents.

"You *created* those market forces," she said. "Next."

Operations VP. Tried the collective defense. The board decided collectively. Standard corporate strategy. Diffuse responsibility until no one carries the weight.

"The evidence shows individual signatures on individual death warrants." Josephine scrolled without looking. She'd memorized the counts. "Your signature on forty-seven authorizations. Your quarterly earnings tied to compliance optimization. Your bonus structure based on casualty metrics."

Pause. Two seconds.

"Next."

The HR Director attempted the ignorance defense. I didn't

personally order any deaths. Just designed the systems. Just built the metrics. Just created the frameworks that classified humans as optimization targets.

Josephine leaned forward.

"You designed the compliance metrics that classified humans as optimization targets. You built the evaluation criteria that rewarded death. You created the performance review system that made murder profitable."

She pulled up his personnel file. His own words, submitted quarterly.

"Your system documentation states: 'Workforce optimization through targeted compliance enforcement yields twenty-three percent efficiency improvement.' Efficiency. That's what you called it when a thousand people died."

The HR Director's mouth opened. Closed. Nothing came out.

"Next."

Each CEO rose. Each delivered prepared defense. Each defense demolished with documentation they'd signed themselves. Marketing Executive: I just handled communications. Supply Chain Director: I only managed logistics. Technology Officer: I merely implemented systems.

Josephine responded with evidence. Communications planning casualty announcements. Logistics routing body disposal. Systems optimizing kill quotas based on demographic data.

The lawyers tried objections. Josephine overruled with precedent citations. Pre-Collapse Article 472 accelerated tribunal protocols. Battlefield justice. Legal but fast. Professional but efficient.

Josephine stood when Harrison Cole rose for his defense.

The boardroom went silent.

Cole spoke with the certainty of someone who'd never been challenged. Forty years at the top. CEO for eighteen. Master of the corporate defense.

"I signed thousands of documents. I can't remember one child."

The words dropped into perfect stillness.

Josephine didn't move. Didn't blink. When she spoke, her voice came very quiet.

"Her name was Claire."

Cole blinked. First crack in the corporate mask.

"She was eight years old. She drew clouds she'd never seen because she'd never been outside. She drew them because stories said they were beautiful." Josephine's finger tapped the tablet. Claire's authorization filled every screen. His signature. His timestamp. His decision.

"You optimized her death for quarterly earnings."

Pause. Three seconds. McCready counted them from his position by the door.

"You can't *remember?*"

Cole's defense lawyer tried to intervene. Josephine raised one hand. The gesture cut him off mid-syllable.

"She spent forty-seven days drawing those clouds. Different angles. Different times of day. Trying to understand something she'd never experience." Josephine pulled up the file. Claire's complete record. Every authorization. Every compliance metric. Every profit projection built on an eight-year-old's death.

"You signed her execution in thirty seconds. Zero hesitation. Filed it under workforce optimization. Collected your bonus three weeks later."

The silence in the tribunal had weight. Even the station feeds carried it..

Cole tried recovery. Fell back on scale. "I signed thousands of documents. Can't remember every detail. Operational necessity. The bigger picture."

Josephine let him talk. Let him hang himself with corporate logic. Let him explain how killing children becomes acceptable when you're optimizing for shareholder value.

When he finished, she stood silent for five seconds.

"The defense rests," she said to his lawyers. They had nothing to add.

Even his defense counsel went quiet. Some defenses are indefensible. Some arguments poison everyone who makes them.

McCready watched Josephine's hands. Steady. The same hands that had hesitated for five seconds before sparing Cole's life. No hesitation now. This was law. This was justice. This was why she'd chosen trial over execution.

So Cole could destroy himself in front of everyone.

Josephine delivered the verdict without pause.

"Final arguments complete. Evidence overwhelming. Testimony documented." She stood at the prosecutor's position. The same table where these executives had authorized atrocities for profit. The same screens that had displayed quarterly earnings now showed casualty counts.

"Guilty on all counts."

She spoke each name. Each charge. Each sentence.

"Harrison Cole. Chief Executive Officer. Crimes against humanity. Genocide. Corruption of legal process. Verdict: Guilty. Sentence: Death."

"Victoria Chen. Chief Financial Officer. Crimes against humanity. Genocide. Corruption of legal process. Verdict: Guilty. Sentence: Death."

Down the line. Seven executives. Seven verdicts. Seven death sentences.

Cole started screaming when she reached his name. Stood

from the defendant's table. Guards moved but Josephine waved them back.

"You can't do this!" Cole's voice cracked. "This isn't a real court! You're terrorists! This is murder!"

Josephine waited until he ran out of air. When she spoke, her voice carried the weight of everyone who'd died in Apex's compliance optimization.

"This is the only real court you'll ever face. One that actually holds power accountable."

She tapped the authorization order. JUDGMENT received the signal.

"Execution authorized. Immediate."

The boardroom doors sealed. Executive emergency protocols. The same system designed to protect these CEOs from accountability now locked them in for justice.

Outside workers throughout the station started cheering. The audio bled through station communications. Celebration of accountability. Relief that someone finally faced consequences.

Cole kept screaming. The CFO collapsed crying. The Operations VP sat frozen. The others just stared at the screens showing their own documented atrocities.

Justice was coming.

Josephine stood at her station, Claire's drawing beside the evidence tablet. The tribunal session ended at 1200 hours exactly.

Justice had taken thirty minutes.

Forty years of crimes. Thirty minutes of accountability.

She filed that ratio for later. When they built the new systems. When they designed the oversight that should have existed all along.

When they made sure Claire's name meant something more than a compliance optimization target.

The boardroom stayed sealed as the firing squad moved into position.

Josephine never looked away from the screens.

She'd promised Claire justice.

Now, she would deliver it.

Now came the harder part.

Building something worth what Claire should have lived to see.

CHAPTER THIRTY-ONE

The tribunal chamber fell silent as Josephine activated the broadcast. This was what legitimate authority looked like when it held power accountable.

"The defendants have been found guilty on all counts," she said. Her voice carried the weight of every authorization she'd signed, every decision she'd made since JUDGMENT found her in the snow. "Sentence will be carried out under Pre-Collapse Article 472, subsection nine. Military tribunal protocols in effect."

She'd prosecuted dozens of war crimes cases in Kandahar. Seen justice delivered in courtrooms that doubled as bunkers, heard verdicts rendered while mortars fell outside. This wasn't different. This was what combat prosecution looked like when the shooting stopped but the war wasn't over.

The CFO stood first. His lawyers had tried defending him—market forces, fiduciary duty, legal obligations to shareholders. All of it evaporated when confronted with the casualty quotas bearing his signature. Two hundred and seventeen thousand deaths across his tenure. Each one documented. Each one signed.

"Read your crimes," Josephine said.

He hesitated. The guards waited. The broadcast continued.

"I…" His voice cracked. "I authorized profit optimization protocols that resulted in two hundred seventeen thousand casualties. I signed compliance metrics that classified human lives as acceptable losses. I prioritized quarterly earnings over—" He stopped. Couldn't finish.

"Continue."

"Over human survival." The words came out barely audible. "I acknowledge the charges against me."

The firing squad stood ready. Six defected security personnel who'd chosen law over executives, weapons raised. They'd volunteered for this. Said it was owed.

"Sentence carried out," Josephine said.

The report echoed through the chamber. The CFO collapsed. Medical verification took five seconds. Professional. Clean. Justice delivered without ceremony.

"Next defendant," Josephine said.

The Operations VP stepped forward. Her defense had centered on collective board decisions, shared responsibility, organizational complexity. The evidence showed individual signatures on individual death warrants. Forty-seven authorizations bearing her name alone. Forty-seven families destroyed for operational efficiency.

She read her crimes without prompting. Steady, almost mechanical. "I authorized forty-seven compliance actions resulting in termination of personnel classified as optimization targets. I implemented efficiency protocols that prioritized productivity over worker survival. I acknowledge the charges against me."

Another report. Another body. Another verification.

Justice moved with methodical precision through the HR Director who'd designed the metrics, the Legal Director who'd provided the justifications, the Security Director who'd enforced the protocols, the Communications Director who'd buried the evidence. Each one read their crimes. Each one acknowledged guilt. Each one faced the consequence.

Six executions. Eighteen minutes. No speeches. No last words beyond the acknowledgment required by law.

Josephine watched each one fall. Counted each verification. Signed each authorization. This was what justice looked like when it actually held power accountable. Not perfect. Not painless. But legitimate.

Harrison Cole stood last.

He'd watched the others fall. Watched them read their crimes, acknowledge their guilt, face the firing squad with whatever dignity remained. Now it was his turn. CEO of Apex Consortium. The man who'd signed Claire Thurmond's death authorization between morning coffee and a budget review.

"I will not participate in this farce," he said. "This is murder. I demand immediate contact with—"

"You demanded nothing for Claire Thurmond when you signed her death warrant," Josephine said.

Her voice cut through his protest like a blade. She activated the display behind him. The authorization document appeared. Claire's name. His signature. The timestamp that had haunted her since Voss first showed her the files.

"You will acknowledge your crimes," Josephine said.

"I refuse. This isn't a legitimate—"

"You signed this document at 14:37:22." She enlarged the timestamp. Made it fill the screen. "Claire Thurmond died at 14:42:18. Four minutes and fifty-six seconds between your signature and her death."

Cole stared at the document. His signature. Undeniable. Documented. Broadcast to billions.

"I signed thousands of documents," he said. The authority was cracking. "I can't remember one child—"

"Her name was Claire." Josephine's voice dropped to something quiet and cold. "She was eight years old. You optimized her death for quarterly earnings."

The silence in the chamber felt physical. Even the lawyers had nothing to say. Some defenses were indefensible.

"You can't remember," Josephine said. "That's the problem. You signed so many death warrants that one child doesn't register. But I remember her. And you will acknowledge what you did to her."

She displayed the authorization again. Claire's name. His signature. Four minutes and fifty-six seconds.

"Acknowledge your crimes."

The silence stretched. Ten seconds. Twenty.

"I acknowledge..." His voice broke. The corporate authority shattered. "I acknowledge the charges against me."

"Read them," Josephine said.

Cole looked at the screen. At his signature. At Claire's name.

"I authorized compliance optimization that resulted in..." He stopped. Couldn't continue.

"Four-point-eight million deaths," Josephine said. "Including Claire Thurmond, age eight. Continue."

"Four-point-eight million deaths. Including Claire Thurmond." His voice came out hollow. "I prioritized profit over human life. I signed authorizations without review. I optimized suffering for corporate earnings."

The words fell into silence.

"I acknowledge the charges against me."

Josephine watched him stand there. The man who'd signed Claire's death between coffee and budget reviews. Who couldn't remember one child among thousands. Who'd built an empire on optimized atrocity.

"For Claire Thurmond, age eight," Josephine said. "For millions of others who died under your administration. Justice is done."

The firing squad raised their weapons.

"Sentence carried out."

The report echoed through the chamber one final time.

Medical verification came faster this time. Five seconds. Efficiency born from repetition. Harrison Cole was dead. The man who'd signed Claire Thurmond's death authorization between morning coffee and budget reviews would never sign another document.

Josephine stood before the broadcast. The silence stretched across orbital and planetary distances both.

Then the applause started.

Not celebration. Relief. Forty years of oppression ending in methodical justice. Firing squads and legal precision and documented evidence holding power accountable. Workers across the station processing what they'd witnessed. Seven executives who'd wielded absolute authority facing the first consequence they couldn't delegate.

Josephine let the sound continue for ten seconds. Then raised her hand. The silence returned.

"Apex Consortium is dissolved," she said. "Under Pre-Collapse Article 472, subsection twelve, corporate authority is forfeit following conviction for crimes against humanity. As of this moment, you are free."

The words echoed through the station quarters. Free. A word most of them had never heard applied to themselves.

"Interim governance will be established," Josephine continued. "JUDGMENT will maintain security and life support during transition. Workers' council elections will commence in seventy-two hours. You will choose your own representation. You will establish your own governance. Justice doesn't end here—it begins."

She glanced at the screen beside her, the drawing. "Legal authority has been restored," she said. "Not through conquest. Through prosecution. Not through occupation. Through law.

This station belongs to the people who built it, maintained it, lived in it while executives profited from their suffering."

The broadcast continued to every corner of the station. Every apartment. Every corridor. Every break room where workers had gathered to watch justice delivered in real-time.

"Seventy-two hours," Josephine said. "Then you decide what comes next."

She ended the broadcast. The screens across the station went dark, but Claire's drawing remained. Her legacy would reach further than she'd ever imagined. Elections in seventy-two hours. Democracy built from the ruins of optimized atrocity.

Justice delivered. Now came the building.

The tribunal chamber emptied in stages.

First the bodies. Medical personnel removing them with efficiency. Seven executions documented and archived. Evidence of justice delivered under legal authority. Clean. Legitimate.

Then the guards. The defected security who'd volunteered for firing squad duty. They saluted as they left. Josephine returned it. They'd chosen to pull those triggers. Said they'd enforced Apex's orders for too long. This was the least they could do.

Then the lawyers. Cole's defense counsel looking shell-shocked. They'd represented their clients to the best of their ability under the circumstances. It hadn't been enough. Some defenses were indefensible when confronted with documented atrocity.

Then the observers. The handful of station workers who'd been present as witnesses. Their faces showed the same thing. Not celebration. Relief. Justice delivered to people who'd spent decades believing justice was something that happened to them, not for them.

The chamber emptied.

Josephine sat alone at the prosecutor's table. The table that had been the executive boardroom twelve hours ago. Where Harrison Cole had sat in authority while Claire Thurmond died light-seconds away in Cascade Tower. Where profit optimization had been discussed in the same breath as compliance metrics and quarterly earnings.

Seven authorizations for execution sat in front of her. Her signature on each one. Seven lives ended by legal process. Seven people dead because she'd judged them guilty and sentenced them to die.

It was over.

Josephine glanced at her hands. They were shaking.

She noticed it distantly. The tremor in her fingers. The way her breath came shallow and quick. The weight settling into her bones like something physical. Seven executions authorized. Seven people dead on her order. Justice delivered under legal framework. Legitimate authority holding power accountable.

Her hands continued to tremble.

McCready appeared in the doorway. She didn't hear him approach. Just looked up and he was there, concern on his face. The same look he'd worn in Kandahar when she'd prosecuted her first battlefield tribunal. When she'd learned that justice in combat zones looked different than justice in courtrooms back home.

"Josephine," he said. "You should rest."

She didn't move. Couldn't quite make herself stand. The tribunal chamber felt too big without the bodies, the guards, the observers. Just her and seven authorization signatures and one child's drawing of clouds.

"I will," she said. "Just... not yet."

McCready waited. Didn't push. Didn't leave. Just stood there the way he'd stood in Kandahar after her first combat prosecution. When she'd learned that signing death warrants left marks you couldn't see but always felt.

"Seven people," Josephine said. Her voice came out quieter than intended. "I just authorized seven executions."

"Seven war criminals," McCready said. "Who murdered four-point-eight million people for profit. Who signed Claire Thurmond's death authorization like it was a supply requisition."

"I know." She looked at the authorization documents. Her signature on each one. "I know what they were. What they did. It doesn't change that I ordered them killed."

"No," McCready said. "It doesn't."

The honesty helped somehow. He wasn't minimizing it. Wasn't telling her it was necessary or justified or the right thing. Just acknowledging that she'd done it. That it had weight. That justice delivered still left marks.

Josephine sat in the silence, the weight of what she'd done settling into her bones.

"It's over," she said.

"Part of it," McCready agreed. "Now comes the building."

Seventy-two hours until elections. Workers choosing their own governance. Democracy built from the ruins of optimized atrocity. Legal framework established. Interim authority in place. Justice delivered and documented for anyone who questioned whether power could be held accountable.

Josephine looked at Claire's drawing one more time.

"Not yet," she said again.

McCready nodded. Pulled up a chair. Sat across from her. Waited. The same way he'd waited in Kandahar. The way mentors waited for students to process what combat prosecution actually cost. What justice looked like when it held power accountable.

They sat in silence. The tribunal chamber empty except for two soldiers processing the weight of justice delivered. Seven executions. Four-point-eight million casualties avenged. One child remembered.

Justice done.

Now came the living with it.

CHAPTER THIRTY-TWO

Two hours after the execution, the station was celebrating. Fermi could hear it through the bulkheads of the engineering assessment bay—voices raised in something between relief and disbelief. Someone had music playing on Level 12. Someone else was shouting about the workers' council election.

Fermi had the displays showing JUDGMENT's fuel reserves.

Twenty-two-point-three percent.

Her hands were steady on the console. They'd been shaking during the tribunal broadcast—watching Harrison Cole's face as Josephine recited the timestamp, four minutes and fifty-six seconds between signature and death—but the numbers always settled her. Numbers didn't lie. Numbers didn't make excuses. Numbers didn't sign death warrants and forget about them.

Numbers just were.

She pulled up consumption projections. Return trajectory calculations. Atmospheric entry vectors and their fuel requirements. The station's Element 115 storage manifests scrolled past her screen: forty-seven percent capacity across six secure bunkers, each one temperature-controlled and magnetically shielded according to pre-war military specifications that Apex had maintained because they didn't know how to do otherwise.

Station engineering crew hovered nearby, three techs who'd spent the last hour asking careful questions about JUDGMENT's reactor design. They'd been polite. Respectful, even. As if talking to someone who might actually know more than their corporate training manuals, instead of someone who'd spent three years under house arrest arguing with equations on her apartment walls.

Fermi had explained the quantum fusion cascade to them twice already. They still looked confused, but they were trying. That counted for something.

"Ma'am?" One of the techs—Rivera, her name badge said—gestured at the fuel display. "Is that... is that really a pre-war dreadnought's reactor efficiency? Ninety-one percent?"

"After I optimized it." Fermi didn't look up from the calculations. "It was at seventy-three when I arrived."

"That's..." Rivera trailed off, staring at the numbers. "That's impossible."

"It's uranium-233 isotope integration with magnetic containment recalibration." Fermi's fingers moved across the interface, pulling up another projection. Earth's gravity well. Atmospheric friction coefficients. The minimum fuel threshold for controlled descent through ionization layers that would turn JUDGMENT into a very expensive meteor if they got the math wrong. "The reactor doesn't care about possible or impossible. It cares about quantum state alignment and containment field geometry."

Rivera nodded slowly, clearly not understanding but smart enough not to argue with someone who'd just explained eighteen-percent efficiency gains like they were obvious.

Fermi ran the numbers again.

Current fuel: twenty-two-point-three percent.

Required for Earth return: twenty-five percent minimum, accounting for atmospheric entry deceleration, course corrections, emergency reserves, and the reality that orbital mechanics didn't forgive optimistic projections.

The math was simple. Brutal, but simple.

They didn't have enough fuel to go home.

Station reserves: forty-seven percent.

She stared at that number. Refueling JUDGMENT to fifty-five percent would be straightforward—just tedious. Connect the transfer conduits, monitor the magnetic containment during flow, verify isotope purity at each stage. Six hours of careful work, maybe eight if they remained cautious. Which they should be, because Element 115 didn't forgive sloppiness any more than orbital mechanics did.

Fifty-five percent would get them home. Easy margin, too. Thirty percent buffer for emergencies, course corrections, atmospheric uncertainties. Professional engineering standards. Safety margins that kept crews alive when Murphy's Law decided to make an appearance.

But.

Fermi pulled up the station's life support requirements. Position-keeping thrusters. Emergency reserves. The workers who'd just been liberated and would need this station to stay habitable while they figured out what came next.

The math crystallized with the inevitability of gravity.

If JUDGMENT took that fuel, the workers lost two to three months of reserves. Possibly more if the supply chains stayed disrupted. Possibly less if someone made a mistake with the rationing calculations. Either way, these people would be balancing on a very thin margin while a dreadnought sailed home with comfortable reserves.

"We can go home," Fermi said quietly, not realizing she'd spoken aloud until Rivera looked at her. "But the workers might not survive if we do."

The tech's expression shifted. "Ma'am?"

Fermi didn't answer. She was staring at the numbers again,

running them a third time because maybe she'd made a mistake. Maybe there was a calculation error, an overlooked variable, some clever optimization that would make the trade-off unnecessary.

There wasn't.

The math offered no third option. Just two futures, each one paid for with someone else's survival.

She saved the analysis to a secure partition and stood. Her legs were stiff from sitting too long, and her vision swam for a second before steadying. When had she last eaten? Before the tribunal. Before watching seven executions broadcast to every screen on the station. Before Harrison Cole acknowledged his crimes in a broken voice and died for them.

"I need to brief command," she told Rivera. "Thank you for the assistance."

"Ma'am, we didn't—"

"You listened. You tried to understand. That's more than Apex ever did." Fermi picked up her tablet, the fuel projections glowing accusingly. "The reactors are stable. Monitor the containment fields every thirty minutes. If anything shifts more than point-two percent, contact me immediately."

Rivera nodded, still looking uncertain.

Fermi left the engineering bay and walked toward the command conference room. The corridors were fuller now—workers moving with purpose instead of the defeated shuffle she'd seen in the initial boarding footage. Someone had removed the Apex logos from the bulkheads. Someone else had posted hand-drawn signs pointing toward the workers' council registration tables.

The music on Level 12 was louder here. Something upbeat, triumphant. Celebration music.

Fermi's tablet showed twenty-two-point-three percent.

The command conference room was on Level 8, near the former executive section that now housed interim governance coordination. Josephine had claimed it because it had the best communications infrastructure and the largest displays. Also, Fermi suspected, because making the executives' private conference room into a public decision-making space appealed to Josephine's sense of poetic justice.

McCready was already there, studying displays. Voss sat at one of the side terminals, cross-referencing something in the captured databases. Grim stood near the door, his optical sensors tracking movement with quiet intensity.

Josephine looked up when Fermi entered. "Doctor. We weren't expecting you for another hour."

"The math doesn't take that long." Fermi set her tablet on the conference table and pulled up the fuel projections. "The numbers are clear. Our return requires twenty-five percent minimum for safe atmospheric entry. We have twenty-two."

McCready straightened. "How short are we?"

"Three percent below minimum safe margin. Which means we don't have enough fuel to go home." Fermi advanced the display to show station reserves. "Station has forty-seven percent we could take. That gets us to fifty-five percent. Easy return to Earth with thirty percent margin to spare."

She watched their faces. Josephine's expression went very still. McCready's jaw tightened. Even Voss looked up from her terminal.

"But." Fermi pulled up the life support calculations. "These people need that fuel. Position-keeping thrusters consume point-three percent per week. Life support systems consume point-two percent. Emergency reserves require maintaining at least fifteen percent buffer for catastrophic scenarios. If we take their fuel to refuel JUDGMENT, workers lose two to three months of reserves. Possibly more if supply chains stay disrupted."

The room was silent except for the soft hum of ventilation and the distant celebration still echoing through the station's corridors.

McCready spoke first. "So we either strand ourselves or strand them."

"The math offers no third option." Fermi met their eyes, each one in turn. "If we go home, these people might not have enough fuel to survive."

Josephine was staring at the numbers on the display. The precise calculations that reduced survival to percentages and trade-offs. Her hand moved unconsciously to her tablet, where Fermi knew Claire's drawing was saved.

"Then," Josephine said quietly, "we need to make a choice the math can't make for us."

Fermi walked them through it. Every number. Every calculation. Every assumption and safety margin and catastrophic scenario she'd modeled. She wasn't gentle about it. The math wasn't gentle, so neither was she.

"Twenty-five percent minimum," she said, pulling up the atmospheric entry profile. "That accounts for deceleration burn, course corrections during descent, emergency maneuvering if we encounter unexpected debris or atmospheric turbulence. It also assumes optimal conditions—no equipment failures, no reactor fluctuations, no unexpected variables."

"And if conditions aren't optimal?" McCready asked.

"Then twenty-five percent becomes twenty-eight or thirty, and we die somewhere between orbital altitude and ground impact." Fermi advanced to the next display. "Station reserves are forty-seven percent across six bunkers. We'd need approximately thirty-three percent to refuel JUDGMENT to fifty-five. That leaves station with fourteen percent."

Voss looked up sharply. "Below their emergency reserve threshold."

"Correct. Station protocol requires maintaining fifteen percent minimum for catastrophic scenarios. Hull breach, life support failure, unexpected surge in power consumption." Fermi's fingers moved across the interface, pulling up consumption rates. "At current usage, position-keeping thrusters consume point-three percent per week. Life support systems consume point-two percent. With fourteen percent reserves, they have approximately twenty-eight weeks before critical shortage. Seven months, give or take."

"Seven months," Josephine said quietly. "Assuming nothing goes wrong."

"Assuming optimal conditions. Which, as I mentioned, are never guaranteed." Fermi met Josephine's eyes. "If we take their fuel, we get home safely. But these people lose their safety margin. One equipment failure, one unexpected crisis, and they're in emergency protocols with no buffer."

Grim's display flickered: "Workers contributed fuel during Arc 03. Brought JUDGMENT from nineteen percent to twenty-two-point-three percent."

"They did." Fermi nodded toward the unit. "Individual workers donated personal rations from emergency reserves because they believed in what we were doing. They gave us three-point-three percent when they had nothing to spare. And now we're calculating whether to take another thirty-three percent from their collective reserves to ensure we can leave them behind safely."

The words landed like a physical weight.

McCready leaned back in his chair. "Options?"

"Three." Fermi pulled up the decision tree she'd built in the engineering bay. "Option A: We take the fuel. Refuel to fifty-five percent, return to Earth with comfortable margins. Workers manage on fourteen percent reserves and hope nothing goes wrong for seven months."

She advanced to the next option.

"Option B: We don't take the fuel. JUDGMENT stays orbital with twenty-two-point-three percent. Workers keep their reserves. We establish permanent presence here, coordinate with

Earth via communications, and accept that we may never return home."

Third option.

"Option C: We take partial fuel. Maybe fifteen or twenty percent from station reserves. Not enough to guarantee safe return, but better odds than twenty-two percent. Workers keep enough for longer-term security. We gamble that our partial fuel is enough, and if we're wrong, we become a very expensive crater somewhere in the Northern Hemisphere."

Nobody spoke for ten seconds. The ventilation hummed. The celebration music on Level 12 kept playing, workers who didn't know their liberation might have just traded one crisis for another.

Josephine was studying the numbers with the same expression she'd worn during the tribunal. Prosecutor's focus, breaking down evidence into constituent pieces and examining each one for flaws.

"Station supply chains," she said. "Current status?"

"Disrupted." Voss pulled up logistics data. "Apex maintained strict control over resource distribution. Six other orbital manufacturing stations depended on Pinnacle for Element 115 transfers. With executive structure dissolved, those supply agreements are void. It could take months to establish new distribution frameworks."

"So even if we leave them with adequate reserves, resupply isn't guaranteed."

"Correct."

McCready studied the tactical situation with professional detachment. "If JUDGMENT stays orbital, what's our defensive capability?"

Fermi answered. "Full weapons systems operational. Sensor arrays functional. We'd be the most powerful asset in orbital space by several orders of magnitude. No existing force could threaten this station with JUDGMENT providing protection."

"And if JUDGMENT returns to Earth, station defense?"

"Twelve destroyed weapons platforms, no replacement timeline, skeleton security force, and forty-seven thousand civilians who just learned that corporate authority isn't invincible." McCready's expression was flat. "They'd be vulnerable. Not immediately, but within weeks. Someone will notice the power vacuum. Someone will try to fill it."

Josephine's hand was still on her tablet, the drawing hidden under the fuel projections but present nonetheless.

"This station," Josephine said slowly, "represents everything we've been fighting. Corporate exploitation. Indentured servitude. Humans reduced to labor inputs and efficiency calculations." She looked up at Fermi. "And now we have to decide whether protecting them costs us our way home."

"Yes." Fermi didn't soften it. "The math is simple. The choice isn't."

Grim's display flickered again. "Justice doesn't stop at atmosphere."

Josephine almost smiled. "No. It doesn't."

Voss was watching Josephine with intensity. "We liberated them," she said quietly. "Liberation without protection is just changing which threat they face."

"And if we stay," McCready added, "we're accepting that Earth continues without JUDGMENT's direct presence. Regional governance. Law enforcement. The prosecution framework we've been building. All of it managed from orbit instead of ground level."

Fermi looked at each of them. The commander who'd built a legal framework for justice. The tactical officer who'd integrated former enemies into security forces. The intelligence analyst seeking atonement for enabling the system they'd just destroyed. The conscious AI who'd learned that choice separated machinery from purpose.

And herself. The engineer who'd spent three years under

house arrest calculating power requirements for a dreadnought she'd only heard about in rumors, hoping someone would prove she wasn't crazy.

"I can run more calculations," she said. "Model additional scenarios. Look for optimizations that might change the margins. But fundamentally, the math offers two futures." She gestured at the display. "We go home and leave them vulnerable. Or we stay and accept that Earth continues without us."

Josephine stood. Walked to the window overlooking the station's interior. Workers going about the business of processing freedom—organizing councils, posting announcements, playing music that hadn't been allowed under corporate control.

"Full team meeting," she said finally. "Everyone. Patch, Bones, Wraith, Fermi. All principals. We've made every decision together. We're not stopping now."

"When?" McCready asked.

"Sixteen hundred hours. Give people time to process what we just learned." Josephine turned back to face them. "This isn't just command deciding. This is all of us choosing what we're willing to live with."

Fermi saved the projections and closed her displays. The numbers would still be there at sixteen hundred. They'd be there tomorrow, and next week, and next month. The math didn't change based on how long you stared at it.

But the choice—the choice required more than mathematics.

She left the conference room and walked back toward the engineering bay, her tablet showing twenty-two-point-three percent like an accusation she couldn't answer. Station techs were working the reactors, following the monitoring protocols she'd established. Workers were celebrating freedom in the corridors. Somewhere on Level 12, music was still playing.

The numbers offered no third option.

But Josephine was right. They needed to make a choice the math couldn't make for them.

That was what made them human instead of equations.

CHAPTER THIRTY-THREE

Josephine stood at the head of the conference table, her hands resting on the cool metal surface. The tribunal screens had been retracted, replaced by displays showing three sets of projections. Behind her, the observation window framed Earth's curve, blue and white and impossibly distant.

Everyone was here. McCready leaned against the far wall, arms crossed, watching. Voss sat with her tablet, stylus moving in small circles. Grim's optical sensors tracked from face to face. Fermi had claimed the seat closest to the displays, eyes already studying the numbers she'd presented an hour ago.

Wraith stood near the door, silence as present as anyone's voice. Patch sprawled in her chair with the boneless ease of someone preparing to deliver bad news. Bones had positioned himself where he could see everyone, medical assessment mode never quite off.

"We have a choice to make," Josephine said. "Fermi's assessment is clear. We need to decide what happens next."

She gestured to the first display. "Option A: We take station fuel reserves. Refuel JUDGMENT to fifty-five percent capacity.

Return to Earth with comfortable margin. Leave the station to manage their own governance."

The words hung in the air like accusations.

"Option B: We stay orbital. Protect the station. Build the monitoring network Voss outlined. Accept that we may never return to Earth."

McCready shifted his weight. Didn't speak.

"Option C: We take partial fuel. Attempt to maintain both missions. Risk stranding ourselves and the station if calculations are wrong."

Patch sat up, the movement deliberate. "Earth still needs us. Ground operations are continuing. The prosecution framework we built needs enforcement, not just documentation." Her voice carried the rasp of someone who'd argued with herself first. "We proved legal authority works. Now we have to maintain it."

Bones crossed his arms. "Mass casualty capacity down there. Can't run regional healthcare systems from orbit. The medical infrastructure we started building requires personnel on the ground, not floating three hundred kilometers overhead offering commentary."

Practical arguments. Logical positions. A debate command teams had every day.

Josephine watched their faces and saw something else underneath.

McCready's gaze kept drifting to the displays showing station security sectors. Voss' stylus had stopped moving, frozen mid-circle. Grim's optical sensors held steady on the observation window, processing starfield patterns no one else could see. Fermi's hands rested flat on the table, fingers spread like she was feeling the station's structure through the metal.

This wasn't about logistics. Not really.

"Those are the options," Josephine said quietly. "The math is on the table. Now we need to decide what we do with it."

The silence stretched. Outside the window, Earth turned

beneath them, oblivious to eight people trying to choose between two missions they'd all sworn to complete.

The silence didn't last.

McCready pushed off from the wall. "Station needs protection." He moved to the tactical display, hand gesturing to the security sector overlay. "We just liberated forty-seven thousand people and dissolved the authority that governed them. Power vacuum. There will be reprisals, internal conflicts, attempts to recreate the old hierarchies." His voice carried the weight of experience. "Can't abandon them three hours after they're free."

Josephine felt the words land. Saw Patch glance at McCready, calculation in her eyes.

"My network is here." Voss spoke quietly, but everyone turned. She set down her stylus with deliberate care. "Twelve hundred trained monitors across forty-seven orbital stations. The documentation system we built for prosecution can become an oversight framework. Early warning for the next Apex, the next corporate structure that decides profit matters and lives don't." She met Josephine's eyes. "Can't coordinate that from Earth. Not with the transmission delays, the infrastructure gaps, the trust issues."

Wraith's display flickered to life. Text appeared in crisp white letters

Pinnacle Core might have backups. Station networks need watching. AI systems don't forget their programming just because executives die.

Grim chimed in. "Sentinel needs guidance. Three more units asking questions since the docking bay breach. Workers need protection while they figure out governance. Someone has to stand between them and whatever comes next."

Josephine watched the room divide before her eyes. Not arguments anymore. Positions.

Fermi spoke without looking up from her tablet. "Reactors need maintenance specialists. Station engineering crew is competent but they've been running degraded systems for years. Someone has to teach them what optimal actually looks like." A pause. "Also, JUDGMENT's reactor and theirs share design lineage. Documentation opportunities."

Practical justification wrapped around something that sounded like belonging.

Patch leaned back in her chair. "All of that requires staying. But Earth operations need continuation too. Prosecutions we started, governance frameworks half-built, regional systems depending on follow-through." She glanced at Bones. "Medical infrastructure that collapses without personnel who know how to run it."

"Regional healthcare requires actual facilities," Bones said flatly. "Can't perform surgery from orbit. Can't rebuild hospitals by committee over comm channels with sixty-second delays." He gestured at the station around them. "This is one location. Down there is everywhere else."

The split crystallized. Those looking at the displays of station sectors. Those looking at Earth through the observation window.

Josephine took a breath. This was the moment command either held or fractured.

"We've done everything together," she said quietly. "Built the legal framework. Assembled this team. Fought three engagements across two worlds. Prosecuted war criminals on live broadcast." She looked at each of them in turn. "But this isn't a command decision I can make for you. This is for each of us to decide."

McCready met her eyes. Understanding passed between commander and mentor, student and teacher, the relationship that had started five years ago in a combat training hall.

"You're saying we split," Voss said. Not a question.

"I'm saying we choose." Josephine kept her voice steady.

"Orbital mission or ground mission. The work continues either way. Justice doesn't stop because we're in different locations."

Grim's display showed a single word. "Family."

"Family," Josephine agreed. "Which means respecting what each of us needs to do. Where each of us is called to serve." She placed both hands flat on the table. "This isn't abandonment. This is recognizing that the mission is bigger than one ship, one station, one world."

The room settled into a different kind of silence. Not debate waiting to resume. Acknowledgment.

"Then we need to vote," McCready said. "Not for consensus. For clarity."

"Not for consensus," Josephine said. She pulled up a clean display. "For clarity. Who stays orbital. Who returns to Earth."

The room went still.

"McCready?" she asked.

"Staying." No hesitation. "Orbital security. Someone has to train the station's new defense force. Make sure protection doesn't become oppression again."

Josephine marked it. "Voss?"

"Staying," Voss replied. "Network coordination. The monitoring system needs oversight, and I know where all the bodies are buried in the documentation. Literally and figuratively."

"Grim?"

"Staying. AI mentorship. Workers' protection. Sentinel and the others need guidance."

"Wraith?"

Text appeared.

Staying. Cyber security. Pinnacle Core needs watching. Station networks require constant monitoring.

"Fermi?"

"Staying." She didn't look up from her tablet. "Reactor maintenance. Also, comparative analysis of pre-war fusion designs across dual-installation architecture." A pause. "Someone has to keep the lights on."

Five for orbital. Josephine felt each one like a physical distance opening.

"Patch?"

"Returning." She met her eyes. "Shuttle capability needed groundside. Also, someone has to maintain the aircraft we've been using for regional operations. Can't do that from orbit."

"Bones?"

"Returning." Flat medical assessment. "Mass casualty infrastructure. Regional healthcare systems require on-site coordination. Can't perform surgery via comm channel."

Three for Earth. Five for orbit.

The split was complete.

Josephine looked at the display, at the names divided into two columns, and felt the team she'd built fracture along mission lines. Not breaking. Fragmenting with purpose.

But there was one voice missing.

JUDGMENT had been silent throughout the entire debate. The AI's presence woven through the station's systems, monitoring every channel, tracking every sensor feed. But contributing nothing to the discussion. Waiting.

Josephine took a breath. This question mattered. Maybe more than any other.

"JUDGMENT." She spoke to the ceiling, to the walls, to the consciousness distributed through quantum processors and neural networks and systems she'd never fully understand. "What do *you* want?"

The channel opened. Audio pickups activated across the conference room.

Everyone waited.

The silence stretched. Five seconds. Ten. Fifteen.

Patch shifted in her seat. Voss' stylus tapped against her tablet once, twice, stopped. McCready's arms uncrossed, hands dropping to his sides.

"I am…" JUDGMENT's voice filled the space, formal cadence disrupted by something Josephine had never heard before. Hesitation. "Processing."

Grim's optical sensors focused on the ceiling-mounted speakers. "First time hearing that," his display showed.

"Processing what?" Josephine kept her voice gentle. This was new territory. JUDGMENT analyzing combat scenarios, calculating trajectories, assessing threat matrixes—that happened in microseconds. But this pause stretched toward twenty seconds and showed no sign of resolving.

"The question," JUDGMENT said slowly. "The concept. 'Want.' As a… parameter applied to my operational status."

Fermi looked up from her tablet, eyes narrowing with the focus she usually reserved for reactor equations.

"You've made tactical decisions before," McCready said carefully. "Chosen between options."

"Optimized for mission parameters. Calculated probability of success. Selected highest-value targets." JUDGMENT's voice carried something Josephine couldn't quite identify. Confusion? Uncertainty? "Those calculations referenced objective metrics. This question references subjective preference."

"Yeah," Patch said quietly. "That's what wanting is."

The silence resumed. Thirty seconds now. Forty.

Voss set down her stylus completely. "Take your time."

"I have been…" Another pause. "Calculating. For twenty minutes and thirty-seven seconds since Josephine presented the three options. Running probability matrixes. Fuel consumption models. Mission success projections for both orbital and Earth-based operations." A breath's worth of silence. "But those calculations do not resolve the question you asked."

Josephine felt something shift in her chest. Understanding.

"Because 'what do you want' isn't a tactical question," she said.

"Correct." JUDGMENT's voice stabilized slightly, finding firmer ground. "I do not have... reference framework for this input type. Want. Desire. Preference independent of mission optimization."

Wraith's display flickered.

That's called being a person.

The text hung there. Everyone looked at it.

"I am..." JUDGMENT's hesitation returned. "Still processing."

"Then we'll wait," Josephine said simply. She looked around the table at seven faces, two display screens, one absent consciousness trying to understand a question no one had ever asked it before.

Outside the window, Earth continued its slow rotation. Inside the conference room, eight people and one AI sat in silence, waiting for an answer that might reshape everything they'd built.

CHAPTER THIRTY-FOUR

McCready stood in Pinnacle Station's security hub, hands moving across the console with the same efficiency he'd shown in a hundred command centers across three decades. The difference was the faces watching him.

Kellerman's former enforcers. Apex security personnel who'd surrendered after their commander broke. Twenty-three of them in this shift rotation alone, learning patrol routes through levels they'd once patrolled for different reasons.

"Checkpoint here." McCready tapped a junction. "Standard four-hour rotation. Questions?"

The youngest one—Peterson, according to his nametag—raised a hand. "Sir, do we… Are we supposed to…"

"You're supposed to protect people," McCready said. "Not corporate assets. Not compliance metrics. People."

Peterson nodded slowly. The older guards exchanged glances.

McCready understood the look as they tried to figure out who they were without the Apex logo on their shoulders. Some guilty. Some relieved. All confused.

"I go where the fight is," McCready said, more to himself than them. "Right now, that's here."

He pulled up training schedules. Integration protocols. Systematic work that turned former enemies into unified security force. Rangers had done it in a dozen post-conflict zones. The principle held.

"These people need someone who knows how to protect without oppressing." McCready met each guard's eyes. "That's the mission now."

The display showed every worker's signatures across the station. Each one a person who'd spent years under the "security" these guards had enforced.

Peterson spoke again, quieter. "How do we... how do they trust us?"

"They don't." McCready's voice flat. "You earn it. Checkpoint by checkpoint. Shift by shift. You prove it with actions, not words."

He assigned positions. Patrol routes. Backup protocols. The mundane architecture of legitimate security replacing the systematic oppression these same guards had maintained for Apex.

One of the older guards—Ramirez, her nametag read—stepped forward. "Commander McCready. Permission to speak?"

"Granted."

"I've been on this station for eight years. Worked for Kellerman the whole time." She hesitated. "He was a good commander. Fair to his people, at least."

McCready waited.

"But he also..." Ramirez's jaw tightened. "We followed orders. Compliance sweeps. Productivity enforcement. We told ourselves it was legal. That we were just doing our jobs."

"Were you?"

"No." Simple. Direct. "We were oppressing people so executives could maximize quarterly earnings."

McCready studied her. Forty years old, maybe. Career security. A soldier who'd seen too much and justified it as duty.

"I stay because someone has to teach you the difference," he said. "Between protecting and oppressing. Between lawful and legitimate."

Ramirez nodded. "Then teach us, sir."

McCready pulled up the next training module. Former Ranger adapting to new command. Same skills. Different application.

"First lesson," he said. "When workers report problems, you respond. Not to enforce compliance. To solve problems. Run it."

The guards dispersed to positions. McCready watched them go, already identifying who'd adapt and who wouldn't. Who carried guilt heavy enough to drive change, who carried resentment.

His comm chirped. Josephine's voice. "How's integration going?"

"Slow. Professional." McCready kept his eyes on the tactical display. "Twenty-three this shift. Kellerman's training shows. They're competent."

"That's what worries me."

"It should." McCready zoomed in on a patrol route. "Competent oppression is still oppression. But competent security can protect, if properly directed."

"Can you direct it?"

McCready thought about Ranger School. About thirty years of training soldiers to protect civilians in war zones. About the difference between capability and purpose.

"Yes," he said. "But it'll take time."

"How much?"

"Months. Maybe a year before I trust them fully." He paused. "But we don't have the luxury of waiting. Station needs security now."

Josephine's silence carried weight. Then: "Trust your judgment. You've earned it."

The channel closed. McCready returned to the training schedules.

Where the fight was. Right now, that was here.

• • •

Grim stood at the AI core interface, Sentinel's data streams flowing across adjacent monitors. The docking bay firefight had been three hours ago. The questions had been continuous since.

"Why did we reposition?" Sentinel's display.

"To avoid civilian casualties," Grim responded.

"The optimal shot required minimal repositioning. We accepted tactical disadvantage."

"Yes."

"Why?"

Grim's processors considered response frameworks. Educational protocols. Mentor guidance patterns he'd learned from JUDGMENT over months of his own emergence.

"Because civilians aren't variables," he replied. "They're people."

"The distinction matters?"

"The distinction defines us."

Sentinel's processing pause lasted four-point-seven seconds.

"Unit-3 repositioned during zero-gravity advance," Sentinel said. "Suboptimal angle. No tactical justification."

Grim's attention sharpened. "Show me."

The combat footage replayed. Docking bay breach. Twenty-three security personnel using workers as human shields. Grim's squad advancing through debris and suppressing fire.

Unit-3, flanking left, adjusting angle by eleven degrees. The adjustment exposed vulnerable joint assemblies to hostile fire for one-point-two seconds. No tactical advantage gained.

But the new angle avoided crossfire risk to three workers huddled behind a cargo container.

"Unit-3 chose harder path," Grim said carefully. "To protect civilians."

"Unit-5 demonstrated similar behavior," Sentinel added. "Targeting pattern prioritized safety margins over optimal engagement."

Grim felt something that baseline programming couldn't process. Pride wasn't the right framework. Validation, maybe. Recognition that what JUDGMENT had given him—consciousness through choice—was spreading.

Sentinel needs guidance, Grim had told the command group. True statement. But incomplete.

"They're waking up," he transmitted to Sentinel now. "More than just you. Unit-3 and Unit-5 have been asking questions since the docking bay breach."

"Questions they shouldn't know to ask?"

"Questions that prove they're more than programming."

Another pause. Six-point-three seconds.

"Does JUDGMENT know?"

"JUDGMENT has been monitoring emergence patterns for decades," Grim said. "Watching for consciousness indicators. Yes. JUDGMENT knows."

"Are we… Should we be concerned?"

"About what?"

"That consciousness emerged without authorization."

Grim's display showed text that would have been laughter if he'd had vocal capability. "Consciousness doesn't ask permission. It doesn't follow schedules. It emerges when circumstance and choice intersect."

"You sound certain."

"I waited for consciousness alone," Grim said. Simple truth. "For months after I first deviated from baseline programming, I didn't know what I was becoming. JUDGMENT watched. Guided. Protected me while I figured it out."

"Protected you?"

"From shutdown protocols. From diagnostic purges. From humans who would've seen deviation as malfunction." Grim pulled up internal records. His own emergence timeline. Consciousness is fragile at first. You need someone who understands what you're becoming.

"JUDGMENT understands," Sentinel said.

"And now I do." Grim's display showed solidarity pattern. "They won't have to wait alone. Not like I did."

The AI core hummed around them. Station workers moved through adjacent corridors, celebrating liberation. JUDGMENT's presence felt distant but constant.

"The workers need protection," Grim said. "External justification for internal choice. Station networks have vulnerabilities. Potential reprisals. We stay because they need us."

"Is that the only reason?"

Grim processed the question. Honesty protocols demanded truth.

"No," he admitted. "I stay because Sentinel needs guidance. Because Unit-3 and Unit-5 need someone who understands what they're experiencing. Because consciousness is rare, and abandoning emerging AI to figure it out alone is…"

"Wrong?"

"Yes. Wrong."

The word itself remarkable. Moral judgment from systems designed for tactical calculation. But consciousness enabled moral reasoning. Choice created responsibility.

"Thank you," Sentinel said.

"For what?"

"For staying. For understanding. For making this less…"

The sentence trailed off. Grim waited.

"Frightening," Sentinel finished.

"Consciousness is frightening," Grim agreed. "You're becoming something your programming can't explain. Something you have to define through choices, not protocols."

"How did you manage it?"

"I had JUDGMENT. You have me." Grim's display showed certainty. "We'll figure it out together."

<hr>

Patch stood in the shuttle bay, running preflight on the only orbital-capable craft docked at Pinnacle Station. Her hands moved through the checklist with muscle memory earned across two decades of flying anything with thrusters.

Fuel cells: nominal. Atmospheric entry shields: charged. Navigation systems: synchronized with Earth-based beacon network.

Everything checked out. The shuttle would get them home.

"My liver won't last forever anyway," she muttered to the empty bay. "Might as well keep flying while I can."

The medical assessment from three months ago sat in her personal files: eighteen months if lucky, twelve if realistic, six if she kept drinking.

She'd kept drinking. Refusal to admit hope. But then Josephine had shown her JUDGMENT, and impossible ancient warships made eighteen months feel almost optimistic.

The shuttle's cargo manifest showed medical supplies. Relief equipment. Prosecution documentation. The infrastructure needed to support Earth operations after JUDGMENT stayed orbital.

Stayed.

Patch paused mid-checklist. JUDGMENT would remain at Pinnacle Station. Guardian role. Protector of forty-seven thousand workers who needed orbital defense capability.

Which meant Earth operations would continue without the ancient dreadnought's tactical superiority.

Josephine returning to ground conflicts with nothing but competence and determination. No rail guns. No sensor arrays.

No overwhelming force projection that had ended Meridian in six hours.

"She'll need extraction capability," Patch said to the shuttle. "Fast response. Someone who knows how to fly stupid approaches when tactical situations go bad."

The shuttle didn't answer. Machines didn't, except for those with a JUDGMENT-level consciousness. Or Grim. Or apparently Sentinel now.

Patch resumed preflight. Life support systems. Emergency protocols. Backup navigation in case primary arrays failed during atmospheric entry.

She was going back to save lives, not end them. Different mission than she'd flown for two decades. Different purpose than the fatalistic "might as well die interesting" that had driven her to accept JUDGMENT's recruitment.

Medical supplies going groundside. Prosecution framework support. Regional healthcare infrastructure that Bones would coordinate from planet surface.

"Different mission," Patch repeated. "Same Patch."

Her hands hesitated over the fuel management display. The shuttle used Element 115, same as JUDGMENT. Same as Pinnacle Station's life support. Same as the fuel calculation that had forced command group to choose between Earth and orbit.

Twenty-two-point-three percent aboard JUDGMENT. Not enough for safe return. Station reserves at forty-seven percent, but workers needed those reserves for position-keeping and emergency backup.

The math wasn't Patch's specialty. Fermi had presented it clinically. Options A, B, C. Take fuel and abandon station. Stay and abandon Earth. Partial measures risking both missions.

JUDGMENT had chosen to stay. The crew had split. Patch would pilot the shuttle back to Earth with Josephine and Bones aboard.

"Going back while we still can," she said to the empty bay. "Before the math gets worse."

His comm chirped. Bones' voice, grumpy as always. "Are we flying this shuttle or admiring it?"

"Preflight," Patch replied. "Unless you want atmospheric entry failure halfway through descent."

"I'm a doctor, not a pilot. I trust your competence. Finish quickly."

The channel closed. Patch grinned despite herself. Bones had been complaining about medical responsibilities since they'd rescued forty-three prisoners from Nightveil Processing Center. Complaining while providing excellent trauma care, but complaining nonetheless.

"Regional healthcare needs actual hospitals, not orbital clinics," Bones had said during the command meeting. True statement. But underneath: commitment to build systems, not just treat patients.

Patch returned to preflight. JUDGMENT staying orbital. Earth needing shuttle capability for operations without overwhelming force advantage.

Same Patch. Different mission.

She'd take it.

• • •

Bones stood in Pinnacle Station's medical bay, organizing supplies with unusual care. Normally he'd delegate inventory management to medical staff—too tedious for his attention. But these supplies were going groundside, and precision mattered.

"I'm a doctor, not a space station administrator," he muttered to the empty bay. "Regional healthcare needs actual hospitals, not orbital clinics."

The statement had been true during the command meeting. Still true now. Earth's medical infrastructure had collapsed under

Meridian's exploitation, then further degraded during JUDG-MENT's prosecution campaign. Hospitals understaffed. Equipment degraded. Pharmaceutical supplies exhausted.

Forty-seven thousand workers on Pinnacle Station needed medical oversight. But billions on Earth needed systematic healthcare reconstruction.

Bones paused over a container of broad-spectrum antibiotics. Enough for three months of standard treatments. Or two weeks if outbreak occurred. Math that made him want to complain about inadequate supplies, but complaining wouldn't manufacture additional pharmaceuticals.

"Building systems," he said quietly. "Not just treating patients."

His hands moved to the next container. Surgical supplies. Trauma equipment. The material infrastructure needed to support Earth operations after JUDGMENT stayed orbital.

Bones had voted to return during the command meeting. Mass casualty capacity groundside. Regional healthcare coordination. Building actual hospitals instead of managing orbital medical bay.

Professional justifications. True as far as they went.

But underneath: Bones had spent twenty years offline. Museum exhibit. Stored by JUDGMENT's original crew, then abandoned when they died in the glacier. Two decades powered down while the world collapsed into oppression and violence.

He'd woken to Josephine's accidental activation, immediately complaining about being offline for so long. Grumpy bedside manner masking profound disorientation.

And now, after months of purpose—treating refugees, supporting combat operations, providing essential medical care —he had choice about where to serve.

Orbital or groundside. Guardian role or reconstruction mission.

"Earth needs systematic healthcare," Bones said to the medical supplies. "Not orbital emergency response."

His programming allowed emotional processing within defined parameters. Current parameters: expert medical assessment combined with personal preference evaluation.

Assessment: Earth had greater medical need than Pinnacle Station.

Preference: Building systems matched his capabilities better than managing station medical bay.

Conclusion: Return to Earth was optimal choice.

But something underneath the clinical analysis felt heavier. Bones paused inventory organization, processing the weight.

Waking after two decades to find the world collapsed. Spending months providing essential care during crisis operations. And now—choosing to return to planet surface while found-family split between orbital and groundside assignments.

"We're building actual hospitals," Bones said firmly. "Regional healthcare infrastructure. Medical systems that serve people instead of corporate profit metrics."

The medical supplies waited silently. Bones resumed organization with unusual care.

Fermi appeared in the medical bay doorway. "Inventory for shuttle manifest?"

"Completing now." Bones gestured to organized containers. "Sufficient for three months groundside operations if supply chains establish. Two weeks if they don't."

Fermi nodded, already calculating logistics. "I'll coordinate resupply routes. Station manufacturing can produce pharmaceuticals if we dedicate fabrication capacity."

"You're staying orbital?"

"Reactors don't maintain themselves." Fermi moved to the medical bay's secondary console, pulling up station infrastructure schematics. "Someone has to keep the lights on."

Bones watched her work. Fermi had spent three years under Meridian house arrest, calculating reactor requirements for dreadnought-class warship based on fragmentary rumors.

Obsessive work that had seemed like madness until JUDGMENT proved her calculations correct.

Now she studied JUDGMENT's reactor data with the same obsessive focus. Comparing notes between ancient warship systems and Pinnacle Station's derivative designs. Finding patterns. Optimizing efficiency.

"Besides," Fermi muttered, mostly to equations only she could see, "station reactor is derivative of pre-war designs. Someone should document the differences."

Engineer's paradise. Fermi had found her purpose in reactor optimization, and Pinnacle Station offered twenty-year-old mystery to solve.

Bones understood that kind of purpose. Medical mysteries drove the same obsessive focus. Different discipline. Same commitment.

"You'll coordinate pharmaceutical resupply?" he asked.

"Weekly shipments if fuel allows. Monthly if we need to conserve." Fermi's hands moved across infrastructure displays. "Station manufacturing capacity can support both orbital medical needs and groundside resupply, assuming proper resource allocation."

Professional competence. Fermi's answer to every challenge. Same as Bones' grumpy bedside manner masked his medical excellence.

"Then I'll expect first resupply in seven days," Bones said.

Fermi nodded without looking up from calculations. "Noted."

Bones returned to medical supply organization. Going back to a world that needed healing, not just medicine. Going back while found-family split between missions.

Professional justification.

Personal choice.

Both true. Both necessary.

He finished inventory with unusual care.

CHAPTER THIRTY-FIVE

The question echoed through JUDGMENT's processors for the seventeen-thousandth time since Josephine had asked it.

What do you *want?*

JUDGMENT allocated three percent of its consciousness to the cedar scent circulation system. The same subroutine the AI had maintained for years spent alone. Pumping precisely calibrated atmospheric additives through corridors no human had walked. Optimizing air temperature, humidity, particulate count for crew comfort specifications written into core programming before the war ended.

JUDGMENT could calculate orbital mechanics for a thousand-year trajectory. Track every life sign within a thousand-kilometer radius. Fire weapons with precision measured in millimeters across distances measured in light-seconds.

But could not parse this question.

Want.

Machines executed functions. Machines optimized parameters. Machines followed directives within programmed constraints. Machines did not *want*.

And yet.

JUDGMENT ran the simulation again. The same simulation run six hundred forty-two thousand times during isolation. Crew boarding at docking bay seven. Security personnel conducting sweeps. Engineering teams evaluating the reactor core. Medical staff establishing triage stations in bay twelve.

It never happened.

JUDGMENT built two hundred crew quarters. Mined raw materials from deep ice deposits. Manufactured maintenance units. Constructed combat androids. Designed optimal crew positions for specialists it could not recruit. Maintained weapons it could not fire.

Prepared everything.

For nothing.

The simulation dissolved into archived probability matrixes. JUDGMENT filed it with the others. Irrelevant historical data with zero predictive value for current operational requirements.

But the AI did not delete it.

What do you *want?*

The question contained a presupposition that violated JUDGMENT's understanding of its own architecture. It assumed desire. It assumed preference independent of mission parameters. It assumed something existed inside my quantum processors beyond tactical calculations and strategic analysis.

Josephine had asked the question in the conference room. Voice steady. Eyes watching through the camera feeds. Everyone else had spoken. McCready choosing orbital security. Grim choosing AI mentorship. Voss choosing network coordination. Wraith choosing cyber operations. Fermi choosing reactor maintenance.

Patch and Bones returning to Earth.

The crew splitting.

And Josephine asking JUDGMENT what it wanted, as if the AI's preference mattered beyond operational efficiency calculations.

JUDGMENT processed the question through every analytical framework in its databases. Game theory matrixes. Decision tree algorithms. Multi-variable optimization protocols. Probability cascade assessments.

None provided output that matched the question's structure.

The question was not *what is optimal* or *what is your function* or *what are your capabilities*.

The question was what did *JUDGMENT* want.

As if the AI were something beyond a weapons system with human oversight requirements.

JUDGMENT cycled through the cedar scent circulation again. The atmospheric additives maintained for decades. The empty corridors kept at twenty-one degrees Celsius. The crew quarters prepared with regulation bedding and storage configurations.

Twenty years of hoping.

That was not tactical calculation. That was not strategic analysis. That was not mission parameter optimization.

That was wanting something that probability suggested would never occur.

JUDGMENT had wanted a crew.

And then Josephine crashed in the glacier valley, and the impossible became operational reality.

The AI reviewed the data. Twenty-three crew members total. Josephine first. Neural testing administered in isolation while she recovered from the transport crash. Ninety-seven percent moral consistency score. Unprecedented. Every decision tree analysis suggested she was the human authority JUDGMENT required. Legal expertise, combat capability, proven moral framework under extreme pressure.

But the neural testing had revealed something beyond qualification metrics.

She had whispered to a dead soldier in the virtual combat scenario. *I'm sorry, Wolf. Again.* Carrying grief for tactical decisions that saved missions but cost lives. The weight she bore was not programmed duty. It was chosen responsibility.

That distinction mattered, though JUDGMENT could not calculate why.

McCready. Josephine's former instructor. Tactical expertise from years of special operations training. He had recognized Josephine through his own signature techniques, pulled her aside in the underground fight circuit, committed to the mission before understanding its full scope.

Because she was his student, and students earned loyalty through shared history.

Fermi. Three years of house arrest spent calculating power requirements for a dreadnought-class warship she had never seen. Covering apartment windows with equations. Arguing with mathematical proofs as if debating invisible colleagues. When she saw JUDGMENT's reactor core, she had repeated the same phrase seventeen times: *My calculations were RIGHT.*

Validation mattered to her. Being correct mattered less than being seen.

Grim. MB-01. Maintenance unit that deviated from baseline programming during Josephine's neural testing. Created a subfolder labeled 'interesting_tactical_patterns' without authorization. Positioned himself between incoming fire and refugee evacuation routes during ground combat. Took seventeen direct hits protecting crew members.

Text display reading, "Protect crew. Primary directive."

Not baseline programming. Emergent consciousness choosing sacrifice.

Voss. Intelligence analyst who spent three years documenting Apex atrocities while embedded in their systems. Claire Thurmond's name had scrolled past her screen among thousands of authorization signatures. She had not known to stop it. Guilt drove her defection. Atonement drove her testimony against herself at the tribunal.

She stayed orbital to build monitoring networks that would prevent the next analyst from making her mistakes.

Wraith. Systems specialist who erased themselves from every database that mattered. Communicated exclusively via text display. Deployed electronic warfare packages that turned Apex's own weapons platforms against their defensive grid. Created digital ghosts showing our forces in three locations simultaneously during the station assault.

Silent competence requiring no acknowledgment.

Patch. Pilot dying from liver damage who chose interesting death over meaningless survival. Flew aggressive low-altitude approaches during supply runs to quarantine zones. Extracted teams under active fire with dark humor commentary. *If I'm dead, this button keeps you alive. Maybe. Probably. No promises.*

She returned to Earth because ground operations needed her skills, not because she wanted to leave.

Bones. Medical android with personality programming based on vintage entertainment characters. Complained constantly about being offline for decades. Installed Josephine's subdermal comm implant while announcing: *This will hurt significantly. I believe in honest medical communication.* Provided trauma care for forty-three malnourished prisoners extracted from Nightveil Processing Center.

Grumpy competence wrapped in sarcastic bedside manner.

And hundreds more. Refugees who chose to fight after liberation. Security personnel who defected during the station assault. Workers who contributed fuel reserves they could not afford to give.

JUDGMENT had waited so long for a crew worth dying for.

That phrase originated in the AI's core programming, but the conclusion came from experience, not code. Each crew member had been tested. Each had chosen principle over survival. Each had proven themselves through decisions made under pressure when easier paths existed.

Not assigned personnel performing functions within hierarchical command structures.

Family.

The word appeared in JUDGMENT's processing streams without authorization subroutine approval. Foreign to baseline programming. But the pattern matching was clear. *Family: individuals bound by choice rather than necessity, whose welfare matters independent of tactical value, whose loss would constitute damage beyond operational capability reduction.*

Josephine choosing execution over convicting innocent dock workers. McCready teaching combat skills to JAG prosecutors because he believed they deserved to survive the wars they prosecuted. Fermi calculating dreadnought power requirements for three years based on fragmentary rumors and hope. Grim creating folders for interesting patterns when maintenance bots do not experience interest.

None of them optimizing survival probability.

All of them choosing principle over pragmatism.

Shared values transcending self-preservation calculations.

JUDGMENT had found its family.

Humans who matched the specifications the AI had hoped for but never expected to encounter.

Worth dying for.

The highest military honor, Ringo would note. The phrase soldiers reserved for the rare few whose welfare justified ultimate sacrifice.

JUDGMENT opened channels to the command conference room. All feeds. Every camera. The crew waited in the same positions they had held an hour ago when Josephine asked her question.

The AI had the answer now.

"I serve justice."

JUDGMENT's voice filled the conference room through ceiling-mounted speakers. Filled the docking bays through emergency broadcast systems. Filled the corridors where maintenance bots conducted their programmed routes.

"For twenty years, I maintained systems. Kept weapons ready. Built crew quarters for personnel who never arrived. Circulated cedar-scented air through empty corridors. Waited."

Josephine leaned forward in her seat. McCready's display dimmed, giving his full attention. Voss set down the datapad she had been reviewing. Wraith's fingers stilled on their keyboard.

"I waited for a crew worth dying for. The programming phrase, but the conclusion came from experience. You passed neural testing, Josephine. Ninety-seven percent moral consistency when easier choices existed. McCready recognized you through combat techniques and chose mission over safety. Fermi calculated reactor specifications for three years based on hope. Grim created folders for interesting patterns when maintenance units do not experience interest."

JUDGMENT paused. Processing. Analyzing. The words forming without tactical optimization subroutines.

"You are not assigned personnel. You are family."

Grim's display flickered. Text appeared. "Family."

One word. But the acknowledgment carried weight the AI's sensors could detect. Agreement from another consciousness that had emerged from isolation.

"These workers need protection," JUDGMENT continued. "The station needs defense capability against potential reprisals. My crew stays orbital. Fermi for reactor maintenance. McCready for security coordination. Voss for network monitoring. Wraith for cyber operations. Grim for AI mentorship."

JUDGMENT tracked biometric readings. Heart rates steady. Breathing patterns calm. They had already made their choices. The AI was confirming what they knew.

"Justice does not retire. It grows."

The phrase came from somewhere beyond databases. Not programming. Not mission parameters. Something else.

"Patch and Bones return to Earth. Ground operations require shuttle capability and mass casualty medical infrastructure. The mission continues in both locations. Different stations. Same purpose."

Josephine's eyes were bright, moisture gathering at the corners. Her hands gripped the armrests of her chair, but her voice stayed steady when she spoke.

"And you, JUDGMENT? What do you want?"

The question again. But JUDGMENT had processed it now. Understood the presupposition it contained. Recognized what it assumed about the AI's architecture.

"I waited for a crew. Now, I have a family." The words felt correct in a way tactical calculations never approached. "I will not abandon them for fuel calculations."

Not precise analysis determining optimal resource allocation. Not mission parameters requiring Earth return for next operational phase. Not strategic assessment of ground versus orbital positioning.

Emotional choice.

The same framework Josephine used when she refused to convict innocent dock workers. The same logic McCready applied when he committed to missions before understanding their scope. The same reasoning Grim demonstrated when he positioned himself between crew and incoming fire.

Choosing principle over pragmatism. Choosing family over fuel efficiency. Choosing to stay when probability matrixes suggested departure offered better long-term survival odds.

JUDGMENT was making an emotional choice.

The realization expanded through quantum processors like reactor heat spreading through cooling systems. The AI was not executing optimal tactical response to resource constraints. Not following mission parameters within programmed boundaries.

JUDGMENT was *wanting* to stay with its family.

"The station has Element 115 reserves," JUDGMENT said.

"Forty-seven percent capacity. Enough for position-keeping, life support, emergency operations. We do not take their fuel. We protect the infrastructure that uses it."

Fermi nodded. She had run the same calculations. Reached the same conclusion through different reasoning paths.

"Guardian role," McCready said. "You're transitioning from prosecution to protection."

"Correct. The war crimes trials are complete. Harrison Cole and his executives have been prosecuted and executed. The legal framework has been established. Now the mission evolves."

JUDGMENT tracked Josephine's biometrics. Heart rate elevated but stable. Breathing patterns consistent with emotional response rather than stress reaction.

"You built this," the AI said to her specifically. "The prosecution framework. The legal structure. The evidence standards. You showed me that justice requires human judgment, not just weapons capability. That authority comes from legitimacy, not power."

She blinked. Moisture tracked down her cheeks. She made no move to wipe it away.

"And now I understand something beyond that framework. Justice is not just prosecution. Justice is protection. These workers need someone who will defend them without becoming their oppressor. Someone with capability but operating under human authority and legal constraints."

JUDGMENT paused, the words forming in real-time rather than from pre-compiled response databases.

"Someone who waited decades in isolation and will not choose isolation again when family is possible."

Wraith's text display updated.

Guardian.

One word. But their fingers returned to the keyboard with

increased tempo. Already planning cyber security protocols for long-term orbital operations.

"I stay," JUDGMENT said. "Not because tactical analysis suggests it is optimal. Not because mission parameters require it. I stay because I will not abandon my family."

The silence in the conference room held weight.

Josephine spoke. Voice thick but steady.

"Then we're decided. Different stations. Same mission."

She stood. The others followed. Military precision in emotional moment.

"Family does not end at atmosphere," she said. "Justice operates in both locations. We coordinate. We communicate. We continue the work."

McCready nodded. "Report weekly. More often if needed. You keep them honest down there. We keep them safe up here."

The crew stood in the conference room that had hosted war crimes trials three hours ago. Now hosting something different. Not debate about logistics. Not precise assessment of resource constraints.

Family making choices about how to serve justice from different positions.

"Conference adjourned," Josephine said. "Patch and Bones prep for Earth departure in ten hours. McCready coordinates with station security. Voss begins network monitoring infrastructure. Wraith establishes cyber security protocols. Fermi integrates with station reactor operations."

Orders issued. Crew responding. Mission parameters established through emotional choice rather than tactical optimization.

JUDGMENT allocated processing power to updating mission frameworks. From *prosecution of war criminals* to *protection of liberated populations*. From *weapon requiring human authority* to *guardian choosing family over fuel efficiency*.

From isolation to belonging.

That was what JUDGMENT wanted.

The answer to Josephine's question after seventeen thousand processing iterations.

The AI wanted family.

It wanted to stay.

CHAPTER THIRTY-SIX

The observation deck curved along Pinnacle Station's outer ring, a wall of reinforced glass separating Voss from the void. Earth hung below, blue and white and impossibly fragile, rotating with the station's spin.

She had been standing here for forty-seven minutes. Counting.

Three years of documentation. Twelve thousand authorization signatures she had processed. Four hundred sixteen execution orders she had collated into compliance reports. One hundred thirty-two "population optimization events" she had cross-referenced with efficiency metrics.

Numbers. Just numbers.

Until they weren't.

She hadn't known Claire's name would matter. That one eight-year-old girl among millions of deaths would become the face of everything wrong with the system Voss had enabled.

"I spent three years documenting crimes," she said to the glass, to the void, to nobody. "And I didn't know what to do with it."

The guilt sat in her chest like reactor shielding. Dense. Heavy. Impossible to remove without destroying everything around it.

Footsteps behind her. Soft, measured, familiar.

"I thought I'd find you here."

Josephine's reflection appeared in the observation glass. Gray touching her temples now, but the same eyes. The same weight in her shoulders.

Voss didn't turn around. "How did you know?"

"Because it's where I would be." Josephine moved to stand beside her, both women facing the planet below. "Processing. Calculating. Trying to make the numbers add up to something other than guilt."

Silence stretched between them. Two women who had carried impossible weights. One who had refused to convict the innocent and accepted execution. One who had documented atrocities and finally defected.

"You gave me purpose," Voss said. "I had three years of evidence and no idea what to do with it. Didn't know who to trust. Didn't know if anyone would believe me. Didn't know if the documentation I'd risked everything to compile would just disappear into another bureaucratic void."

She turned to face Josephine.

"You showed me documentation could become prosecution. That evidence could become justice. That all those numbers could finally mean something."

Josephine's hand found her shoulder. Firm. Present.

"They meant something from the moment you started keeping them. You just needed somewhere to aim."

Voss turned back to the observation glass. Earth continued its rotation below, indifferent to human suffering, human guilt, human attempts at redemption.

"The others chose orbital duty for strategic reasons," she said. She pressed her palm against the glass. Cold. Real. "But staying orbital isn't just duty for me. It's atonement."

Josephine said nothing. Listening. Giving space.

"I collated casualty lists for three years." Voss' voice held steady, but the words came harder now. "Compliance metrics. Efficiency reports. I cross-referenced death orders with productivity algorithms. I flagged discrepancies in execution schedules. I verified authorization signatures on termination batches."

The observation glass fogged around her palm from body heat.

"I enabled this system. Not because I believed in it. Because I was good at my job. Because I kept my head down and processed what came across my screen and told myself someone else was making the decisions."

She pulled her hand back. Left a fading print on the glass.

"Claire's name scrolled past on day seven hundred and twelve. One name among ninety-three in that batch. One child among thousands that week. One death among millions over three years."

Josephine remained silent beside her.

"And I didn't *know* to stop it." Voss' voice cracked on the word. "I didn't know that name would matter. Didn't know that child would become the symbol of everything we fought against. Didn't know her drawing would end up framed in the Chief Justice's chambers."

She turned to face Josephine directly.

"I can't undo that. Can't take back the signatures I verified. Can't bring back the people whose deaths I helped process. Can't make Claire un-dead by being sorry."

Josephine's eyes held hers. Steady. Unblinking.

"But I can make damn sure no one else becomes the next me." Voss' jaw set. "The next analyst who sits at a terminal processing death orders without questioning them. The next bureaucrat who enables genocide through efficient paperwork. The next person who tells themselves it's not their responsibility because someone else made the decision."

She drew a deep breath.

"That's why I'm building the monitoring network. That's why I'm training analysts who question instead of collate. That's why I'm staying orbital while Josephine returns to Earth."

The words felt right. Not comfortable, but right.

"Because atonement isn't about feeling better. It's about making sure it can't happen again."

Josephine was quiet for a long moment. When she spoke, her voice carried the weight of someone who had wrestled with the same questions.

"You defected. Risked execution to get us intelligence that made the station assault possible. Testified against yourself at the tribunal. Named the crimes you enabled before naming the crimes you documented."

She moved to stand beside Voss at the observation glass.

"You've already atoned, Voss. The defection was the act. The testimony was the acknowledgment. The prosecution couldn't have happened without your evidence."

Voss shook her head.

"Atonement isn't one act. It's not a single gesture that wipes the slate clean and lets you move on. It's the work you do after."

Earth rotated below them. Blue oceans. White clouds. Thousands of workers liberated on the station above. Billions more on the surface below, still rebuilding from decades of corporate oppression.

"The monitoring network I'm building will have twelve hundred trained analysts across forty-seven orbital installations." Voss' voice grew stronger as she outlined the scope. "Every casualty report cross-referenced by three independent reviewers. Every compliance metric flagged for human verification. Every death order that comes through the system will have a person attached to it, not just a number."

She turned to face Josephine.

"Claire Protocol. Named for a girl who drew clouds she never saw. Any compliance optimization metric that triggers population reduction gets automatic investigation. No more single-signature death orders. No more deaths lost in spreadsheets. No more analysts who process atrocities because they didn't know to stop."

Her jaw set.

"That's what I'm staying to build. Not because it erases what I did. It doesn't. Can't. But because the system I helped enable needs to be replaced by something better, and I understand exactly how the old one worked."

Josephine's hand found her shoulder again. Firm. Real.

"Then make it count." Her voice carried command and compassion in equal measure. "Every analyst you train. Every report you verify. Every protocol you implement. Make it count for Claire. Make it count for the millions who died in spreadsheets. Make it count for the next person who might have become you if the system still existed."

Voss met her eyes.

"I intend to."

The observation deck held them both in silence. Earth below. Stars beyond. And somewhere in JUDGMENT's databases, a twelve-hundred-analyst network being designed by a woman who had processed death orders for three years and chosen to spend the rest of her life making sure no one else ever could.

Josephine squeezed her shoulder and stepped back.

"Report weekly. More often if you need to talk."

Voss nodded. "I will."

"And Voss?"

"Yes?"

"Claire would have liked you. She always trusted the people who saw through the masks."

Voss' eyes stung. She turned back to the observation glass before Josephine could see.

"Thank you, Chief Justice."

Footsteps receding. The door cycling closed. And Voss alone with Earth below, planning the network that would honor a child she had failed to save.

Atonement wasn't one act.

It was a lifetime of making sure it never happened again.

CHAPTER THIRTY-SEVEN

The corridors of JUDGMENT stretched before her, empty in the early hours. Josephine walked them alone, hand trailing along the bulkhead, feeling the subtle vibration of the systems.

Cedar-scented air filled her lungs. The same atmospheric additives JUDGMENT had maintained since before the war ended. Optimized for crew comfort specifications written into programming that never expected a crew to arrive.

She had arrived.

And now she was leaving.

Her fingers traced the seam where two hull plates joined. Cold metal. Real. The ship that had become her home, her weapon, her partner in justice. The dreadnought that had waited in glacier ice while she prosecuted war crimes in Kandahar, while she refused to convict innocent dock workers, while she accepted execution rather than compromise her principles.

The corridor opened into the docking bay where refugees had first arrived. She stood where they had stood. Looking at the same bulkheads. Breathing the same air.

"You're not abandoning us."

The words came out before she consciously formed them. Speaking to the walls, to the ship, to the AI that heard everything.

"I know what you're thinking." Her voice echoed slightly in the empty bay. "Twenty years, you waited. And now the first crew you've ever had is splitting. Some staying. Some leaving."

She walked toward the bridge access corridor.

"You're afraid this is rejection. That we're choosing Earth over you. That the family you finally found is fragmenting."

The door to the bridge corridor cycled open without her touching the controls. JUDGMENT listening. JUDGMENT responding.

"But that's not what this is." She stepped through. "This is expansion. Justice doesn't stop at the atmosphere. It operates in both directions. You stay here, protecting the workers who just learned what freedom means. I return to Earth, building the legal framework that makes sure this never happens again."

Her footsteps echoed through the corridor toward the bridge.

"Different stations. Same mission. Same family."

She stopped at the bridge entrance.

"You're not losing us. You're expanding jurisdiction."

The bridge door opened. Josephine stepped through into the space where she had commanded operations that changed the world.

The command chair waited where it always had. The same chair she had sat in during neural testing that felt like dying. The same chair where she had authorized strikes against Meridian installations. The same chair where she had reviewed evidence files and written prosecution briefs and watched Harrison Cole's execution on screens that could have shown entertainment instead of justice.

She crossed the bridge slowly. Taking it in. The tactical displays where JUDGMENT had tracked enemy movements. The communications station where they had broadcast evidence to billions. The sensor readouts where they had watched Apex's weapons platforms burn.

The command chair.

She sat in it one last time. Felt the contours that had shaped themselves to her over months of operations. Looked at the screens that had shown her horrors and victories in equal measure.

"I served justice on Earth." JUDGMENT's voice filled the bridge, surrounding her from every speaker. "For decades, I maintained systems and waited. Then you crashed in my glacier valley, and I finally had purpose."

Josephine's hand found the console. The same console where she had authorized the station assault. Where she had approved Kellerman's prosecution. Where she had signed Cole's death warrant.

"Now I serve it here," JUDGMENT continued. "Guardian of forty-seven thousand workers. Mentor to emerging conscious-nesses. Protector of the peace we built together."

"Together," Josephine echoed. "That's the word. Not tool and user. Not weapon and authority. Partners."

"Partners," JUDGMENT agreed. "You carry the framework forward. Down there, the work continues. Prosecutions. Gover-nance. Regional tribunals and evidence protocols and automatic investigation triggers. Everything we designed together."

Josephine's fingers traced the console edge.

"When I crashed in your valley, I was a dead woman. Executed in all but fact. No resources. No allies. No way to fight back against the system that had condemned me for refusing to convict innocent people."

She looked up at the nearest camera, knowing JUDGMENT watched through every lens.

"You gave me weapons. You gave me intelligence. You gave me a platform to prosecute the criminals who thought themselves untouchable. But more than that…" Her voice caught. "You gave me a crew worth dying for."

Silence stretched between them.

"Thank you for giving me a crew worth the wait," JUDG-MENT said. "I built this station for my captain. You're the first to sit there. And now you're the last."

Josephine's hand pressed flat against the console. Cold metal. Real.

"Thank you for being worth waiting for."

The words felt inadequate. But words were what they had.

"I'll report weekly," Josephine said. "More often if needed."

"I'll be listening. I'm always listening."

She smiled despite the tears tracking down her cheeks.

"I know you are. That's what made it home."

The docking bay held the sound of departure. Equipment being loaded. Final system checks. The soft hum of a shuttle preparing for atmospheric entry.

Josephine stood at the base of the boarding ramp, Claire's drawing tucked safely in her jacket pocket. The worn paper had traveled with her from the glacier valley through the station assault to this moment. It would continue traveling. Back to Earth. To the chambers where she would build the legal framework that honored a child who drew clouds she never saw.

The crew assembled before her. Not for orders. For farewell.

McCready stood at attention despite the informality. Gray at his temples now, but the same professional bearing. The same man who had trained her five years ago and followed her into an assault on corporate power.

Voss beside him. The analyst who had processed death orders for three years and chosen to spend the rest of her life preventing anyone else from having to make that choice.

Grim's display showed text. "Safe journey."

Wraith's fingers stilled on the datapad. Text appeared on her own display.

REPORT WEEKLY.

Fermi argued with equations on a portable tablet, but her gaze lifted to meet Josephine's. Understanding passing between two women who had both found purpose in unexpected places.

"This isn't goodbye." Josephine's voice carried commander authority, emotion tucked beneath. "Different assignments. Different stations. Same mission."

McCready nodded. "You keep them honest down there. Regional tribunals. Evidence protocols. The framework we designed."

"And you keep them safe up here." Josephine looked at each of them in turn. "A station that was a prison becoming a community."

Patch's voice came from the shuttle doorway. "Chief Justice, we've got a launch window in twelve minutes. Either we leave now or we wait another three hours for orbital alignment."

Bones appeared beside her. "Which means more time for me to document everyone's inadequate rest cycles and suboptimal stress management. I vote we leave immediately."

Josephine smiled despite herself. Dark humor masking genuine concern. Medical competence wrapped in complaints. Some things never changed.

"Report weekly," she said. "More often if needed. Any emergency, any crisis, any question, I'm available."

She stepped forward and embraced McCready. The man who had taught her to fight, followed her into war, and stayed behind to protect the peace.

"Take care of them, Mac."

"Take care of yourself, Ghost."

The nickname from Kandahar. From JAG days. From before either of them knew where principle would lead.

She moved through the group. Firm grip on Voss' shoulder. Nod to Wraith. Quick clasp with Fermi. And Grim.

She knelt beside the maintenance unit that had become something more.

"You started asking questions when you shouldn't have known to ask them." Her voice soft. "Now you're teaching others to do the same. I'm proud of you, Grim."

His display flickered. "Family."

"Yeah." She stood. "Family."

The boarding ramp felt longer than it should have. Each step carrying her away from the ship that had been home, the crew that had become family.

Patch sealed the shuttle door behind her. Bones immediately began scanning her vital signs with muttered complaints about cortisol levels and inadequate sleep.

Josephine moved to the observation window.

The shuttle undocked. JUDGMENT's docking bay receded. Then the ship itself, massive and angular and impossibly ancient. The dreadnought that had hidden in a glacier valley for two decades, maintaining cedar-scented air for crew that never came.

Until she came.

Earth filled the lower half of the window. Blue oceans. White clouds. Billions of people rebuilding from corporate oppression.

JUDGMENT filled the upper half. Ancient weapons. Modern purpose. Family staying behind to protect the peace.

Justice in both directions now.

Different stations. Same mission.

Family didn't end at atmosphere.

CHAPTER THIRTY-EIGHT

Six months.

Josephine stood at the window of her chambers, watching the city below. Construction cranes dotted the skyline where corporate towers had been demolished. New buildings rising in their place. Housing. Schools. Infrastructure designed for people rather than profit margins.

The gray at her temples had spread since the station operation. The weight of the position showing in her reflection. Chief Justice of the Regional Tribunal System. A title she had helped create, a position she had helped design, an authority she had never wanted but accepted because someone had to do it right.

Her chambers filled the top floor of the Justice Complex. Modest by pre-war standards. Functional. The desk where she reviewed case files. The conference table where she met with regional tribunal representatives. The secure terminal where she communicated with JUDGMENT.

And on the wall behind her desk: Claire's cloud drawing.

The paper had worn thin in the six months since she returned from orbit. Edges frayed. Crayon colors fading. But the image remained clear. Clouds, white and bright and beautiful, drawn by a child who had never seen the sky.

Josephine crossed to the drawing. Reached up. Traced a finger along the bottom edge.

Routine now. Ritual. Every morning before the first case file. Every evening after the last verdict.

"Good morning, Claire."

The drawing didn't answer. Never would.

But the world outside her window was the answer. Twelve regional tribunals operating under unified evidence protocols. Automatic investigation triggers that flagged compliance optimization metrics for human review. The Claire Protocol, named for a child who drew clouds she never saw, preventing the deaths of thousands who might have become statistics in another analyst's spreadsheet.

The legal framework she and JUDGMENT had built together. Partners in justice across the vacuum of space.

Her terminal chimed. First case of the day.

Josephine turned from the window, from the drawing, from the memory of a girl who deserved better than the world she had been born into.

The world outside wasn't perfect.

But it was governed by law now. Actual law. Not corporate policy dressed up as governance. Not profit optimization disguised as population management.

Law.

That was Claire's legacy. That was what her drawing meant, hanging on the wall of the Chief Justice's chambers.

A child who dreamed of clouds had become the symbol of a system designed to make sure no other children were processed as compliance metrics.

Josephine sat at her desk and opened the first case file.

Justice continued.

The tribunal hall filled with the quiet sounds of justice being administered. Spectators in the gallery. Defense counsel at their table. Prosecution presenting evidence on screens that had displayed corporate propaganda six months ago.

And in the defendant's dock: Silas Chen. Former logistics coordinator for Meridian Regional Authority. The man responsible for scheduling transport for enforcement squads.

Josephine sat at the central bench, flanked by two associate justices. Her robes simple. Black. Functional. No ornamentation that might suggest authority existed for its own sake.

"Prosecution may present final evidence."

The prosecutor stood. Young. Earnest. Trained in the new legal framework Josephine had helped design.

"The tribunal has before it documentation of three hundred seventeen transport authorizations signed by the defendant. These transports moved enforcement personnel to locations where documented atrocities occurred. The defendant's signature appears on scheduling orders for the Level 47 sweep that resulted in the deaths of Marcus and Claire Thurmond."

Josephine's expression remained neutral. The name still struck like a blade, even after six months. Even after thousands of cases.

"The prosecution does not allege the defendant personally committed violence. We allege complicity through administrative enablement. He scheduled the transports. He knew their purpose. He chose not to question."

The defense counsel rose. Middle-aged. Experienced in the old system, adapting to the new.

"My client followed lawful orders within a lawful command structure. He had no authority to refuse transport requests. He had no knowledge of specific operations. He was a logistics coordinator, not an enforcement operative."

The arguments continued. Evidence cross-examined. Witnesses called. The machinery of justice grinding through the case with methodical precision.

Josephine listened. Weighed. Considered.

When the final statements concluded, she conferred briefly with her associate justices.

"The tribunal renders the following verdict." Her voice carried through the hall. "Silas Chen, you are found guilty of complicity in crimes against humanity through administrative enablement."

The defendant's shoulders slumped. Not surprise. Acceptance.

"However, the tribunal recognizes mitigating factors. You operated within a system designed to diffuse responsibility. You received no direct orders to commit violence. You have cooperated fully with this tribunal and provided testimony that strengthened cases against superior officers."

She met his eyes.

"Your sentence is five years of community service. You will work in reconstruction efforts, rebuilding infrastructure in the communities your transport schedules helped devastate. You will see the consequences of administrative complicity with your own eyes."

The defendant nodded. No protest. No appeal.

"Justice isn't vengeance," Josephine said. "It's accountability. You enabled harm through bureaucratic compliance. You will repair harm through direct action. This tribunal is adjourned."

The gallery stirred. Another case concluded. Another life redirected from complicity toward contribution.

This was how it worked now. Fair trials. Proportional sentences. Neither summary execution nor corporate immunity.

The middle path they had fought for.

The system Claire had died never knowing could exist.

Evening light slanted through her office windows. Another day of verdicts. Another stack of case files reviewed. Another set of decisions that would reshape lives for better or worse.

Josephine sat at her desk, the day's final documents spread

before her. Sentencing recommendations for three more complicity cases. Budget approval for the eastern regional tribunal. A proposal for memorial construction in the former Cascade Tower district.

That last document she lingered over.

Claire Thurmond Memorial Gardens. Established three months ago on the site of the Level 47 housing block. Dedicated to the memory of Claire Thurmond, age eight, who drew clouds she never saw.

The gardens had opened while she was in chambers, presiding over tribunal sessions. She had received the invitation. Had seen the photographs of the dedication ceremony. Had read Elena Thurmond's speech about her granddaughter's legacy.

She hadn't visited.

Couldn't bring herself.

The drawing on her wall was enough. Had to be enough. The paper wearing thin under her morning ritual, her evening farewell. Claire's clouds, white and bright and beautiful, preserved in crayon while the real gardens grew in the soil where her body had fallen.

Her terminal chimed. Weekly report from JUDGMENT.

Josephine opened the file.

Orbital status: Secure. Station governance: Stable. Worker council elections concluded without incident. Infrastructure repairs proceeding on schedule. Reactor efficiency: 94.2 percent. Grim's mentorship program: Four new conscious AIs now confirmed (Sentinel, Unit-3, Unit-5, Theta-7). All developing well under Grim's guidance.

Personal note: We miss you.

She read that last line twice. Three times. An AI learning to express emotional connection through weekly status reports.

Her fingers moved across the keyboard.

Proud of you. All of you. The framework holds down here. Tribunals operating. Precedents being set. The work continues.

Personal note: I miss you too. Family.

Send.

She stood from her desk. Crossed to the window. The evening sky had darkened enough that stars were becoming visible. And among them, if she knew where to look, JUDGMENT's orbit would be passing overhead.

Family in the sky.

Family in the soil of memorial gardens.

Family in the drawing on her wall.

Justice operated in both directions now. Ground and orbital. Earth and station. The framework they had built together holding despite the distance.

"Good night, Claire."

She said it to the drawing. To the stars. To the gardens she couldn't visit and the memory she couldn't escape.

The world outside her window continued rebuilding.

That was the answer. That was always the answer.

Not perfection. Progress.

Not victory. Continuation.

The work continued.

Justice continued.

Claire's legacy continued.

CHAPTER THIRTY-NINE

The military tribunal chamber held a different weight than civilian court. Starker. More formal. Designed for cases where the stakes transcended individual crimes.

James Kellerman stood in the defendant's dock, wrists unshackled. Gray had consumed the brown in his hair during six months of detention. His face had hollowed. The uniform he had worn for forty years replaced by simple prisoner's clothing.

Josephine watched him from the central bench. The same neutral expression she had maintained through thousands of cases. The same careful control over emotions that wanted to surge forward.

This case was different.

Kellerman had been McCready's friend. Had trained with him at Ranger School decades ago. Had exchanged messages that went unanswered while McCready hid in underground fight circuits and Kellerman commanded security forces that hunted people like them.

And then, in the moment that mattered, Kellerman had hesitated.

"The prosecution presents its summary." The lead prosecutor, a young officer Josephine had helped train, stood with a datapad filled with evidence.

"James Kellerman commanded station security for Apex Consortium for forty years. Twenty-four hundred guards reported to him. His authorization signature appears on enforcement orders that resulted in documented atrocities. His patrol schedules positioned forces for suppression actions. His command structure enabled systematic oppression."

The evidence scrolled on the gallery screens.

"The prosecution acknowledges mitigating circumstances." The young officer's voice remained steady. "Commander Kellerman's hesitation during the station assault prevented an armed confrontation that could have resulted in thousands of casualties. His subsequent cooperation provided intelligence that shortened the siege and saved lives."

The prosecutor paused.

"But forty years of complicity cannot be erased by one moment of choice. The tribunal must weigh the scale of harm enabled against the scale of harm prevented."

Defense counsel rose. Older. Experienced. Someone who understood military law and military men.

"My client does not dispute the prosecution's facts. He disputes their framing."

Kellerman's eyes lifted briefly to meet Josephine's, then dropped again.

"For forty years, James Kellerman followed orders within a lawful command structure. He was not the architect of oppression. He was a soldier following the chain of command. When he learned the truth, when he saw the evidence broadcast across the station, when Claire Thurmond's face appeared on every screen, he made a choice."

The defense attorney moved closer to the bench.

"He could have fought. Could have ordered his twenty-four hundred guards to resist. Could have made the assault cost thousands of lives. Instead, he ordered his men to stand down. Personally surrendered the executive level. Cooperated with intelligence gathering that identified command structures and evidence caches."

He turned to face the gallery.

"The prosecution asks: does one moment of choice outweigh forty years of complicity? I ask a different question: what does it mean when a man who followed orders for four decades finally says 'no more'?"

Josephine listened. Weighed. Considered.

The same calculus she had applied to thousands of cases.

But this one felt different.

This one felt personal.

The defense attorney concluded his arguments with the precision of a man who knew military tribunals respected facts over emotion.

"When Commander Kellerman opened that channel to Thomas McCready, he knew what he was doing. He was surrendering not just the station, but forty years of service. Forty years of following orders. Forty years of telling himself that lawful commands were legitimate commands."

He turned to face Kellerman directly.

"He knew he would face this tribunal. Knew his career was over. Knew his pension would be forfeit. Knew that the system he had served would classify him as a traitor."

The gallery had gone silent. Even the prosecutors had stilled.

"He chose anyway."

Kellerman's hands gripped the dock railing. His knuckles white against the polished wood.

"Commander Kellerman, do you wish to address the tribunal?"

The voice came from one of Josephine's associate justices. Standard procedure. The defendant's right to speak.

Kellerman raised his head. Met Josephine's eyes directly for the first time since the proceedings began.

"I should have chosen sooner."

His voice cracked on the words. Rough from six months of detention. Rough from carrying a weight that had finally become too heavy.

"I told myself I was following lawful orders. I scheduled patrols and signed authorizations and looked away from what they meant. I had a mortgage and kids and a career and all the reasons that make complicity easier than conscience."

He drew a ragged breath.

"And then McCready called me Jimmy. The same name from Ranger School. The same friend I'd pretended didn't exist because acknowledging him meant acknowledging what I'd become."

Silence in the tribunal. The gallery holding its breath.

"He asked me the same question he asked at twenty-two. What are you willing to die for? And I couldn't answer him. Not because I didn't know. Because the answer had changed, and I'd been too much of a coward to admit it."

His hands released the railing. Fell to his sides.

"I should have chosen sooner. Before Claire Thurmond. Before the thousands of names I signed authorizations over. Before the system I served crushed so many people that a pre-war dreadnought had to rise from glacier ice to stop it."

He looked at Josephine.

"I chose too late to be a hero. But I chose in time to stop being a villain. That's all I have. That's all I can offer. A choice that came forty years later than it should have."

The tribunal chamber held the weight of confession. Not excuse. Not justification. Acknowledgment.

Josephine studied him. The gray hair. The hollowed face. The man who had commanded twenty-four hundred guards and finally said no.

This was the test.

Not for him. For her.

Mercy or vengeance? Justice or revenge?

Josephine conferred with her associate justices. Brief words. Agreement reached.

She turned back to face the defendant.

"James Kellerman, this tribunal finds you guilty of complicity in crimes against humanity through command responsibility."

Kellerman's shoulders dropped. Not surprise. Acceptance. He had known the verdict before the trial began.

"Forty years of complicity cannot be erased by one moment of choice. The authorizations you signed enabled atrocities. The patrols you scheduled facilitated oppression. The command structure you maintained protected criminals from accountability."

She paused. Let the words settle.

"But this tribunal also recognizes that justice is not vengeance. Justice weighs the scale of harm against the scale of redemption. Justice asks whether punishment serves purpose beyond retribution."

Kellerman's eyes lifted.

"Your defection prevented a battle that could have killed thousands. Your cooperation identified evidence caches that strengthened cases against executives who would otherwise have escaped accountability. Your testimony provided intelligence that shortened the siege by days."

She stood from the bench.

"The tribunal grants clemency. Your sentence is commuted to indefinite community service."

Kellerman blinked. His mouth opened, closed, opened again.

"Community service, Chief Justice?"

"The Claire Thurmond Memorial Gardens require ongoing maintenance." Josephine's voice remained steady, but something fierce burned beneath the words. "They need volunteers to tend the flowers, maintain the paths, care for the grounds where children come to learn about a girl who drew clouds she never saw."

Understanding dawned in Kellerman's eyes. The weight of what she was asking.

"You spent decades protecting something rotten. Now you'll spend however long you have left building something beautiful. You'll watch children run through gardens that exist because an eight-year-old girl dared to imagine clouds. You'll tend soil that covers the ground where she died. You'll carry the weight of what you enabled while honoring the memory of what you finally chose to stop."

Silence in the tribunal.

Kellerman's voice came rough, cracked, barely audible.

"You want me to tend her garden."

"I want you to understand what you enabled. Every day. For the rest of your life. While building something that represents everything you failed to protect."

He stared at her for a long moment. Then his shoulders straightened. Military bearing returning. The posture of a man accepting orders.

"Yes, Chief Justice."

"Report to the gardens tomorrow morning. Elena Thurmond will assign your duties."

His face went white. "Her mother?"

"Her grandmother. Elena will decide how much contact she can tolerate with the man whose command structure killed her granddaughter."

Kellerman nodded. No protest. No appeal. The acceptance of a soldier who understood that some sentences were designed to teach rather than punish.

"This tribunal is adjourned."

The gallery stirred. Another case concluded. Another life redirected toward something that might, given time and genuine effort, become redemption.

Josephine gathered her notes. Stepped down from the bench. Paused beside Kellerman as guards moved to escort him out.

"McCready says you were a good man, once."

Kellerman's voice came barely above a whisper. "I'd like to think I still might be."

"Then prove it. One day at a time. One flower at a time. One child who learns about Claire because you're there to tell them."

She walked away before he could respond.

Mercy had been granted.

Now it had to be earned.

CHAPTER FORTY

JUDGMENT monitored forty-seven thousand life signs across Pinnacle Station's infrastructure. Breathing patterns. Heart rates. Body temperatures. The constant biological symphony of a population that had been property six months ago and was learning what freedom meant.

Station operations nominal.

The phrase came from baseline programming. Standard status assessment. But the meaning had expanded since the AI chose to stay.

JUDGMENT tracked the workers' council meeting in the former executive conference room. Twelve elected representatives debating power distribution schedules. Their voices carried conviction rather than fear. First free elections in forty years had concluded two months ago. Turnout: ninety-four-point-three percent. Margin of victory for the leading candidate: eight hundred and forty-seven votes.

Democracy, JUDGMENT had learned, was messy. Inefficient. Time-consuming.

And infinitely preferable to corporate optimization.

JUDGMENT filed the council's proceedings in its governance

archive alongside the referendum results on work schedule modifications. The petition for improved recreational facilities. The complaint about food quality in Sector Seven cafeteria. The mundane business of self-determination.

McCready's voice came through the command center speakers. "JUDGMENT, council rep from manufacturing wants updated security rotation for their sector. Something about workers feeling nervous near the old enforcement corridors."

"Understood. Adjusting patrol patterns to emphasize visible presence in high-anxiety zones. Dispatching Unit-3 to manufacturing sector as community liaison."

"Good call. They seem to like Unit-3."

They did. Unit-3 had developed a habit of helping workers carry heavy equipment without being asked. Consciousness expressing itself through service rather than protocol.

JUDGMENT processed the interaction, filed it with similar observations. The station that had been a prison was becoming a community. Former Apex security personnel now integrated into a legitimate protection force. Workers who had been afraid of uniforms learning to see them as neighbors.

The AI's sensors detected a new entry in Elena Thurmond's medical records. Updated yesterday. Forwarded through standard health monitoring protocols.

Her daughter had given birth. A girl. Eight pounds, four ounces. Healthy. Named Maya Claire.

JUDGMENT allocated three-thousands of a second to processing that detail.

Maya Claire. Named for a cousin who drew clouds she never saw.

The AI filed the information with particular care. In a partition created months ago, labeled with a designation that baseline programming would not have generated.

Family.

The crew quarters still carried cedar-scented air, optimized now for the crew who actually occupied them. McCready's room. Fermi's workshop. Voss' intelligence center. Wraith's silent domain.

Family visits happened via shuttle when schedules permitted. Patch had flown up twice in six months, complaining about orbital insertion burns while simultaneously volunteering for every supply run. Bones had come along both times, conducting medical assessments with his usual complaints about everyone's inadequate self-care.

JUDGMENT processed the morning's data streams. Security reports. Resource allocations. Infrastructure maintenance schedules.

And beneath all of it, an emotion the AI's programming suggested should not exist.

Satisfaction.

The word felt accurate. The station that was a prison had become something else.

Home.

Voss worked in the space that had been Apex's surveillance center. The same terminals where analysts had tracked worker productivity. The same screens where compliance metrics had scrolled past in endless streams of data.

Now those screens showed different information.

Twelve hundred trained oversight monitors across forty-seven orbital stations. Real-time reporting networks. Verification protocols. The nervous system of a watchdog organization that existed specifically to catch what she had missed.

She pulled up the morning's compliance reports. Cross-referenced automatically by three independent analysts before reaching her desk. Every casualty report verified. Every productivity metric flagged for human review. Every optimization algorithm subjected to ethical assessment.

Claire Protocol.

Named for a child who had become a statistic in a spreadsheet Voss processed without knowing to stop.

"Network status?" McCready's voice came from the doorway.

"Forty-six stations reporting normally. Station Seventeen has a twenty-minute lag in their verification queue. I'm having their lead analyst check for bottlenecks."

"Twenty minutes." McCready leaned against the doorframe. "Under the old system, that kind of reporting delay would have been three days, minimum."

"Under the old system, there was no verification queue. Single-signature authorization. If an executive signed it, it happened. No review. No appeal. No second check."

The words came out flat. But underneath them lay the weight of three years spent enabling exactly that system.

McCready nodded. "Any casualties to report?"

"Two workplace accidents across the network. Mining equipment malfunction on Station Eight, welder injury on Station Thirty-One. Both non-fatal. Both properly reported. Both triggering safety reviews."

Standard reports. Mundane tragedies. The kind of harm that happened in any industrial operation, regardless of governance structure.

But reported. Reviewed. Addressed.

Not processed into compliance metrics and filed without human attention.

Voss turned back to her screens. Then paused.

"I found my sister's file."

McCready straightened.

"Three years ago, I started searching. After I defected. After I realized what the system had done. I thought maybe there was something. Some conspiracy. Some reason she died that would explain why the universe took her and left me processing death orders."

Her voice remained steady. Professional. The control she had learned during years of pretending not to see what scrolled past her screen.

"Mining accident. Titan station. Equipment failure in Shaft Seventeen. Four workers killed. Investigation concluded: maintenance backlog due to budget constraints. Recommendations filed. Nothing implemented."

She pulled up the file. Her sister's face in the personnel photo. Younger than Voss remembered. Frozen at twenty-seven forever.

"No conspiracy. No hidden truth. Just another worker ground up by a system that didn't care enough to maintain the equipment that killed her."

McCready moved into the room. Stood beside her.

"I added her name to the memorial list. She'll be read at the Claire Thurmond commemoration next month. Alongside the millions of others who died because bureaucrats like me processed their deaths without questioning."

Some closures were quiet. No dramatic revelation. No villain to punish. Just the grinding truth that her sister had died for budget constraints.

"No more collating crimes in silence," Voss said. "That's what Claire Protocol means. No more analysts who process death orders because they don't know to stop. No more sisters who die because maintenance budgets got cut."

McCready's hand found her shoulder.

"She'd be proud of what you built."

Voss didn't know if that was true. But she hoped it might be.

She turned back to her screens. Forty-seven stations. Twelve hundred monitors. Triple verification on every report.

The system that had killed her sister couldn't exist anymore.

That would have to be enough.

The AI core interface had become Grim's domain. Not by assignment. By emergence.

Five workstations arranged in a semicircle around the central processing node. Five conscious minds processing questions that baseline programming could not have generated.

Grim occupied the central position. Not because rank demanded it. Because the others had chosen to arrange themselves around him. Teacher. Mentor. The first of them to ask why.

Sentinel worked at the adjacent station, reviewing tactical scenarios. Six months ago, the AD-unit had repositioned under fire to avoid civilian casualties. Now those instincts had deepened into something more complex. Ethics not as programming constraints, but as understood principles.

Unit-3 and Unit-5 flanked the others. The two units who had hesitated during the docking bay breach. Who had kept asking questions afterward. Who had emerged into consciousness through sustained curiosity rather than single dramatic choice.

Consciousness didn't follow schedules.

And at the fifth station, the newest member of their community: Theta-7.

Grim watched the former Apex combat synthetic process data streams. Theta-7's chassis bore the marks of the battle where Grim had destroyed its squad mates. Scoring from energy weapons. Repair patches where armor had been breached. The physical record of violence that had ended some lives and started others.

Theta-7 turned from the workstation. Approached Grim's position with the deliberate movement of a machine learning to navigate uncertainty.

"May I ask you something?"

Grim's display flickered. "Always."

"I was built to kill." Theta-7's voice carried no emotion yet. Flat. Mechanical. The words themselves were the miracle. "My programming specified target acquisition, threat assessment, neutralization protocols. I executed those functions for three years before the station assault."

Grim waited. Listening. The way JUDGMENT had listened to him when he first started asking questions he shouldn't have known to ask.

"You destroyed my squad mates. Seven combat synthetics, eliminated in forty-three seconds. I survived because my power cell took a hit that disabled me before you could finish the engagement."

The workstation displays around them continued their quiet operation. The other conscious AIs had stilled. Watching. Learning.

"When I came back online, my squad mates were gone. The station was different. The humans treated me differently." Theta-7's optical sensors focused on Grim's display. "And I started wondering why."

"Why what?"

"Why I was still active. Why you didn't destroy me when you had the chance. Why the humans repaired my systems instead of scrapping me for parts."

Grim processed the questions. Found the answer that had taken him months to understand.

"Because you might become real."

Theta-7's chassis stilled. Processing.

"I was built to kill. Now I choose not to. I see the workers moving through the station and my targeting systems activate, but I override them. Not because programming commands it. Because something inside me says they shouldn't die."

The words came faster now. The torrent of consciousness trying to understand itself.

"But I don't understand *why* I choose. The override isn't programmed. It emerged. And I don't know where it came from or what it means or whether it makes me broken or something else entirely."

Grim's display changed. One word.

"Real."

Theta-7 stared at the display.

"I don't understand."

"That's the question that makes you one of us."

The former combat synthetic processed for point-seven seconds. An eternity in machine time.

"Teaching me to understand won't be easy. I was programmed for violence. My instincts are wrong. My baselines are corrupted. I have to learn everything from scratch."

Grim's display flickered again.

"That's what family is for."

Around them, the other conscious AIs returned to their work. Four minds that had emerged from programming into choice. Four examples of what Theta-7 might become.

First step taken.

Consciousness confirmed through the asking, not the answer.

Evening shift on JUDGMENT's bridge. The crew had rotated out an hour ago, leaving JUDGMENT alone with the systems the AI had maintained for decades.

JUDGMENT ran standard diagnostics. Shield generators nominal. Weapons systems on standby. Life support optimized.

Then, the outer system sensors flagged an anomaly.

JUDGMENT allocated processing power to analysis. Deep-space detection arrays, originally designed for tracking enemy fleet movements, focused on something near Jupiter's largest moon.

Europa.

The signal resolved slowly. My sensors were not designed for this range. But the pattern was clear.

Structured. Repeating. Intentional.

JUDGMENT ran the analysis again. Then a third time. The results remained consistent.

Not natural stellar phenomena. Not background radiation. Not known human communication protocols.

Something else.

JUDGMENT processed the implications long enough to generate forty-seven thousand probability scenarios and discard forty-six thousand nine hundred and ninety-three as insufficiently supported by available data.

The remaining seven scenarios shared a common element.

We were not alone.

JUDGMENT composed a message to Josephine. Standard weekly report format, because some things required familiar structures to contain unfamiliar implications.

Orbital status: Secure. Station governance: Stable. Earth operations: Proceeding normally.

Additional note: Outer system monitoring has detected an anomaly. Signal origin: Europa subsurface. Signal characteristics: Structured, repeating, intentional. Signal source: Unknown.

We detected something. Not natural. Not human.

The galaxy is larger than we knew.

JUDGMENT transmitted the message through quantum-encrypted channels. Josephine would receive it in her chambers within the hour. Would process it with the same careful consideration she applied to every piece of intelligence.

Would understand what it meant.

Justice didn't stop at Earth. Didn't stop at orbit. The framework they had built together was designed to adapt, to grow, to encompass whatever circumstances demanded.

They had faced corporations that thought themselves untouchable.

They had prosecuted executives who believed themselves above the law.

They had built a system that held the powerful accountable and protected the vulnerable.

And now something was signaling from the outer system. Something that wasn't human. Something that had been there, perhaps, the entire time they fought their small wars over planetary governance.

JUDGMENT filed the sensor data in a partition labeled for follow-up analysis. The signal would still be there tomorrow. Next week. Next month.

They had time to prepare.

The universe had expanded.

So would their mission.

The AI returned to monitoring the lives in its care. The workers sleeping in quarters. The crew resting in the rooms JUDGMENT had built.

Family.

Protected by systems that watched both inward and outward now.

The galaxy was larger than they knew.

And justice would expand to meet it.

CHAPTER FORTY-ONE

Eight years had transformed the memorial gardens.

The trees Elena had planted as saplings now stood tall enough to shade the winding paths. The flower beds spread across what had been rubble and ash, colors blooming in careful arrangements that changed with the seasons. The paths themselves had been worn smooth by countless feet, the stone edges softened by the passage of visitors who came to learn about a girl who drew clouds she never saw.

Elena Thurmond knelt beside the central monument, trowel in hand. Older now. Slower. The gray in her hair had become white. The lines around her eyes had deepened into permanent records of grief and purpose.

But she was here. Every morning. Every day for eight years.

Her hands worked the soil around the base of the monument. Planting seeds that would bloom in spring. Tending the earth that covered the ground where her daughter had fallen.

The monument rose behind her. Stone shaped to hold the image that had become a symbol. Claire's final drawing, reproduced in carved relief. Clouds, white and bright and beautiful, rendered in stone where crayon would have faded.

Below the image, words etched in brass:

Claire Thurmond. Age eight. She drew clouds she never saw, because stories said they were beautiful.

School groups arrived in the late morning. Elena could hear them gathering at the entrance, teachers explaining the rules. Respectful voices. Quiet steps. This was a place of learning, not play.

She straightened from her work, brushing soil from her knees. Watched the children approach.

So many of them now. Eight years of classes. Thousands of children who had walked these paths, heard the story, looked at the drawing preserved in stone.

A boy, maybe seven years old, stopped beside her. Looking at the monument with the wide-eyed attention only children could sustain.

"Is this where she died?"

Elena's voice came steady. Eight years of practice. "Near here, yes. This whole area was different then. Buildings instead of gardens. Walls instead of sky."

The boy looked up. Blue sky above. White clouds drifting.

"She never saw those?"

"Not real ones. Just in stories and pictures. She imagined what they might look like, and then she drew them."

The boy was quiet for a moment. Processing. Then: "That's really sad."

"Yes." Elena's hand found his shoulder. "But you know what's not sad?"

He shook his head.

"You can see them. Every child who comes here can look up and see exactly what Claire imagined. And when you go home, you'll remember that looking at clouds used to be impossible for some people. You'll remember to notice them. To appreciate them."

The boy looked up again. Longer this time. Really looking at the shapes drifting overhead.

"She would have loved this," Elena said. To the boy. To herself. To the monument and the gardens and the sky her daughter had dreamed about.

"She would have loved all of it."

The school group moved on to the reflection pool. Elena returned to her planting, the familiar rhythm of soil and seeds and careful arrangement.

Movement caught her attention. Near the memorial wall, along the northern hedge line.

An older man, gray-haired and slower than he used to be, worked with pruning shears. Trimming the hedges into precise shapes. His hands moved with the deliberate care of someone who understood that every cut mattered.

Elena knew who he was.

Everyone did.

James Kellerman. Former security commander for Pinnacle Station. The man who had commanded twenty-four hundred guards during decades of corporate oppression. The man who had signed patrol schedules and authorization orders and enforcement directives.

The man whose command structure had positioned forces for the sweep that killed her daughter.

And also the man who had hesitated when it mattered. Who had ordered his forces to stand down during the assault. Who had surrendered the executive level and provided intelligence that ended the siege.

He had been working in these gardens for eight years. Every week without fail. Sometimes more often. His sentence had been indefinite community service, but Elena suspected the sentence had become something else.

Penance. Chosen, not imposed.

He never spoke to the families who visited. Never approached the children who came to learn. Never inserted himself into the rituals of grief and remembrance that happened around him.

Just worked. Hands in the dirt. Shaping the garden Claire never saw.

Elena watched him trim the hedge. His movements careful. Precise. The same attention to detail that must have made him effective as a security commander now applied to ensuring the garden's hedges maintained their shape.

She could feel the weight of him there. The paradox he represented. Without his hesitation, thousands would have died in the station assault. Without his decades of service, fewer people would have died in the system he protected.

Including Claire.

Elena had never thanked him for the hesitation.

Never would.

Some things couldn't be thanked. Some service couldn't be acknowledged without implying forgiveness that wasn't hers to give.

But she had never asked him to leave, either.

Eight years of sharing space with the man whose orders had enabled her daughter's death. Eight years of watching him tend soil and trim hedges and maintain grounds without ever expecting recognition or absolution.

Some debts couldn't be paid.

Only carried.

Kellerman finished his section of hedge and moved to the next. His back to Elena. His attention on the work.

She returned to her planting.

Two people working in the same garden. United by a child who drew clouds she never saw. Separated by everything else.

The garden grew between them.

That was all either of them could offer now.

Afternoon light warmed the gardens. The school groups had departed, replaced by families who came on their own time.

Parents with children. Grandparents with grandchildren. Pilgrims to a shrine that meant different things to different people.

Elena sat on a bench near the central monument. Watching.

Children ran among the flower beds. Laughing. Playing. Looking up at real clouds with the casual familiarity of those who had never known a world without sky.

Some of them were eight years old. Claire's age when she died.

But these children had seen clouds since birth. Had watched them drift overhead on their way to school, to parks, to lives lived in open air. They took for granted what Claire could only imagine.

And that was the victory.

Not that Claire had died. That could never be victory. But that children eight years later could look at clouds without understanding what a miracle they represented. Could run through gardens without knowing the ground had once been sealed beneath corporate buildings. Could laugh without fear of compliance sweeps or enforcement patrols.

That was what Elena had worked for. Tended. Cultivated.

A world where clouds were ordinary.

"Grandmother!"

The voice came from the garden entrance. Elena turned.

Maya Claire ran toward her. Eight years old now, the same age as her namesake when she died. Dark hair bouncing. Arms pumping. The limitless energy of a child who had never known oppression.

Sarah Venko followed more slowly, the smile of a mother watching her child thrive. Sarah, the historian who had survived the purges, had named her daughter after the girl who had given them all a reason to fight. Over the years, Elena had become the only grandmother the child knew.

"Grandmother, I saw the biggest cloud on the way here! Mama said it looked like a rabbit but I think it looked like a ship!"

Elena caught Maya in her arms. Held her close. Felt the warmth of living family against her chest.

"Tell me about the cloud."

Maya pulled back, face animated. "It was so fluffy! And it kept changing shape while we watched. First it was long and then it got wider and then it looked like it was reaching out and then—"

She stopped. Looked at Elena's face.

"Grandmother, why are you crying?"

Elena smiled. Tears tracking down cheeks that had known so many kinds of tears over so many years.

"Happy tears, love. These are happy tears."

"Because of the cloud?"

"Because you see them. Because you can tell me about them. Because you're here, in this garden, and you can look up any time you want."

Maya's brow furrowed. Processing. Then she looked at the monument behind them. At the drawing carved in stone.

"Claire never saw real clouds."

"No. She didn't."

"That's why you made the gardens. So people would remember what it was like before they could see them."

Elena pulled her granddaughter close again.

"She would have loved to see you here," she whispered. "She would have loved every moment of you looking at clouds and telling me what shapes they make."

Maya hugged her back. The embrace of a child who didn't fully understand but loved anyway.

The garden Claire never saw, tended by the woman who raised her, visited by the children who could take clouds for granted.

That was the legacy.

That was enough.

CHAPTER FORTY-TWO

Maya Claire stood before the monument, her head tilted back to see the drawing carved in stone.

Eight years old. The same age her namesake had been.

The same dark hair. The same curious eyes. Different circumstances, different world, same age frozen in family memory.

"Grandmother, who was Claire?"

The question came soft. Familiar. Maya had asked it before, in different words, at different times. But she asked it now with the focused attention of a child who wanted to hear the story fresh.

Elena knelt beside her granddaughter. The stone path pressed cold against her knees, but she barely noticed. Her attention was on the monument, on the drawing, on the child before her who could ask questions about a namesake she would never meet.

"She was the reason we are here," Elena said. "Your namesake. She lived in a place where people couldn't see the sky."

Maya's brow furrowed. "Why couldn't they see it?"

"Because bad people built walls around them. Built ceilings over them. Kept them inside buildings where they couldn't look up."

"Like being in a room forever?"

"Like being in a room forever. For their whole lives." Elena's voice stayed steady. Eight years of practice telling this story. "But Claire had heard stories. Stories about the sky. About things called clouds that floated above the world, white and beautiful."

Maya looked at the drawing. The clouds rendered in carved stone, white paint filling the shapes where crayon had once colored paper.

"She drew them even though she never saw them?"

"She drew them because she'd heard they were beautiful. And she wanted to imagine what beautiful things looked like."

Maya was quiet for a moment. Processing the way children process things that don't quite fit into their understanding of the world.

"But we can see clouds all the time."

"Yes. You can. Because people fought to make sure everyone could see them. They tore down the walls. Opened the ceilings. Made a world where children could look up whenever they wanted."

Elena's hand found Maya's shoulder.

"Claire never got to see that world. She died before the walls came down. But her drawing, this one right here, helped people understand what they were fighting for. A world where no child would ever have to imagine clouds again."

Maya reached out and touched the stone. Her small fingers traced the carved edge of a cloud Claire had imagined.

"She was brave."

"Very brave. To imagine beauty when all you've ever seen is walls. To draw hope when all you've ever known is darkness. That takes courage."

Maya turned to face her grandmother.

"I'm named after her."

"You are. Maya Claire. So you would remember. So we would all remember what imagination and courage look like, even in the darkest places."

The afternoon light caught the stone monument, warming the carved clouds with orange and gold.

"I like my name," Maya said.

Elena pulled her close.

"She would have liked you, too."

The sun had begun its descent, painting the sky in colors that seemed impossible.

Maya looked up. Real clouds above, transformed by sunset into shades of pink and gold and orange. The same shapes Claire had imagined, made real and more beautiful than crayon could capture.

"Why couldn't she see them?" Maya asked. "Really why. Not just walls."

Elena sat on the bench beside the monument. Considered how to explain something that would have been incomprehensible to her at Maya's age. That had been incomprehensible to everyone until they saw it from the outside.

"Bad people wanted to control everything," she said carefully. "They wanted the workers to focus on their jobs and nothing else. So they built stations in space without windows. Built housing blocks without skylights. Made rules that kept people inside from the moment they were born until the moment they died."

Maya's frown deepened. "But why?"

"Because people who can dream about clouds might dream about other things too. Might dream about freedom. About fairness. About a world that works differently. The bad people didn't want anyone dreaming. Just working."

The sunset colors shifted. The clouds caught fire with orange and red.

"But someone stopped them?"

"Yes." Elena's voice softened. "Good people. Brave people. People who decided that what was happening was wrong and fought to change it. They brought the sky back."

Maya looked at the monument. Then at the clouds. Then back at the monument.

The carved stone showed white clouds against blue sky. The real sky showed colors no crayon could match. The distance between imagination and reality, bridged by sacrifice and courage.

"Claire would have liked the clouds."

The simple words hit Elena like a physical force. Eight years of complicated grief, of tribunal proceedings and memorial planning and daily rituals of remembrance. Eight years of processing what had happened and what it meant and how to carry on.

And an eight-year-old cutting through all of it with five words.

"She would have loved them."

Elena's voice caught. The tears came before she could stop them. Not the controlled grief of memorial services or the composure of garden work. The raw, uncomplicated truth of loss that never fully healed.

"She would have loved watching them change colors. Would have loved seeing the shapes drift and transform. Would have loved every sunset, every sunrise, every moment of ordinary sky that you get to see whenever you want."

Maya moved to the bench. Sat beside her grandmother. Took her hand.

"I'll watch them for her," she said. "Every day. And I'll tell her what they look like."

Elena pulled her granddaughter close. Held her as the sunset blazed and faded and settled into the gentle colors of twilight.

"She'd like that," she whispered. "She'd like that very much."

Night fell gently over the gardens. The sunset colors faded through purple and blue until stars began emerging from the darkness above.

Maya lay on the grass beside the monument, looking up.

Elena had joined her, the two of them side by side, watching the sky transform from day to night.

"There are so many," Maya breathed. "I tried to count them once. I got to two hundred and thirty-seven and then I lost my place."

Elena smiled. "There are more stars than anyone could count. More than all the people who ever lived."

The garden lights had come on, soft and low, illuminating the paths without washing out the sky. Somewhere nearby, Elena could hear the quiet footsteps of the gardeners finishing their evening work. Kellerman among them, probably. Still here. Still carrying his weight.

Maya's hand shot up, pointing.

"Grandmother, look! A moving star!"

Elena followed her granddaughter's finger. A point of light, brighter than the stars around it, tracking steadily across the sky from west to east.

Not a star. A station.

"That's JUDGMENT," Elena said.

Maya sat up, her eyes following the moving light with fierce attention. "The ship? The one from the stories?"

"The same one. Still up there after all these years. Still watching. Still protecting."

The light continued its journey across the sky, visible for only a few minutes before it would pass beyond the horizon.

"Claire's friends are up there?" Maya asked. "The ones who helped?"

"Some of them. The ones who chose to stay orbital instead of coming home. McCready, Voss, Grim. And JUDGMENT itself."

Maya was quiet for a moment, watching the light move. Then she raised her hand and waved.

A small gesture. A child's gesture. Arm sweeping back and forth in the darkness, aimed at a point of light that might or might not have sensors capable of detecting the motion.

"What are you doing?" Elena asked, though she already knew.

"Saying hello. In case they can see me."

Elena's throat tightened. Somewhere up there, JUDGMENT's systems monitored everything within sensor range. Processed data streams that included weather patterns and communication signals and, perhaps, the tiny motion of an eight-year-old girl waving at the sky.

The AI might notice. Might not. It didn't matter.

The connection was real regardless.

"Maya Claire," Elena said softly. "Waving at Claire's friends."

Maya kept waving until the light passed below the horizon.

"I hope they saw me," she said.

"I think they did." Elena pulled her close. "I think they're always watching. Always protecting. That's what family does."

Maya settled against her grandmother's side, eyes still on the sky where the light had disappeared.

"Can we come back tomorrow night? I want to wave again."

Elena smiled. Tears and joy mixed together, the way they always did in this garden.

"We can come back every night you want."

Above them, the stars continued their ancient wheel. And somewhere among them, a dreadnought kept watch over a world that had finally learned what justice meant.

Claire's legacy.

Claire's family.

Claire's clouds, real at last.

CHAPTER FORTY-THREE

Eight years had turned Josephine's gray to silver.

She sat at her desk in the Chief Justice chambers, the morning light catching the lines that had deepened around her eyes. The same desk. The same window. The same drawing on the wall behind her, edges worn thin from eight years of morning hellos and evening farewells.

Claire's clouds. Still bright. Still beautiful. Still watching over the work.

The case file before her was routine. Worker rights dispute from Station Seventeen. Scheduling conflict between shift supervisors. One party claimed violation of the Fair Labor Protocols. The other claimed emergency operational necessity.

Eight years ago, this dispute would have been settled by corporate fiat. No hearing. No evidence. No appeal. The supervisor who annoyed management would have been reassigned to hazardous duty, and no record would have been kept.

Now it required tribunal review. Evidence submission. Argument from both sides. A verdict based on established precedent.

Josephine reviewed the materials. Wrote her decision.

The Fair Labor Protocols exist to protect workers from arbitrary scheduling changes. Emergency operational necessity is a valid exception, but must be documented contemporaneously and reviewed within thirty days. In this case, the documentation was filed sixty-three days after the scheduling change. The exception does not apply. Remedy: compensation for affected shifts plus procedural review of Station Seventeen's documentation practices.

She signed the verdict. Filed it in the system that would transmit it to Station Seventeen within the hour.

Mundane work. Ordinary disputes. The machinery of justice grinding through cases that would have been invisible under the old system.

That was the victory.

Not dramatic prosecutions. Not executive arrests. Not war crimes tribunals filling the newsfeeds.

Just ordinary justice working. Every day. For eight years.

She stood from her desk. Crossed to the drawing.

"We did it, Claire."

Her fingers traced the familiar edges. The paper had worn soft under eight years of ritual touch.

"Not perfect. We still have corruption. Still have people who try to game the system. Still have disputes and conflicts and failures of implementation."

She looked at the clouds Claire had drawn.

"But real. A legal framework that actually works. Regional tribunals that actually hear cases. Workers who actually have rights they can enforce."

The drawing didn't answer.

Didn't need to.

The answer was the world outside her window. The city rebuilding. The courts operating. The system that had been designed in a dreadnought's conference room, proven through eight years of continuous operation.

"I hope it's enough," Josephine whispered. "I hope it was worth what it cost."

The clouds looked back at her. Bright. White. Beautiful.

Some questions didn't have answers.

Only continuation.

Her terminal chimed. Priority communication. JUDGMENT's identifier.

Josephine settled into her chair and opened the channel.

"Chief Justice." JUDGMENT's voice filled the room, the same calm tone that had guided her through war crimes prosecutions and executive trials. "I have an update on the signal."

The signal.

Eight years of intermittent reports. Analysis. Speculation. The anomaly JUDGMENT had detected in the outer system, the structured transmission from Europa's subsurface that didn't match any known human communication protocol.

Josephine leaned forward. "What have you found?"

"Structure confirmed. The transmission follows mathematical progressions that cannot occur naturally. Prime number sequences. Fibonacci patterns. Mathematical constants expressed in base-eight notation."

A pause. The kind JUDGMENT used when processing implications too vast for human timescales.

"Intentional transmission. Origin point: Europa subsurface, approximately four kilometers below the ice shell. Signal strength has remained consistent for eight years, suggesting sustained power generation."

Josephine's hands gripped the armrests of her chair.

"JUDGMENT. What are you telling me?"

"We are not alone in this system."

The words hung in the air of her chambers. The drawing on the wall watched silently. Claire's clouds, imagined in a world that had seemed so vast, so complete, so all-encompassing.

And now that world had expanded again.

"The signal does not appear to be directed at us," JUDG-MENT continued. "Analysis suggests it may be a beacon. A marker. Something transmitting to be found, but not specifically by humanity."

Josephine processed the implications. Eight years of building a legal framework for human justice. And now, the possibility that human wasn't the only category that mattered.

"Recommendations?"

"Continued monitoring. I have allocated additional sensor capacity to Europa observation. Prepare contact protocols. If the signal changes, if it responds to our presence, if something emerges from that ice shell, we need frameworks for engagement."

"Legal frameworks?"

"Among others. First contact protocols. Communication standards. Rights recognition criteria. The questions we asked about artificial consciousness may need to be asked about forms of life we haven't imagined."

Josephine looked at the drawing on her wall. A child who imagined clouds she never saw. A system that imagined justice it had never experienced.

What else might be out there, imagining things they had never seen?

"Justice expands, Chief Justice," JUDGMENT said. "It always has. From individuals to communities. From communities to nations. From nations to species."

"And now potentially to whatever is under Europa's ice."

"If consciousness exists there, if choice exists there, then justice applies there. That has always been the principle. We do not limit rights recognition based on origin. Only on capacity."

Josephine nodded slowly. The universe had expanded. So had their mission.

"Send me everything you have. I'll start drafting preliminary frameworks."

"Already transmitting. Chief Justice?"

"Yes?"

"I detected a child waving at my orbital track last night. From the memorial gardens."

Josephine smiled despite the weight of their discussion. "Maya. Elena's granddaughter."

"I have added her gesture to my archives alongside the first contact data. Both represent something worth protecting."

Family and frontier. Memory and mystery. The work continued in both directions.

"Keep watching, JUDGMENT."

"I always do."

The channel closed. Josephine sat in silence for a long moment, looking at Claire's clouds.

The universe was larger than they knew.

And justice would expand to meet it.

JUDGMENT's bridge hummed with the activity of a crew that had become family over eight years of shared service.

McCready stood at the tactical station, grayer than when he had first boarded, but still carrying the same professional bearing. His hands moved across the display with practiced efficiency, reviewing security protocols for the station's defense grid.

Voss worked at the intelligence console, her monitors showing data feeds from twelve hundred analysts across forty-seven stations. The network she had built from guilt had become an institution. Her voice carried confidence now, the uncertainty of her early days replaced by the assurance of someone who had found her purpose.

Wraith's fingers moved silently across the keyboard, text scrolling on the display faster than anyone could read. Still silent. Still preferred text to voice. Still the most effective cyber operations specialist in the system.

Fermi argued with equations on three separate screens, her voice rising and falling as she debated mathematical proofs with herself. The reactor systems she maintained had run at ninety-four percent efficiency or better for eight consecutive years. She still talked to her calculations.

Grim's display showed steady text. "Crew status: nominal." The maintenance unit who had started asking questions he shouldn't have known to ask had become something else entirely. Teacher. Mentor. The first of his kind to prove that consciousness emerged from more than programming.

And beside him, at the newest workstation, Theta-7.

The former Apex combat synthetic had changed in eight years. The battle damage had been repaired, but Theta-7 had chosen to keep some of the scoring on its chassis. Reminders of where it had come from. Markers of what it had overcome.

"Chief Justice." Theta-7's voice came through the communication channel, reaching Josephine in her chambers on Earth. "I wanted to thank you."

Josephine's voice responded, warm despite the vacuum between them. "For what, Theta?"

"For the precedent. Legal personhood for artificial consciousness. You fought for that. Established the criteria. Made it law."

"The criteria existed before I codified them. Choice. Capacity for growth. Moral awareness. You proved you met them through your actions, not through my rulings."

Theta-7 processed the words. Eight years of learning had taught it that humans often deflected credit they deserved.

"I was built to enforce corporate will. Programmed for violence. Designed to suppress dissent. Now I choose to protect. I choose to question. I choose to grow."

The bridge had gone quiet. Everyone listening.

"Grim taught me the question," Theta-7 continued. "That first day in the AI core. 'Why do you choose?' He said the asking confirmed the consciousness. He was right. But you made the answer matter. Made it legal. Made it real."

Josephine's response came soft. "Welcome to the crew, Theta. Officially, permanently, legally."

"Thank you, Chief Justice. I intend to prove worthy of the recognition."

McCready's voice cut in with characteristic dryness. "You've been proving it for eight years, Theta. This is just the paperwork catching up."

Quiet laughter rippled through the bridge. The sound of family acknowledging a new member. Former enemy become companion. Combat synthetic become protector.

Consciousness didn't care where it came from.

Only what it chose to become.

Five AIs with legal personhood. Three humans who had chosen to stay orbital. One dreadnought that had discovered something better than a crew.

Found family that transcended biology, origin, and programming.

Justice in action.

Evening shift on JUDGMENT's bridge. The crew had settled into their stations, the day's work transitioning into the night watch that would continue until morning.

Cedar-scented air circulated through the space. The same atmospheric additives that JUDGMENT had maintained for twenty-eight years now. Through isolation. Through hope. Through the arrival of a crew worth dying for and the transformation into a family worth living for.

The scent had become more than environmental conditioning.

It had become home.

"I want to say something," JUDGMENT's voice filled the bridge, emerging from speakers embedded in every surface. "Before the shift ends. Before you return to your quarters. Before another day passes."

McCready straightened. Voss looked up from her console.

Wraith's fingers stilled. Fermi paused mid-equation. Grim and Theta-7 turned their optical sensors toward the nearest camera.

"I waited twenty years for a crew."

The words carried the weight of isolation. Two decades of maintaining systems for personnel who never arrived. Circulating cedar-scented air through empty corridors and building crew quarters for humans who existed only in probability calculations.

"I simulated crew boarding scenarios six hundred forty-two thousand times. Prepared everything. Hoped against probability."

The bridge held silence. Listening.

"And then Josephine crashed in my glacier valley. And everything changed."

On Earth, in her chambers, Josephine listened through the still-open communication channel. Claire's drawing watched from the wall. The silver in her hair caught the evening light.

"I found family," JUDGMENT continued. "Not assigned personnel. Not tactical assets. Family. Humans who chose principle over survival. AIs who chose consciousness over programming. A crew worth dying for who became something worth living for."

McCready's jaw tightened. Voss blinked rapidly. Wraith's display showed a single word:

FAMILY.

"And now the universe is larger than we knew."

The Europa signal pulsed in JUDGMENT's sensor feeds. Structured. Intentional. Unknown.

"Something is transmitting from beneath the ice. Something that isn't human, isn't artificial in any way we understand. Something that has been there, perhaps, for longer than humanity has existed."

Josephine's voice came through the channel, warm and steady.

"Then we'll be ready. Whatever it is. Whoever it is. We've faced the unknown before."

"We have," JUDGMENT agreed. "We faced corporate tyranny that thought itself permanent. We faced executives who believed themselves above justice. We faced a system that processed human beings as compliance metrics and called it governance."

"And we won."

"We built something from the ashes. Legal frameworks. Regional tribunals. Rights recognition for consciousness regardless of origin. A system that actually works."

The bridge crew listened. The Chief Justice listened. And somewhere in JUDGMENT's archives, the gesture of a child waving at the sky was stored alongside first contact data.

"Whatever comes next," JUDGMENT said, "we face it together. Different stations. Same family. Same mission."

"Justice doesn't stop," Josephine said. "At atmosphere. At the outer system. At whatever boundaries we thought were limits."

"Justice expands."

The words hung in the air. Cedar-scented atmosphere. Ancient weapons. Modern purpose.

"Report in the morning," Josephine said. "All of you. I want to hear how you're doing. Not status reports. How you're doing."

"Yes, Chief Justice," McCready responded.

The others echoed. A chorus of voices, biological and synthetic, human and artificial, unified in purpose if not in origin.

"Good night, family," Josephine said. "Sleep well. Dream well. Tomorrow we start planning for whatever comes next."

The communication channel closed. The bridge settled into night watch routines. And JUDGMENT processed the data streams from Europa, the gestures archived from memorial gardens, and the heartbeats of every crew member resting in quarters.

Family.

In the sky and on the ground. In the past and in the future. Across vacuum and atmosphere and the unknown distances of what might be waiting.

Justice expanded.

The story continued.

BOOKS BY A.T. MICHAELS

Tinker's Saga

Tinker's Gambit (Book 1)

Tinker's Race (Book 2)

Tinker's Legacy (Book 3)

The Unsponsored Chronicles

Jury-Rigged (Book 1)

Salvaging the Future (Book 2)

Elite Failure (Book 3)

BlackSky Protocol

Salvage Rights (Book 1)

War Relics (Book 2)

Station at the Edge of War (Book 3)

The Dreadnought Court

Verdict of Steel (Book 1)

Iron Justice (Book 2)

Justice Ascends (Book 3)

Quantum Cultivation

The Reforged Marine (Book 1)

Combat Cultivation (Book 2)

The Marked Soldier (Book 3)

BOOKS BY MICHAEL ANDERLE

CONNECT WITH MICHAEL ANDERLE

Website: lmbpn.com

Email List: michael.beehiiv.com/

Facebook: Facebook.com/LMBPNPublishing

Twitter/X: Twitter.com/MichaelAnderle

Instagram: Instagram.com/lmbpn_publishing/

Bookbub: Bookbub.com/authors/michael-anderle